Praise f

"A smart, taut, mind-blowing thr ... ayal that moves along at breakneck speed. Ellison has outdone herself with this one. Readers will be obsessed!"

—Mary Kubica, *New York Times* bestselling author of *Just The Nicest Couple*

"Betrayal, obsession, and familial ties that bind create a tension-filled story with an intriguing theme. Readers will race through the pages to an end they didn't see coming."
—*Library Journal*, starred review

"A riveting domestic thriller full of twists and turns, but also heart and emotion. You'll root for Olivia Bender every step of the way, as soon as a knock on the door brings shocking news that threatens her marriage and her world. You won't be able to put this novel down!"

—Lisa Scottoline, *New York Times* bestselling author of *Loyalty*

"Expertly explores the intensely complex emotions surrounding infertility, loss, and marriage. Throw in murder, a vivid cast of characters, and shocking secrets, Ellison masterfully mines the human heart in this treasure of a thriller that will keep readers turning the pages long into the night."

—Heather Gudenkauf, *New York Times* bestselling author of *The Overnight Guest*

"Don't miss this layered, emotional, and twisting thrill ride."

—Lisa Unger, *New York Times* bestselling author of *Secluded Cabin Sleeps Six*

'Keeps you turning pages with an ending you'll never see coming. I loved it!"

—Liv Constantine, bestselling author of *The Last Mrs. Parrish*

'An extremely compelling thriller shot through with twists and turns, a strong emotional pulse, and heartfelt exploration of the pressures of marriage and starting a family."

—Gilly Macmillan, internationally bestselling author of *The Long Weekend*

'The secrets snarled in the threads of an unraveling marriage and a heroine who wholly won me over put this one on my keeper shelf—you are going to love it!"

-Joshilyn Jackson, *New York Times* bestselling author of *With My Little Eye*

One of the most compelling psychological suspense stories I've read in years."
—Jacquelyn Mitchard, #1 *New York Times* bestselling author of *The Deep End of the Ocean*

Also by J.T. Ellison

HER DARK LIES

GOOD GIRLS LIE

TEAR ME APART

LIE TO ME

FIELD OF GRAVES

WHAT LIES BEHIND

WHEN SHADOWS FALL

EDGE OF BLACK

A DEEPER DARKNESS

WHERE ALL THE DEAD LIE

SO CLOSE THE HAND OF DEATH

THE IMMORTALS

THE COLD ROOM

JUDAS KISS

14

ALL THE PRETTY GIRLS

IT'S ONE OF US

J.T. ELLISON

Recycling programs for this product may not exist in your area.

ISBN-13: 978-0-7783-1095-2

It's One of Us

First published in 2023. This edition published in 2024.

For questions and comments about the quality of this book, please contact us at CustomerService@Harlequin.com.

Mira
22 Adelaide St. West, 41st Floor
Toronto, Ontario M5H 4E3, Canada
BookClubbish.com

Printed in U.S.A.

For our starlight fireflies.

And for Randy, who was there for it all.

PROLOGUE

A STORY

A woman is missing.

Unbeknownst to those who love her, a placid lake holds her deep in its clutches. Its inhabitants watch her drift and dance in tune to gentle currents. They sneak little bites of her flesh, becoming one with this intrusion until they are no longer startled by her. They coexist. They play. They nestle deep in her hair and build ecosystems in the crevasses of her body. She gives of herself; she becomes their home. Generations are born that never knew a time without her. She is as much a part of their lives as the water around them, as familiar to the decomposed effluvia as the fallen trees and the limestone lake bed.

When the sun shines at just the right angle, and a small breeze ruffles the water, those magic days after heavy rains when the algae blooms disappear to the edges of the bank, the shadow of her can be seen from the surface. A ghostly flicker; here, then gone.

She exists for them now.

A woman—missing, or otherwise—is best viewed in parts. It takes away her power. It eliminates her strength. If she is broken into pieces, dehumanized, depersonalized, she is no longer a threat. She is only eyes. Breasts. Hips. The number on the tag in the back of her jeans. The color of her hair, especially when enhanced. Bejeweled, adorned, shaved, plucked, contoured. Acceptable only when twisted into someone else's ideal.

A woman is told so many things. Cross the street when you feel uncomfortable. Smile, you're so much prettier when you smile. Don't wear that ponytail. Learn to defend yourself. Here, drink this. You said yes. He didn't mean it.

A woman feels so many things. More than emotions. The hand on the shoulder, knuckles grazing a breast. The accidental nudge from behind when bent over. The laughs, the whistles, the fumbled passes, the never-ending worry, the dirty jokes. The stares.

Yes, when viewed in parts, a woman no longer matters.

And sometimes, as now, this kills her.

She cannot rise with a boot on her chest. She cannot move when her body is straddled by an immense weight. She cannot breathe when large, rough hands encircle her delicate throat and squeeze, squeeze, squeeze.

A woman always knows when the end has come. She has always known it would end this way. Scrabbling in the dirt with a beast larger, bigger, more determined. Be it man or psyche, disease or time, she fights to live because she must.

Breathe. Live. Survive.

Women are, at birth and death, closest to their basest instincts.

Women begin, and end. Alive, they are a compilation of moments. But when they're dead, if there's something in between, something good, or something bad, or something left behind, ultimately, it doesn't matter.

This particular missing woman, this compilation, this aggregate of body and hair and smile and sweet and brains and misconstrued affirmations, a sum of her parts, is no longer.

And near her, a man despairs.

He's never been this close to someone dead before.

He can't look at her, not directly, not without remembering everything, so he looks at her in parts.

Feet, bare, toenails painted a vivid red. A tiny shaving cut on her ankle.

Knees, scuffed, the flesh torn, gravel embedded deep in the flesh.

Hips, exposed, her dress rucked up and floating, underwear missing. She groomed herself for him.

Breasts, pale half-moons spilling from black lace.

Collarbone, four dark circles; a ring of black around her throat.

Eyes, open and unseeing.

He relives the moment her breath stopped, over and over. It is a nightmare. A fantasy. A favorite show he binges again and again. A horrifying wreck he can't look away from.

She smiled, until she didn't. Said kind words, until they turned sour.

He panicked.

He didn't mean to do it.

Did he?

Into the water. He needs to weigh her down, but how? Options parade through his mind, none good. He knows she will rise eventually. He can only hope that with enough time in the water, any evidence of him will sluice away.

What has he done?

Can he be blamed?

The idea of it has consumed him, and now…

Corrosive fear, day after day. He cannot eat. He loses weight. He dreams of her there. Alone.

But she is not alone. Not really.

Her terrestrial family worry, then panic, then grieve, then come to uneasy terms with her loss. They hold out hope that she is still alive while knowing in their hearts that she is gone. A light dimmed in the foyer the night she went missing, and her mother, ever attuned to her daughter's soul light, knew something was dreadfully wrong. It was then she sent the first text. A reply was started, but nothing ever materialized.

Hours later, the mother called the police. Days later, weeks later, months later, there is still no word. Only those three small dots flickering on her screen, haunting the mother's every waking moment.

What was her daughter trying to say?

The police search, diligently, in all the wrong places.

They follow dead-end leads. They interview everyone who knew her, and many who didn't.

They lose sleep, are barked at by superiors, fight back the urge to quit this job, this daily devastation.

They drink too much. They rail against an unjust God. They get up with the sunrise and do it all again.

They search, and search, and search.

They do not find her until it is too late.

Despite the despair, or perhaps because of it, he visits. Often.

The lake is almost always calm, serene. It is used to keeping secrets. It has held his for weeks. The idea of her there, her many parts quiet now, fills him, with joy or fear or pleasure, he is not certain. He just knows he is better when he is near, and when he is apart from her, he can only remember her in pieces. Remember the moment she was his no longer.

A noon sun shines on the lake's glossy surface, reflecting into the leaves, making their undersides gleam and shine. He's learned the paths, the vantage points. He knows what lies beneath that murky water, imagines her decay. He walks for hours, circling her, drawing an invisible target for them to find.

Some days, he is happy. Some days, he is sad. Some days, he is afraid.

Some days, he brings his fishing gear, and casts, again and again, not sure what he is trying to catch.

When the police come, at last, searching, searching, he pants with the effort to keep himself still, to not run away screaming. He can't risk drawing attention to himself.

Will they find her today? Will she rise at last?

Every day, every visit, always the same irrational concerns.

What if her blood is still on him? What bits of her cling to his clothes, his skin?

And what of him resides in her?

And when they find her, what then? What happens?

He walks the path around the lake like all the others to make sure he's not noticed, and remembers.

Her screams bleed away. The scuffle has ended. Silence now. Nothing but the breeze, rustling the early fall leaves, urging them toward their own death. The creatures of the forest are still, waiting, watching, to see what he will do.

He waits with them, quiet, calming himself. Looking at her. As the initial disgust wanes, he is suffused with curiosity.

When she first sagged in his arms, head lolling back, mouth agape, hair matted with blood, he'd panicked and dropped her with a cry of revulsion.

Now she seems peaceful. Desire mounts. But no. There is no time. He must end this.

He ties rocks into her dress, wades into the water, the shale at the shoreline loose and glistening under his feet, and heaves her body as far from solid ground as he can manage. The moonlight shows her bob on the surface, feet, hands, and head rising as if to wave a last farewell. Then she slips under the cool, dark water, and is gone.

He stays until the sky begins to lighten, listens to the forest come back to life, watching, waiting, in case she breaks the surface. But she does not.

A woman is found.

At last, she is going home. Disrupting the watery life she's been forced to create in favor of a new one nourishing the earth nearby. Her grave will be less peaceful, near a divided highway, under dirt and grass and soot from the air. A poorer resting place. She will be missed by her aquatic brood.

Her mother is relieved, in a way. To know is so much better than to imagine.

And now, we begin anew. Attention circles, first, from the one who knows the truth, and then, from the rest. The heartbroken, and the curious. The determined, and the furious. From the one who prays not to be caught.

A new obsession is born by her new, exposed, too exposed, grave.

Will they find him?

Will they find him before he does it again?

1

THE WIFE

There is blood again.

Olivia forces away the threatening tears. She will not collapse. She will not cry. She will stand up, square her shoulders and flush the toilet, whispering small words of benediction toward the life that was, that wasn't, that could have been.

She will not linger; she will not acknowledge the sudden sense of emptiness consuming her body. She will not give this moment more than it deserves. It's happened before, too many times now. *It will happen again,* her mind unhelpfully provides.

There is relief in this pain, some sort of primitive biological response to help ease her heavy heart. Olivia has never lied to herself about her feelings about having a child. She wants this, she's sure of it. Wants the experience, wants to be able to speak the same language as her sisters in the fertility arts, her friends who've already birthed their own. And she loves the idea of being pregnant. Loves the feelings of that early flush of success—the soreness and tingling in her breasts, the spotty nausea, the excitement, the fatigue. Loves remembering that moment when she realized she was pregnant the first time.

She'd known even before she took the test. She could feel the life growing inside her. Feel the quickening pulse. A secret she held in her heart, managing several hours with just the two of them, alone in their nascent lives. Every room of the house looked new, fresh, dangerous. Sharp corners and glass coffee tables, no, no, those would have to be tempered, replaced. The sun glancing off the breakfast table—too bright here, the spot on the opposite side would be best for a high chair. The cat, snoozing in the window seat—how was she going to take an interloper? The plans. The plans.

After a carefully arranged lunch, fresh fruit and no soft cheeses, she'd driven to the bookstore for a copy of *What to Expect When You're Expecting*, accepted the sweet congratulations of the bookseller—think, a complete stranger knew more than her family, her husband. She tied the plastic stick with its beautiful double pink lines inside two elaborate bows—one pink, one blue—and gave it to Park after an elegant dinner.

The look on his face—pride and fear and terror and joy, all mingled with desire—when he realized what she was saying. He'd been struck dumb, could only grin ear to ear and pat her leg for the first twenty minutes.

So much joy between them. So much possibility.

Olivia replayed that moment, over and over, every time she got pregnant. It helped chase away the furrowing, the angles and planes of Park's forehead, cheek, chin, as they collapsed into sorrow when she'd miscarried the first time. And the next. And the next. Every time she lost their children, it was the same, all played out on Park's handsome face: exaltation, fear, sorrow. Pity.

No, the being pregnant part was idyllic for her, albeit terribly brief. It's only that she doesn't know how she feels about what happens ten months hence, and the lifetime that follows. The stranger that comes into being. But that's normal—at least, that's what everyone tells her. All women feel nervous about what comes next. Her ambivalence isn't what's killing her babies. She can't help but feel it's her fault for not being certain to her marrow what she wants. That God is punishing her for being cavalier.

Of course, this internal conversation is moot. There is blood. Again.

She hastily makes her repairs—the materials are never far away. If she stashed the pads and tampons away in the hall cabinet, it would be bad luck. Too optimistic.

Not like they're having any luck anyway. Six pregnancies. Six miscarriages. IUIs and IVF. Needles and hormones and pain, so much pain. More than anyone should have to bear.

With a momentary glance at the crime scene in the toilet, she depresses the handle.

"Goodbye," she whispers. "I'm so sorry."

Olivia brushes her teeth, then pulls a comb through her glossy, prenatal-enriched locks, rehearsing the breakfast conversation she must now have.

How does she tell Park she's failed, yet again, to hold the tiny life inside her?

Downstairs, it is now just another morning, no different from any over the past several years. Just the two of them, getting ready for the day.

The television is on in the kitchen, tuned to the local morning show. Park whistles as he whisks eggs in a bright red bowl. Park's breakfasts are legendary. Savory omelets, buckwheat blueberry pancakes, veggie frittatas, yogurts and homemade granola—you name it, he makes it. Olivia handles dinner. If she cooks three nights out of seven, she considers that a success.

They eat like kings in the morning and paupers at night, and they love it.

She pauses at the door, watching him bustle around. He is already dressed for work, jeans and a button-down, black lace-up brogues. His "office" is in the backyard, in a shed Olivia converted for his use. A former—reformed—English professor on a semipermanent sabbatical, Park has launched a second career ghostwriting psychological thrillers. He claims to love the anonymity of it, that he can work so close to home, and the money is good. Enough. Not obscene, but enough. They've been able to afford four rounds of IUI and two in vitros so far. And as he says, writing is the perfect career for a man who wants to be a stay-at-home dad. There's no reason for him to go back to teaching. Not now.

A pang in her heart, echoed by a sharp cramp in her stomach. They are throwing everything away. She is throwing everything away. This round of IVF, she only produced a few retrievable eggs, and this was their last embryo.

My God, she's gotten clinical. She's gotten cold. Babies. Not embryos. There are no more frozen *babies*. Which means she'll have to do it all again, the weeks-long scientific process of creating a child: the suppression drugs, the early morning blood tests, the shots, the trigger, the surgery, the implantation. The rage and fear and pain. Again.

The money. It costs so, so much.

She has frozen at the edge of the kitchen, thoughts roiling, and Park senses her there, turns with a wide smile. The whisk clicks against the bowl in time with her heartbeat.

"How are my darlings feeling this morning? Mama and bebe hungry?"

She is saved from blurting out the truth—mama no more, bebe is dead—by the ringing of the doorbell.

Park frowns. "Who is here so early? Watch the eggs, will you?"

Even chickens can do what she cannot.

It's infuriating. House cats escape into the woods and sixty days later purge themselves of tiny blind beings. Insects, birds, rats, rabbits, deer, reproduce without thought or hindrance. Nearly four million women a year—a year!—manage to give birth.

But not her.

She's not depressed, really, she's not. She's come to terms with this. It happens. Today will be a bad day, tomorrow will be better. They will try again. It will all be okay.

Mechanically, Olivia moves to the stove, accepts the wooden spatula. Park disappears toward the foyer, shoulders broad and waist nearly as trim as the day she met him. She will never get over his handsomeness, his winning personality. Everyone loves Park. How could you not? He is perfect. He is everything Olivia is not.

The television is blaring a breaking news alert, and she turns her attention to it, grateful for something, anything, to focus on beside the intransigent nature of her womb and the fear her husband will abandon her. The anchor is new, from Mississippi, with a voice soft as honey. Tupelo? No, Oxford, Olivia remembers; Park took her to a quaint bookstore there on the square one summer, long ago.

"Sad news this morning, as it has been confirmed the body found in Davidson County earlier this week belongs to young mother Beverly Cooke. Cooke has been missing for three months, after she was last seen going for a hike at Radnor Lake. Her car was found in the parking lot, with her purse and phone inside. Metro Nashville Police spokesperson Vanda Priory tells Channel Four Metro is working with the Tennessee Bureau of Investigation and Forensic Medical to determine her cause of death. The Cooke family released a statement a few minutes ago. 'Thank you to everyone who has helped bring Beverly home. We will have more information on her burial soon. We ask for privacy during this difficult time.' Metro now turns their attention to identifying a suspect. In this morning's briefing, Homicide Detective William Osley stated that Metro has a lead and will be pursuing it vigorously. Next up, time to break into the cedar closet, it's finally sweater weather!"

Olivia sighs in regret. That poor woman. Like everyone in Nashville, Olivia has followed the case religiously. To have a young mother—the kind of woman she's so desperate to mold herself into—disappear into thin air from a safe, regularly traveled, popular spot, one Olivia herself hikes on occasion, has been terrifying. She knows Beverly Cooke, too, albeit peripherally. They were in a book club together a few years ago. Beverly was fun. Loud. Drank white wine in the kitchen of the house and gossiped about the neighbors. Never read the book.

Olivia stopped going after a few meetings. It was right before she'd started her first official fertility treatments, had two miscarriages behind her, was hopped up on Clomid and aspirin, and all anyone could do was talk babies. Beverly had just weaned her first and was drunk for the first time in two years. She alternated between complaining and cooing about the trials and joys of motherhood. Olivia couldn't take it, this flagrant flaunting of the woman's success. She stood stock still in the clubhouse kitchen, fingers clenching a glass of Chardonnay, envisioning the myriad ways she could murder Beverly. Cracking the glass on the counter's edge and swiping it across Beverly's pale stalk of a neck seemed the most expedient.

Honestly, she wanted to murder them all, the sycophantic breeders who took their ability to procreate for granted. They had no idea what she was going through. How she was tearing apart inside, month after month. How she felt the embryos detach and knew it was over. How Park's face went from joy to disdain every time.

Some people wear their scars on the outside.

Some hide them deep, and never let anyone in to see them.

Olivia is still staring at the screen, which is blaring a commercial for car insurance, processing, remembering, fists balled so tightly she can feel her nails cutting the skin, when she hears her husband calling her name.

"Olivia?" His voice is pitched higher than normal, as if he's excited, or scared.

Park enters the kitchen from the hall between the dining room and the butler's pantry.

"Honey, they found Beverly—" she starts. But her words die in her throat when she sees two strangers, a man and a woman, standing behind him, people she knows immediately are police officers just by their wary bearing and shifting eyes that take in the whole room in a moment, then settle on her appraisingly.

"I know," Park says, coming to her side, shutting off the gas. She's burned the eggs; a sulfurous stench emanates from the gold-encrusted pan. He takes the spatula from her carefully. "It's been on the news all morning. Liv, these detectives need to talk to us."

"About?"

The man—stocky, slick smoky-lensed gold glasses, perfectly worn-in cowboy boots and a leather jacket over a button-down—takes a small step forward and removes his sunglasses. His eyes are the deepest espresso and hold something indefinable, between pity and accusation. It's as if he knows what she is thinking, knows her uncharitable thoughts toward poor dead Beverly.

"Detective Osley, ma'am. My partner, Detective Moore. We've been working Beverly Cooke's case. I understand you knew her? Our condolences for your loss."

Olivia cuts her eyes at Park. What the hell has he been saying to them?

"I don't know her. Didn't. Not well. We were in a book club together, years ago. I don't know what happened to her. I'm sorry I can't be of more help."

"Oh, we understand. That's not why we're here." Osley glances at his partner. The woman is taller than he is, graceful in the way of ex–ballet dancers even in her street clothes, with a long, supple neck, hooded green eyes devoid of makeup and blond hair twisted into a thick no-nonsense bun worn low, brushing the collar of her shirt.

"Why are you here, exactly?" Olivia asks.

Park frowns at her tone. She's come across too sharp, but my God, what she's already handled this morning would break a lesser woman.

"It's about our suspect in the Cooke case. Can we sit down?"

Olivia reigns in her self-loathing fury and turns on the charm. The consummate hostess act always works. Park has taught her that. "Oh, of course. Can I get you some coffee? Tea? We were making breakfast. Can we offer you some eggs, or a muffin? I have a fresh pan here—"

"No, ma'am, we're fine," Moore demurs. "Let's sit down and have a chat."

Olivia has a moment of sheer freak-out. Was it Park? Had he killed Beverly Cooke? Was that why they wanted to talk, because he was a suspect? If he was a suspect, would the police sit down with them casually in the kitchen? Wouldn't they want something more official? Take him to the station? Did they need to call a lawyer? Her mind was going fifty thousand miles an hour, and Park was already convicted and in prison, and she was so alone in the big house, so lonely, before she reached a hand to pull out the chair.

She needs to knock off the true crime podcasts. Her husband is not a murderer. He is incapable of that kind of deceit.

Isn't he?

Sometimes she wonders.

"Nice kitchen," Osley says.

"Thank you."

Olivia loves her kitchen. It is the model for all her signature looks. Airy, open, white cabinets with iron pulls, leathered white marble counters. A black granite–topped island just the right size for chopping and serving, light spilling in from the big bay window. A white oak French country table with elegant cane-backed chairs. It was the heart of her home, the heart of her life with Park.

Now, though, it is simply the site of his greatest betrayal. Forevermore, from this morning—with the burned eggs and the somber police and Park's face whiter than bone—until the end of her tenure here, and even then, in remembrance, she would look at this precious place with fury and sadness for what could have been. The ghosts of the life they were supposed to have clung to her, suckled her spirit like a babe at her breast never would. Everywhere she looked were echoes of the shadow existence she was supposed to be living. Here, a frazzled mother, smiling despite her fatigue at the children she'd created. There, a loving father, always ready to lend a hand tossing a ball or helping with homework. And look, a trio of towheaded boys and a soft blonde princess girl, the teasing and laughter of their mealtimes. How the table would seem to grow smaller as the boys got older and took up more space. The girlfriends came, the boyfriends. The emptiness when it was just the two of them again, the children grown with their own lives, the table bursting at holidays only. The grandchildren, happiness and racket, the noise and the joy creeping out from the woodwork again.

She is alone. She will always be alone. She will not have this life. She will not have this dream.

Park made it so.

As the detectives continue to speak, softly, without rancor, and her world splinters, Olivia hardens, compresses, shrinks. She watches her husband and holds on to one small thought.

I have the power to destroy you, too. Dear God, give me the chance.

2

THE HUSBAND

"Mr. Bender, we have a problem," the detective begins, and Park feels Olivia's sable eyes rest on him. He ignores her. He has no idea what's going on, why these detectives are sitting in his kitchen gravely preparing him for…something. Olivia is fairly vibrating with suppressed excitement. She will feel important that the police have come to them for information. She's been obsessing about the woman's disappearance, about her peripheral connection to Beverly Cooke. She will be on the phone the second they leave, sharing this news with Lindsey, her best friend, who also happens to be his sister, or her mother, Gwen, who retired down in Mexico with Olivia's father last year. Maybe someone he doesn't know. Whoever she can raise on a moment's notice on an early Tuesday morning. His wife the extrovert. She complements him, he knows that. Opposites attract. Isn't that what they say?

Park is quiet with those outside his family. He left the classroom because when it came right down to it, he hated having to get in front of a group and talk, especially to impressionable kids. He wants nothing more than a good cup of coffee and a quiet morning with his words. And a baby, of course, to break the silence in ways he can understand, to bring Olivia down to earth. An anchor: not a weight, but a lodestone for the two of them to create and share.

He needs to approach his agent about another deal. He is getting too short for comfort. They burned through all the money from his last advance on the fertility treatments. Olivia doesn't know how precarious things have become. He's sheltered her as much as possible, created a nest of warmth and finery for her, given her his attention, his money, his essence, anything so she will get and stay pregnant, and not look too closely at what they don't have.

He feels her presence next to him, their presence, and his heart lightens. Those days are over. No more shots and pills and surgical interventions. No more *Penthouse* and jacking off into a cup to the Muzak-twisted strains of "Sweet Home Alabama." The indignities he's suffered. No one takes the men into account when the journey to artificially conceive is started. They have the easy part, after all. It's only when the couple can't conceive properly that things get interesting.

It isn't him. This they know unequivocally. His swimmers are Olympic caliber.

Thank God it's all over, thank God she's held onto this one. Twelve weeks. Heartbeats heard and avuncular grins from the doctors. Her skin glowing like a pearl, the little smile she walks around with, gently touching her stomach when she doesn't know he's looking. He loves her more now than when he married her. His beautiful, mercurial Olivia. She is giving him everything he's ever wanted.

But babies cost money, too. He needs to make the call to New York today.

"Mr. Bender," the detective says again, clearing his throat as if the words he's about to speak taste bad. "In the Cooke case, a small amount of alien DNA was found in her car."

DNA.

Park feels sweat pop on his brow, despite the chill outside and the temperate air inside. It's sunny but not warm; the fall has been mild and they haven't had to turn on the heat to the house yet. They keep it on the cool side, costs less that way. There is no reason for him to be sweating, and he hopes like hell the detectives don't notice.

Olivia does. She nudges him with a foot, slides a napkin his way. He ignores her, and the sensation of damp continues unabated.

Detective Moore picks up her partner's thread. Her voice is surprisingly husky.

"We found a partial DNA match to our suspect in the system. What we've discovered—"

"Park didn't do this," Olivia cuts in. "There must be a mistake."

The cop shakes her head. "The DNA is irrefutable."

Confusion. Panic. Olivia grasps his hand and just as quickly releases it, as if her instinct is to comfort and then she's realized what they're saying. A DNA match. To him. From a dead woman. He sees Olivia watching him aghast. Sees the thought form as if in a cartoon bubble above her head.

My husband is a killer.

But he doesn't know Beverly Cooke. He's never met her before. Has he? There must be some mistake.

"I—" he starts, but the ballerina detective raises a hand.

"This is where things get complicated. The DNA is not a direct match to you, Mr. Bender. It belongs to your son. Do you know where he is at this moment?"

"I…my… A son?" His voice breaks on the last word, and his lips twitch. His initial confusion is chased away by deep, abiding, palpable relief. He resists a smile but blows out a breath hard through his nose. "I see. Well, I hate to argue, but clearly there has been a mistake. I have no children. My wife is pregnant, though." He touches Olivia's shoulder. "We're due in late June."

Two sets of interested eyes take in Olivia, who is staring at him open-mouthed. They haven't told anyone she's expecting. They've learned not to, after all the miscarriages. And here he's shared this secret with strangers in some sort of defense mechanism? He's going to get an earful later, but it seems very important to make note of this impending fatherhood versus the idea that he already has a living, breathing child.

"Many best wishes, ma'am," Osley says. "It's an exciting time."

"Yes," Olivia replies, eyes now on her hands.

Moore isn't as bonhomie as Osley. She's tensed, coiled, like a snake about to strike, and Park braces himself. There's more. He can feel it.

"I'm afraid there is no mistake. We've been running down this DNA sample for several weeks. A paternal link has been established. The suspect in our case is your biological son."

Park shakes his head. "This is all very interesting, but it's impossible. Like I said, I don't have any children. But I have a brother. A twin. This could be his kid, couldn't it? Since we're twins?"

"Identical or fraternal?"

"Fraternal."

"Then no, Mr. Bender. If he was an identical twin, there could be some question, but as a fraternal, you have distinctly individual DNAs."

Park shakes his head. "It's a mistake. There's no way."

"You aren't aware of a child?"

"No. I'm not."

"You're not covering for him, are you?" Moore asks, frost dripping from her words.

That pisses him off. "No, I'm not covering for him. There is no him. I don't know how this could happen."

"Park?" Olivia is still staring, her mouth a small O of shock. He takes her hand, and she lets him.

"It's okay, honey. It's all some big mistake."

"I think I'll take you up on that coffee," Osley says, flashing a smile, and Olivia jumps to her feet and pulls two cups from the cupboard, tipping one toward Moore in a silent offer. Moore waves her off.

"I don't understand," Olivia says, handing Osley the cup of steaming coffee and rejoining them at the table. "How could this be possible? Park doesn't have any children. I think I'd know. I think he'd know."

"My wife is right. I'm sure this is just a misunderstanding," Park starts again, but Moore shakes her head.

"I'm afraid there's no mistake. Mr. Bender, you are the father of the suspect we're seeking. That you're not aware of the child makes things more complicated, but it doesn't change reality."

Moore glances sideways at Osley, who finishes his coffee with a slurp and sets the cup on the table hard enough to rattle. "We know this is awkward, Mr. Bender. We'd like to take another sample from you, so we can run the tests once more, just for certainty."

Olivia is crumbling now. "This is impossible. Tell them, Park. Tell them they've made a mistake." She's crying; there's a thickness in her voice, a long, slow sniffle. "You can't have a child with someone else. You can't."

The coffee is burning in his stomach, acid crawling up into his throat. Her tears are making it worse. Shut this down. Now.

"Detectives, you need to give us a moment."

"Sir—"

"A moment. Please. My wife is in a delicate condition. She needs to lie down."

"I don't. Tell them. Tell me," Olivia wails. He hasn't seen her this emotional since the first miscarriage. She's been so strong through it all. Stoic. Numb, maybe. Damn it, why can't she fall apart *after* they leave?

He stands, fighting the urge to grab her arm and yank her out of the room. Gently, oh so gently, he cups her elbow, says, "Come with me," and, relieved when she complies, leads her from the kitchen toward the staircase in the hallway.

He hears the police murmuring, ignores them. Tears are pouring down Olivia's cheeks, her gorgeous dark eyes swimming. He stops at the base of the stairs, knuckles one hefty tear away. "Go lie down. I'll figure this out. I promise."

"I don't need to lie down." A choking cry. "I'm not pregnant anymore. I lost it. This morning."

The twin blows are too much to take. He has a biological child out in the world, one he had no idea existed. His wife has lost their baby. Sorrow spills over him, and he pulls her to his chest. Her hair smells like freshly cut hay on a summer day, clean and grassy, and now that he's paying attention, he scents the blood. He's always been especially attuned to her cycle. How had he missed this?

"God, Olivia. Why didn't you come get me when it happened?" he says.

"There are some things you don't need to experience firsthand, Park. Trust me."

The quiet desolation, the haze in her eyes. She's already back there, remembering, reliving it.

"Then why didn't you tell me, honey?" he asks, softer now.

"I was about to when they rang the bell," she whispers, body drooping in defeat. "Park. I'm so sorry. I'm sorry I failed you again."

He grasps both shoulders—he can feel the sharp edges of

her collarbones under her sweater; if she'd only gain a little weight, maybe she wouldn't keep miscarrying—and makes her face him. "Oh, hon. No more talk like that. Remember what Dr. Henry says. This is not a situation of blame. It's a biological anomaly."

"Apparently, you're the biological anomaly, Park. What will the neighbors say? How will you explain this to our families? Do you even have any idea who the mother might be?"

No, I don't. I don't have a clue.

"I'm sure this is some sort of lab screwup," he says. "They've made a mistake."

"They don't make mistakes with DNA. They wouldn't be here if they weren't sure."

"Just… Olivia, go upstairs, okay? Let me talk to the police, let me straighten this out. You do need to lie down, you look very pale. Take an iron pill, and maybe a little something to relax you. Since you won't hurt the baby—"

Her face crumples, and he trails off. The tears have ended—Olivia is too strong for her own good—but she needs to temper things. No woman should have to go through what she has. He feels a spike of guilt for his uncharitable thought about her weight being to blame for the babies. Of course this isn't her fault. It's a terrible circumstance, that's all.

"No numbing," she says finally. "I have to work today. The Jones build. And you owe me an explanation of what the hell is going on. When you finish telling them whatever it is you need to say without me in earshot, I expect you to share with me, Park Bender. Is that understood?"

This last is said fiercely, and he nods. Without another argument, Olivia moves soundlessly to the stairs and floats up, small feet soft on the runner. He watches her go, heart twisted, mind whirling.

This absolutely cannot be happening.

The detectives are still in the kitchen. He half hoped they'd see his family was suffering and quietly let themselves out, but no, here they are, the Black cowboy sitting at the table calmly sipping away and the cold white chick with the swan's neck standing at the window, looking out at the backyard. The feeders are nearly empty, and the squirrels are up to their usual hijinks, hanging upside down, tails straight out as the feeders spin wildly. Olivia always laughs when they do this, says it's their way of going on a roller-coaster ride. Moore seems to agree, is more animated, at least. He doesn't know how Osley can stand being with her all day; she's so intense, so disapproving.

Osley has helped himself to another cup of coffee. He sets down the cup with a small click and smiles, gesturing for Park to take the chair opposite, as if this is *his* kitchen, *his* home, and Park the honored guest.

Park hesitates a moment, drops into the chair. Moore stays by the window.

"Sorry things are so confusing, sir. Your wife okay?"

"She will be. Listen, she's in a fragile state right now. We've lost several pregnancies, and it's been very difficult. We're both in therapy, trying to make sense of it all. You can imagine this news coming as more than a shock. That I have…a kid." He shakes his head like a wasp is flying near. "How old is he?"

"We don't know for sure. Old enough to ejaculate. Now that your wife's out of earshot, who's the mother?"

Park shakes his head again. "I told you. I honestly have no idea. I don't have a lot of exes. Olivia and I dated in high school. I had a girlfriend in college, then Olivia and I got back together."

Osley's eyes glitter. "Speaking of the girlfriend in college—"

"She's dead. Which I assume you already know, or else you wouldn't be here."

3

THE WIFE

"The suspect in our case is your biological son."

That word, that word. Olivia wants a son. She wants sweet-smelling baby skin to cuddle. She wants so much, more than she's ever going to get. More than she deserves.

Who has birthed her husband's child? Is he telling the truth that he doesn't know? He's been faithless before; has it happened again, and again, and again? When did this anonymous woman spread her legs for him to sow his seed?

She opens the cabinet, assesses the array of bottles. It is tempting, too tempting, to seek the oblivion of a pill. How easy it would be to just check out of this situation.

Park has a child.

If this was happening to anyone else, the irony would be delicious. They'd lie together on the couch, legs intertwined, watching some random documentary about the story, a mysterious child who murders women, drinking wine and giggling at the absurdity of it all.

Can you imagine? Poor guy. He had no idea.

Poor guy? Poor kid!

But this is their chaos. There is no way they're going to keep it a secret. If Park doesn't cooperate, the police will just leak it to the media, and he'll be forced to confront the story in the press. They are going to be scrutinized, pitied, torn asunder. She can already hear the screams from the street as she slams the door—*Mr. Bender, how does it make you feel to know you're father to a murderer? Mr. Bender, why didn't you tell your wife you had a child with another woman? Mrs. Bender, how are you still living under this roof knowing your husband lied to you all these years—*

"Jesus."

Olivia shuts the cabinet, scrubs her face, twists her chocolate hair into a bun, changes from her yoga pants and T-shirt into leggings, boots, and a blazer. Her therapist is going to be pissed at her for normalizing things again. She'll want both Olivia and Park to sit down and discuss their "feelings" about the miscarriage immediately, add entries to the dog-eared journals they're both supposed to be keeping, sharing those words between them, but damned if she's going to put herself through another round of *who's fault is it?* That's all their conversations are anymore anyway. Olivia—I'm so sorry, the money, it's me, we can't keep doing this; Park—it's fine, it's not your fault, we have plenty, we'll try again. Reassuring, cajoling, tender, conciliatory, while inside she can feel him blaming her.

At some point, he will want a baby enough to try with someone else, and he'll divorce her, leave her the house maybe, as a consolation prize, with its sterile bathrooms and haunted toilets, while he sets up shop across town with a leggy blonde who produces two-point-three perfect towheaded little beasts within the first five years.

Now he has his deepest desire. It doesn't matter how. It only matters that he is a father, and she is not a mother. Maybe she can just get her tubes tied so she doesn't have to go through the agony of hope anymore. She won't tell him. She'll just never get pregnant again, and they can go back to their lives before they became *those people,* the people she felt sorry for, the people she pitied. The statistics. The anomalies. The curiosities. Infertility is fascinating to those who seek to break its back. The doctors and the therapists who get rich at the expense of those desperate to procreate. Oh, they care. But they're still rolling in it.

Stop. Stop. You're not getting anywhere with this line of thinking.

She swipes on a little lip stain, then heads for the front door. Let Park deal with the police. She needs to get out of here.

The detectives' Crown Vic sits at the curb like a great black buzzard hovering over a freshly dead deer. Her Jeep is in the driveway—since Park put a gym on her side of the garage, her car was nominated to sit outside in the weather. "It's more rugged than mine," he'd said at the time, dismissing the fact that hers was much more interesting to people who might want to break in. "Who wants to steal tile samples?" he scoffed, laughing at the very idea, so she's been parking in the drive for the better part of two months. She is grateful for it now; she can slip away without raising the door and drawing everyone's attention.

She leaves the car in Neutral and lets it roll backward out of the drive, then whips the Jeep around, heading toward Belmont. The Jones build will give her plenty of distraction today.

She feels only a little guilty about leaving him with the cops.

Work. Focus. Escape.

Between teardowns and new builds and the renovation boom, she has five houses currently underway and a wait list of ten more. Nashville is slammed with new construction right now. She can't drive a block without seeing a construction site. The big boom downtown, multiple skyscrapers going up at once, gave the town the nickname Crane City, but now, with the influx of tech jobs and the vagaries of the COVID pandemic, the push is out of the city into HDH—high-density housing, also known as "tall and skinnies"—on the fringes of downtown, and the suburbs beyond. Add in new builds, renovations, additions—every craftsperson in Nashville is spoken for.

She is grateful she has her own crew who've been working with her for years, grateful she has the jobs lined up to keep them busy, because finding new and reliable tradesmen in this environment is like casting a line into the final hour of an end-of-season salmon spawn. Everyone is looking for people, and anyone worth their salt is committed for months.

Though there are plenty of craftsmen who will do whatever Olivia Bender wants, just to have a chance at the publicity. OHB Designs is regularly featured in all the magazines around town and many national publications. There's even been talk of a television show, but she's resisted. She hates the idea of losing her privacy, of having to conform to others' ideals of what her life and work should look like. Anyway, trying to have a baby is a full-time job, as she's told Park numerous times. *I'd rather be a mom than have a show.* How many times has she said it? Twice? Three times? At some point, she's going to start believing it. Though now...police on the doorstep, the phone ringing, the neighbors staring. Murder, and scandal. A child, not of her blood. What of their privacy? Their lives are being upended, and it is only going to get worse.

Maybe now *is* the time to open negotiations. Maybe she should capitalize on this.

Olivia Hutton, you are a horrible person. Human, but horrible.

Stay the course. Do your work, your way. That's what will get you through. It always has.

Olivia has a reputation for creating elegant, livable spaces that are at once homey, personal, as minimal or maximalist as her clients want, but always done with taste and restraint. She understands space and color, knows how to take down a wall and make the room come together, knows when an exposed beam or shiplap wall or quad-level crown molding or orange velvet barstool will do the trick. With her architectural design background, she is not just sought after, she is the crowning glory for anyone who gets her on their job.

She's worked her ass off to get to this point, and she's loved every minute. She has nurtured her talent to create livable spaces out of thin air, lives and breathes color and texture and mixed metals and raw wood and stone. Her perfect day involves hammers and nail guns and paintbrushes and rug placements and jovial shouts in colloquial Spanish and Romanians singing lullabies as they caulk bathtubs. Why would she ruin a good thing by having a kid?

This is why you keep losing the babies, Olivia. You don't really want them.

A shudder runs through her. That isn't true. Of course she wants them. She wants them so badly she can pretend to herself she doesn't. Lying to yourself is the greatest lie of all, isn't it?

She flips on the radio to drown out her thoughts, but they are breathlessly covering Beverly Cooke. It figures that brash woman was going to be a part of Olivia's life forever. It's always the ones you don't want around who stay with you ad nauseam. Beverly wanted to be Olivia's friend. She'd tried everything—texting invites to bunko nights, sending referrals, asking for advice. Olivia was just turned off by her from the very beginning. Yes, she was being judgmental, yes, she was being spiky and unfriendly. Who cares? It was not Olivia's responsibility to make a stranger trying to force her way into her life feel better. Therapy has given her permission to take what she needs from life, from the people around her, and leave the rest. She is not going to apologize for simply not liking the woman.

But Beverly is dead, and Olivia feels bad about this, she truly does. As aggravating as the woman was, Olivia didn't want her to die. Not really. Not like that. Raped, murdered, and submerged in the lake? It's the stuff nightmares are made of.

If Park's child has done this, what does that mean? What does that say about Park?

The arrow-to-the-heart thought leaves her breathless again. Will she ever not feel the betrayal at the words? *Park has a child. A son. At least one son. Who knows, maybe there's more.*

Now there was a nightmarish thought.

And if her handsome, loving, giving husband could create a child who grew up to be a killer? She needs to rethink everything. She knows there's a difference between nature and nurture, between passing on homicidal genes and creating monsters out of neglect and abuse, but plenty of kids are abused and don't kill things. Don't kill people. Maybe they're all just seething like she is. Maybe they're all just so sad. But they don't go through with it. They don't act on their whims.

Can she have children with a man who's taken part in creating a monster?

Her cell rings, the caller ID popping up on the screen in the car. She expects it to be Park, but it's Lindsey. Park's little sister is his polar opposite and has been Olivia's best friend since they were kids. She debates letting it go to voice mail in case Park has reached out to her, but no, there's been no time. Park would call his wife first, not his sister.

"Hey, Linds."

"Hey, yourself. You will never believe what I just heard."

Olivia tenses. It's already out there, it's too late to contain it. Their lives, upended, ruined. "What did you hear?"

"Perry is coming home."

4

THE PAST

Nashville, Tennessee
April 1999

“He’s here, he’s here. Oh my God, wait until you see him, he’s gorgeous.”

Olivia’s mother drops the curtain and flits around her bedroom like a demented butterfly. Her father is downstairs, waiting with the camera for Olivia to make her grand entrance.

“And so are you, my darling girl. You two will be the talk of prom.”

Olivia smiles, swallows back her nerves, and gives her nose one last sweep with the powder brush. A few grains fall onto the strapless bustline of the pale chrysanthemum organza, and she carefully brushes them away. Prom. Rite of passage. She will be going through many rites of passage tonight. First corsage. First black-tie event. First time.

It's been planned for weeks. They have a hotel room—ostensibly, the whole crowd is going to be there, but they've managed a suite with an adjoining bedroom, so they'll be able to sneak off for privacy once people start passing out. She's not nervous to lose her virginity, not to him. They're going to be together forever, she knows this in her heart. They have a tie that will see them through everything, a link that's been in place since the day they met. The day the Benders moved to town, and she saw the boys across the street for the first time, she'd felt it, that zing, an invisible thread that crossed the street and tied her to him. He'd seen her lingering on the porch, threw up a hand in a jaunty wave, already so comfortable with his new surroundings. Then he punched his brother in the arm—she knew it was his brother, they looked alike, not exactly, but they were similar in the ways that counted—and the other boy made brief eye contact with her, then looked shyly away. The girl, younger, pretty, had come tearing around from the side yard screaming about a rope swing, and the three of them had disappeared through the hedge without a word. But the moment was ossified for her, clear as amber in her mind's eye.

And here they are, six years later, vivacious, elegant Olivia Hutton and studious, athletic Park Bender, the most popular couple in school, about to embark on the most important night of their lives, the night that will change everything, and they both know it. Not just know it, accept it, encourage it, relish it. They've been counting down the months, weeks, days, hours—and now minutes, and it's finally here, the life-altering moment has arrived in the back of a limo with his brother Perry, flying solo despite myriad options, and two other couples, and she's never been more ready for anything in her short seventeen and a half years on this earth.

The night does not go as planned.

Oh, it starts well enough. The photographs are perfect, Olivia sweeping down the grand staircase (she's always wondered if her mother insisted on buying the house in preparation for this moment). Her mother cries a little. Her father looks ridiculously proud. Park charms them both, and they sign the pledge that they won't drink and drive—a family tradition before every date—even though they've paid for the limo for the whole night and the following morning.

Thank heavens there are no more pledges to make to the parents. If they knew what was planned…

They arrive to the adulation of their friends and teachers—their clique mobbing them like typical adolescent sycophants, with squeals of admiration and high-fives and knowing looks.

The band is great, they dance and take photos, and someone manages to spike the punch so they're all too merry and the teachers are pissed off.

No, it doesn't start to go south until it's time to crown the King and Queen and Perry Bender is named Prom King instead of Park. He was on the court, sure, of course he was, but no one expected it. Park is the King of the school. Everyone knows it. Perry hadn't even bothered with a date.

So it is Perry standing next to Olivia in her gaudy store-bought crown being photographed and cheered, looking both thrilled and bashful and not a little shocked, while Park storms from the gymnasium with a scowl, followed, as Olivia catches out of the corner of her eye, by Alison Banks. Alison is moving surreptitiously, as if heading toward the bathrooms but instead ducking left at the last moment, out the door Park slammed through.

It is Perry who kisses Olivia's hand gallantly to the cheers of the student body, who takes advantage of the King-and-Queen dance to hold Olivia in his arms in the most confusing way. Perry has been as much a brother to her as Lindsey has been a sister, and suddenly, he is taller than Park, leaner; his arms are strong and warm and feel similar to his brother's but different, too. He smells of cedar and woodsmoke, so alien in this proximity. He's always been a handsome boy, but tonight he looks rakishly charming in his tuxedo, his too-long hair in a tight ponytail at the nape of his neck, his braces recently expunged from his bright white teeth, and his eyes, gray with the barest hint of blue around the edge of the iris, heavily lashed—staring deep into her own in ways that make her stomach twitch. When had he gotten so good-looking?

She's never seen Perry in this light, never.

It was her fault, of course. She should have shunned the dance, escaped after Park immediately, smoothed over the ruffled feathers, abdicated, perhaps, to someone else on the court, but something about how Park handled the situation, not with good humor or even begrudgingly, but throwing a small tantrum and stalking out, does not endear him to her at this moment. Yes, it was a disappointment, but still, she's been crowned Queen, and he could at least acknowledge this coup de grâce for her.

When the dance is over, Perry stops staring soulfully into her eyes, squeezes her arms, and returns to his regularly scheduled brotherly state. "He's pretty pissed. Let's go talk to him."

And it is the two of them—Olivia and Perry—who seek out Park. The two of them who find Park with his hand up Alison Bank's slinky black dress, her hair spilling out of its hundred-dollar updo and her eyes clenched in ecstasy.

The two of them who flee—Olivia first, Perry right after her, with Park stammering and calling, and Alison stamping away unfulfilled—to the parking lot, where Olivia breaks down, and is comforted by Perry, Perry the second brother, the friend, the witty jouster of puns and illicit six-packs, who tells her the affair has been going on for a month at least and holds her in his arms as she weeps.

It was inevitable that he would brush away her tears, inevitable that he would run a finger across her lower lip, inevitable that he would kiss her.

Inevitable that they would lose their virginity to each other in the back of the limousine—Olivia in a sheer, unadulterated rage fuck, Perry in something else, something deeper and quieter, but no less intense, no less strong.

Inevitable, the regret. The recriminations. The scandal. The breakup.

Inevitable that Park dumped her, and she didn't want Perry, who was more than happy to play the chivalrous knight, being half in love with her himself, and always had been.

Inevitable that nine weeks later, pale and clammy and borderline hysterical, she was driven to Knoxville by her best friend, where no one would know or see or stop her, and had the life they'd created that night carved from her belly.

5

THE WIFE

Olivia brakes, hard, the car behind her shrieking to a stop just shy of her bumper. She waves a hand in apology and yanks the Jeep to the shoulder, the wheels skidding on the loose gravel.

Lindsey's voice shouts through the car's speaker. "Are you okay? I heard the brakes—"

"I'm fine. All good. Car in front of me braked at the yellow."

She is not fine. She is not all good. She is numb. And numb she must stay, or the whole world will crumble around her.

She can't handle Perry on top of all of this.

Perry, with his soft gray eyes and floppy blond hair. Perry, with his rangy body, hard and lean in all the right places. Perry, with his heart of gold and silly laugh and velvet lips.

Perry, Park's brother. His twin, for God's sake.

"I assume he called?" she hears herself ask, voice sounding calm and cool. Disinterested.

"Texted. He needs to be in New York next week. He thought he'd fly here first, before he heads up north, then back to Europe. He has a shoot in a month. He has to climb the Matterhorn. Can you believe that?"

Perry, swathed in gear, goggles on, his beard crusted in ice and snow, grinning from the top of the world, arms outstretched as if to say—I rule this place.

That image, burned into her brain from the climb when they almost lost him.

You'd think almost dying in an icy crevasse would deter him. Losing two toes, three friends, a Sherpa guide, and thousands of dollars of the best camera equipment the BBC's money could buy would convince him to stay home, to give up the dangerous lifestyle of a nature photographer. Olivia has never understood his compulsion to fling himself heedlessly into harm's way.

He has a shoot in a month.

Clearly it hadn't.

The two of them, her husband and his brother, so different—in looks, in temperament, interests, attitudes. Even politics. How they'd shared a womb was beyond her. Park was so settled in comparison to Perry, who was more comfortable lying on his stomach in a mud puddle with a long-lens camera waiting to see if a leopard would come to a drinking hole than having a simple conversation. Yin and yang.

"Olivia?"

"Sorry, Lindsey. Zoned out."

"What are you up to right now?"

"I'm on my way to a client's house."

"Pick me up? You can drop me at Fido's on your way. I can grab a coffee and work from there for a while."

"All right. See you in five."

"Liv?"

Olivia pulls the car back onto Hillsboro, careful to make

sure there is no oncoming traffic in sight. She doesn't need to be anywhere near other drivers like this. "Yeah?"

"Are you really okay? You sound off."

"Yeah."

She punches the button on the wheel to cut the call before Lindsey pushes further. Non-answers don't work with her. She's a lawyer and she's literal, wants every detail broken out, likes her stories told sequentially, but always forgets the punchlines of jokes just when she gets to the good part. Olivia loves her. Olivia is afraid to be alone with her now, because there's no way they aren't going to go there, going to dig into the past that Olivia has so carefully fortressed, especially when she shares there's been another miscarriage.

But who else can she talk to about this...betrayal? This monstrous betrayal? Who else knows her as Lindsey does?

She makes all the lights, a miracle in this town, turns into Forest Hills, then onto Lindsey's street, sees an icy, remote blonde with the profile of a Russian princess and calves that could cut glass standing at the intersection. She must have run down the hill.

Lindsey, wrapped in an oatmeal cashmere sweater and black tights against the early fall morning chill, sipping from an Ember travel mug. Great. Already caffeinated.

There is not enough caffeine in the world to handle this morning.

Olivia maneuvers the car to the curb, putting on her hazard lights so no one accidentally plows into them, and depresses the lock button. Lindsey opens the door with a lascivious wink.

"Hey, lady. Wanna date?"

Olivia can't help the smile. She has always been astounded by Lindsey's bawdiness. You'd think after all these years...but no. Olivia will always be the girl who blushes at the inappropriate remark. It's who she is.

"You know it."

Once her seat belt is dutifully clicked into place, Lindsey sets her thermos in the cupholder and turns ice-blue lasers on her best friend. "Spill. What the hell is going on?"

Olivia explains as succinctly as possible. Just the facts, ma'am. Be dispassionate.

"Park is at the house with the detectives who are working on Beverley Cooke's murder. There's a DNA match to a suspect, and they've traced it through some database to Park."

The gasp is satisfactory. "Park? That's impossible."

"Not Park." Olivia doesn't take her eyes off the road. "Apparently he has a child. A son."

She risks a glance. Lindsey is staring out the window, shoulders tense.

"Did you know?"

"Know?"

The tone… "Lindsey. Tell me."

"No. Of course not. It's nothing. Really. I was just thinking about Chapel Hill. You know, everything that happened with Park while y'all were broken up. Hey, you just drove past Fido's."

"Dang it."

Chapel Hill. She hasn't thought about that for years. Not really. A chapter of Park's life she wasn't directly involved in until after the fact, but a chapter closed, nonetheless.

Of course. That's how the police put him together with Beverly's killer. His DNA was in the system.

She takes the next left, circles the block, then enters the parking lot. She makes no move to get out of the car, and Lindsey, taking the hint, takes a pull on her mug and twists in her seat to face Olivia.

"There's more. Talk."

"I lost the baby this morning."

Lindsey doesn't touch her, knows even the gentlest caress would be unwelcome, but she closes her eyes briefly and blows out a heavy breath. "Shit. That sucks. I'm sorry."

This is comforting to Olivia, who is so used to people falling all over themselves with obsequious platitudes when they find out about the fertility issues that sometimes, a simple declarative statement makes it all better. At least Lindsey isn't going to follow up with "It will be okay. You can just adopt." Or some other horrifying brush-off. Olivia had nearly punched the no-longer-a-friend who said it first, but was shocked to hear it echoed again and again—from friends to doctors to parents to strangers.

No one understands what it is like. No one can possibly understand unless they've been through it themselves. Olivia has been put on this earth to fulfill one essential biological duty—procreate—and she isn't going to be able to do that, isn't ever going to get past the first few months of the quickening, and it's all her own damn fault.

Lindsey, though, has an inkling of what's behind Olivia's self-flagellation. They haven't talked about it, not out loud, but Olivia knows Lindsey gets it without having to lay it out. Lindsey is the only one who knows. A mistake made in haste as a child has cost Olivia her entire future.

It's all my fault.

Park has a child.

"Liv? You okay?"

"Yeah. Sorry. Drifted off there. Anyway. I need to get to work."

Lindsey takes the hint. "I'm sure this is just some sort of lab screwup. Hang in there. If you want to talk later, call me."

"When is Perry showing up?" She's surprised by the bitter curiosity in her tone, but Lindsey doesn't seem to notice.

"He's going to send me his itinerary. I'm picking him up from the airport. Want to—"

"No."

"You didn't even know what I was going to ask."

"If it involves Perry, the answer is always going to be no."

6

THE HUSBAND

Park hears Olivia running water upstairs, hears the door click closed, hears the Jeep's engine turn over. He is hurt that she's running but doesn't blame her. Not really.

Detective Osley raises a brow, and Park shrugs. "Let her go. She needs time to process. This must have been a terrible shock. What else can I answer for you?"

"Obviously, Mr. Bender, your time in Chapel Hill, the case of your dead girlfriend, it's of interest to us."

"That case is closed. I had nothing to do with Melanie's death."

"Oh, we know. But the similarities are uncanny. And your son—"

"Quit calling him my son. I don't know this person. He is your *suspect*. And I don't care for the insinuations you're making. I know nothing about this, and I want to be kept out of it, do you understand? I won't let you go ruining my life to chase down a dead-end lead."

Both cops watch him, a thousand times more interested now. *Stop reacting. You're making yourself look guilty.*

He blows out a breath. "I apologize. This is hard for me. Olivia…she doesn't need any drama right now."

"Fair enough. Is there anything you can tell us, anyone who might be able to help? There's gotta be a mother." Osley leans forward with a conspiratorial grin. "You know it only takes once. Could be a drunk hookup. Could be a short relationship. Could be you pushed someone into it, and she was scared afterward…"

"Except I don't make drunk hookups. And I don't force myself on women. I'm a married man, for Christ's sake. I want to help. I really do. I just don't—"

But he does. Oh, God. He does. He needs the cops out of here, now.

Moore catches his hesitation. "Mr. Bender?"

"It's nothing. Truly, I'm sorry. Please let me know what happens. I'd like to…well, I'd like to know who he is, regardless of what he's done. I'm so sorry we had to meet under these circumstances. Please, if you can avoid dragging my family into this, I'd appreciate it. Olivia is having a hard enough time without having this thrown in her face."

"That's not really up to us, Mr. Bender. Your wife does know about your history in Chapel Hill, doesn't she?"

There's the shot across the bow he's been waiting for. Chummy it up, then strong-arm him into giving them something, anything. An oblique threat to ruin his life, all he's gutted it out for, the toehold he's gained in the community, into the lives of his students, his family, his secret readers. He's done a damn good job of becoming as anonymous as possible. A few well-placed words and poof, everything reverts, and you are again the person from that horrific year, the object of scorn and derision, the one women cross the street to avoid walking past. People forget they enjoy having you over for dinner, instead want to gossip and scheme and point fingers.

"Of course she does. It was national news, for a time. That's how Olivia and I found each other again. She knew I had nothing to do with Melanie's death."

"Want to run us through what happened there?"

"In Chapel Hill? Not particularly. That part of my life is over, and I prefer to keep it that way. You have all you need from the files, I'm sure."

End this.

He stands. The detectives gather their things, drop cups in the sink, leave cards on the table.

"We'll be in touch," Moore says, eyes cold as the ocean. "And if you do remember anything, Mr. Bender, you give us a call, okay? A woman's dead, and we need to find her killer. That's all we care about."

"That's all I care about, as well."

He waits until their car has turned at the corner before shutting the door and quietly making his way to his office in the backyard.

He will not think about how similar the crimes are. Will not think about a girl, found dead in a lake, more than twenty years ago, and a woman, now, also found dead in a lake, only miles from where he is standing.

How long was Beverly Cooke in the water? He wanted to ask details, wanted to know more, but he couldn't ask, not without looking weird, or guilty.

They'd sensed his eagerness to hear more, hadn't they? Moore had, at least. He needs to be careful around her. He can imagine just how easily she can spin lies from truths.

No, he has bigger problems.

The combination safe in the closet of his office is keyed to the date of Olivia's first miscarriage. Morbid as hell, he knows, but a sequence no one outside the family would ever latch onto.

He moves aside the stack of emergency cash, the contracts, the envelope with the small gold ingots his mother left him in her will, the gun, and pulls out a file from the bottom of the stack, one he never in a million years thought to need again, cursing himself.

So naive. You've always been so naive. Of course this could happen.

The file is laminated, has a cheery yellow cover with a hand-drawn house, smoke rising from the chimney, a white picket fence, and two genderless people in shadow, holding hands. A child's drawing, commissioned from an adult artist, he's sure of that.

The red print is subdued, elegant in contrast with the childish drawing.

Winterborn Life Sciences.

He closes the safe and takes the file to his desk, shoving papers out of the way. He puts on his glasses and goes through the paperwork.

A copy of the questionnaire, his medical records, blood work. The release forms. IQ tests. He was healthy. Smart. Handsome. Attractive as hell to anyone who wanted to use him. The perfect donor. Especially because he wanted no contact from the children he might sire. *I give to you my essence and expect nothing in return.*

Of course, he wasn't expecting one of them to become a killer.

He slams shut the file, tosses it on the desk. There's nothing here to give him answers. There's nothing to tell him what he needs to know. And he can't exactly call them and demand answers, can he?

Well, that's not true. He could…

He needs Lindsey. She'll know what to do.

But his sister's phone goes to voice mail. She's either driving or in a meeting. He leaves her a brief message—"Call me, it's urgent"—and sets his phone gently on the table, facedown.

He is overwhelmed. The thoughts are coming so fast he can't keep track of them.

Olivia.

She is the priority.

He chastises himself—he's called his sister for help before calling his wife to offer solace. No wonder Olivia ran. She'd just gone through hell—another miscarriage, the news he had a child, the police on their doorstep, the death of a friend—and he'd let her leave. What sort of monster is he?

He starts to dial her number, puts the phone back on the table.

How can he face her? What is he going to say?

He should have told her, should have confessed immediately when she'd made the damn gracious offer a year ago for him to donate sperm so he could leave a piece of himself behind. He should have fessed up immediately when the police said he had a kid.

Instead, he lied to her, he lied to them, and now what is he going to do?

Olivia will be devastated.

More devastated than she already must be.

Good job, asshole. You're going to ruin her life, on top of everything.

She has every right to be rocked by this news, news that should not have been a surprise.

God, why did he lie? It was knee-jerk, immediate. Hide the truth, no matter what.

You didn't lie. You omitted. The cops will get it. You needed to have a heart-to-heart with your wife. You needed her on your side before you revealed the truth.

He fingers the edge of the phone. *You love her. She's your wife. You don't have to say the right thing, you just have to say something.*

"I'm not pregnant anymore. I lost it. This morning."

The chasm in her eyes as she broke the news.

His heart is bruised. Another baby gone. Another life unled.

It's not Olivia's fault. He knows this. So why does he resent her so much?

Things have been hard lately. It's not just losing the babies. Their lives, their relationship, have become singularly focused. There's nothing like basal thermometers and missionary-style timed sex to make the heart go wild.

It wasn't always like this. Their *before* was incredible, full of travel and excitement and impulsivity. And when they started trying, it was a heck of a lot of fun.

Even when it became clear they weren't going to get pregnant without professional help, Olivia devised naughty games to make the stud calls—as she referred to them—sexy instead of drudgery. The doctor's office wouldn't let her in the room with him when he was giving his samples, so she wrote him dirty letters he could read while he masturbated instead of rifling through the skin mags left on the small side table. They both agreed there was something singularly gross about wanking off with the same magazines as the guy he'd sat next to in the waiting room who'd been called in first, the two of them stiff-shouldered and avoiding eye contact.

But as she lost pregnancy after pregnancy, all the little touches disappeared. She sank deeper into her grief. There were no more notes, no more jokes. Things were serious now. She reeked of desperation. He saw the way she looked at young families and pregnant women. He saw the avarice in her eyes, the way her lips tightened, the smile becoming a rictus, even as she pretended things were fine. After the fifth miscarriage, he'd said the magic words—why don't we consider adoption—and she'd gone ballistic.

She didn't want someone else's kid. She wanted her own. Their own. She was torturing herself for him, damn it, so he could have a child to call his.

The irony of this moment is not lost on him.

He starts to dial her, again. Puts the phone down, again.

He just doesn't know what to say to the stranger who is his wife. To the crying, desperate, unhappy woman he saw earlier. He will never forget her face when she heard the news. The betrayal he's done to her. To them.

Again.

7

THE WIFE

Olivia manages to swim deep in her work and avoid Park until dinnertime. He's called several times, each message progressively more intense.

"Please come home. Please."

"I have to talk to you."

"I have to explain."

"Please, Olivia, let me explain."

"Damn it, quit ignoring me or I'll come to the build, and we'll talk this out in front of the crew."

With every call, it sounded more and more like he'd figured out who the mother of his mysterious son was.

You can't ignore him forever, Olivia.

She is tired, hungry, crampy, and sad. So sad. She'd managed to keep things together until the call to the clinic to let them know about the baby. The nurse who answered had burst into tears, a very unprofessional but entirely human response, and that had set Olivia off, too. They'd cried together, two women separated by a few miles and an unbreachable gulf. The nurse, a sweet lady named Brigit Blessing, had suffered her own trauma, her own loss, a few years before Olivia and Park started working with the clinic. A child born who lived for only a few hours. That loss, Olivia felt, was a thousand times harder than anything she had faced. The needles, the pills, the terrible side effects, the days she had to lie in bed before and after the harvesting while her ovaries filled with blood and fluid, swelling her belly to comical proportions and making her incredibly sick, the blood in the toilet, again, and again. No. It didn't compare. There had been no breaths. No opening of eyes, no flexing of limbs, no touching of fragile, translucent skin. Olivia's tragedies are amorphous blobs, swept away on a current. If she'd held one in her arms and watched them die? No. She would not be able to go on. That Brigit was able to continue working with young mothers and their own many disappointments was a testament to her strength.

Olivia felt a measure of peace when they hung up. No one but another woman who's lost a child can truly understand. Even Lindsey's unflagging grace isn't quite enough.

She needs a glass of wine and a good night's sleep. Maybe some Ativan, after all. She wants to check out for a little while. And she must face Park, and his terrible secret, and try not to blow up her marriage.

Kill him with kindness, her mother always says. Olivia misses her. Her parents are on a monthlong sailing cruise at the moment. They should be rounding Cape Horn and off into the seas to Antarctica this week. A lifelong dream to see the South Shetland Islands. They're relatively unreachable, or Olivia would have been on the phone to her all day, asking for advice.

She's rather proud of herself for weathering the storm without her mother or her husband. She tends to want to fix Park's emotions, to make him feel like things are okay when inside she is tearing apart, but today, she decided to allow herself a few hours of genuine self-pity without worrying for him.

She calls ahead to their favorite restaurant and orders dinner to go. Steak frites for him, halibut for her, some prosciutto and figs to start, crème brûlée to finish. A celebration meal. For some reason, it feels appropriate to have something delicious in her stomach that she hasn't made herself to tackle the evening's conversation. It is not a reward for bad behavior, it is a bolster.

Traffic is light, and she pulls into the parking lot of 360 Bistro before the meal is ready. No problem. She'll have a glass of wine at the bar while she waits.

She's greeted and seated, and accepts a luscious, minerally cab franc and a glass of water. The restaurant is dark and quiet. Service has just begun. They'll hit their stride later; right now, it's only two tables in the back, the four-top at the door, and her. The television is showing a golf match, but the sound is off, and she can hear the conversation from the four-top easily.

The older couple are regulars. She's seen them in here before. They're joined tonight by a younger couple who've apparently recently married. The young bride is wearing a massive diamond that shines brilliantly in the dim light. Paterfamilias calls for a bottle of champagne, and when the waiter pours out, the young woman coyly puts her hand over her glass. A moment of shock—"We could have wine instead, or a cocktail," he says—but the girl continues her silent Madonna smile and shakes her head. Then the table erupts in congratulations.

"Oh, my goodness, a baby! When are you due?"

"April," she crows, grinning at her husband, clearly thrilled at their surprise. She has a small strip of paper in her hand. "We had the first ultrasound this morning. Here, you can see—"

"Olivia? Dinner, hon."

She drags her attention back, and the bartender hands her the brown bag and the check. Olivia's hands are shaking. She signs her name in an untidy scrawl and downs the wine.

"You okay, hon?"

"Fine," she says, her voice unnatural, high. There is a steak knife in the place setting next to her, a beautiful piece of metal, flowing lines and wicked sharp edges. She could plant it in the back of the girl's neck as she passes. It would take no effort at all to—

"You tell Park I said hi, won't you?"

"Oh. Yes. Of course. Thank you."

She manages to get to the car, throw the bag on the seat, and drive away, all without looking at the smug-as-shit face of the pregnant little bitch by the door. The fact that her key may have slid oh so surreptitiously along the door of the BMW the young couple pulled up in as she went to her own car, well, that was just poor placement of her hand, right?

Olivia blows out a breath, slowly.

These urges of hers. She knows it's the hormones they're pumping through her body, first the shots and pills to get pregnant, then the natural accumulation of estrogen and progesterone that nourishes her small, broken womb, but oh, these urges. She has some PTSD, at least that's what her therapist says. Olivia thinks that's nonsense, it's not like she's been to war or was abused or anything.

Only last week: "I'm so angry, Dr. Benedict. All the time. I feel this rage pulsing inside me anytime I see a pregnant woman."

"Olivia. You've gotten pregnant six times in the past two years. You've lost five of those pregnancies. They have what you so desperately want. It's normal to feel upset when you see a woman who's carrying a child. It's okay to be angry that you haven't been able to carry a child to term. It's unfair, and it's sad. But you're farther along than you've been before. I have a good feeling about this one."

Olivia casts her thoughts back to her bathroom, the scene of the crime. *So much for your good feeling, Doc.*

Home belongs to a stranger. She sees it from a new perspective. Not the graceful lines of the pitched roof and the gable with its cedar posts anchoring the front porch, nor the French country charm of the white brick and graphite shingles, the front elevation bedecked with boxwood and laurel. Maybe it's something in the water. Or there's lead paint. Or radon. Maybe they should move. She's probably ingesting or breathing some sort of poison, and that's why she keeps killing her babies.

Sitting in the drive, she pulls up her shopping app and orders a new water filter, a lead paint test kit, and emails her inspector to drop off a meter for a radon check. Small things, but they make her feel better.

You can do this. You're strong, Olivia. You can face him.

She's not supposed to feel revulsion when she thinks of her husband's handsome face. Is this what he's done to them? Or is this the betrayal of her body?

She knocks her door closed with her hip and carries the food inside. The kitchen, with its cheery white cabinets and leathered marble and black-framed windows, no different than it was this morning, feels alien. Like she's never seen it before. Maybe she's coming down with something. Maybe she's caught some sort of virus and that's why she lost the baby.

She busies herself with plating the food and throwing the bags in the trash, then sets the plates in the oven and puts it on Warm.

Park hasn't shown himself.

She opens the door to the garage; his car is inside.

In his office, then.

The phone rings, startling her.

"Hello?"

"Is Park Bender available?"

The voice, female, young, a hint of flirt.

"Who is this?" Olivia asks, not caring about being abrupt. Is this the sainted mother of the creep who killed Beverly? She's worked fast, discovering how to reach out to her child's father.

"Ma'am, this is Erica Pearl from Channel Four. I'd like to speak to Mr. Bender, please."

Oh.

"About what?"

"Are you Mrs. Bender? I'd love to sit down with you both and talk about the Cooke case. There's—"

Olivia smashes End with her thumb.

Didn't take them long. How did the news get out? Damn those cops.

The phone rings again, and she ignores it, fury driving away her worry. She trails through the house to the back door, out onto the porch, through the garden, and pushes open Park's office door.

"A reporter from Channel Four just called."

"Huh?" Park looks up, unseeing for a moment, until his brain clears of whatever he's writing, and he is able to focus on her again.

"Honey. You're home," he says, leaning back so quickly that the chair tips precariously.

"A reporter just called."

He pushes away from the desk and stands as if to hug her, but she steps back, and his arms hang empty in the air, a parenthesis of confusion, before dropping to his side.

"They've been trying my cell, too. I haven't answered. I don't know what they want me to say. And I thought you and

I should talk first, before I discuss anything with anyone outside the family."

She crosses her arms on her chest. "All right. Talk. Who is this mysterious mother who's had your child?"

"I honestly have no idea. I swear. Please, will you just sit down for a minute? You're making me nervous."

She blows out a breath and sinks into the chair across from his desk. It is dark brown leather, cracked in multiple places, missing nails along its border, and needs to be replaced. She hates it. He loves it.

Welcome to marriage.

"I need to tell you something," Park says.

He looks as nervous as he did the night she confronted him about screwing Alison damn Banks the summer after their senior year.

He hands her a file.

"Winterborn Life Sciences? Park, what is this?"

"My second year in grad school, one of the guys from the fraternity who was in medical school reached out to see if I'd be interested in donating sperm."

She drops the folder on his desk. "You didn't."

He rounds the desk and kneels at her feet. "I did."

She pulls her feet under the chair to stop herself from kicking him in the groin. The rage is bubbling again, just below the surface. She already knows what he is going to say.

"And?"

"And it's possible there are more children."

8

THE DAUGHTER

Scarlett Flynn was eight years old when she realized something wasn't right about her family. To start with, she had no father. All of her friends had fathers. Some had two fathers, an indulgence she couldn't imagine. All Scarlett had was a mother who worked the night shift at Vanderbilt's children's oncology unit, a brother who was five years older and imperious as hell, and a nanny who liked to sneak cigarettes on the back porch and watch R-rated horror movies with the sound down.

As a result, teenage Scarlett hates both horror films and cigarettes, and is wildly jealous of families with fathers.

Your donor. That's how her mother refers to Scarlett's father. "Your donor was a college graduate with blond hair and blue eyes and a clean medical family history. What more do you need to know?"

What more?

Does he have a beard? Does he play Frisbee? Does he like dogs? Cheese pizza, or the works?

Did he sire other children?

It was that last thought that drove Scarlett to save up all of her allowance money and buy the DNA kit that you send off to learn your heritage. Not that Peyton isn't enough; he is a good brother, for the most part, unless teasing her about her first bra or withholding the remote, but Scarlett sensed there was more. She has talents that her mother's biology can't explain. She is destined for great things, this she knows in her heart, and finding out who she is? That's the key to everything.

It doesn't feel like much to ask, learning who her biological father is. She is proud of her mother, the sacrifices Darby's made, how she managed to keep both Scarlett and Peyton in private schools and build them substantial college funds. Darby is smart and hardworking and a lovely, fun mom, but intransigent when it comes to answering the real question—why have two kids with a sperm donor? She is pretty. She is smart. She is straight, for all that Scarlett knows, not that it matters one way or another.

And yet, she'd chosen to raise two kids by herself. Siblings. She wanted a boy and a girl, Darby said, and that's why she'd chosen this route. She wanted children she knew were healthy, and that's why she had chosen this route. Could you blame her, spending all day with sick kids, that she'd want ones of her own not afflicted?

None of the answers were satisfying to Scarlett, who yearned for the whole story.

Plus, there was one glitch in her otherwise detailed and well-executed plan. Peyton and Scarlett were supposed to have the same father, but technically, she and Peyton are only half siblings.

Scarlett asked, but why not use the same guy for both? Isn't that the normal thing to do?

The answer was another one of cool logic—"I wanted to, but his sample had been retired. They only allow the samples to be used a very limited number of times so a client doesn't end up with five hundred kids."

"You hear of that happening all the time, though," was Scarlett's argument, and her mom would simply smile and say, "I worked with the best clinic in town, one that was extremely ethical and would never do something like that."

Whatever DNA Peyton's father and Scarlett's had provided, clearly her mother's was the stronger of the two, because both of them look just like her.

Which is another strange thing. Her friends with fathers all have elements of both their parents. No one is a dead ringer, but both Darby and Peyton have their mom's heart-shaped face, cleft chin, lime-green eyes and thick, dark curls, though Scarlett's are auburn.

What her mom doesn't know is the management of her extremely ethical best clinic in town isn't quite as aboveboard as she thinks. Scarlett hasn't broken the news to her just yet, because there's going to be huge fight when she finds out Scarlett went behind her back, got her DNA checked, and discovered the truth: there are a whole bunch of kids out in the world with the same dad DNA. She has been conversing online with her half siblings for the past few months. Unethical or illegal, whatever it is labeled, Scarlett knows there are a lot more siblings than there should be. Now she has a lifetime membership to the Donor Sibling Registry, and any matches that pop she invites to a Discord server so they can talk freely in a safe, private environment. More matches seem to pop up weekly.

The first step every one of them took was to try and secure the DNA of their own siblings, if they had any. Scarlett has broken the rules and hasn't reached out to Peyton. She really needs to tell him what's going on and do it in person. But Peyton will tell their mother, and Scarlett can't let Darby know what's happening just yet. Her mom's going to hit the roof.

Scarlett had always been driven by sussing out information about her donor. Peyton had always shrugged it off. He didn't want to know. Didn't want a dad. He was perfectly fine without one, always had been. Handsome, gregarious Peyton, with that curly hair just the same shade as their mom's, the matching dimple in his chin a little more pronounced, his laughing baritone and string of girlfriends. He is a junior at MTSU and loving every minute of school so far. She needs to drive to Murfreesboro to talk to him about this—FaceTime won't do. The rest of the bio-kids are pushing her to get him tested. She doesn't know how much longer she can put them off. But really, what does it matter? She's been in her mom's filing cabinet. She's seen the donor profiles and all the paperwork. She and Peyton have different biological fathers. There is no need to involve him in this part of things. The science part.

She has half an hour before she needs to leave for school. Mom isn't due home until 9:00 a.m. at the earliest, so she can log into Discord and check in with the group, see if any more people have popped up as matches.

Morning, she types in the small box to the right of her photo—a cartoon owl, a wise owl. She isn't dumb enough to put her face on this profile. She knows there are creepers out there who love to chat up pretty teenagers. Even if she controls who enters this server, that doesn't mean one of the halves couldn't get hacked.

How's everyone today?

Did you hear? comes an immediate comment from the other group moderator.

Hear what?

There's been another DNA match to our dad.

Scarlett feels the adrenaline rush she always gets when a new kid pops up.

Who is it? Did anyone reach out?

Uh, yeah. The police. It's at the crime scene of a dead chick. It's all over the news.

What dead chick?

Cooke.

Beverly Cooke? Holy cow. She's from here in Nashville, she's been missing for a while.

What's happening hits her. A DNA match.

Are you saying our dad killed someone?

No, comes the answer.

It's one of us.

9

THE MOTHER

Darby Flynn, all five-feet-three of her, five-five with her curls loose, stands on the ladder in the nurses' station, stringing the farewell sign for little Patti Finley, who is officially in remission and going home after months in the oncology unit. In that time, they've lost five kids to the insidiousness of cancer, but Patti is their success story, a darling six-year-old cherub who's borne all her treatments with a smile and a kind word for the people around her, even when the medicine made her violently sick.

Patti has been a personal favorite of Darby's simply because she reminds her of her own daughter at that age. Scarlett was—is—feisty as hell, full of deep questions, quick to smile and laugh. There is no physical resemblance, but their spirits are the same.

Patti is going home this morning, which makes this a wonderful day, the end of a cycle of ups and downs, of whipsaw emotions and terrifying physical scares. Patti is a strong kid; she's going to do well back in the real world. She's licked the cancer, and she told Darby earlier tonight she wanted to be an oncology nurse, just like her. Darby was beyond flattered.

Darby is tired. She's at the end of her twelve-hour shift and her feet are sore, but she's going to stick around to see Patti off before she retreats to her ten-year-old Honda Civic and takes the meandering path from the hospital back to the house for a few hours of rest before tackling the remainder of her day. She's due back on the ward at eight tonight, and she needs to get in a stop at the grocery store for cupcakes and a birthday present for one of Scarlett's classmates. A gift card will have to suffice. A small gift card. Scarlett may be attending Bromley West, but she's on a full ride, and Darby doesn't have change to spare to make a spoiled little rich girl happier than she already is.

"Darby?"

The shift supervisor and her boss, Eileen Warner, pops around the corner, startling Darby, who nearly falls off the ladder.

"Good grief, you scared me. What are you doing sneaking up on me?"

Eileen doesn't smile. "Sorry. Can you step into my office for a moment?"

Uh-oh. Darby climbs off the ladder, annoyed that one end of the sign is a full two inches lower than the other. Could Eileen have not waited until she was finished?

Down the hallway, looking neither right nor left, Darby follows Eileen to the end, where her desk is situated in a little office—with a door, mind you, a luxury of privacy none of the other nurses enjoy—that has a wide window overlooking the quad. It is a lovely space, one Darby always likes to linger near, because after looking at the yellow walls and pained expressions of a ward of sick kids for twelve hours a night, any glimpse of trees, even those lit up by solar lights in the black of night, is worth a few moments of her precious time.

"Have a seat."

Eileen's voice holds a note of concern, enough that Darby goes on alert. A complaint? Did someone, a parent, a coworker, say she's done something wrong? Darby is so conscientious, she can't imagine—

"Darby, I'm sorry. We have to let you go."

She freezes. "Excuse me?"

"Budget cuts. I argued against it, we can hardly afford to lose a nurse, especially now, especially one as good as you. But the orders come down from the administration, and it's out of my hands. You're the most expensive salary."

"Eileen, no. You can't. I'll take a pay cut. You can furlough me for a few weeks."

Eileen is shaking her head, her eyes sad. *This isn't happening. This just isn't happening.*

"What am I supposed to do? Scarlett, Peyton, they—"

"Darby, I truly am so sorry. I will write you a glowing recommendation, and the moment you find a new opportunity, you have them call me immediately, and I will tell them how wonderful you are. With your background, your skills, you'll get picked up somewhere quickly, I just know it. In the meantime, there's a small severance package, and you'll be eligible for unemployment. HR has all the paperwork waiting for you, but I wanted to tell you myself instead of one of them dragging you out of here. I owe you that much, at least. You're my best nurse."

Eileen seems genuinely upset, voice cracking and lower lip wobbling, which makes Darby feel even worse. They've always gotten along, had great respect between them. But this, the power imbalance suddenly exposed, is untenable.

"Can I stay for Patti's going away?"

Eileen nods. "Technically I'm supposed to take your badge and ask you to leave immediately, but what HR doesn't know won't kill them. But promise me you'll see HR as soon as we're done? And don't talk to anyone on the floor? I have one more cut to make, and I don't need the whispers starting. This is hard enough."

Tell me about it.

Darby nods, unable to speak anymore. Who else is Eileen letting go?

That doesn't matter. My God, what is she going to do? This is a good paycheck, and to have it disappear with no warning... She has planned for this, of course, has enough to last several months, and there's the kids' college funds... No, she can't raid them. A new job is the only way to survive. Oncology nurses aren't a dime a dozen; the field is small and the opportunities limited, at least here in Nashville. With all the specialized training she has, she is an expensive proposition. She'll be able to get another job, sure—hopefully—but this is the best gig in town, even if she does work nights.

Damn. She is now a single mother with two kids in pricey schools and no job.

Eileen has given her a swift hug and ushered her out of the office, and Darby realizes she's been standing, frozen, in the hall, running scenarios through her head: rack and ruin, the kids starving, losing the house, living on the street. She has the fallback of six months' savings, but that's it. She's alone in the world, just her and the kids. She wanted it that way. She wanted to do it herself. But now...

There are cheers coming from the other end of the hall, bells ringing and people shouting congratulations. Darby hurries toward the cacophony, arrives just in time to blow Patti a kiss before the doors close on the elevator and it's over, the sweet child is gone, and now Darby must collect her coat and bag and keep her chin up, get the paperwork from HR, and follow her young charge out of the hospital, not looking back.

She manages the exit with dignity, makes it to her car in the parking garage before the tears come. She is sobbing with her arms folded on top of the steering wheel when she hears the breaking news alert that the body of Beverly Cooke has been found at last.

Could this day get any worse?

She listens, head still pillowed on her arms. She knows—knew—Beverly from a private group on Facebook for local mothers who've used sperm donation to have children. It is an intimate enclave, a very safe space. It is the one place these women have to express their hopes and fears—into the waiting arms of anonymous friends who are always there to lend succor. Beverly was unique in the group because she was married, and her husband doesn't know the baby isn't his. The lengths she went to in order to save face for that man, the crazy details she'd shared—how she mixed the donor's semen with her husband's so they would never truly know unless they did testing, how guilty she felt at times for tricking him, for doing the testing to find out it was him, not her, and making the drastic decisions to catapult them both into the unique world of donation; exultant in others, especially when it became clear the baby she conceived was going to have her husband's coloring—she'd done so much research, been so very careful to find a donor who would fit the physical bill so her husband would not become suspicious…

And then she went missing, and now she's been found dead, and God knows what's going to happen. Beverly's husband, Dan, is by all accounts a kind, gentle man, incapable of harming his wife, but it's always the husband, Darby knows this. He must have found out and lost it.

The police ask for any tips, and Darby sighs, turning off the radio, and puts the car into gear.

She stops at Five Daughters for gluten-free donuts on her way home. She shouldn't spend the money, but she's exhausted and heartsick and needs something sweet to help get her through the rest of the morning. She will have a nice cup of the cinnamon-spiced decaf she likes, and a donut, or maybe two, and then she will take a deep damn breath and figure out what she's going to do.

Traffic is light. The sun is out. She listens to the *All Things Considered* podcast, as she always does, pretending this is a normal drive home. Despite her exhaustion, she takes the long way, as if delaying her arrival will change anything. The drive is surprisingly pleasant, so she keeps going past her street and down to Centennial Park. Eats a donut sitting by the lake, listening on her headphones. She never gets through a full episode; it normally takes her three morning commutes home. Today, she indulges. Watches the ducks bob and dunk. Feels her nose growing pink in the bright sunshine.

Finally, the show over and her gas tank reduced by one quarter, she pulls into the driveway, surprised to see Scarlett's beat-up Volvo still in its spot. Normally Scarlett drives herself to school—the deal they made when Darby bought her the car, no more lingering in bed and missing the bus so Darby has to rush her to school when she comes home from her shift—and she's stuck to it until today. Maybe she's ill. Damn, just what they need. Doctors' bills.

She gathers up her things—she's always very careful not to leave anything of value in the car—and trundles to the door. It is unlocked, another breach of family rules.

"Scarlett?" she calls. "Are you okay?"

There is a shuffle, and Darby's mom radar goes off. Scarlett is up to no good.

Please don't let some random kid come down the stairs with rumpled hair and a sheepish smile. Please, not yet.

"I'm up here, Mom. Just running late. No big."

"You won't be as sanguine when you have Saturday school. I'm not calling you in. You'll have to take the tardy."

"Yeah. Whatever."

Darby has not been impressed with Scarlett's attitude lately.

She knows it's just teenage rebellion brought about by hormones, but Scarlett's favorite phrase is suddenly "yeah, whatever," and it's like waving a red flag in front of Darby's eyes. She is the bull, Scarlett the inept but enthusiastic matador. Guess who wins?

"Get down here, young lady. Right now."

Scarlett comes flying down the stairs like a startled cat, school uniform skirt askew, Dr. Martens unlaced, thick, curly hair spilling out of its sloppy bun. She holds her laptop like a shield, eyes huge in her lovely elfin face.

"Pull yourself together, child," Darby says, fighting back a laugh despite herself.

"Mom. Did you hear they found Beverly Cooke?"

Ah. That explains it.

"I did. Have you been upstairs reading the news sites again? I thought we talked about that."

"Well, it's everywhere. I could hardly miss it. I mean, aren't you freaked out? They're saying she was murdered. Oh, are those donuts?"

Darby shakes the bag. "I was going to surprise you when you got home from school."

"You're the best mom ever. I'd be happy to be surprised now."

"You need to get to school. I'll save one for you."

"Mom." How her child has learned to inject a single-syllable word with four layers of inflection is beyond her. Her own fault, probably, letting Scarlett stream *Schitt's Creek* again. She'd been in Alexis mode for weeks the first go-round.

"Fine. Here." Darby hands over the bag, and Scarlett eases out the small brown box reverentially.

"Oh, my kingdom for a donut."

"You have no kingdom, Richard. Eat, and scat. Drink some milk, too. You need the calcium."

"Ugh." But she pours a glass and downs it. Scarlett's been

hanging around with the other Bromley girls at Starbucks lately and insists she's too old for milk. She wants coffee in the mornings now, God save us all.

A quick, missed, peck on the cheek and she's out the door, flying to the car. Thank God she hadn't noticed anything was wrong. Darby doesn't have her parental walls up yet; she would have broken down in front of her daughter and scared them both.

"Drive carefully," Darby calls, heart swelling with love despite being annoyed as hell. Kids. Mixed emotions weren't the half of it. At least they hadn't had a fight. That happens more often than not these days. Donuts working their magic. Sugar and spice and everything nice.

Darby makes herself a cup of coffee, takes another donut because damn it, she's having a bad morning and she deserves the treat, and sits down at her tiny desk in the corner of the kitchen. She ignores the tall stack of bills sitting neatly on the ledge just at eye level and brings up Facebook. Sees the burgeoning fight in her donor group, logs out. She can't do this, not now. She has bigger problems.

Humiliation streaming through her, she pulls the unemployment papers from her bag and navigates to the website to file her claim.

Later, fortified with coffee, sugar, and a nap, Darby logs into Facebook again. She is met with a knotty philosophical discussion among the moms about whether they need to tell the police what they know in case there's something related to the donor that might shed light on Beverly's death.

On this, she has many feelings, and now she's willing to share.

Our privacy is sacred, Darby types. It's all we have. If we expose Beverly, we expose all of us. We will never have peace. The police, then the media, will hound us and we will be a part of this story. Our group will become the story. Tempers are high. Fear does that. We should stay out of it, at least for now.

The moderators chime in, suggesting we all take the night to think it over, and convene in the morning to vote on our course of action. Darby tries once more, already sensing this is a moot point.

Their lives are already ruined, she types. Dan's, and the baby's. What do we gain by tearing them apart? What do we gain from Dan learning his son probably isn't his? That his wife was hiding such a huge secret from him? Because that's what we need to think about today. It's one thing to pull back the curtain and expose ourselves. The baby is innocent, and the baby will suffer. Dan might not want him anymore. Trust me, I've seen it happen.

Trust me.

A flurry of responses, some agreeing, some not. The Nots are vociferous. It's amazing how quickly friends turn on each other. The moderator pops in again.

Ladies, seriously. We need to cool off. I'm closing this thread to comments.

Darby's private message notification lights up immediately, but she logs out. No sense bickering. She needs to make dinner, and she might as well do some laundry since she'll be home tonight to put it in the dryer. She's superstitious about putting clothes in overnight and going to work with the dryer running. House fires are all too common.

She glances in Peyton's room as she passes. Two decades of habit is hard to break. She misses him. It had been the two of them against the world, her little man and his single mom, until they decided he needed a sibling. He was almost four, precocious and lively, when he announced she should have another baby. She hadn't been considering it; work was going well, she had managed to load up on certifications and was planning to go back to school for a physician's assistant degree. More money, better hours. She could work in a clinic instead of the hospital.

But Peyton's announcement gave her the bug. She loved babies. Loved being pregnant, loved holding Peyton's sweet, warm body to her breast. Loved watching him grow. Two would be hard, but boys need brothers.

She went back to Winterborn because they'd made the process so easy with Peyton. Clear instructions, nonjudgmental coordinators, and, let's be honest, they weren't as pricey as some of the other banks she contacted. Privately funded, they kept costs low by allowing bulk purchases—it usually takes more than one insemination to achieve a pregnancy—and had a robust buyback program.

She'd held onto two vials of Peyton's donor in case she decided to have another child. Winterborn had it in their cold storage and drop-shipped it to her with hearty congratulations. She was a nurse. She knew exactly how to do the intracervical insemination—ICI was simple, really, all she needed was a needle-less syringe and a good bottle of lube—and tracked her ovulation for three months so she had a solid idea of her moment of prime fertility. The limitations astounded her; considering how small a woman's window of achieving pregnancy actually is, at best twelve hours within a single monthly cycle, it's a miracle there are so many people on this earth, especially those conceived by accident.

The day of, she got a babysitter for Peyton, poured a glass of wine, let the sample defrost, took one more ovulation test to confirm she was ripe and ready, and inseminated herself. With the sample in place, she masturbated herself to orgasm to ensure the sperm got farther inside her (a fun trick she'd learned from the forum), and lounged in bed, sipping the wine and watching a Nora Ephron marathon.

She bled right on schedule two weeks later.

Undeterred, she tried again. Bled, again.

All her earlier ambiguity ended. Now she was in it and couldn't stop.

She called Winterborn to purchase more samples, only to learn that Peyton's donor had been retired. She didn't want two kids by two different fathers. She wanted her version of a family, with full-blooded siblings, but the consultant convinced her what mattered was the mother. *That's why you're using a donor anyway, right? So* you *can have this experience. We have the perfect man for you. A match to all your wants.* They sent the paperwork and the donor interview, and they were right. This donor was exactly what she wanted—and even bore a resemblance to Peyton's donor. She agreed, took receipt of the samples, and the third time was a charm.

Scarlett was born early eight months later, during a snowstorm that almost saw her slip out on the side of the interstate, and both Darby and Peyton fell head over heels in love. Scarlett charmed all the doctors and nurses in the NICU with her rosebud lips and wispy hair. She was perfect and tiny and adorable.

Darby enters Scarlett's sanctum. The opposite of her orderly brother's, Scarlett's room always looks like a confetti bomb has just gone off in happiness. Darby gathers what clothes she can find from hither and yon, loading her arms, straightening as she can. She bumps the desk chair with a hip as she moves ungainly to the door. A piece of paper falls on the floor, and she stops to pick it up. A Gmail log-in and passcode—a string of letters and numbers no hacker could ever access. It is not Scarlett's email; she's not allowed to have a private email address. But this certainly looks like it belongs to her somehow—scarfly414—Scarlett Flynn, and 414 is their street address.

Darby confiscates the paper and bumbles downstairs with the laundry. She drops the note on the table and gets the clothes in the washer and started, then retrieves it and heads to her desk.

She pulls up her Gmail, logs out of her own, and logs into the strange account. The inbox is confusing at first, full of Discord notifications. She back traces to the first email and sure enough, Scarlett has herself an illicit Discord account, too.

Oh, girl. You are in so much trouble.

It takes Darby exactly thirty seconds to find the private group. The more she scans, the more horrified she is.

Scarlett is not her donor's only child.

And one of her siblings has been tied to Beverly Cooke's murder.

10

THE DAUGHTER

After gym, while the rest of the girls are changing back into their skirts and button-downs, Scarlett takes her phone to the bathroom, closes the door on the stall and downloads the app. She's not allowed to have Discord; she has to download the app and delete it every day so her mom doesn't get suspicious. She's been busy, hasn't had a chance to go back in and look to see what they're saying about the Cooke murder since her mom came home and busted her for skipping homeroom. She's dying to see what's going on.

The group is buzzing. Her private messages are full. She goes immediately to the last one, the only other kid in Nashville—the rest are spread around the South, mostly, with a few off in other parts of the country. It's weird to think she has a sister in town she's never met. They'd talked about meeting up, revealing their real identities, but neither had gotten up the guts yet. Now, though, she needs to reach out and find out what's going on.

Jezebelle: It's one of us.

Jezebelle: Man, I drop a bomb and you ghost me.

Scarlett types quickly, thumbs flying over the screen.

Scarfly414: Sorry, mom came home early. I'm totally weirded out about one of the halves being a killer. How did you find out?

Sits for a minute, chewing a nail, waiting.

Jezebelle: Mom works for Metro labs. There was a match to our dad. Don't tell anyone.

Scarfly414: Wait, so your mom knows you know?

Jezebelle: No. I was snooping. I have a flag on her account so I can see any activity that might match our DNA. Wrote the code myself. She has no idea. Though now...

Before J can answer, a message pops up from a strange account, one she doesn't recognize.

Hello Scarfly414. This is your mother. We'll discuss this when you get home. Straight home from school, do you hear me?

"Oh, shit!"

Not only has her mom found her private account, she's read every message that's come through. She knows everything that's being said.

She knows that one of the siblings is a killer.

It's not like Scarlett was going to be able to hide this anyway, not with that kind of news. But damn, her mom will go ballistic.

The bell rings. She needs to get to chemistry.

Scarfly414: JZ, I think I'm busted. Talk later?

Jezebelle: Yeah.

Scarlett scrolls quickly through the rest of her messages, tendrils of panic coursing through her. Everyone is concerned about the same thing. Speculation, fear, are we in danger?

Do you know who it is?

We should shut this down. I don't want to be a part of this.

Do we know it's not one of us on this group?

Could the person responsible for this woman's murder be on their server already? Watching them? That's like her worst fear ever.

You have only one chance to do the right thing in this world, baby girl.

Scarlett knows what the right thing is. She should call the police. She should tell them everything she knows. Everything she's learned. She's done nothing wrong. There's nothing to be afraid of. She should get Jezebelle, whatever her real name is, to act as well.

Unless someone on the group is the killer, and they know she ratted them out.

Scarlett needs her mother.

A bit of peace settles upon her. Even if she's furious, her mom will know what to do. This is too big a decision to make without her. It was one thing finding out who Scarlett is, genetically speaking. Something else entirely to know she may be related to a killer.

Screw chemistry. She'll make up the quiz later. Scarlett goes to the office, tells the nurse she's not feeling well, and checks herself out of school for the rest of the day.

The drive home doesn't take long enough. Her mother is in the kitchen, on her computer. Great.

"What are you doing home?"

Scarlett opens the fridge, gets out a bottle of lemonade and a piece of string cheese.

"I feel sick."

Darby stands with a sigh. "Let me get the thermometer."

"Not sick like that." She sits down at the table, gestures for Darby to do the same. An eyebrow raised, her mother sits.

"You're missing a quiz in chemistry, you know. They might not let you make it up."

"This is too important. We need to talk. I need your advice."

Darby is clearly trying not to detonate. "On your little Discord group? My God, Scarlett. How dare you go behind my back like this?"

"How dare you snoop in my room?" Scarlett shoots back. "I thought we were past that."

"I wasn't snooping, I was getting your laundry. I was doing you a favor, and what do I see? You've been hiding the truth from me, living a secret life, and God knows what else—"

"Don't you dare, Mom. I haven't done anything wrong. I wanted to know who he was, that's all."

"And you couldn't have come to me, made a plan with me? You went online and confided in a bunch of strangers? This could all be some sort of huge lie, some sort of scam, you realize that. To prey on donor kids."

"It's not. I'm not an idiot. And see, that's the problem right there. You won't ever say anything about him other than calling him *your donor.* Your donor, your donor, your donor. He's my father. I've always wanted a father, and you tore that dream away from me, and now I have a chance to meet him, and I bet he loves me more than you do."

They are both shocked by that outburst.

"Want to take that back?" Darby asks.

"No," she cries, lower lip stuck out like a petulant five-year-old, though the tears are coming, her lip wobbling, and Darby sighs and pours herself a glass of water while Scarlett erupts into a shower of tears.

"Why couldn't I have a father? Why did you have to do this alone? All I ever wanted was to be a proper family, and instead it was the three of us and people laughed and said nasty things and—"

"They did?" Darby puts the water pitcher back into the fridge.

"Yes."

Darby hands Scarlett a tissue. "What did they say?"

A shuddery sigh. The fight has gone out of her as quickly as it arose. Her mother is so calm, so logical, so unruffled all the time. She doesn't fight with passion like Scarlett. She's almost robotic. It's infuriating. Sometimes Scarlett wants to scream and smash things. The pressure builds inside until she needs to explode. When she was little, she'd punch or bite the kids around her, completely out of control, but as she's grown older, she's learned to master her feelings. She usually takes it out on her pillow, or on the pitch, against the soccer ball. Right now, though, it's come to a head, and she's forcing it away. They have bigger problems than her own emotions.

"It doesn't matter."

"If it hurt you, honey, it matters. People talk, people say things, because they don't understand other people's choices, especially on something as personal as building a family."

"Didn't you want a husband? Or a wife? I mean, a partner of some kind?"

Scarlett claps a hand over her mouth. This is as close as she has ever come to inquiring about her mother's sexuality.

"I assume there's been talk?" Darby asks evenly.

"Speculation is more like it. Because people are cruel and can't mind their own damn business. But I never knew what to say. Not that it matters, Mom. People were just curious."

Darby runs a long finger across the top of her water glass. It sings a tiny note of squeaky joy. "I wanted kids. I wanted you. You know my dad wasn't the greatest, right? I've told you I had a rough upbringing. He drank, and he hit, and he threatened, and my mom wouldn't walk away, and she was always so miserable. I couldn't do that to myself. I never wanted to be beholden to someone else for my happiness. I decided early on that I was going to be a single mother, and I never strayed from that."

"But aren't you lonely? I mean, it would be so hard to be alone all these years."

"How could I be lonely when I have you and your brother? You're my world, and always have been."

"I don't know. It doesn't matter. I have a bigger problem."

"All right," Darby says, leaning back in the chair. "Shoot."

"It's about the group. The match to the murder. I think we need to go to the police. Normally I would have said it on the page because the Halves—that's what we call ourselves—we've been making most of the decisions together. But if the killer is a part of the group—"

"Slow down. Back up for me a moment, all right? You want to run me through how in the world you got hooked up with them—the Halves—in the first place?"

"Through the DNA website. You know, the one you send off your DNA and they send you your history?"

"I'm aware of such sites."

"I did a lot of research on the science of this before I jumped in, and I used the DSR—that's the Donor Sibling Registry—for advice, too. Anyway, right away I had a match that was, like, too close to be a cousin. It had to be a sister. I reached out, and she told me she was a donor kid. Several more had popped up by then. I sent them each a message, asked if they wanted to talk. It got unwieldy in the program, so I suggested we create our own server on Discord, where we could talk as a group."

"So you did this publicly?"

"No, of course not. It's a private server. It's totally unfindable unless we give the link."

"And you were the ringleader? You set all of this up?"

"I mean...technically?"

Darby sighs and shakes her head. "I don't know whether to kill you or be proud, Scarlett. What have I told you about talking to strangers online?"

"These aren't strangers, though. Not really. They're my blood. They're my siblings. We all have the same dad. We all want to meet him."

"Not going to happen."

Scarlett gives her mother a small smile. "Well, technically, it's not your choice."

Darby's face darkens. "This isn't about what I want or don't, little darling. This is a legal issue. He—the donor—signed away his rights and was very specific that he didn't want to be contacted by any potential offspring. You must respect that, Scarlett. You can't meet him. He doesn't want to meet you."

"Harsh, Mom. You don't know that. He might have changed his mind. He—"

"Is an anonymous donor. You know what the word means, yes?"

Scarlett bites her lip. Her mother isn't usually sarcastic with her. Darby rubs the spot between her eyebrows with a thumb. She looks so tired. There are new lines around her eyes, and a sprinkling of silver in her curls. Scarlett puts a hand on her mother's arm. The skin is papery and dry; she needs lotion.

"Listen, Mom, this is a bad situation, and I don't want to fight with you. But I think we need to go to the police and tell them about the Halves."

Darby drops her hand. "And paint a target on your back? No. Absolutely not."

Then: "Who even figured out that there is a DNA match between someone in the group and Beverly Cooke? Tell me that?"

Scarlett sits back in her chair. "I don't know. It was in my messages this morning."

"You don't know who that person is?"

"We're all there under fake names. Just to keep us safe in case someone from our real lives gets wind of things before we're ready to say anything."

"Scarlett. Darling. This goes from bad to worse. Anyone can be posing as a sibling. Do you not get that?"

"Just...quit being so judgy. They can't, we actually do have some controls. And it seemed smart at the time. There were some people who were worried about their names getting out on social media. I can probably cross-reference a few of them who I've gotten friendly with, just based on location and stuff. So we can check them out and see if they're legit."

"You can do that? You know how to track people on the internet?"

"Duh. It's not exactly hard."

"Scarlett Flynn, if I find out you've been doing anything illegal..."

"Mom. Seriously. People put their lives online. They aren't hard to find."

Her mother sighs, heavy and long. "We don't need you playing detective. And we don't need anyone in that group coming after you."

"You're right, we don't. But Mom, if one of us is a killer, we have to tell the police."

Those strong, capable arms cross on her chest. Scarlett is losing this argument.

"I don't want you getting involved. Not until we know how that little tidbit got planted. It could be completely false, and you'll open a can of worms that ruins lives."

"I am already involved. We can't pretend that I'm not. And you've always told me to do the right thing. This is the right thing."

"Oh, Scarlett."

Scarlett knows that tone. She's worn her mother down and she's won. She feels a spark of excitement, tries to keep herself in check. This is happening, it's really happening. She's going to find out who her father is. She can just tell.

"There's probably a tip line," Scarlett says, careful not to seem too ebullient. "Or we can just call the non-emergency number and tell them we have some information related to the Cooke case."

"I should never have let you listen to those true crime podcasts," Darby groans, but Scarlett already has her laptop open and is searching for the number she needs.

"Got it, here on the story from WSMV. They have the tip line. It says we can leave an anonymous tip. Would you rather me do it like that?"

Darby thinks for a moment. "Let's just call and see what they ask. They'll have your phone number regardless. If they want to hunt you down, they probably can. If people are as easy to track as you say they are."

Scarlett ignores that crack, dials the number and puts her phone on Speaker.

"This is the right thing to do, Mom. I know it."

11

THE DETECTIVES

Joey Moore closes the lid on her laptop and stretches. "I'm getting nowhere fast. I don't think we're going to get anything else out of Chapel Hill PD until tomorrow. Anything back from the family? I'd really like to have a chat with them. I know it's been twenty-plus years since their daughter died, but you never know what they might have to say."

Will checks his phone. "Nothing."

"Want to call them again?"

He does, leaves another message. "Mr. and Mrs. Rich, this is Detective William Osley in Nashville again. I'd like to speak to you about your daughter's murder. Please call me back." He leaves his number and shakes his head. "That's five messages and no returned calls. They might not want to rip open this wound."

"I know. Let's pick it up in the morning, okay? Maybe once

we talk to Chapel Hill, they'll reach out to the family and tell them our intentions are pure."

Osley gnaws on a toothpick. His booted feet are up on the edge of her desk, so she has a great view of the tattered, scraped soles.

"Yeah, all right." He doesn't drop his feet to the floor. She waits. It's quiet in the homicide offices today. She can hear the soft screech of a marker; someone is writing on a white board across the cubicles.

"What's wrong now?"

Osley sighs. "That dude knows something."

"Who, Bender? Oh, I agree. But about what? The kid? The girl from Chapel Hill? His wife?"

"I thought without the wife there he might cave and admit who he had the affair with."

Joey senses a longer conversation about to break free. Some of their best ideas come when they're just shooting the shit like this, so she indulges Osley, even though she's tired as hell and just wants an old-fashioned and maybe a pile of spaghetti.

"You're assuming he knows," she says. "It's not out of the realm of possibility that he truly isn't aware of a child."

"You think you wouldn't know if someone had *your* kid?"

"Interestingly, Will, this is a phenomenon limited to the males of the species. While we might be in a situation where we don't who a father is, we do have a tendency to know when a kid is ours or not. Considering we give birth to them."

"Point taken," he says, saluting with two fingers. "Still. Something just smells wrong about this. The way he reacted. Like it was inevitable that we'd come calling."

Now she leans back in the chair and joins his makeshift footstool. "Don't you think that's got a lot to do with his past? He was a suspect in a murder. Even though it turned out to be someone else, that's gotta fracture a guy, right? He was a kid, and it went unsolved for a while. That's hung over his head all these years."

"Yeah. Still—"

Joey's phone rings. "Moore. Yeah? Let's hear it."

She sets her phone on the desk and hits the speaker. "Tip line got a call about Cooke. Says it's a live one."

A girl's quiet but excited voice plays through the speaker.

"I need to report something that might help with the Beverly Cooke case."

"Would you like to identify yourself?"

"Nooo. Um. So. There's this group of people who are all related. And they are related to the killer, though I don't know who that is."

"A group, ma'am? Can you be more specific? You know the killer's family?"

"Um, sort of. We…all have the same dad."

"I see. So you believe your brother is the suspect in the Cooke case?"

"Oh, no. Not my brother. A half brother. A half sibling. We all have the same donor father. I don't know who that is, though."

"Donor father?"

"Yes. A sperm donor. There's a whole group of us, and apparently, one of us is the suspect in the Cooke case."

"Ma'am, I'm going to need more information. Would you please at least give me a callback number so the detectives can contact you?"

Whispers, then the girl clears her throat. "615-555-8796. But I'd like to stay anonymous. Thank you."

"Thank you, ma'am. We will do our very best with this information, and the detectives will probably be in touch."

"Probably?" Osley says, reaching for the phone. "Shit, call her now."

Moore is already dialing the number.

"That didn't take long," a voice says. It is not the girl's voice from the tip line, but an older woman.

"Ma'am? Detectives Moore and Osley from Metro Nashville homicide. I understand you consented to be contacted about a tip regarding the Beverly Cooke case?"

"Yes, but I must insist that we stay out of this."

"Understood. The suspect we're looking for, you're saying he's one of a number of children, all fathered by the same sperm donor?"

"Yes. My daughter is a member of an online forum that is comprised of multiple children from the same donor, all who've found each other through an DNA database. One of them is apparently matched to the woman who was found in the lake."

"Ma'am, it sure would make things easier if you could give us some concrete details. Can we come talk to you and your daughter?"

"We prefer to talk by phone. For now."

Osley gives Moore a thumbs-up.

"Fair enough. We're all ears, ma'am. Tell us what you can, and we'll investigate."

At the end of the call, they hear whispering, then a sigh from the woman they've been talking to.

"Fine. Here. Talk to them."

A young woman's voice comes on the line, tremulously excited.

"We've agreed to give you our information. My name is Scarlett Flynn. And if you speak to our donor, tell him I'd like to meet him."

12

THE PAST

Chapel Hill, North Carolina
University of North Carolina
April 2001

Park Bender, lanky, lean, fraternity heartthrob, catch of the century and knew it, strolled across the campus with his backpack on one shoulder and a hand in the pocket of his North Face, trying to look cool. He had a vicious hangover, compliments of the PKA party the night before. The Pike house had been thumping; someone had passed around a dose of mushrooms at the pregame, and he always drank too much when he was tripping. After the semester he'd had so far, no one blamed him for overdoing it.

No one blamed him at all.

Because Melanie Rich was missing.

Still missing.

When the police had questioned him, the weekend she disappeared, about his perky young on-again, off-again freshman girlfriend, about the fight they'd had that Thursday night at the KD house, witnessed by Melanie's roommates, he blew it off. He figured they'd find her sleeping off a bad drunk in one of her friends' apartments or discover she'd gotten homesick and gone home to her parents' place in Raleigh for the weekend. But hours became days, which stretched to weeks, and suddenly she'd been gone for two months, and the semester was ending. Everyone from the students to the media speculated about when her body would show up. There were even betting pools in some of the frat house basements with Las Vegas–style oddsmaking, though no one would admit that publicly. Odds that Melanie was dead: four to one. Odds that Park killed her? Ten to one, as of last night, which was why he'd gotten so smashed. Last weekend, they'd been riding at thirty to one. His favor among his compatriots was slipping.

When the cops finally came and took his DNA, he gave it willingly, without making a fuss or asking for a lawyer; he had nothing to hide. But after that, tired of the sideways glances and sudden ends to conversations when he came in the room, Park decided to head home the moment finals were over, instead of lingering for the end-of-semester parties.

He'd been more than relieved to be back in Nashville over winter break, something he usually avoided because it made him sad. Holidays just weren't the same now that they were all grown and his mom was gone. He missed the excitement of Christmas Eve, he and Perry whispering under the covers, timing their descent down the big staircase so they could catch Santa coming out of the chimney. Missed the gentleness of Christmas Day, when kids and parents all had their presents and were playing before the big dinner. Missed what it was like before things fell apart.

He missed the way it was before their mom got sick and Perry bailed for Europe, and it was just him and Lindsey and his dad, who had checked out when his mom died, and the family's descent into depression was too much to bear.

This year, though, two months after Melanie went missing, he'd thrown himself into the holidays, doing all the things his mom used to love. Put up a tree, dragged out the ornaments they'd made as kids, hung wreaths on the garage doors. Lindsey, relieved to have at least one brother around to temper their dad's benign neglect, helped cheerfully, and even his dad seemed to pull out of his funk for a while Christmas morning.

Melanie was still missing when he got back to campus. While he was home, the police had cleared him, and the media reported his innocence, and now people weren't quite so jittery around him. The odds, though, getting tighter and tighter as the semester went on.

Sometimes he missed Melanie, though most of the time, he tried not to think about her. She went into the bucket of emotions that included his mom's death and the med school rejections and the hopelessness that his life was going nowhere. It wasn't that he forgot about her. The posters all over campus made that impossible. But they'd dated for only a little while, and he hadn't even liked her all that much. She'd wanted more than he was willing to give.

Back in his apartment, he dropped the sunglasses on the kitchen counter, adding to the crowded mess of backpacks and mail and empty beer cans, and downed four ibuprofens with the lukewarm remnants of a Moosehead. He needed to go shopping. He needed to do laundry. He needed to clean up the wreck that was his apartment, and he desperately needed to study. He needed a lot of things. Instead, he got a fresh beer from the fridge and plugged in his brand-new Xbox, a Christmas present. A few rousing kills in *Halo* would set him straight.

The door crashed open half an hour later, making him jump.

His roommate, Peter Johnson, burst into the living room looking like he'd sprinted all the way from the arboretum. Johnson's hair was a drenched mess, and his face was red as fire. Park hit Pause on the game.

"Dude. Did you hear?"

Park pulled down his headphones, pointed sarcastically at them. "Hear what?"

"They found her. They found Melanie."

A crappie fisherman had caught the edge of the girl's cardigan and dragged her from the depths of University Lake. Her bloated body was put through an autopsy, which determined she'd been murdered. Cause of death, either a subdural hematoma, or manual strangulation. Or both.

The students on campus held prayer vigils and Take Back the Night rallies. Park attended them all. Then they had September redux: the questions from the police, the stares from the coeds, the suppositions from his professors. This time he handled things more soberly. No more drugs, no alcohol. He wanted to be clearheaded, clear-eyed, in case someone thought to try and hang Melanie's murder on him.

Melanie, no longer missing. Murdered.

The funeral was awful. He went, buttressed by his loyal fraternity brothers, but it didn't feel right, listening to her parents crying in the front pew, the oversized portrait of Melanie in her high school graduation gown, wispy bangs and a secret smile, and NSYNC on the church speakers singing "Bye Bye Bye"—Melanie's favorite song, but really, it seemed too on the nose for a funeral—and at the wake after, her sister got drunk and screamed at him to leave, which he thought was totally unfair, since he wasn't a suspect and no one thought he'd actually killed her. He was a good target for fury, though, and he understood the need to blame someone when there is no one to blame.

★ ★ ★

Melanie's murder stayed unsolved through his graduation, through his tenure in graduate school. It was still unsolved when he got his first teaching gig. Still unsolved when he hooked up with Olivia again.

He assumed they'd never know the truth about what happened the night Melanie Rich died.

He was wrong.

Peter Johnson was arrested a year after Olivia and Park married.

Park couldn't believe it.

The roommate.

Peter couldn't either. He claimed innocence. The police claimed they had a DNA match. The police won.

Peter went to prison, his lawyers promising him he'd be released on appeal because the case was so thin. But six months later, he got shanked in a dispute over three cigarettes, died of sepsis in the prison's grungy hospital wing, and the case was closed forever.

Melanie, dead. Peter, dead. Park, out in the world with his lovely young wife, trying for a baby.

Life is strange sometimes.

13

THE WIFE

Morning sun stretches across Olivia's comforter. Normally a happy lark in the early hours, now she feels gritty and exhausted. She's been sleeping poorly, tossing and turning after going to bed alone, wondering if Park is going to join her or if he is going to sit in his shed all night, avoiding her, avoiding them, hoping for the latter but strangely needing the former. Each night, she's given up waiting and shut off the light, sinking alone into the darkness before the dawn. Her dreams are full of amorphous beasts and heartbreaking visions, and she wakes feeling utterly unrested.

It is chilly this morning, despite the sun. Park isn't beside her, but she smells coffee; he must be in the kitchen. She snuggles on the bed with a cozy blanket and her phone, idly scrolling through Instagram, looking at her favorite accounts. Her feed is full of architecture and design. Vision boards and paint schedules and herringbone marble patterns. French country home tours and farmhouse chic renovations. All relevant to her business, and to her life.

And a few others. The hashtags are preprogrammed; she's looked at them so often all she needs to do is press the little magnifying glass that indicates Search and up they come, a parade of want and need. Happy tags: #motherhood #momsofinstagram #momslife #pregnantbelly #pregnantlife #maternityshoot #pregnantstyle #IVFlife #babygirl. (She does want a girl, no matter what she tells Park—and herself—about not caring what gender their little darling is. A boy would be lovely, of course. But a mini-me would be precious.)

She loses herself in this rabbit hole of glorious, distended bellies and cradled hands and fingers in the shape of hearts and radiant joy and sometimes even feels happy for the mothers-to-be in the photos. It certainly isn't an issue for her. She isn't addicted. There are just moments when she finds comfort in the idea of what might be.

Today, though, it is punishment, and she won't pretend otherwise. Seeing the joy and happiness on these strangers' faces makes her ache inside. For the past few months, she's scrolled these hashtags full of excitement and wonder, cataloging the changes in her own body with comparisons to #12weekspregnant and #excitingnews. Now she wonders why there aren't more hashtags that deal with the trauma of losing a child. The horrors of miscarriage. The injustice of a body's biological betrayal. Something more visceral than #rainbowbaby.

#bleedingagain #lostit #loser #wonteverbeamother.

She's handled this one well, she thinks. She's been strong. She hasn't whined. She hasn't obsessed. She hasn't gotten obliterated on white wine and screamed at Park. The Ativan is helping, for sure. Every evening, half of a small round tab lingers on her tongue, sweetening her own bitter recriminations.

Park comes into the bedroom carrying a cup of coffee for her as if this is just any other day. He hurries to her side, placing the coffee on a coaster by her phone. "Honey? Are you okay? Tell me why you're crying."

Park is so good at asking the hard questions. He's never shied away from her sadness, probably because he doesn't know it's driven by her own guilt. She did this to them. She is responsible.

She wipes her face, surprised to feel the wetness. "I hadn't realized I was."

He joins her on the bed, pulls her to his chest. He is strong, and warm, and despite herself, she snuggles in, letting the tension release from her body. She is still mad at him—furious, in fact—but she wants comfort more than rage right now.

She feels him relax as well. They need this. The touching. It's so easy to forget the importance of a simple hug. The chemicals that release when they love each other, making them both feel better. They haven't spoken more than the necessities in days. They certainly haven't touched.

Park takes a deep breath. Despite herself, she tenses. *Here we go*, she thinks, and mentally slaps herself. He's lost something here, too.

"Olivia, I'm so sorry. I've made a mess of things. I didn't tell you about donating before because I was a coward. I should have said something the moment you offered to let me donate. That was so magnanimous of you, and you were hurting, and… I just couldn't admit what I'd done. Not right then. I felt like I'd be hurting you even more, kicking you when you were down. Please, honey. Please forgive me."

She sighs. Her brows are drawn together so tightly she can sense the divot in the tender flesh above her eyes. She idiotically waits for the morning sickness to come so she can surge out of the bed, away from his strong arms, but it's absent. She is empty. It's the weirdest feeling. Breasts no longer sore. Womb no longer swelling. Stomach solid as a rock. Hungry. She's actually hungry.

Life goes on, damn her.

Park is still talking. "We're going to get through this. I know it's going to be rough, but I swear, Liv, we're going to get through this."

Focus on your husband.

"I'm not sure what there is to get through, Park. This situation is terrible, but we've done nothing wrong."

"No, darling, we haven't. You're absolutely right. But there's probably going to be more press. We've gotten lucky they aren't swarming, but in case they do, we need to decide what we want to say."

A tiny purl of panic flows through her. "We don't have to say anything. I don't want to talk to the media, Park. No one's called the past few days. They won't, I'm sure of it."

"I understand where you're coming from. I do. But when they put it all together…the suspect notwithstanding, Beverly was your friend."

"No, she wasn't. She was someone I knew, that's all. An acquaintance at best. I'm certainly not going to talk to the media about her."

Because I might tell them the truth, that I hated her to the marrow for what she had that I did not.

"Okay. Okay." He holds her again in silence. She has a sudden realization. *We are never going to be parents together. This is the end for us.* It hurts, but not as deeply as it should. She should be searing with pain at the loss of her marriage, of her husband, of the man she loves, but instead she feels nothing. She has been desensitized by grief. These past few years, the horrors, the high and lows, the pain, the shots, the indignities… she can't help it; she resents him. He can't give her what she needs. He never has. Instead, he's given it to God knows how many other women. Park Bender's world-class sperm. The gift that keeps on giving.

She shifts restlessly and he releases her, leaning back against the pillows so he can see her face again. Has he sensed her thoughts? Does he know the moment they've just had? What feels like their last moment as a team? Does he know he's killed them dead?

She thinks that yes, he does, especially when he clears his throat and stands.

"I have to call the police and talk to them about Winterborn. I've been doing some research. If I give my approval, Winterborn will be able to release the names of the women who received my donations over the years. They will be able to track down my...the children, do testing, and discover who killed Beverly. It's pretty simple, actually. There can't be that many of them. There were limits, ethical limits."

My children, he'd started to say. Was there the tiniest bit of a boast in his tone?

She rolls away, facing the window, letting the sun pour onto her face. "Then call and let's get it over with."

This time, Olivia is prepared for the cops. She has dressed carefully, an oyster shell under a dark gray blazer, wide-legged gray pants with an alligator belt cinching her waist, gray suede pumps. She has done her hair and put on makeup. Her armor is on. She is ready for the stares, the questions, the insinuations.

There will be no tears. There will be no drama. She will sit quietly by as Park exposes his transgressions, and then she will go to work.

The doorbell rings. Park comes thundering down the stairs. He looks ragged, his hair uncombed, yesterday's jeans. "Clean yourself up," she snaps as she enters the kitchen. "I will get them settled."

She is the general now. She is in control. She is the Martha fucking Stewart of this chaos.

The cops are much as she left them, though she notices Moore watches her closely as if waiting for her to crack. Not happening.

"Detective Osley. Detective Moore. Please come in."

She ignores the stare of the gossipy neighbor across the street, a woman named Terrie Lavender, who despite seeing the police has shockingly not intruded on them yet. At least, as far as Olivia knows; she's been avoiding everyone, so it's possible Terrie did come over, looking for news to spread to the rest of their neighbors. The odds of not getting a knock today are slim to none.

"Good morning, Mrs. Bender," Osley says with a tip of his hat. His boots today are brown ostrich. Moore wears the same tonal outfit as before. A capsule wardrobe, most likely. She seems the type. Olivia is especially glad she looks so very put together and stylish, she of the warrior wardrobe, not one of convenience and boredom.

Judgy judgy, Olivia. You know nothing about this woman. Stop making assumptions.

The kitchen is sparkling clean. She's made an extra pot of coffee, laid out the cups and the special biscotti she gets from the bakery in Green Hills, brought out the dessert plates from their wedding china. The gold-rimmed edges glow in their tidy stack.

Park enters the kitchen from the back stairs. Hair combed, a freshly ironed shirt, lace-up brogues. They are put together. They are cool, calm, and collected. They are innocent.

"Officers," he says, helping himself to a cup and biscotti. He, too, seems more in control, and Olivia can tell it puts the police on edge. Their show of strength and unity has not gone unnoticed.

Coffee all around this morning. The ballerina pulls out a notebook.

Olivia speaks first. "We have some information we'd like to share with you."

"And we have some to share with you," Moore says. "Maybe we should go first."

"By all means," Olivia says, scooting deeper in the chair. She doesn't have any idea what is going on, but the ballerina and the cowboy both seem about to burst with some sort of news.

"We find ourselves in an interesting moment in time in criminal investigation. Many new resources have presented themselves in the past few years. Resources we didn't have access to before. Databases are better linked, which is obviously how we were able to tie the DNA from the Cooke crime scene to you, Mr. Bender, from the case in Chapel Hill. But a few days ago, we received an interesting tip, and because of it, our lab has rerun the data. We've been waiting for confirmation because this is an extremely delicate matter."

Park nods. "I assume you're talking about Winterborn. That's why we asked you to come over this morning."

"Winterborn?" Osley asks, innocence personified.

Park sounds like he's teaching in front of his class, not sitting in his kitchen. Smug. She's never liked it when he does that, condescending to protect his fragile ego. "Yes. I was caught off guard when we first spoke, and with everything we've been going through…this is obviously a very personal line of questioning, but in the spirit of full disclosure, we've been struggling with infertility. Olivia's lost several babies—"

"Park!" Olivia slaps a hand down on the table. They don't talk about this. Not with anyone. This is their own crucible.

He glances over, seeking approval to continue. She shakes her head, teeth gritted. *How dare you?*

If they weren't broken before, this…this is the last straw. She did not agree to reveal their problems. He's supposed to be sticking with *his* past, damn him, not dragging her into it.

Park ducks his head in false apology.

"I'm sorry, ma'am," Osley says with such compassion that she blinks back sudden tears.

"Thank you," she forces out. "But this is irrelevant to the situation we are discussing."

"It is, and it isn't," Moore says. "The thing is, we've identified a number of individuals who share significant DNA markers with our suspect. All with paternal matches to you, Mr. Bender. I'm sorry to be the bearer of complicated news, but you are the father of multiple children. And you're without question the father of the suspect we're seeking."

Moore sips gently from her coffee, watching Park's reaction over the edge of the cup.

Park fiddles with his napkin, and nods. "I figured that was the case. That's what we wanted to tell you. That I donated sperm, years ago. To Winterborn Life Sciences. How many are there?"

Olivia can feel Osley studying her, waiting for her reaction, and tenses. This isn't going to be good news.

Moore clears her throat and slaps a thick manila folder down on the table. "At last count? Twenty-eight."

Park drops his cup on the table, coffee spreading everywhere, muddling the edges of the folder with wet brown. Olivia and Osley jump up, tossing down napkins to catch the spill. The contents of the file fall onto the floor, a sea of faces swirling across the hardwood. Olivia stoops to pick up the papers and catches a glimpse of one flame-haired girl who looks so much like Lindsey she wants to scream.

Moore takes the folder and pages from her with a gentle nod. Olivia holds on to one, fingers bent protectively around the edges, still staring at Park's daughter. She sees a name and part of an address before the page is gently tugged from her hands.

"Twenty-eight?" Park says, voice laden with incredulity. "I have twenty-eight children? How is this even possible? Surely—but that's completely unethical. There's no way they—"

"It's not a mistake," Osley says. "There very easily could be more. Ethics and upsets aside, our job is pretty straightforward. We need to identify the suspect. Right now he's just an anonymous marker on a spreadsheet. But he's real, he exists, and we need to find him."

"How are you going to do that?" Olivia asks, gathering up the remainder of the mess and throwing the napkins in the trash. She has gone totally numb.

"One kid at a time, Mrs. Bender. One kid at a time. One male kid, I should say. There's nineteen of 'em."

This detail. They need to know it, of course, but it feels as sharp as a slap.

"This seems pretty implausible," Park says, regrouping. "I can't imagine… Winterborn is a first-class outfit. They aren't just some crappy sperm bank that anyone can get into. They have standards."

Olivia wants to laugh. Park *would* toss that out there. He wouldn't give his precious sperm to just *anyone*.

But Moore nods. "Not implausible. Unethical, without a doubt, on the part of the doctor who facilitated the matches. To confirm our findings, we have sent a warrant to a DNA database in question to access their information. These databases are very private, and it's possible they will decline our request. We're hopeful, though, that because of the nature of the situation, they will cooperate. There's clearly a sense of urgency for us to catch this killer. We hope that's enough to sway them.

"Now, if we can get some details from you? Mr. Bender, when did you donate to Winterborn?"

Park slumps back in the chair, clearly rocked. She can almost hear his thoughts. *This isn't possible. This isn't happening.*

Yeah, I feel you, buddy.

From one child to twenty-eight. From one son to nineteen. All of them his, and none of them hers.

What a nightmare.

Park is back in professor mode. "It was during graduate school. I was friends with a couple of guys at the med school. They said I fit the profile the doctors were looking for. Healthy, intelligent, you know. They said there were limits on how many times I could be used. They mentioned the ethics of it, right up front. I also signed the paperwork that I didn't ever want to be contacted. I was fine helping out some families who couldn't have kids of their own. It felt—"

"Noble?" Moore provides helpfully.

"I didn't think of it like that. Maybe. But I was meant to stay anonymous. That was the deal."

Olivia's phone chimes discreetly. She glances down. Work beckons.

"Well, Mr. Bender. I don't know that anonymous is in the cards anymore. One of the kids has been reaching out to the others to try and identify and contact their biological father. How you interact with her—with them—going forward is not our problem. We need to identify our suspect. It would be a big help, Mr. Bender, if you could give us all the information you have about Winterborn Life Sciences."

14

THE HUSBAND

Olivia is up out of her chair before the echoes of the *ding* from her text are entirely gone.

"So sorry, I have to run. An emergency at one of my sites. Fill me in on the rest later, okay, honey?" She busses him briefly on the forehead and is out the door a moment later, leaving Park staring.

He listens to Olivia's Jeep drive away, feeling very small, and very alone. Abandoned in his moment of need. Embarrassed in front of the cops who are already eyeing him like he's a juicy steak and they haven't eaten in weeks.

The ballerina especially. "So, Mr. Bender, if we could go into more detail about Winterborn—"

"Hold up," he says, trying to get control of the conversation again. "My—she—this girl. Who is she? Where is she?"

"She's here in Nashville," Moore says, a little gentler now. "She and her mother are willing to meet you, if you want."

"Of course I want to meet her. My God. What kind of man do you think I am?"

"No one's saying you're anything but an honorable guy, so don't freak on us," Osley says. "I know this is an extraordinary situation, and you've had some bad experiences with the police in the past. Just...hang in here with us for a bit, so we can get through the rest. Then we'll give you her information, and you can do with it what you will."

Park manages to get through the remainder of the interview with the detectives, giving them everything he can about the donation process he'd undertaken, the names of the doctors, assuming they were still there, of course, all these years later. The names of the friends who talked him into it, the interviews he went through, every single detail he can spit out.

Now, an hour later, Osley finally stands and stretches like a cat, complete with yawn. The ballerina cuts her eyes at her partner and sets a card and a piece of notebook paper down on the table. "We'll do what we can to keep this quiet, Mr. Bender," she promises, and the two leave.

They will be back. He knows they will. They are on the scent; they sense a bigger story here.

Olivia, the baby, lost again. Their lives upended. The dwindling bank account, and now this.

A son who is a murderer. Twenty-eight children. Nineteen boys and nine girls.

Nineteen suspects.

That they know of.

To think this will stay quiet...there's no way.

Park's head spins, worse than before. Now that the news has had time to settle in his bones, in his soul, and the elation he feels at the thought—twenty-eight children!—is drowned by the knowledge that one of them is a murderer, and his child with Olivia is dead.

What hath he wrought?

He picks up the piece of paper and looks at the handwritten note. They live in Belmont. His daughter lives in Belmont. She is less than fifteen minutes away. Has he ever seen her before, at a grocery store, or a park? He and Olivia love the restaurants around 12th South. The chances that he has seen her are off the charts. Nashville is not that big of a town; even with the influx of tourists, it isn't uncommon to run into friends everywhere you go.

His *daughter.*

The joy at that moniker almost outweighs the gravity of this situation. His daughter—and his son. His son, who might have killed a woman.

He wants to call the girl right now, but he must respect Olivia here. He needs to get her permission—this feels very important to him. He can't stomach upsetting her more. As upset as he is that she bailed on him this morning, he understands.

The doorbell rings, a stab of annoyance. The cops back, forgetting something?

He opens the door to find a woman he vaguely recognizes standing on the porch.

"Hi, Mr. Bender? I'm Erica Pearl from Channel Four. I'm so sorry to come by unexpectedly, but I tried to call and couldn't get through. Would you have a few moments to talk to me? We could go inside and chat? Off the record, if that's more comfortable for you."

"This isn't a good time," he says, wary.

"I understand this might be awkward. I know that you've been talking with the homicide detectives—"

"I don't know anything about the Cooke case."

A small smile on her perfect rosebud lips. "Would you be more comfortable talking out here?" She gestures toward the two chairs across from their porch swing.

"I don't have anything to add."

"Mr. Bender, I think once you hear what I have to say, you'll want to talk to me. I know that you're tangentially tied to the Cooke case through a DNA match. I want to give you the opportunity to tell all of us how you feel about this."

"How do you know that?" Park feels the rage begin to bubble, and steps outside, shutting the house door behind him. "You need to leave, right now. I'm not kidding. I have no comment about this."

"Why don't we sit down and talk this through?"

He is tempted. Set the record straight. He knows nothing about the case, nothing about the suspect—his supposed son. Nothing has been proven, nothing.

But just as he opens his mouth, he spies the van down the street, and the flash of what looks like a camera.

"Are you taping this?"

"It's just my photojournalist," Pearl says, smooth as silk. "For my safety. I can signal him, and he can come—"

"Your safety? What, do you think I'm going to hurt you? That because I'm the biological father of a suspect in a murder case, I'll suddenly attack you? That I passed on some sort of murder gene to a stranger I don't even know?"

Shut up, shut up, shut up.

Pearl, softer now, "Of course I don't think that. But you raise so many interesting points. I'd love to talk to you further. Get your side of the story. Let me just get my photojournalist and you can go on the record and—"

Park steps inside and slams the door in Erica Pearl's perfectly lovely face.

In the kitchen, Park is mildly alarmed to see his hands are shaking. His mind is racing, and he shuts his eyes and takes three deep breaths to calm himself. *Fix this, Bender. Fix it now.*

Part of him wants to talk to the reporter, to deny knowing anything about Beverly Cooke and his son, the suspect in her murder. But he's not stupid. He's seen enough true crime shows—Olivia is obsessed, he can't avoid them—to know you never talk to the media. Never. Besides, the last time he talked to a reporter, at a vigil for Melanie, he'd gotten himself in seriously hot water. Granted, he was a kid, and the situation was fraught, but he'd handled it badly. A friend brought the reporter over and introduced Park as Melanie's boyfriend. Candle wax spilling down his hand, burning the crap out of his thumb, Park was quick to point out they'd not only broken up, but he was the one who'd dumped Melanie, and it happened well before she went missing, and that unsolicited admission brought the police straight to his door. All he needed to say was they were no longer dating, that he was devastated and hoped she was found alive and unharmed, and instead, he'd painted a target on his back as an insensitive creep.

Never again. Erica Pearl can go to hell.

Despite the jitters in his hands and a griping in his belly, he gets a fresh cup of coffee and flees the oppressive emptiness of the house for his office. No matter what's happening, before he does anything else, he needs to get some money flowing in, and he needs to do it quickly. He's ahead of schedule on the latest manuscript. Maybe he can get a partial payment if he turns in the pages early.

He unlocks the shed and steps inside. The huge computer screen is dark, the desk littered with papers and research books and pages of the latest novel, detritus of the creative life.

Something, though, is off. The holder of his beloved Pilots is broken, the pens scattered on his desk. The filing cabinet stands open. Glass litters the floor, shards sparkling in the sun like a handful of diamonds dashed across the Batik rug. The desk drawer is ajar, and the key and combination to the safe are missing.

"Shit." He goes first to the safe to see if it's been opened, and sure enough, it has. The door has been pushed closed, but the lock hasn't caught. The cash is gone. So are his contracts and annual income statements, birth certificate, passport, and the Glock. What else was in here yesterday? The tiny gold ingots are still in their envelope, but the Winterborn files, they're missing. His backup thumb drive, too.

Who would want those files?

The shed is alarmed, but he disengaged it when he entered. Didn't he? He always locks the shed at night and sets the alarm, but is it possible, with everything happening, he forgot?

He sets the mug down on the desk but misses the edge, and spills coffee all over the papers. Cursing, he tries to mop up the mess and only succeeds in making the brown liquid drip down the leg of his desk.

Good job, asshole. That's twice this morning. And now you've probably destroyed evidence.

He takes a picture of the space with his phone, then backs out, closing the door with his elbow. Though what's the point? He's already touched the handle, already smudged whatever prints might have been left behind.

The sense of being watched creeps up his spine, and he whirls around to the woods, searching, searching, for whatever—whoever—is there, watching him.

He sees nothing, only the darkness peeking between the thick trees. But the birds have stopped chittering, and the forest is still. Waiting.

Shaking off the eerie feeling, he hurries back to the house. He needs to call the detectives.

He needs to call his wife.

Needs to avoid the reporter.

Instead of picking up the phone, he walks the house, just to be sure no one has gotten in. He sees nothing amiss on the first floors, no windows unlocked or screens askew. The second floor is too warm, reinforcing why they don't turn on the heat until it gets damn cold out.

He stops at the room they've slated to be a nursery when the time comes. The first pregnancy, they'd gone hog wild, moving out the guest bed and furniture, painting the room a soft green, adding elegant animal murals—an artist friend of Olivia's who does the nurseries in her houses came by one sunny afternoon and sketched the animals—giraffes, lions, an elephant peeking from the corner. The sketches are simple lines, just a few strokes, almost a shadow of what they could be. Fitting, really, to have shadow animals in this desolate space.

They haven't touched it since the first miscarriage. No more blankets and booties bought, no more paint and lampshades. No crib. No nursing chair. Just a shaggy throw on top of the gray carpet and the lurking animals with no one to watch over.

He stands there, leaning against the frame, letting his imagination fill in the blanks of what he should be seeing, until his eyes blur with unshed tears and he has to close the door to lock in the possibilities.

Their lives are coming apart, and he can do nothing to stop it.

15

THE WIFE

Olivia's phone chiming halfway through Park's recitation of his moments of glory in graduate school gives her exactly what she needs. With half-hearted apologies and promises to check in later, she excuses herself from the meeting. She has never been as grateful for an expedited granite delivery as she is this morning.

Park looks astonished, but the cops only glance at her, don't push back at all. She is not their primary target, this she knows. They'll take advantage of having Park to themselves to dive deeper into his sordid past, all the things he can't—won't—admit in front of her. She hadn't been with him when the murder happened in Chapel Hill. She'd been pining away here in Nashville, going to design school and trying to decide which Bender brother she hated more.

She's managed not to think about it, but God, Perry is coming home. Could he have picked a worse time to make his grand re-entrance into their lives?

She can't fathom this situation they've found themselves in, and the only way she can cope is to work. She will lose herself in samples and glory in architectural drawings. It is the only way she knows to move forward.

On the way to the build, she dials Lindsey, who answers on the first ring.

"Hey, girl. What's shakin'?"

"Have you talked to Park?"

"No. I was trying to give y'all some space. Why, what's happening?"

"Oh, it gets better. Or worse. I don't know what to call it. Did you know Park donated sperm back in grad school?"

"Um…no. And eww. Sorry, talking about my brother's sperm isn't something high on our chat list. So that's how he has a kid, huh? That's wild."

"Yeah. Wild."

"Are you okay, hon? You sound stressed."

"Finding out my husband lied to me does that. No big."

"I thought you said you'd encouraged him to donate at one point during all the fertility stuff."

"I did. I didn't want him to be left with no one if we couldn't stay pregnant, and I was pretty clear with him that if something happened to me, I wanted him to find someone and have a family. That's not what's going on here. He did this when he was younger. The kids are nearing adulthood. Some already are. And obviously, one is a murderer."

"All right. That's arguably very bad. But why are you mad at him? How is it different? Explain it to me."

"Technically…" Olivia gathers her thoughts. Lindsey is right. She's being a bit hypocritical. What difference does it make that he donated sperm then, or now? "When I brought it up, he didn't tell me. That's the issue. He had every opportunity to say hey, Liv, just FYI, I donated years ago, don't worry, my evolutionary trail is covered."

"But you would have been upset."

"Damn straight. I'm upset now."

"Understandable. I'm not defending him, truly. But I can see him not wanting to mention it to you simply because he knew it would set you off. It would set *me* off. Wait. You said *kids*, plural. There's more than one?"

"Are you sitting down? There's twenty-eight of them. And counting, apparently."

The string of invectives is enough to make Olivia blush. God, if only she could cut loose like that.

"I feel the same way. I…saw one of them. A girl. In the police file. She's here in Nashville. She looks just like you, except her hair is red and curly."

Silence. "Aw, Liv. I'm sorry. This has to be impossibly hard. What can I do? How can I help?"

"I don't know. I don't know what I need right now. It's all been too much—first I miscarry, again, then Park has a kid who's a murderer, now there's twenty-eight of them—it's like a bad joke the universe is playing on me. All I can do is wonder why. What have I done to deserve this? Why am I being punished?"

She sounds childish and peevish, but she doesn't care. For God's sake.

Curly hair, a crooked smile, that dimple in her chin.

"All this aside… Lindsey. One of these kids—your nephew, technically—murdered a woman. What does that mean?"

Lindsey has gathered herself. Olivia can hear the scratching of pen on paper in the background. "It means there's going to be a media shitstorm. We need to be prepared. I want to reach out to my friend Lucía Perez. She's one of the best crisis management attorneys I've ever seen. She'll—"

"Wait, what? You think we need a crisis management lawyer? Why can't you handle things? I don't want a stranger digging into our lives." Olivia slumps in her seat, a tear glistening in the corner of her eye. "No. Keep this between us. Please." She sniffs. "I can't believe this is happening. As if we aren't under enough stress."

"Honey, I hate to be the bearer of bad news, but this is going to be off the charts. The headlines write themselves. *Sperm Donor Child Murderer*, *The Man with a Thousand Kids*, you get the idea. Once they put together the current situation and Chapel Hill? There's going to be press, and there's going to be more police, and it's going to be absolutely insane. I want you protected. You need to have someone who can run interference, who can put together a plan to get you through this. Both of you."

She trails off.

"What?"

"The mothers...can you imagine how they are going to feel?"

Olivia quietly and carefully hangs up.

A few moments later, her phone chirps discreetly from the dashboard, and seeing it is neither Lindsey nor Park, she depresses the button to attach the call to the car's speaker.

"OHB Designs."

"Olivia? Oh, I'm so glad you answered. It's the crazy cat lady! When are you coming to the beach to redo my house?"

Annika Rodrigue is hardly a crazy cat lady, though she is very rich, and very eccentric. She earned the moniker by having a human-size bronze sculpture of a stalking Siamese commissioned to place by her pool house. Thanks to a clever system of automated pulleys that Olivia designed for her, Annika's guests would open the door to find the massive cat blocking their path, ready to pounce. Annika thought it great fun to scare her friends with the looming beast.

"Annika. How are you? It's been ages."

"It has been. You promised you'd get me on the schedule when I was ready and girl, now is the time. I won't take no for an answer. We're heading down to the beach house tomorrow, and you must come with. We'll make a long weekend out of it. I'll give you a blank check and free rein…" This last is sung with a cajoling two-note cadence.

"Such a seductress. I wish I could pick up and come with—"

"You can, and darling, you should." Annika's voice drops to a conspiratorial level. "A little bird told me you're having quite the drama. Sneak away now before the media latches onto you. You'll never shake them otherwise."

Uh-oh. "I don't know what you're talking about."

"Now, now, dear. You know I am Nashville's most omniscient hostess."

"You're something, Annika. I'll give you that."

The woman laughs like a waterfall. "I'm serious, my love. If what I'm hearing is true, you're going to need an exit ramp, and I'm happy to provide it for you. You don't even have to work if you don't want. You can just use the house as an escape. I'll text you the code to the front door and alarm system, and whenever you need to bolt, the house will be there, waiting. Deal?"

"I—" But Annika is already gone.

Olivia's phone dings with a text, the information promised.

How in the world has Annika Rodrigue, of all people, found out about the police visits to their house?

And why offer up such a kindness? An escape is all Olivia wants right now. But running won't solve a thing. She's going to have to face Park, and the police, and the horror of this situation. (And Perry. Don't forget Perry.)

On impulse, she calls for an emergency appointment with her therapist. An afternoon slot secured, she pulls into the Joneses' gravel driveway and jumps from the Jeep, relieved to be able to lose herself in work, if only for a few hours.

As she unlocks the door, the thought grabs her. What exactly does Annika think she knows? That Park has multiple children? That the police think one of them killed Beverly Cooke? The police had been quite clear they were keeping things quiet, that they didn't want this news out there for fear of muddying the investigative waters. So, what has Annika scavenged from the rumor mill?

Lindsey was right. They're going to need a professional to help.

OK, she texts, juggling the phone with her sample bag. *Get in touch with your friend. We can talk to her this afternoon after I get out of therapy.*

10-4 comes the quick reply, followed by thankful hands and a smiley face blowing a kiss.

16

THE MOTHER

After they called the police, Darby and Scarlett had a long and serious conversation about why Darby felt Scarlett had betrayed her trust, and Scarlett explained how growing up without a father made her a target. The emotions ran too high until they began to bicker, and then things blew up. A fight to remember, one that will live in infamy between a mother and daughter forever. The things Scarlett said. The replies Darby made. The doors slammed. The silence between them charged with lightning. Days of this. It was too much to bear.

Darby and Scarlett rarely fight, but when they do, it's the knock-down, drag-out of two lionesses with too-similar buttons being pushed. Things were tense enough before the blowup; Darby hadn't told Scarlett she lost her job yet. She didn't want her daughter worrying, naturally, but in truth, she'd been too consumed with learning the hideous news that her child had multiple siblings and said child had been hiding that information from her mother. For Scarlett to go behind Darby's back was such a betrayal. Such a lie.

And it hurt. It hurt terribly.

Yesterday, watching Scarlett through the kitchen window, her legs drawn up underneath her on the front porch swing, the *creak, creak, creak* of the metal S-hook that she's needed to hit with oil for months now, Darby realized there was more to it.

Darby spent her whole adult life staying in control, staying on top of things. She is organized, dedicated, reliable. When she says she's going to do something, she does it, right away. She's raised her children to be just like her—compassionate, capable, and considerate.

They are not liars. They do not hide things from her. They are expected to be honest, forthright, and kind—especially with her.

But is Scarlett searching for the identity of her donor really a lie? Is it really a betrayal? Can she blame the girl for wanting to know where she comes from?

Yes, she can. If Darby's being honest, she knows exactly why she's upset. Scarlett wanting to know her father means Darby—as a mother, as a parent, as a friend—isn't enough. And when did that happen? It used to be the two of them against the world. Especially when Peyton left for school, she and Scarlett were inseparable.

Darby thought she was doing a stellar job. Clearly, she isn't.

And despite herself, she keeps going back to something Scarlett said during their initial argument. *"But aren't you lonely? I mean, it would be so hard to be alone all these years."*

Of course she's lonely. But she's never been alone, and that's a very different thing.

And it doesn't matter anymore. The police have their names; the donor will be notified that they exist. So as soon as Scarlett leaves for school today, Darby is going to talk with the head of Winterborn. She is going to demand an explanation. Later, once she knows the whole story, once she has a plan in place, she'll explain to her daughter what's happened at the hospital.

Darby glances at the clock on the microwave, goes to the stairs and calls up.

"Scarlett Flynn, you get out of bed this minute. You're going to be late."

"I don't want to go today," comes the plaintive reply.

"Tough. Get up and get out of here."

A yawning Scarlett arrives in the kitchen. "Is there coffee?" Her daughter's hair stands on end, like she slept upside down.

"There's milk."

"Yeuch."

She drops into her chair, head bowed. Darby softens, the breath leaving her, and with it, the tension from their fight. She can't stay upset with Scarlett. This isn't the girl's fault.

"I'll make you a deal. No more forcing me to drag you out of bed, and I'll make an extra cup in the morning. But only one, you hear me?"

Scarlett brightens and blows her a kiss. "Mwuah! Thanks, Mom!"

"Go brush your hair. You look like a wild woman."

Truce.

After a cheerful Scarlett leaves with coffee heavily laden with milk and stevia sweetener in her thermos, Darby spends half an hour on the Winterborn website, searching for anything that might help her argument, then another hour with her files, picking through her privacy statements, her agreements, what she's allowed to ask for regarding the identity of her donor and what she is not, taking copious notes, before she picks up her phone. She is going to get to the bottom of this. She wishes the original founder was still alive; a quick search shows he passed away almost a decade earlier. Him, she knew, and liked, though considering, realizes he was the one who'd let this happen. She's going to have to talk to someone who will certainly deny any responsibility or culpability, but at least there's a chance she can get more information.

She dials the phone, puts it on speaker, tapping the pen against her teeth, frowning slightly. Gearing up. Resting bitch face.

"Winterborn Life Sciences. Amanda speaking. How can I help you today?"

The chirpy voice sets Darby on edge.

"My name is Darby Flynn. I am a client, and I have an appointment to speak with Mr. Slade."

"Oh hello, Ms. Flynn. It's wonderful to hear from you. I hope you're well?"

Like they're friends. Like they've met. Like she's called to have a chat.

"I'm not well. I need to speak with Mr. Slade, right now."

Chirpy Amanda turns sad in a heartbeat. "I'm so sorry. He's not available. Can I leave a message for him?"

"We have a meeting."

"Yes, unfortunately, I was about to call you and tell you he's tied up. He asked that we reschedule for next week. But if there's a message I can relay in the meantime?"

Darby sees red. "Tell him he needs to get on the call with me immediately. I've just discovered Winterborn has been selling my donor's sperm to multiple families."

"Well, you know our policy—"

"Amanda, right? Seriously. Either get him on the phone for me or the police will be calling you in five minutes. I'm surprised they haven't called you already."

"The police?"

"Get me Slade. Now."

A click. Has she hung up? No, there's the burble of elevator music, soft and sibilant in the background.

Darby takes a deep breath and blows it out slowly. She needs to be careful here, not come in guns blazing. But now that she's on the phone, now that she's opened the door, she's furious, beside herself with anger. There are rules to these delicate matters. Ways to handle things. How dare they create such a terrible situation?

"Thomas Slade. Sorry for that miscommunication. How may I be of service?"

Let it go, let it go.

"Mr. Slade, I'm a client of Winterborn, and I've just discovered my donor's sperm has been disseminated well past the number of times it's allowed to be used. Per the contract we signed, no more than ten individual families are allowed to purchase the same donor."

"Mrs. Flynn, is it?"

"Ms."

"Ah. Yes. Ms. Flynn. I'm sure this is a simple misunderstanding. Our protocols—"

"As of this moment, there are at least twenty-eight ancestry matches to my daughter. They range in age from two years to twenty. One of them is the suspect in a murder. Now, would you like to explain your protocols?"

Silence, then a brisk, no-nonsense tone.

"May I have your donor's profile number, please."

Darby hangs up wondering if she's done the right thing by calling. Slade seemed concerned, yes, but he'd shuffled her off the phone almost as quickly as he'd gotten on with promises to look into the situation and return her call. And he seemed surprised by her announcement. Why hadn't the police been in touch? Or was he simply a fine actor, used to keeping hysterical parents calm in a crisis?

She pours a fresh cup of coffee. She has constructed a beautiful world and she's happy, they're all happy, and suddenly, the cracks are showing along the edges, and she has no idea how to mend things.

On impulse, she dials Peyton. They established ground rules when he left for school—calls on Sundays only, no surprise visits, all the things she knew he needed to have comfortable boundaries and autonomy. It's worked well for the first two years he's been at school. But she wants to hear his voice. She wants to warn him of the storm to come.

He answers on the first ring.

"Mom? Are you okay?"

His voice is so deep, it sometimes surprises her. She's made a man. He's still a boy, her little boy, but he's a man now, too.

"I just wanted to say hi. Sunday felt like a long way off."

"Well, hi." He laughs. "I always like hearing from you."

"Anything exciting happening on campus?"

"Nothing unusual. I have an early midterm, so I've mostly been in the library, studying."

"Aren't you a good boy?"

"You brought me up well."

She hears voices in the background, a murmur, and what sounds like crying. "Do you have people over?"

The noise stops. "Sorry. YouTube. An ASMR room to help me focus. I don't want to rush you off, but I am in the middle of something. Want to tell me what's really going on?"

She explains as succinctly as she can. "I can't imagine this isn't going to be big news locally, maybe even nationally, and I'm sure people will seek you out."

"Wow. Is Scar okay?"

"She's justifiably upset."

"I bet. I'll text her, see if I can calm her down. But, you know, it doesn't affect me otherwise. He's not my donor. The media and police shouldn't bother me at all."

"You know how the press is, sweetie. They will hunt down every angle they can. Proximity will be enough."

"I wouldn't worry so much about the press. I'd be more concerned about the lawyers."

"What do you mean?"

"Winterborn will most certainly be sued, I would assume in some sort of class action, and there will be discovery, and every family who's used their services regardless of whether they belong to Scarlett's donor or others will be scrutinized."

Darby sighs. "I suppose you're right. You planning to go to law school now?"

"I've considered it," he says lightly.

A spike of pride in her heart. This is news. She won't think about the money, the time, the effort, the challenges, will only be happy for him finding his own path, deciding the course of his life.

"That's great, honey." The background noise starts up again, his video coming off pause. "I better let you go."

"Okay. Keep in touch, though. I can come home this weekend if you want. I have plans, but I can break them. It might be good for Scar to have someone to talk to. You know, someone that she doesn't blame. Sorry, Mom, that sounded bad. I just assume she's upset with you? Though you haven't done anything wrong," he adds quickly.

"No. You're right, she is upset. I'll text you, all right, honey? I love you."

"Love you, too, Mom."

There is a squawk as he hangs up, and Darby can swear she hears a woman's voice calling as the phone dies.

She freezes, listening, as if the connection hasn't been cut.

Nothing.

Good grief, Darby. Your imagination is really running wild these days.

Later, exhausted, Darby decides a nap is in order. She wraps the blankets around her and falls into a fitful sleep, startling at every creak, dog bark, engine whine, door slam. These are the sounds that have always comforted her before, and now they are ominous, frightening. A woman has died, been murdered, and while she hasn't fixated on Beverly Cooke's death, suddenly it is all she can think about. What it must have been like to know you were about to die. The panic, the fear, the hypoxia.

She wakes to the sounds of lapping water and shattering glass, but quickly realizes it was just a dream, just a nightmare. Her imagination on overdrive.

As she drifts back to sleep, she hears something from her dreams.

A woman's voice.

A woman's voice, calling for help.

17

THE WIFE

At the Jones build, Olivia shuts the door behind her and walks carefully between the stacks of flooring and paint buckets to the kitchen.

A flash of red. A hoodie, draped over the counter, next to a leaking to-go cup of coffee. The cup is perched atop her unfinished four-inch-thick slab of Statuario marble, and even from here she can see the dark ring that's formed on the stone's porous surface.

"No!" she cries, leaping for it, just as a head pops up from behind the island. She screams in surprise and knocks the coffee cup off the slab, where it immediately begins to soak into the subfloor.

"Oh my God, it's ruined."

And there goes the budget, and the timeline. They'd ordered this piece directly from the quarry in Italy, had it specially cut striato, so the veining formed a swoosh pattern that ran over the waterfall edge, and waited three months for it to show up, and now some idiot has managed to ruin it by putting his coffee cup on the raw marble? She knew they should have polished and sealed it the moment it arrived. They were waiting for the owners to decide on a finish. *Never again.*

"Hey, sorry." The owner of the hoodie—young, bearded, rumpled, sweat-stained—calmly picks up his coffee cup. The stain is dry. He's been there for a while. "I'm sure we can get that out. I can just buff it up." He starts for his toolbox, which she notices is perched precariously on the edge of the island, ready to fall and ruin something else.

"No. Stop. Don't touch it. I'm calling my guy. Who the hell are you, and what are you doing on my job site?"

"Griffin White. I work for Dave."

"Which Dave? I have three."

He mutters a last name that sounds like Hartwell, and she narrows her eyes. "Dave Hartwell is a carpenter, not an installer. Plus, he isn't working this job. Who are you really?"

He doesn't answer, only stares at her, his brown eyes unfathomable. His voice is cold. "Like I said, I'm Griffin. And I work for Dave *Cas*well. I'm supposed to be pouring footers for your porch."

"Then you should be outside, not in here ruining my kitchen. How did you even get the code?"

His dark eyes are flat and assessing, like a snake. Pools of black in a bone-white face. He might be handsome if not for those awful eyes.

She points to the door. "Go. Now. And I'm letting Caswell know you helped yourself to my interior and ruined thirty thousand dollars in marble. You'll have to pay for the damage. I'll leave it up to him how to make it right. You better hope his insurance is up to date."

When he doesn't move, she waves a hand at him. "Leave. I have work to do."

He takes his sweet time, gathering up the toolbox and putting on the hoodie. He retrieves the coffee cup from the floor. When she sees his back, she dials her counter guy, Eddie, who answers on the first ring.

"Oh, boy, do we have a problem."

"Everything is fixable," he replies. "What happened?"

Olivia hears the back door to the property open and close softly and looks over her shoulder to see the young man who just screwed up her day, her life, her career, staring at her again from outside the glass. The second she deals with this, she is calling Caswell and having the asshole fired. He gives her the creeps, standing there staring. Why the hell has he gone out the back instead of the front?

"Hold on a sec."

She marches to the door and flicks the dead bolt.

He grins. His lips are chapped, and he licks them, slowly. They stand there a moment, locked in a battle of wills. Her inside, him outside. Both of them pretending he couldn't just smash a rock through all that glass and put a hand around her throat. He flicks up the hood on his jacket and draws the zipper in exaggerated slowness, all the way to his neck.

"Olivia?" Eddie says through the phone's speaker, and she breaks eye contact with Griffin White by reflex, glancing down at the black screen of her phone. When she looks up, he's gone, and she is alone in the massive open space that will eventually be the kitchen and living room for the Jones family.

On impulse, she walks quickly to the front door and bolts it, too, then pops the back off the Kwikset and removes one of the four batteries so no one can use the code to get in. She is never afraid on her builds, and she has protection in the form of pepper spray and, if all else fails, at the bottom of her bag, a nonlethal Byrna that looks like a gun but fires projectiles instead of bullets. But something about this guy gives her the willies.

"Hey, Eddie, come on over, will you?"

There must be a note of concern in her voice because he doesn't ask any more. "Yeah, I'm at Frothy Monkey. Be there in five."

She clicks off, a shiver running through her at the idea of more coffee inside her build. An engine turns over, and she sees a decrepit white van with an extension ladder on top pulling away from the site.

What in the world just happened?

She is still asking herself this when Eddie knocks a few minutes later, making her jump.

When did she get so edgy?

Maybe when people you know started getting murdered?

"Why are you locked in here? The code wouldn't work."

"Because some idiot decided to come and ruin the slab, and I kicked him out." She lets Eddie in, shows him the marble, listens to him cluck over the stain.

"I might be able to fix it if it's not too deep. Want me to try?"

"Might as well."

"Well, if I can't get it out, maybe we'll leather it to match the granite. Or flip it? The veins won't be the same—"

"And won't match the waterfall. Maybe we turn both pieces upside down… God, I am so pissed off."

While he works on the stain, she calls Dave Caswell to rip him a new one for not only letting someone from his crew into the house, but ruining things by being stupid.

But Caswell is confused. "I don't have anyone by that name on my rolls, Liv. I've never heard of him. And we aren't supposed to pour those footers until Friday."

"Are you sure you're not covering up an expensive mistake?"

"I swear. You know me, Liv. I don't lie. At least not to you." He laughs a little, and she feels some of the tension leave her.

"Honestly, I don't recognize his description, either. If someone was in the build that none of us know, but he knew you, and lied about working for me? That's creepy." A pause. "I think you should call the cops."

"You think I should? Isn't that a little extreme?"

"Yeah, I do. I don't like a stranger using my name, and from what you're saying, he was trying to intimidate you. Plus, someone gave him the contractor code, or he was watching and got it that way, which means he could come back. Won't hurt. Change that, too, okay?"

She hangs up and weighs her options. Considering what's already happened this morning? Caswell is right. She needs to report this. But she feels like an idiot. *911? Some guy was in my build and spilled coffee on the marble.*

Hardly a crime.

But that grin. Licking his lips, the reverse strip tease with his hoodie. Standing there on the other side of the glass, staring at her like she was a display case of cupcakes…

"Hey, Liv? You left some papers here on the floor. Probably want to put them in your bag so you don't forget them."

"What?"

Eddie ambles out of the kitchen with a sheaf of papers. "Looks like some personal stuff."

She knows she didn't leave any paperwork here. She snatches it from him and leafs through. Park's birth certificate. An old passport application. A pile of disclaimers and legal documents from Winterborn Life Sciences, in Chapel Hill.

The place where Park donated.

A stack of photographs falls to the floor. A dazzling smile, one Olivia recognizes.

Melanie Rich.

What the hell?

Eddie is looking at her quizzically.

"These belong to Park. What in the world?"

"I don't know. It was spread all over the place by the butler's pantry. But bad news. That stain ain't gonna come out. We're gonna have to find another option."

"Damn it. I knew we should have gone with the honed Copacabana. That slab's not still sitting in the back of the warehouse by chance, is it?"

"Nope. It'll take six to eight weeks for another Staturario to come. I think if we flip this, and put in the sidepiece upside down, the owners might not be able to tell."

"But the designer will know."

"You know the rules, Liv. Will it bother the client—"

"Or the designer. All right. Thanks, Eddie."

"You okay, Liv? You seem…jumpy."

"All good. I need to think this through and come up with some options for the Joneses."

He nods. "Lock that door behind me if you're sticking around, you hear? I'll be back in a while with the granite."

She locks the dead bolt and waits for him to drive away. Okay, now she's calling the police.

Moore.

She'll call the woman. She liked her better than the man.

She puts the photos of the girl in her purse. She might need them later.

18

THE DETECTIVES

Joey takes the call from Park Bender while Osley is inside Starbucks getting them coffee.

"You're going to want to come back to the house," Bender says. "Someone broke into my office."

"Are they still there?"

"No."

"All right. Have you touched anything?"

"Other than spilling another cup of coffee, this one all over my desk? No." The wry tone is only partially apologetic. The man sounds wrecked, and no wonder.

"Stay put, and don't touch anything else."

"Yes, ma'am," Bender replies smartly.

She hangs up on him, grabs the mic from the computer. "Dispatch, we need an evidence team to meet us at our last address. Possible B and E."

"Copy that, Detective."

Osley is jawing with a pretty girl sitting at the table by the window closest to the door, flashing that ridiculous grin, a booted foot up on the stool by the woman, showing off the latest in a long line of cowboy boots. He's a collector, as he calls it. A shoe whore, she calls it, which makes him laugh. *I got style, lady. You could use some. The eighties called. They want those shoulder pads back.*

Osley has never met a stranger. He's so outgoing, Joey often has to drag him away from interactions. This is no different. She pops the horn with her thumb, laughs a little inside at the shocked, then pissed look he gives her. She gives him a *come here* wave, and Osley takes his sweet time about it. When he finally hits the door with his shoulder, the girl is holding his card, a dazed expression on her face. Half in love or can't wait for him to shut up, who knows.

Joey likes working with him, most of the time. He's shrewd, and loyal. He's had her back for three years now, and they work well together. So long as she's had her caffeine. Of which, at this moment, despite the two cups she had at Bender's place, she is severely deficient.

"Why, in the name of all that's holy, did you just interrupt my soliloquy? She was about to ask me to dinner."

"It looked like she was about to barf on your boots. Gimme that coffee. Bender called. We gotta go back. Someone broke into his office. I've got an evidence team meeting us."

"You're so damn efficient, Moore."

"Give me my coffee, Will, or I swear—"

He hands it to her, already doctored exactly as she likes. "Dark and sweet, like me," Osley cracks.

"Don't be a douche. We need to go."

"You're exceptionally grumpy today, lady. What the hell is up your butt?"

She doesn't answer, because she doesn't know, just has that

awful, itchy feeling that they're missing something. Shakes her head and takes a deep swallow, then puts the car in gear.

Back in Forest Hills, Park Bender stands on the porch of his house, waiting for them to pull up. He is talking to a blonde in pristine yoga clothes who stands on his sidewalk leading to the front porch, a neighbor, most likely. When he sees their car, he nods, and the neighbor shoots a glance their way and scoots off, back across the street, where she sets up a wary watch from her own porch.

"Do you trust this guy?" Osley asks as Joey expertly parallels between the cars on the street.

Joey thinks about it. "Right now, I see no reason not to. As far as we know, he hasn't done anything wrong. It's a terrible circumstance. I'm sure he's been in shock since we rolled up the first time."

"You just think he's pretty."

She flashes him a smile. "Contrary to *some* people we know, I wait to make judgments until I've assembled all the facts."

"Oh, you *do* think he's pretty," Osley crows, and she can't help it, she laughs as she gets out of the car. Osley isn't wrong. Park Bender is pretty. Sensitive mouth, square jaw, unruly hair, tall and trim. But pretty boys aren't her thing. *Never date a man who's better looking than you*, her mother always used to say. It's not the advice she takes so much as the knowledge that most gorgeous men are wrapped up in themselves and their egos, whether obvious or not. They have something to prove. Not to mention he has a stunner for a wife, though she's as skittish as a deer.

"Thank you for coming back," Bender says. Polite. Non-evasive. He seems troubled; she senses the tension running through him, his lips thin, knuckles white around a steaming fresh cup of coffee. She thinks longingly back to the now empty cup in the car's holder. Never enough. It's never enough. But she's wired now; more and she'll shoot off to the moon.

"No problem. Why don't you show us what's happened?"

They tromp into the back yard through a wrought iron side gate—"keyed, always kept locked, the only one who can get through is the mower, and he's done for the season"—into a fenced-in area the size of a small parking lot. Grass, still lush and green, bisected by a gravel path interspersed with wide slate slabs that leads to a charming cedar-and-stone cottage. The scent of burning leaves fills the air, one of the neighbors doing a burn.

"I didn't realize you had so much room back here," Joey says.

"The lot goes back into the woods, all the way to the creek."

"Fenced all around?"

"Yes. There's barbed wire down by the creek. We converted the shed so I'd have a place to work when school was out." At Joey's glance toward the Bender house, which easily runs four thousand square feet, he stammers, "I need quiet and privacy. It's…contractual."

"I'll take a look around," Will says, taking off to the right. He disappears, and moments later, there's a frantic susurrus as the host of sparrows who live behind the cottage take flight, zooming into the air.

Joey follows Bender into the very misnamed "shed"—the small cedar-and-stone cottage has tons of light, space, and natural wood. The desk is live-edge wood and built into the wall, the bookshelves are stuffed, and the Aeron chair is original Miller.

"Olivia designed it for me," he says, ducking his head in humility at her raised brow. "She's an amazing designer. You could give her a cardboard box and five bucks, and she'd make it look like Buckingham Palace. This was a falling-down donkey barn when we bought the place."

Joey takes in the disturbance—the glass shards, the open safe, the pens and papers covered in coffee.

"What did they get?"

"Money. Paperwork. Passport and birth certificate." A pause. "A gun."

"Registered?" she asks.

"Yes."

"Concealed permit?"

"No. Just a regular home protection piece."

She shrugs. *No big deal, dude. Don't be so fidgety.* "Good. If it shows up in a pawn shop or on the streets, we'll be able to track it down."

"Do you think this is a coincidence?" Bender sounds worried.

"Do you?"

He flushes and chews a nail. When he speaks again, his voice is hard and flat. "Listen. You two keep showing up, dropping bombs that end my life as I know it. Reporters are bugging us. Now I find someone's broken into my office and emptied my safe, and earlier, I felt like someone was watching me from the woods. No, I don't."

"Okay. Any cameras to your security system?"

"We have a monitoring system on the front door. Nothing back here, though. Since it's locked inside the fence and has an alarm...."

She doesn't bother stating the obvious—people jump fences all the time—just nods.

"You might want to give it a look, just see if it caught anything out of place overnight. Any more media calls?"

"That woman from Channel Four. She came by the house after you left."

"And you talked to her?"

Bender gives her a look of extreme loathing. "No. Though I can't say I appreciate you telling her about my connection to this case."

Joey holds up a hand. "I haven't talked to any reporters. Not my favorite, you know? And the PIO hasn't made any statements. But they have their ways, their sources. What did she ask you?"

"Just to talk. Like she did when she called. I declined."

"It's going to get out eventually, Mr. Bender. The media

listen to our radio calls. They know when something happens that will be of interest. The Cooke case is high profile. We've been here three times now. Add in your ties to the case, and the fact that someone's been digging around in your personal things? As far as the media is concerned, where there's smoke, there's fire, you know what I mean?"

"There is no smoke, nor fire. I haven't done anything wrong."

Bender is clearly rattled. Interesting. "Right. But a tip can come from anywhere. Neighbors. Work. What did you say you do back here, sir? Something contractually private? Is that something that can be used against you?"

"No, it couldn't." He thinks for a moment, shakes his head again. "No. It's..."

"You're going to have to tell us at some point, sir. Why don't you let me be the judge of whether your occupation has anything to do with this."

"I can't. I'd have to get permission."

"Then I suggest you do that. It could be relevant."

Will appears in the door. "Got some footprints in the mud back here. We'll get the place dusted and take some casts, see what pops." A car door slams. "Oh, team's here. I'll go get 'em."

Joey looks toward the street; though she can't see in front of the house from Bender's office, she does have a view down the road. A derelict-looking white van with a ladder on top cruises by and disappears around the corner. She can hear Osley jawing with the team.

Joey stashes her notebook in her back pocket. "Good. Well, Mr. Bender, if you have no idea why you might be targeted, we will add this to our investigation. You get in touch when you've secured *permission*, okay?"

She is coming across like a bitch, she knows it, but come on, what in the world could a suburban English professor be doing in his back yard that needs this level of privacy and security? And if he does, why in the world would he keep the safe in an outbuilding instead of inside the house where the security system's cameras would cover it? It makes all her radars go on alert.

He's hiding something, her subconscious remarks. *You know it, and he knows you know it.*

Bender is fidgeting again, like a little boy who needs to use the restroom. She waits him out.

"Okay, you can't tell anyone."

She crosses her heart.

"I'm a ghostwriter. And no, I will not say for whom. But there was a thumb drive with a few manuscripts on it in the safe, and that's gone too. I have to call New York and warn them."

"Published or unpublished work?"

"What was taken? Unpublished. Next books in the series. I've been on sabbatical and drafting for the past few months, trying to get ahead so when I go back to work, I'm not overwhelmed."

"I understand."

"Do you?" His eyes find hers, imploring. A desperate man.

Something here...

"Yeah, I do. I have a friend who's a writer. You're not the only one in town. I'll be discreet, Mr. Bender. My job is to solve crimes, not blab people's secrets. Okay?"

His relieved breath comes out in a sour, coffee-tinged whoosh, and she takes a step back involuntarily.

Will, mouth running a hundred miles an hour at the two kids who've come to run the place—they are kids, my God, she's getting old—is barking directions. She lets him give the instructions, then bids Bender and the team farewell. She's not going to stand over them while they do their jobs. Nothing to be gained by hovering. Let Will do that.

No, Joey wants something else.

An audience with Olivia Bender.

19

THE WIFE

Olivia taps a nail against her teeth, waiting for Moore to pick up the call. When the cop finally does, her cool voice saying, "This is Moore," Olivia breathes out a relieved sigh.

"Detective, this is Olivia Bender."

Moore's voice gentles. "I was about to track you down, Mrs. Bender. I was hoping we could have a chat."

"I need to speak with you, too. Something odd's happened at one of my build sites."

"What?"

"A workman was inside when I arrived this morning. He said he works for one of my contractors, but that's not true. I don't know what he was doing here, or what he wanted. I got him out of the house as soon as I could—"

"Are you alone?" There is unexpected urgency in Moore's voice.

"I am, but things are locked up tight. I'm okay for now."

"I'll be there in ten. Stay put. And if he comes back, call 911."

Olivia hears the siren start to wail.

"Okay, now you're scaring me."

"Just clearing people out of my way. Perks of the job. Get to make lots of noise and drive real fast. If we could blow shit up, I'd have the trifecta."

There's a smile in Moore's voice, and Olivia hangs up a little more settled.

She takes a look at the marble, runs a hand over the circular stain, yanks it back as if the stone is burning hot. Could there be fingerprints? Hers and Eddie's, without a doubt, but the mystery man, too?

What else might he have touched?

The back door. He left through the back door. *Did I touch anything but the dead bolt?*

He wasn't wearing gloves, was he? Surely, they'll be able to find his prints and figure out who he is. She doesn't know. She wasn't paying attention to his hands.

She pulls out her notebook and writes up everything as she remembers it—the chapped lips, the toolbox, the red hoodie, the coffee cup… Did he take that with him? A quick look confirms he has. The van with the extension ladder. She line-sketches the flat, serpentine eyes.

A knock on the front door. Moore has arrived.

Olivia lets the cop in. Moore's eyes are guarded as she looks around.

"Any sign he broke in?"

"Not that I've seen, though I haven't checked upstairs yet. Nothing down here. He must have had the contractor code to the door. But look. Here's what's bizarre." She hands Moore the papers. "Park has nothing to do with my business. It's not like he would come here and leave his birth certificate. And this, from Winterborn Life Sciences. I have no idea why these things are here."

Moore nods, lips pursed, looking very interested now. "I do. Someone broke into your husband's shed last night and emptied his safe. I think we can assume your intruder this morning was involved."

"So he stole stuff from Park and brought it here. To me? Why?"

"An excellent question. To make sure you know about Winterborn, is my guess."

Olivia grapples with details, lets them run through her mind as quickly as a flooded creek. There is only one answer, but she needs to ask anyway.

"Detective, are we in danger?"

"Also an excellent question." Moore takes the papers and flips through them, either ignoring or unaware that Olivia is staring. The cop is just so blasé about it all. It's like she's seen everything; nothing surprises her. Olivia doesn't know whether to feel reassured or terrified.

A cramp takes Olivia's belly, and she gasps inadvertently, just a little intake of her breath. She turns away to grimace and rub the spot. Brigit the nurse told her to call if she was having any issues. She's still spotting, and the cramps have been nasty. Maybe she needs to get looked at. She had to have a D&C—"just to clean things up"—after her second miscarriage. It felt a little like this. Insult to injury.

Moore doesn't miss it, though.

"Are you okay?"

Is she? Is she okay? Her world has shattered around her, yet she is still standing. She is strong. But okay? No.

"I miscarried. Right before you arrived the other day. I hadn't even had a chance to tell Park, and suddenly you were there with the news..." She chokes back a sob. "I'm sorry. It's been a lousy week."

Moore looks both horrified and sad. She awkwardly pats

Olivia's shoulder. "I'm sorry for your loss," she says quietly. "Truly. Can I help? Do you want to sit down or something?"

"No. I'm fine. Do you have children, Detective?"

The woman shakes her head. "Always too busy with the job. Kids just weren't my thing."

"They're clearly not meant to be mine, either. And now we find out Park has twenty-eight of them? It's ridiculous to think..."

"Think what?"

"That having one with me will matter to him anymore," she finishes, then dashes a hand against her cheeks and wipes away the tears. *Get yourself together, Hutton. You're letting her in too far.* "Sorry, that is really not your problem. What do you want to do about this guy who was here today?"

Moore seems grateful to return to the break-in. "Can you sit down with a sketch artist for me? So I have an idea what he looks like?"

"Of course."

"Good. I'll have an evidence team look for prints and any other biologicals he might have left behind, too. Now, tell me everything he said, what he did."

Olivia runs the cop through her interaction, shows her the coffee-stained marble, walks to the back door and describes how he stood on the other side of the glass, clearly relishing how uncomfortable he made her.

"It felt like he was trying to send me some sort of message. Though I haven't a clue what. He gave me the willies, though. Something about the way he looked at me. I can't describe it. It felt wrong. I'm making this into more than it is, I'm sure. My hormones..."

Moore shakes the papers. "I don't think you are, Mrs. Bender. Could be something here. I'm not a big believer in coincidences. Especially when women are being murdered. Run me through what happened when he left."

"He got in a van and drove off. Well, I didn't see him get into the van, but it left right after, so I just assumed it was him."

Moore looks at her notes. "'A dirty white van with an extension ladder on top.' Did it have windows?"

Olivia closes her eyes to recall. "No. It was a panel van. There's got to be a thousand just like it, crawling all over town."

Moore looks as if she's trying to make a decision. Finally, she says, "I don't want to alarm you, but I saw a van that matches the description you just gave me cruise by your house while I was there looking into the break-in."

All of the breath leaves Olivia. "My God. He left here and went to my home?"

"Possibly. I'm going to have a car put on your house. And check the cameras coming in and out of the neighborhood here, and there, to see if we can't capture a license plate. We'll print this place, compare the latents to the ones from your husband's office. Put them in the system, maybe get lucky and get ourselves a suspect. This is what we do, Mrs. Bender. Don't worry, okay? We've got your back."

Sure you do. "Do you think this is Park's son?"

Moore pauses before answering, thoughtful and calm. "I honestly don't know. I don't want to jump to conclusions, but I'm going to look into all of this. I promise."

"Have you talked to the people at Winterborn?"

"Sort of." Moore glances toward the door as if to escape but sighs and crosses her arms. She is wearing small gold hoops in her ears, and they catch the light as she moves. "There's a lot we still don't know. Winterborn is the primary source of the multiples, but they have thrown up every wall they can, are insisting on warrants before they release any information. We're working on that. But we have talked to the parents of some of your husband's biologicals, and they all chose him as their donor from Winterborn's catalog."

"What, they go shopping for donors? From a catalog? Like,

J.Jill shows up in your mailbox with sperm donors instead of sweaters? That's insane."

Moore coughs out a laugh. "Something like that, though it's all done online. Mr. Bender seems to have been a popular donor. Winterborn claims an 80 percent live birth ratio, though we've discovered they have no requirements for their clients to report, so that number means nothing. They're a broker. They sell sperm to women who want to have kids. It's that simple."

Olivia's watch buzzes discreetly from her wrist. She glances at it. Park is calling. She declines.

"Don't they have some sort of regulations that stop them from using the same donor a ton of times? I remember a report out of Georgia about a sperm bank that let this happen. But that donor had psychological issues, if I recall, and there are lawsuits."

The watch buzzes again.

"Yes, I know the case you're talking about. This is different, in that apparently your husband only donated a few times, and that was years ago. Frozen sperm works fine, clearly, versus fresh… But in case you're worried about lawsuits against Mr. Bender, no. He never misrepresented himself. There's nothing criminal here. Not on his end, of course. The issue is why Winterborn allowed so many women to buy Mr. Bender's sperm. Sadly, it's a relatively unregulated industry, one that depends on the ethics of the sperm banks and the doctors running it to do the right thing and limit the number of times a donor is used. Most do. Some don't. Winterborn is clearly one of the ones that doesn't. It's not illegal. Unethical as hell, but not illegal. Many states are starting to change the laws, but as of now, they are untouchable."

"And you're sure one of Park's children is a killer?"

"I am."

"So it stands to reason Beverly's killer broke into Park's office and brought me the paperwork to discover the truth?"

"That sounds a bit like a mystery novel, but it is possible. Again, I don't like jumping to conclusions."

Olivia's watch continues buzzing. She keeps hitting Decline.

"Why though? Why would… I'm going to ask you again, Detective. Am I in danger?"

Moore doesn't answer, and Olivia blows out a breath. "Okay. I can get out of town for a few days. I have a job. I can—"

"Let's have you stay here where I can keep an eye on you, okay? I don't want you running off alone right now."

"Maybe I want to be alone." *God, would everyone please just leave me alone?* It's all she wants, space to heal, to throw herself into work, to hide away from her traitorous husband and his illegitimate brood. Getting a start on redoing Annika's beach house gives her a perfect escape on every level. She can push back a few weeks here, especially since the marble is ruined. By the time she returns, this could all be over.

Ah, but you will never be able to separate your husband from the twenty-eight biological brats he has, will you?

Moore is getting antsy. "Understandable. But humor me. I'd prefer not having to investigate any more killings, okay?"

"You think this guy might try to kill *me*?" The sentence ends on an unattractive shriek, one Olivia is embarrassed to make, but the idea that she might have been in real danger sends a flood of adrenaline through her after the fact. Moore puts up both hands.

"No, no, I'm not saying that at all. Bad choice of words, and I'm sorry. But I'd much rather be ten minutes away from you if something goes wrong than six hours. Stay put, okay? I'd really appreciate it."

Olivia nods.

"Great. Let me get you with our artist. Do you have time now?"

Olivia gestures to the half-finished kitchen. "All the time in the world, apparently. I just had a massive setback on this project, crews are going to be here any minute, and—" she points to her wrist "—my husband's been calling incessantly for the past five minutes."

"I hear you. I'll make it quick and painless. I'm going to take another look around if you don't mind."

"Have at it. I need to call my husband."

Olivia scoops her phone out of her purse and dials Park.

"Where are you?" he demands. His voice has the hitch it gets when he is extremely stressed.

"At the Jones build. What's wrong?"

"What isn't wrong?" he says bitterly. "Can you please just come home? We need to talk."

"I can't right now. I had a weird break-in here this morning. I have to go to the police station to sit down with a sketch artist."

"What kind of break-in? Are you okay?"

"I'm fine. Nothing was taken. It was… I'm fine."

"Well, I'm not. I think we're being targeted. Someone broke into the shed last night."

"I heard. Moore is here."

"You called her? God, Liv. I get that you need to punish me, but seriously? You're talking to the cops instead of me?"

"Calm down."

"Don't you always say telling someone to *calm down* is equal to the patriarchy saying *shut up, you ridiculous woman*?"

"Yeah, I do. How's it feel?" she snaps.

She hears him breathe deeply through his nose, mastering his emotions so he doesn't explode. Maybe he needs to explode. Maybe they both do.

"This isn't my fault, Liv. I didn't do anything wrong, and I'm just as shocked as you are about the news. And now someone's breaking in, stealing things. They took my gun, for God's sake. Please. Just…come home so we can talk. We need to make a plan. I know you're still pissed at me. I want to… I don't know. I want to protect you. Protect us. I want to go back to when everything was fine." His voice cracks, and a little piece of her heart shatters.

Her rational mind knows he didn't ask for this, any more than she did, that he's hurting, and she wants to go to him, to hold him, to hear his words of succor. Her pride won't cooperate.

"There's nothing to explain, Park. Lies of omission are just that, lies. Now they're coming back to haunt you. Did you tell the police everything that happened at school?"

"I didn't lie to you, damn it, and Chapel Hill is not relevant at all, and you know it. Why would you even bring it up?"

"I don't know, maybe because a woman was found dead in a lake. And your son is mimicking your past. Oh, and did you hear the other news? Perry is coming home."

She can feel Park go utterly still, imagines his face draining of color, his lips thinning, the muscle twitching in his jaw that pops when he grinds his teeth in anger.

"Low blow, Olivia," he says, and hangs up.

She wishes she could slam down the phone, slam a door, anything to bring the call to a close with crashing finality. *Fuck him. Fuck him!*

It hurts her to yell at him. She's never been a fan of fighting like this. But she feels like she's driven her car into a brick wall. Totaled. She is totaled inside, and she can't pretend things are okay any longer.

Look what he's done to them. He's destroyed their life together, with one terrible lie.

Again.

She bites her lip and shakes her head, anger welling deep inside her. Her life as she knows it is over. Her husband is a liar. Her womb is empty. Perry is coming back, and she's managed to weaponize him before he's even reached the city limits. A killer is on the loose.

And the detective is standing five feet away, going pale as she listens to someone on her phone. She clicks off looking so stricken Olivia is compelled to ask, "What's wrong?"

Moore meets her eyes, steel and worry in their depths. "Another woman has gone missing."

20

THE HUSBAND

He shouldn't have hung up on Olivia, but sometimes she can be so damn irritating he wants to strangle her.

A broken body flashes in his mind, and he hisses in a breath. No, he doesn't mean that. Not like strangle her, strangle her. Sometimes she can just be so annoying, so teeth-gritting annoying that he wants to pound his fist against the wall. He's going through something here, too. She's not alone in her sorrow. To throw Perry at him like that… They've agreed never to talk about him. To excise him from their lives. And his erstwhile brother is going to show up now, after all this time? Wonderful.

Park gets his agent, Neil McKinnon, on the phone on the first try. Sometimes he gets lucky like this. Other days he has to wait, biting his nails, for Neil to return his call.

Though honestly, he would have preferred to wait rather than have to share the chaos that's happened this week.

"Hey, hey, hey. How is my favorite client? Writing hard?"

"I have been, Neil, yes."

"Good, good. Everyone will be happy to hear it." *Everyone* is code for world-renowned bestseller Bartholomew Pekkan, writer of major psychological thrillers that wowed the world in the eighties and nineties and continue to sell like hot cakes even now. In his first decade as a writer, Pekkan sold millions of copies worldwide, made enough money to live comfortably in a small beach town in North Carolina—in a house and grounds that took up most of the town—and started hiring ghostwriters to continue the series. He figured he'd made enough money that it was time to share with some of the new, fresh writers out there.

Neil had found Park in the slush pile after he'd sent him a thriller that was, by all accounts, good enough to catch the eye of an agent but not nearly unique enough to sell into the crowded genre marketplace. In their first call, Neil had said, "Hey, you write an awful lot like Barty Pekkan," and Park had preened, for "Barty" was his favorite writer, and he'd written his story in good old-fashioned Southern thriller style in the hopes that maybe, just maybe, Pekkan would read it and give him an endorsement.

Instead, he read it and gave him a job.

The first time they spoke, the great man to the plebeian writer, Park had walked away from the call vaguely disappointed to find his hero was a boisterous giggler with the hint of booze on his breath even from two states away, but $100,000 richer.

It was not, as they say, the beginning of a beautiful friendship. But Barty gave him free rein as long as the books sold well, and Park was able to feather his nest and supplement his income and plan for his retirement. He taught during the year and wrote during the summers and tried his level best to get his wife pregnant and keep her happy. Keep her pregnant. Do his duty to his marriage, his family, his legacy. It's been a good life, and now?

He fears all of this is about to come to a screeching halt.

You're being punished. You know why.

"You still there, pal?"

"Sorry, Neil. Got lost in thought. There's a problem. I had the thumb drives with the next three manuscript drafts—"

A pause. "*Three* manuscripts?"

"Yes. I've been crashing hard all summer. It's actually a trilogy, but they're just drafts, not even full-length. Just the bones, really."

"Trilogy?"

"Yes. But I had a break-in last night, and they were stolen. The police are aware of the situation—"

This snaps Neil to attention, away from the dreamy idea of work completed ahead of deadline and fresh new stories to reinvigorate the series. "Police? You told them who you're writing for?"

"No. I only said I was a ghost, but that's it. The drives were in my safe along with some paperwork and personal documents. The police are looking for the intruder."

The frost comes in clear through the phone. "Well, this is not good, Park. Not good at all. At least you didn't tell them everything. Though anyone who sees the manuscript will know—"

"Actually, no. Here's the upshot. It's a new character. A spin-off from one of the early books. Like I said, it's just drafted work, so there's a chance that even if it does come out, it won't be tied to him immediately. It would take a true connoisseur of his work to put it together. The odds are incredibly slim."

"I don't recall us discussing you going off piste, Park."

"Don't go all schoolmarm on me yet, Neil. There's more."

When he's done explaining the situation, he can practically feel Neil vibrating through the phone. "Not to be a venal asshole, but you realize memoir is a huge category for us now.

Promise me you'll let me take this out when you're done writing it."

"You're being a venal asshole. A woman is dead. My life has been upended. Someone's broken into my house. My wife is devastated, and... Listen, Neil. Let's focus. I need an advance on the next Barty book. I'll get started on a straight series title now, send you an outline next week, and have the book to you by the end of November."

"Two months? The next one's not due until March. You don't have to rush it."

"It's not a problem. I already know what the story is. I'll grind it out. But I need some cash now. I don't know where things are headed here, and—"

The genial gentleman's deal with a handshake three-martini-lunch agent he knows and loves is back. "No problem, buddy. I trust you. Barty trusts you. But if it gets out that you've been ghosting for him all these years, the spigot will run dry, you realize that. Your NDA is ironclad."

"The police need—"

"What part of *ironclad* did you miss? No way you can tell anyone, Park. Police included."

"I understand."

"Good. I'm glad we're clear. You think about the memoir, and I'll go run some damage control. Twenty-eight kids. Jesus. Hope you don't have to put them all through college."

Park doesn't even deign the joke with an answer, just clicks off and drops the phone onto the counter with a *clunk*. He is rewarded with a small crack in the screen.

"Great."

"Mr. Bender?"

Osley is back.

"Do you want more coffee, Detective?" Edgy, edgy, Park.

"Naw, I'm fine. Just letting you know we're wrapped up in

the shed. It's a bit of a mess, but some wipes will take that dust away. How ya doing? You look wrecked."

"I am wrecked, Detective," he says, running a hand across his jaw. He hasn't showered, he hasn't shaved. He is rumpled and dirty and sad. "Tell me, what are the next steps?"

"Well, first, I gotta get your prints, for elimination." He pops open a small case and sets it on the table. "Just press the pads of your fingers here, if you don't mind."

Park has the sudden urge to say *no, I want my lawyer,* but he complies. He always complies. When you have nothing to hide…

But you do, Park. You do have something to hide.

He presses the pads of his fingers, then his thumbs, watches the loops and whorls assemble into a marker almost as specific to his body as his DNA. Good thing they don't have a way to measure the soul. His would be spilling everywhere right now like blood from a cut.

"Great. Thanks. So now we put everything in the system and see if we get a match. I hear your wife had some excitement this morning, too. With the sketch of the dude, and prints from both places, we might be able to wrap this case quickly. I sure do hope so. Makes me jumpy, having a killer roaming around. You take all the precautions you can, okay? Keep your doors locked and alarms on, just in case. And keep an eye on your wife."

Osley's phone dings with a text, and he glances down at it. The bonhomie cowboy is gone, and Park sees the sharpness inside the man, the face suddenly tense and wary. It's an act, Park realizes. The steady stream of good old boy I'm your buddy we're just havin' a chat patter is just a way to get people to open up, to say something that can be used against them later.

Osley is on the move. "Gotta go. We'll be in touch." And he's out the door, the car whipping away from the curb with a squeal.

Something has happened, that's clear enough. Probably another case. Park knows the cops work on more than one at a time.

As Osley promised, the shed is a mess. Park takes it all in, sighs, then starts cleaning up, stacking paper, wiping off the pens, the doorknob, his phone, the safe. Something bad is happening, something out of his control.

Twenty-eight kids. He's going to sue the shit out of Winterborn. He and Olivia are never going to have to worry about money again.

And as he's examining the facets of that little diamond, he turns it slightly, and the kaleidoscope reveals itself. He's been suffused with excitement and hasn't wanted to admit it. There's nothing he's ever wanted more than a big, boisterous family. Will he meet them all? Will they want something from him? Will he want something from them? Call me Dad, I want to be your friend, walk a few girls down the aisle, all that?

Maybe. And he has to admit, the thoughts fill him with joy.

But. One of them has killed a woman. Where will it end? No place good, that's for sure.

He has no idea how to act, what to think, just feels the simmering emotions inside him. He didn't ask for this. He doesn't want it like this. Like he told Olivia, he wants the weekend back again, wants to stand over the king-size sleigh bed in the early morning sun watching his wife sleep, her lovely face blank with dreams, his son safe and warm in her belly. He wants *her* to birth his children, not a bunch of faceless strangers. And he sure as hell wants the easiness of their earlier troubles. Infertility is a bitch, but fathering a murderer?

He's still holding onto one shred of hope that the police have made a mistake.

The landline rings, and he answers it, hoping it's Olivia, though why she would call the house phone, he has no idea.

"Mr. Bender? This is Erica Pearl again, from Channel Four. We're about to file our story, and I would so appreciate it if you'd talk to me. I know you want your side of the story to be revealed, and I'm just down the street. Could we come talk?"

Shit. The woman is persistent, he'll give her that.

He disconnects the call, then, for good measure, removes the phone from the cord.

A list of questions begins to form in his mind. First among them, what the hell should he do next? The way this is going, a lawyer, definitely. He calls Lindsey, whose phone goes to voice mail.

"Linds, I need your help. Call me the moment you get this."

He looks at the coffeepot, the black sludge accruing in the bottom, opens the cabinet, and pulls out the half-empty bottle of Dalmore 12. It burns going down, but the warmth makes him feel steadier. He drops into his chair, fighting back the urge to scream, and pokes at his cell phone, calling Olivia again.

This time, she answers. "Park, I'm sorry. I'm upset, and I was cruel. I apologize. I should never throw Perry in your face."

The fight leaves him. They have to stick together; they have to be a team. That's how they get through this, how they've always gotten through their troubles. "I'd call it even, then. Apology accepted. Honey, where are you? I need you. We really do have to come up with a plan."

"I'm in the car on the way to meet with the sketch artist. Come to the police station."

"I was hoping we could avoid—"

"Park, another woman has gone missing."

21

THE WIFE

At the police station, Olivia talks and describes and corrects, and it doesn't take long for the artist to put together a reasonable facsimile of the man calling himself Griffin White.

"It's him. His beard is a little darker, though, and the eyes are wrong."

"Okay," the artist says patiently. Thin and narrow-shouldered, his name is Roger, and he gives off a calm, steady vibe that's helping her relax. "Eyes are the hardest to replicate accurately, as I'm sure you can imagine. The windows to the soul. Tell me again."

Olivia appreciates his cool, collected manner right now, because she is freaking out inside, and she just wants Park's traitorous arms around her. She can't take much more of this. She's never been inside a police station before, and the tension coming off the cops is palpable. Until Lindsey answers her damn phone or Park shows up, Olivia is feeling very much alone in the world.

Roger the artist shows her the sketch again. "Better?"

"Closer. If you can draw him without a soul, it would work. He just looked mean inside, you know? Cold. Shrewd. Excited. But flat and empty, too. He's a handsome guy on the outside but void inside. I doubt you can capture that." She wraps her arms around her torso and walks the small room. Outside the open door, phones ring, piercing through the low hum of voices from many people chattering at once. The high-pitched whine of a light bulb about to blow comes from overhead; the fluorescent flickers every few seconds. It's all making her nerves jangle.

"You'd be surprised." Roger tweaks a bit more, and when she looks again, a chill parades down her spine. He's managed Griffin White's emptiness perfectly.

"Yes," she whispers. "Like that."

Moore knocks on the doorframe, making Olivia jump. She has changed into a much more formal black pantsuit with a white silk blouse underneath, which strikes Olivia as strange.

"Court this afternoon," Moore says, noticing Olivia's confusion. "Your husband's here."

Park strides through the door, and Olivia launches herself at him. He catches her in his arms and holds her close, head bent to hers. He is warm, and smells of cedar, and bleach of some sort. She feels safe for the first time in hours. She doesn't understand herself, these wild swings of emotion. Love, or habit?

"I'm so glad you're okay," he says quietly.

"Me, too. I didn't realize there was any danger at the time. I just want to go home. Can we?" she says to Moore.

"In a few. We want to chat a little more. With another woman missing, the case has obviously taken a turn. Things are moving quickly. We'd like to clear up a few more loose ends."

"We're done here, Joey, if you want to use this room," the artist says. "I can give this to Will and let him get started running down this guy."

"Thanks, Roger. Appreciate it."

Joey. What a cute name for a girl, Olivia thinks, cataloging it in her mental filing cabinet of baby name possibilities almost without realizing she's done it. Park grips her hand as if he knows exactly what she's thinking. *Your fault*. She tries to ease her hand from his, but he holds on tight.

Moore gestures to the chairs and nods to Roger when he pauses at the door. He smiles at Olivia and closes it almost tenderly, the latch a gentle click in an otherwise hectic morning. Olivia blows out a breath and sits, still clinging to Park's hand. Under the hawkish eyes of the cop, his grip no longer feels oppressive, but strong, warm and comforting.

They always did do well under pressure, the two of them. She glances at her watch; she has an hour before her therapy appointment. Maybe he'll agree to come. They have been through a lot today. Together is the key. Them against the world. Maybe they are salvageable.

She ignores the little fish nibbling at the edges of her thoughts, a twenty-year-old vision of tangled limbs and fogged windows.

Perry is coming...

"Mr. Bender, we're looking into connections between Beverly Cooke and Jillian Kemp."

"Connections?"

"Unfortunately, yes. Mrs. Kemp is one of the mothers who chose you as her donor."

Olivia's hand jerks away convulsively. "You have to be kidding me."

Park seems dazed, listening to the cops tell him they need to control the message and go to the media before they run with the story, until his face goes red and he starts shaking his head.

"You want to out me as the donor for all these kids? No way,

Detective. I'm not ready to have this made public knowledge. My God, I've only known about it for a few days. I don't even know how I feel about it, and you want to announce it to the world along with the news that a killer is targeting the donor mothers? No. No way. There's a local reporter already hounding me. This will make it all worse."

"Who?" Moore asks.

"Erica Pearl."

"Ah. All right. I understand where you're coming from. We can circle back to that in a moment. There's something else I'd like to talk with you about. Chapel Hill."

Olivia sees the Adam's apple in Park's throat bob. "I don't see how that's relevant to this situation."

"We spoke with Melanie Rich's mother this morning."

Park flinches at the name. She can't blame him. It was so hard on him when Melanie was killed. It was the first thing he told her about when they got back together. Halfway through their first date, he blurted it out. "I had nothing to do with that girl's death. I want you to know that."

"I didn't think you did," Olivia had replied mildly, setting her hand on top of his bigger, rougher one. They were in a lovely Italian restaurant downtown, more expensive than either of them could afford at the time, him on his TA stipend and her still in design school, but he'd been so intent on impressing her that she'd said yes immediately. "Your roommate was a horrible person. I'm just so glad the police figured out it was him."

She remembers how relieved he was. Of course he was telling her the truth. Park didn't have that kind of violence in him. His was more contained. More subtle. The razor's edge instead of a sledgehammer.

Now, though, he's gone quiet at the mention of Melanie's name. Quiet enough that the cop notices, and sits forward, just a touch.

"Mrs. Rich gave us permission to exhume Melanie's body."

"Why would you do that?" Park demands, and Olivia puts a cautioning hand on his arm.

"There was a discrepancy in the blood work in her case. At the time, emotions were running high, and Mrs. Rich held back some information. She was trying to keep Melanie's reputation intact, to make sure her father wasn't shamed. Since Melanie was dead, she didn't see any reason to share."

"Share what?" Olivia asks, dread building in her gut.

"Melanie was pregnant when she died. Or so her mother claims. Did you know?"

Park's face is going red again, and she squeezes his forearm to send a message—stay cool.

"No," he manages. "I didn't."

"There wasn't an embryo reported on the autopsy, so we don't know if the coroner down there missed it or what, but her blood work did show an elevated hCG level. It was sloppy for them not to at least take an embryonic tissue sample and do a paternity test to make sure the DNA matched Peter Johnson. That's a slam-dunk motive for murder, in my mind, but it never came up in the case. Anyway, we thought we should do our due diligence, and go for that sample."

"That's horrible," Park chokes out. "Why would you do that? It won't bring Melanie back."

"No, it won't," Moore says. "But it will put my mind at ease. It's just so strange, all these years later, a murder so similar, tied so closely to you. We're already rerunning the DNA from Melanie's case to make sure we don't have another match in the system. I guess I want to see if Peter Johnson is the daddy. Curiosity more than anything else. I'm just one of those who likes to cross the *t*'s and dot the *i*'s. So, anyway." Moore stands, adjusting the holster on her hip. "I have to get going. I need to be in court. But with all that's happening, we really should go ahead and start talking with the media, letting them in on this situation, or they will be relentless. I can arrange for you to sit down with them, both of you, and you can tell them what this has been like. I know you're being torn apart with worry over this, and now that someone's breaking into your places, you need—"

"What we need is a lawyer," Park says, and the finality in his tone makes the cop sit back down in her chair and cross her arms, a brow hiked to her hairline. "No. I won't go along with this until I've had a chance to discuss the situation with counsel."

Olivia leans over to him. "Park, maybe the detective is right. We've been targeted already. We're the victims here, just as much as Beverly was, and Jillian might be. Just as much as your children. And now someone's broken into both our workplaces. Add in that the police—" she looks sharply at Moore, who smiles blandly at her "—are dragging up the Melanie Rich murder, this is getting out of control."

The look he gives her is of such profound betrayal that she sighs and squares her shoulders, facing Moore again.

Together. Stand together. Talk to Lindsey's friend before this goes any further.

"My husband is right. We need to speak with counsel before any more steps are taken that might share the full details with the media before we are ready for that to happen." Then, softer, "You understand, we've had too many shocks. We need some time to wrap our heads around all of this, and we have to make sure Park is protected in case one of these women decides to… I don't know…talk."

"And say what?" Moore asks, looking genuinely intrigued.

"I have no idea," she snaps. "But it's time for us to go. We'll be at our home if you need to speak with us again and will let you know if anything else happens."

She stands, feeling much less brave than her words imply, and Park follows suit, face stony.

Moore waves a hand toward the door in dismissal. Park grabs Olivia's arm and practically drags her out of the room.

In the parking lot, they confer in heated whispers. Where to go. Who to talk to. Olivia knows their reaction to the cop wanting to release their names to the media made them look furtive, guilty, though they've done nothing wrong. And Park had nearly exploded at the news of Melanie's pregnancy. Another pregnancy.

"Did you know she was pregnant?"

He shakes his head. "We'd already broken up when she went missing. No way it was mine."

"I believe you. Let's get with Lindsey. She'll know what we should do next. She already was planning to talk to the crisis management lawyer."

They call Lindsey, and when she doesn't answer, Olivia says, "Let's try her admin."

"She's not in, Mrs. Bender. She took the afternoon off. Said something had come up and she'd see me tomorrow."

"Thanks, Jennifer." Olivia hangs up, glances at the time on her phone. She's going to be late if she doesn't hurry. "I have a therapy appointment." At Park's anguished look, she says, "You should come with me."

"This stranger who broke into your build, who might have broken into our home, is out there, the police and the media are breathing down our necks, and you want to go to therapy? Aren't you worried about me at all?"

"Of course I am. I'm sick at heart right now, Park. And I have exactly zero ideas how to handle things. Come with me. At the very least, we'll be able to make a plan, get some tools—"

"Screw tools. Olivia, for God's sake." His voice cracks, and she touches his cheek despite the outburst.

"This is definitely one of the worst weeks of our lives, Park. Don't attack me. I'm trying to work with you when all I want to do is slap you. But I am meeting with Dr. Benedict whether you are coming or not. Because I might be strong, but you are breaking me in two right now."

"I'm sorry," he says hoarsely, tears in his voice. "I hate to hurt you like this, Liv."

"Then stop doing it."

"Are you going to call the clinic?" He blurts out the words, and she flinches.

"I already did. I talked to Brigit."

"I mean, are you going to make an appointment to see the doctor? We should talk next steps, shouldn't we? We'll have to start planning—"

"Park. Now is not the time. We have enough to deal with."

"Don't you even want to talk about it?" That mournful tone sends a combination of pain and impatience through her. She's beginning to feel manipulated, a place from where all their worst fights start.

"No. I don't want to talk about IVF right now. I'm not ready. I might not ever be ready again."

She gets in her Jeep and turns over the engine. Park stands by the car, looking like she just stole his puppy. Despite her anger, her instinct is to comfort him, but they're past that. They can fall apart later, once they know the whole story and have a plan to handle what's going to be a huge mess. My God, to think about trying to set herself up for another failure in the midst of this chaos? He's out of his mind.

"Later," she says through the window, and he nods, turning away to his own car.

The way he looks at her, it's like he's finally realizing the schism between them is irreparable.

Why does that spark the tiniest bit of relief inside her?

Because Perry is coming and you want to see him. You traitorous bitch.

22

THE BROTHER

They say you can never come home again, and walking through the Nashville airport, Perry Bender agrees with the sentiment. It's changed more than he could have imagined. This place used to be tiny, two halls and only a few regional flights, local musicians playing the BBQ joint, and now it's full of duty-free brands, multiple terminals, and direct flights to and from the UK and Europe, including the one he's just disembarked from, Heathrow to Nashville. Not a bad flight at all, though he couldn't sleep so he half dozed, half watched four movies, but look at this place. All grown up, just like him. He can only imagine what the rest of the city looks like.

You're an idiot for coming here, his mind helpfully chastises him for the hundredth time. *What do you think's going to happen?* Nothing good, aside from a few days with Lindsey, who he's missed.

It's not like Park will want to see him. He hasn't spoken to his twin in years. Perry stopped trying after it became just too damn hard to be rebuffed, again.

Olivia.

Her name is a stake to his heart, still. She will always be his first love. Maybe his only true love.

He has never understood what happened between them, how it went so south. Yes, he'd stolen her from Park, but Park had done that to himself. Cheating on her, and not even being subtle about it, the little shit. Perry thought he and Olivia had something solid, something real. Yes, they were young, yes, she'd just gotten her heart broken. But they'd had several weeks together between prom and his trip to Oxford, several glorious weeks when they truly connected, and he'd opened himself to her in ways he never thought he could. She blossomed, seemed so happy. Park was off with that girl...what was her name? Oh, it didn't matter. Park abandoned them both, and Perry knew the fissure between them was permanent.

And Olivia hated Park then. No one can pretend that convincingly. They'd been having problems anyway, she suspected him of cheating, and Perry was so relieved to have it out in the open, not having to cover for his jerk-off brother anymore. What an idiot he was to throw Olivia away.

Perry thought he was enough for her.

She promised to be his, always.

She'd begged him not to leave, to defer the Oxford scholarship, but he'd spent everything he had to get there, and though he considered her pleas, there was no way. He had to take this chance. He had to get out of Nashville. It's what his mother wanted for him; it was what she'd put into play for him before she died.

He'd written Olivia every day—every bloody day—and she'd written him back faithfully, for quite a while. They talked when he could afford to call, but it was the letters where they pledged themselves. Young love is a ridiculous thing, full of such highs and lows that no one should ever take it seriously, because it can never maintain such a high temperature, burns away eventually, but theirs seemed destined for success. He believed in her. He believed in them.

He came home for Christmas and things were different. She couldn't look him in the eye. She dropped his hand when he took hers. When he kissed her, the passion was gone. She broke it off an hour before his flight in the parking lot of the bloody airport, and he cried on the plane like a scared child. By the time he boarded his connection in New York, he swore he was never coming back.

He'd only broken that promise to himself once. Until now.

It was Lindsey who told him Olivia had gotten back together with Park. Seven years had passed since their fight in the parking lot. Perry was already making a name for himself in the photography world. He'd taken a position with the BBC doing documentary work and found some peace, at last. It didn't matter the assignment, he'd take it, which made him very popular with his bosses. He'd been to the Arctic, to the deserts. He'd climbed Kilimanjaro and dived the Blue Hole. He'd seen the world, in all her glory, from above and below. Been to places only a handful of people had ever traveled. Been in danger, been in peace, been in wars and labyrinths, been chased by cheetahs and stung by jellyfish and nearly shot by an Al-Qaeda operative in the mountains above Kandahar. He'd even been in love a few times, though the minute things started looking too serious, he got the hell out.

He'd lived. It's what he'd vowed to do the day Olivia broke his heart, and it's what he'd done every day since.

He hadn't had contact since that screwup Park had gotten himself into with the girl at his college, and the media went wild for a time. Perry had given his statements to the police, ignored the media, and sure enough, the story went away.

Then Lindsey gave him the news that Olivia and Park were engaged, and the wedding was in June.

He wrote his true love a letter. Just once.

I'm happy for you. I wish you well. But if you ever need me, I'm here. All you have to do is ask.

He'd even meant it. He'd long since made his peace with Olivia. It was Park he hated.

"Perry!"

Lindsey leaps from her car and runs to him, almost knocking him down when she reaches him, destabilized as he is by memory and camera gear. He catches her and hugs her hard. "It's good to see you."

"You're so big," she says, laughing. "My God, where'd my lanky brother go? You used to be so skinny your chest was concave. Now you're like the Hulk."

"When I was fourteen, maybe. You try lugging all this stuff around and see how skinny you stay. You look great, Linds."

She does. She's grown into a beautiful woman, with her princess hair and ice-blue eyes. She looks just like their mom.

"So do you." She punches him in the shoulder. "Come on, get in the car before the airport cops give me a ticket."

True to her word, a uniformed man is striding toward them with a scowl. She waves and flashes her dimples at him, and the cop shakes his head, face less severe. Lindsey can charm the birds from the trees if she wants.

"Good to know some things never change," he says, snapping on his safety belt.

"What?"

"You flirted your way out of that ticket when you got pulled over the first time, remember?"

"I was not flirting," she says with dignity. "I'd just gotten my braces off, and I couldn't stop smiling."

"That cop is probably still blinded. The wattage was epic."

They laugh, and the ride to her place is filled with little remembrances and jokes and a few fallow moments, two siblings who love each other desperately but don't keep in close touch finding their footing again.

Lindsey's house is a massive white brick-and-stone Tudor with a charcoal roof. He is shocked to see all the new architecture parading through the established neighborhoods. The updated French country designs are so unlike the sweet little one-story brick bungalows that used to line these streets.

When he remarks on this, she replies, "Yeah, styles have definitely changed. It's like this all over town." She looks at him dubiously, dragging his gear from her trunk. "Can I carry anything for you?"

"I got it." He's used to hauling his life around with him. He's the ultimate turtle.

Inside, the design is modern aesthetic, so contemporary that it almost has no personality at all. "You could shoot a magazine cover in here," he remarks, staring at a low sofa that looks like a large gray cube in front of an acrylic coffee table with a clear teardrop vase sprouting a single stem of cherry blossoms. "How do you sit on that thing?"

She laughs. "I don't. It just looks cool. The law is messy. I like things clean and tidy. Besides, I don't need much."

He nods to his bags. "I get it. I'll remember to pick up my socks."

Unsaid between them: *Olivia did it for me.* Perry recognizes Olivia's signature piece, the long marble island with the waterfall edge. Not that he follows her work. He hasn't looked at her website, with its portfolios and blog updates, in at least six months. He has a bone to pick with her photographer, anyway. He shoots everything overexposed so it looks blindingly bright, which, in Perry's not so humble opinion, makes everything look just a touch cold.

Maybe the new Olivia *is* cold. This room is downright frigid. The Olivia he knew was terra-cotta and macrame. The new Olivia is thick Carrara and sea glass. She is impenetrable. Unknowable. Everything in her work is too perfect. Seeing one of her tableaus in person, he understands how much she's changed.

It all feels lonely.

And this from a man who spends a lot of time alone.

Lindsey gets him settled in her guest room which—shocking—has an all-white marble en suite complemented by black leathered-granite countertops and towels. He hits the loo, then meets Lindsey back in the kitchen. She is standing in front of the open Sub-Zero. It's clear she lives here alone by the meager contents of the fridge. He's never asked why she doesn't have a significant other. He knows what it's like being married to your work.

"I've got beer, wine, tea. Water? Coffee? Scotch in the cabinet by your knee, though I have no idea what kind. I still hate the stuff."

"Tea is fine. I need some caffeine. I'm on fumes."

She fills the kettle. "What time is it wherever you came from? Was it Italy? Or were you in London?"

He glances at his watch. "I've been on location in Italy for the past month. It's seven hours ahead. I'd just be sitting down for dinner now."

"At nine o'clock?"

"Oh yeah. We eat late there."

"When's your shoot?"

"Next month. I have some time. I don't have to be back until the thirteenth."

"Are you going to go bonkers, being in one place for so long?"

"It's not the time spent, it's the company kept. I'm sure I'll be fine."

The phone starts to ring. Lindsey looks startled for a moment. "That's my phone."

"I gathered. Might you be answering it?"

"No, I mean that's my house phone. It's only for the alarm system. No one ever calls here. I'm sure it's just a spam caller or something."

The ringing stops, then starts again immediately.

"Oh, for God's sake." She pulls out her cell phone. "Whoops. This is dead. Might be work, trying to reach me. I told them I was taking the afternoon off and not to disturb me unless someone died." She opens a slick maple drawer and plugs in her phone, then picks up a black chunk of metal that looks more like the dark side of the Washington Monument than a phone and puts it to her ear. He's reminded of Maxwell Smart, talking on his shoe.

"Hello? Whoa… Whoa… Stop. Take a breath. I'm sorry. My battery died. I—"

She goes silent, eyes closed, as if memorizing what's being said, breathing in hard through her nose. "No, you did the right thing. Jesus. Go back to the house, I'll meet you there."

She hangs up. Her cell phone has come to life, and he can see the multiple missed calls lighting up the screen.

"Got an emergency? I can handle myself—"

"It's Olivia… And Park… There's been… Oh my God." She sits down on a black leather stool with champagne metal legs and only a few inches of back, biting her lip and running her hands through her hair.

"I'm sorry. I have to go."

"I'm a big boy, Linds. I can hear their names without falling apart. Time heals all wounds, right? What's happened?" She starts to take a breath and he, recognizing a sister about to tell a story, says, "CliffsNotes version."

"Okay. Park donated sperm and has like a gazillion kids, one of them is a murderer, the body was just found this week, the police had both Park and Olivia in for questioning, another woman is missing, a sketch of the suspect is coming out, and we are going to have to move up our press conference."

He assimilates this information. "Press conference?"

"We need to get ahead of the story. That Park is the suspect's dad, all that."

At the look on his face, Lindsey says, "Yeah. I might be late."

Perry is already on his feet. "I'm coming with you."

"Are you sure that's wise, big brother?"

"She needs me."

Lindsey cocks her head to the side like a spaniel. "And how do you know that? You haven't talked to her in ten years."

"She needs me," he repeats, because now he knows why he's come, why Nashville was calling him, why he felt compelled to come home. Olivia's world is spinning off its axis. He is the only one who can put it back.

"I don't think now is the time, Perry. This situation is fraught enough."

"I—"

"Listen. I don't know how much you're in the loop—"

"I'm not."

She hesitates. "They've been trying to have a kid. Doing fertility treatments, the works. Olivia has miscarried multiple times now, and sadly, again just this week. So seriously, stay here. She's already stressed out. Adding her old boyfriend to the mix isn't going to play well, for either of you. Let me ease her into seeing you, okay? I warned her you were coming, and I know she wants to see you. And I know you want to see her, too. But to drop you into the middle of..."

"Of a *family* crisis." His voice is cold; he can't hide the hurt.

Crestfallen, she tries to apologize. "I didn't mean—"

"That's exactly what you meant. I'm not a part of this family anymore. I get it, Linds. You go. I'll stay here like a good dog."

"Perry—"

"Go!"

She hesitates a moment before grabbing her phone and her keys and disappearing out the door.

Good job. Now you've upset her, too. You really do have a way with women, Bender.

A run. He needs to move. It's his normal activity upon arrival at a new location. Settle in, take a run, get the lay of the land. It will work here in his hometown, too.

Outside, he notices the van only because the extension ladder looks like it might fall off, perched so precariously on the top. Apparently, the van's owner has realized the problem, has pulled over to the side of the street to tie it down. But he's struggling with the weight.

"Need help?"

A relieved smile. "Sure."

It's easy to get the ladder back into place with two of them, and five minutes later, the van drives off, the workman sticking a hand out of the window in a wave of thanks and goodbye.

At least he was able to help someone today, Perry thinks, and takes off down the hill in the opposite direction, feet slapping the pavement in time with his heart.

23

THE WIFE

Dr. Benedict's office is designed to be calming. The room is painted a light greige, Sherwin Williams Agreeable Gray—second in popularity in her own designs only to Olivia's favorite, Repose—complemented with a few pen-and-ink silhouettes hanging on the wall. The throw pillows on the plump sofa are lapis lazuli velvet and down-filled, perfect for hugging to your chest as a shield, and the doctor's slipper chair is a lovely dove-gray leather with silver accents beneath a globe floor lamp. Olivia likes the space; there is nothing showy, nothing loud. Quiet and gentle, like Benedict.

But right now, Olivia is deciding whether to rip one of the pillows in two in frustration after Benedict's last probing question, the quintessential therapy staple: "How does this make you feel, Olivia?"

Dr. Benedict watches her, a slight smile on her face, as if she can read Olivia's thunderous thoughts.

"Fine. I'm fine."

"You are anything but." Benedict's smooth, modulated voice is usually hypnotic, but today, she's asking hard questions and expecting honest answers; her tone reflects her impatience with Olivia's obfuscation. She uncrosses her legs and leans forward, the leather of her chair squeaking slightly under the shift of weight. "You can lie to Park. You can lie to yourself. But don't you lie to me. This is a safe place, and you need to open up. Tell me how you really feel about Park's children."

Olivia realizes she is grinding her teeth. She doesn't like therapy. She doesn't like having to dig into her emotions, her past, her feelings. Feelings are difficult for her. Unsafe.

"I'm devastated, okay?"

"I'd be shocked if you weren't. *Devastated* is a good word. Let's unpack that."

Oh, the ridiculous lingo that goes along with trying to repair your psyche. How do you unpack a word? Pull it letter by letter from a suitcase? Here's the *D*, now the *E*, pull harder, that *V* is being tricky. It makes her think of giving birth, those letters flowing out from between her legs, rushing faster and faster. *Red* is a word. *Blood* is a word. And that closes her down again.

"What just happened? Where did you go?" Benedict asks quietly.

Olivia looks out the window. "Can we not do this right now?"

"If you're not comfortable talking about your feelings, let's talk about Park. How do you think Park is feeling?"

A scoffing laugh. "Proud."

"Proud?"

"Yeah. I hear it in his voice. He's trying not to rub it in, but I can practically see the gears turning in his head. He's getting everything he's ever wanted in one fell swoop. It's like handing him a bag of sea monkeys—just add water, insta-family." Olivia holds up a hand. "Don't you dare ask me how that *feels*. It feels like shit, okay? It feels awful. It feels like there's a schism between us that will never be mended."

"Are you jealous?"

"Of course! Jealous and hurt and overwhelmed and—" And just like that, Olivia cracks open wide, sobbing, the façade dropped. She hates herself for breaking down, and that makes her cry harder. Finally, she chokes out the rest.

"The worst thing is, I don't even blame him. I wanted him to do this. I asked him to. Yes, he should have told me, yes, he was trying to protect me, my feelings, my inadequacies. But I was the one who suggested it in the first place. And now the police are digging into our lives, and it's just so damn unfair."

"Being infertile is not an inadequacy, Olivia."

"Whatever. I'm just so upset with him, and really, I have no right to be."

Benedict makes a noise in the back of her throat. "You have no right to feel betrayed that your husband didn't tell you flat out that he had donated years before when you, realizing you might never be able to bear him a child, offered that gift to him? No, don't argue with me. It was a gift, a damn gracious one, too, and he should have told you right then and there. No question about it. Do you understand why he didn't? Why he's hidden this incredible secret from you?"

"He didn't want to hurt me."

"Exactly. So why do you want to be hurt, Olivia? Why do you want to be punished?"

Olivia blows out a breath. "That's harsh."

"It's true. You're punishing yourself for not being able to hold on to a pregnancy. You're punishing yourself for something completely out of your control." A quick glance over Olivia's shoulder. "I hate to end on that note, but our time is up. Please, do me a favor and think about this. Think about why you want to blame yourself for a biological glitch. Would you blame yourself if you got diabetes? If you caught a cold?"

"This is different."

"Maybe. Maybe not." She stands, and Olivia, who has shredded a tissue into confetti in her lap, stands as well, gathering the tiny pieces into her hand.

"Can I give you a hug?

It is the first time Dr. Benedict has offered more than a handshake or a box of tissues, and the gentleness of it nearly breaks Olivia in two. But she holds on, the tears thankfully staying away.

"Strength," Dr. Benedict whispers, and sees her to the door.

Strength. Yes, she'd had another tragedy. Yes, Park has betrayed her. Yes, they are inside a snow globe of personal drama that is about to be shaken, hard.

But Olivia is not a weak woman. She is not going to let circumstance rule her. She's going to try, at least.

In the car, she checks her messages, sees nothing from Lindsey but one from the fertility clinic. She plays the message—it's Dr. Jameson. So many doctors.

"Hi, Olivia. Brigit told me you miscarried. She said it was complete, but why don't you come on in and let us take a look, just to be sure. Put our minds at ease. And we can talk about our next steps. This was the last embryo for this cycle, so we could try a simple IUI since your body is all tuned up or discuss another round of stims and egg retrieval. Either way, whatever you decide, let me know and I'll make a spot for you in the schedule. Hang in there."

Olivia's new life, reduced to a thirty-second voice mail.

The decision hits like a lightning strike—*no more!* No more interference. No more pills and shots and hope and dreams. No more feeling inadequate, no more pitying glances from Park. She can't keep on like this.

She is not going to be a mother, and she will simply need to come to terms with it.

Her heart is pounding, and she has the urge to weep, but there's relief there, too. She's been torturing herself—let's not pretend fertility treatments are anything to laugh at—but it's not that. Desire conflated with stubborn pride is a corrosive beast.

She takes a deep, shuddery breath. *You're okay. Strength.*

24

THE DAUGHTER

The halls of the school are buzzing with girls in hunter-green plaid uniform skirts and white button-downs. Scarlett moves among them, smiling and laughing, waving to her English teacher as he leaves for the day, hugging her BFFs, before they all pile into her car for the after-school Starbucks tradition.

So normal. So right. This is what being a teenage girl is supposed to look like—beautiful, carefree, surrounded by excitement and energy, leggy colts just coming into their sexual and intellectual powers.

She shakes her head, and the fantasy dissipates. Yes, she is standing in the halls of the school, but there is no one with her. She is alone, as usual. She's never felt like she fit in here. Maybe because she doesn't come from the deep pockets of Southern money, maybe because she's not good at playing the game and kissing the ring, maybe because she doesn't have the completeness of a family unit—who knows? She doesn't have any super-close friends, only a few geeky girls like her who smile and chat during chemistry labs. She eats alone, she goes to Starbucks after school alone. She pretends it doesn't bother her, that she doesn't need the companionship of a pod of girls, but sometimes, seeing them screaming and falling all over each other and laughing, it hurts.

She's still not sure what she did that set her apart. Things had started well. She wore the same hairstyle—as much as she could manage with her curls—she wore the right shoes, had the right phone and case and pop socket, watch, even her own car, though not a Mercedes or BMW or Wrangler. There used to be invitations, there used to be open seats. Sometime, somehow, over the past few months, that's changed, and she can't pinpoint what she did wrong.

Maybe she's too smart. Her grades always have been off the charts, and smart women who don't play the game can be terrifying to their peers. She's always been more comfortable behind the screen of her computer or the pages of a book.

Maybe it's her mom. The weirdness started after a sleepover she'd hosted. She'd thought the night went great—Peyton had even shown up. Her handsome, friendly, already-off-to-college brother had been mooned over by several of the girls. Maybe he never returned their texts. Maybe that upset them. But one by one, they started peeling off until it was just her again.

It doesn't matter. Another two years and she's out of here entirely. And now she's found another family, and who needs the approval of the Chastains and Gillians and Ashleighs of the world when you have actual sisters and brothers to discover?

Scarlett skips her normal after school-coffee—*there she is again, lingering by the sweetener and milk, hoping someone asks her to join them, titter, titter*—and uses the library's computer to do some more research. She doesn't want her mother hanging over her shoulder. Now that Darby knows, now that she has Scarlett's password, she needs to find another path to her family.

She knows the email addresses of a couple of the Halves by heart. She opens a fresh email account, sends them notes—my mom busted me, she knows about the Halves, so do the police, and they're looking for the one of us who killed that woman—careful not to share that she is the one who ratted them out, then digs into one of the databases she's been using and looks at the group's structure.

There's a new match. Her heart flutters. Another girl, another sister, and she's sixteen, too. These shadow selves are fascinating to her. There are now four of them, sweet-sixteen half sisters. Scarlett sends her a message—Hi, don't want to shock you, but I'm your half sister. Want to chat?—and leaves her new email address.

The new email pings almost immediately, the subject line four question marks, the message short.

Half sister? What?

Hi! I'm Scar. Yes, you've matched to me because we share a biological father through sperm donation. I don't want to upset you with this news, but there are quite a few of us. We have a support group on Discord. If you give me your info I'll send you an invite. This is going to be very overwhelming for a while–trust me, I know–but we're a super chill group and it's been amazing learning more about each other.

She pauses. Should she tell her all of it? No. It's enough of a shock to find out you have multiple halves without learning one of them is a murder suspect.

Let's start with something easy, though. What's your name and where are you from?

Nothing.

Not unusual, to start.

If the person isn't looking for siblings on purpose, the shock of the news can be upsetting. Some of the kids are searching, with and without permission, but some have no idea they're the result of sperm donation, so not only are their worlds being blown up, the lives of their parents are upended, too.

Using her compromised account, she logs into the Halves group. The chatter has slowed since the news of the murder. Not a huge surprise, since no one knows who did it, and one of them is a part of this group. But she has a DM, from Jezebelle.

Jezebelle: Do you have any idea who it might be?

Scarfly414: No. But the police are looking. We should lay low until they catch whoever it is.

Jezebelle: Our brother. Until they catch our brother. This is freaking me out.

Scarfly414: Has your mom said anything else about the case? Oh, there's a new match, too, another girl. She's my age.

Jezebelle: Another? Wow. No, all I know is they think the suspect broke into a couple of places. They're saying they have a sketch of him, will be on the news tonight. Full-on search getting ready to start. It's wild.

Scarfly414: Have you seen the sketch?

Jezebelle: No. Gotta go. Something's happening. Talk later?

Scarfly414: Yeah.

She looks at her watch, almost four. She should go home. Her mom took the week off work to handle this "situation," as she calls it, so she'll be there waiting, face pinched and hard. Scarlett hates hurting her, but it's too late to back off now.

Especially if there's a chance to identify who killed that woman.

Just as she is logging off, another message pops up.

Jezebelle: Holy shit. Another chick is missing.

Scarfly414: What?

Jezebelle: This is terrifying me. I need to log off for a while.

Scarfly414: Stay in touch, okay?

Scarlett's phone rings. She's not allowed to use it in the library, so she bundles up her things and scoots out the back door into the parking lot. The missed call log shows it was her brother calling. She gets into her car and calls him back.

"Peyton! Hi!"

"Hey, sis. You okay? Mom said you've stepped in it."

"God. Yes. She's so pissed at me." She fills him in, how she sent off the swab, how she's pulled together all the siblings, the rules they were following. "I was supposed to ask you for your DNA, even though I know we're only halves ourselves. It's to map the whole family so no one, like, accidentally marries someone they are closely related to."

"Gross," Peyton says. "No problem, I'll give you a sample. Listen, go easy with Mom, okay? She's having a hard time with this."

"I am, too."

"I know you are, Scar. It's going to be okay, though. I promise."

"It's just all so freaky. And now another woman is missing."

"I haven't heard anything about that," he says sharply, and she kicks herself.

"Insider information."

"If someone else was missing, the police would be all over it. Be careful, Nancy Drew. Just because some strangers say they're related to you doesn't mean they actually are. Have you met any of them?"

"Only online. And that's not how this works. They can't fake a DNA match."

"Still, you don't know who you're dealing with. Anyone could be lurking around. I think it's time for you to step away from this, Scar. This is serious."

"I haven't done anything wrong." And then she's crying, and embarrassed to be falling apart. Peyton does what he's always done, sings a little. John Lennon. "Imagine." Her favorite lullaby. He has a good voice, always has. It calmed her as a kid, and it calms her now. She snuffles to a stop, wipes her face and nose.

"Thanks, Pey. You've always known how to make me feel better."

"Of course. Listen, Scar. I might be out of touch for a couple of days. I have a trip planned with some friends, we're going camping this weekend."

"Didn't you go camping a few weeks ago?"

"Yeah. It was cold as shit but a lot of fun. We're going to the Blue Ridge this time, so my phone probably won't work. It's all going to be okay, yeah? Just be nice to Mom, and I'll talk to you next week, okay? Love you, Scar."

And he's gone before she can say she loves him back. She texts him quickly, a heart emoji.

♥ You're the best brother ever.

The reply is immediate.

Another text, right on its heels.

Are you heading home soon? Momxx

Scarlett sends back OMW, double-checks the Focus mode is on so she doesn't get any alerts while driving, and puts the car in gear. Without traffic, it only takes a few minutes to get to the house from school, and fifteen later, she turns onto her street, narrowly avoiding clipping a car parked right by the stop sign. No one's supposed to park there; the hydrant has a sign. Thank God she had her foot on the brake when she made the turn, or she would have crashed right into them. Her heart races, and she pulls into the driveway with the sense that she's just avoided one of those horrible moments that will change her life forever.

She gets out of the car and debates walking up the street to tell whoever was stupid enough to park right on the edge of the intersection to find someplace else, but as she watches, the car starts to slide away.

Idiot.

More important things to deal with. Another missing woman means everything is going to get frantic, and scary, and honestly, she's glad to be home, where she's safe.

The car from the corner stops at her driveway. In it, she can see a man. He is staring at her, brows furrowed, and without warning, he guns it, and the car squeals away.

She watches him go, not sure what to make of it. A creeper? A killer?

Thoroughly freaked out, she bolts for the house.

25

THE HUSBAND

Park drives the city for a while before making up his mind. He can't help himself. The fear he's feeling, the sense of dislocation he felt watching Olivia drive away, is making him reckless. He wants to see the kid. He wants to see his daughter.

He has the address on the slip of paper in his wallet, though he doesn't need to look, he's already memorized it. He puts it into his phone. Belmont is only ten minutes from his location; he's there before he's decided exactly what he is planning to do or say.

He stops down the street from his daughter's house, and broods. A terrible sense of doom lingers deep in his bones, has since he left the police station. He didn't like how the cops looked at him, as if he were hiding something. He isn't—he has nothing to do with Beverly Cooke's murder—but the very nature of his previous experiences with law enforcement makes him jumpy around all cops. How could it not? When you've been a murder suspect, every interaction is tinged with fear. The idea of being incarcerated, of having his life taken from him, even now, fills him with a deep sense of horror. So close. He'd been so close to arrest, to being blamed.

It's been years since he revisited his emotions from the time when Melanie went missing.

Was murdered.

Was left in a lake near campus.

So similar to Beverly Cooke. Too similar.

But Melanie's murderer is dead, and Beverly was killed by his son. His son!

They're exhuming Melanie's body. She was pregnant. God, to have that revealed all these years later. It isn't his. There's no way. Right?

Honestly, he has no idea. He hadn't lied when he said they'd been on a break. It depended on how far along she was. Two weeks? No chance it was him. Two months? That's different. And what if they dig up her poor body and rip whatever cells remain of her child from her shriveled womb and test it and it does come back to him? Surely, they won't really exhume her. Surely, that was just a threat to make him nervous.

He understands enough about how the legal world works, how law enforcement thinks, from his book research. If he were writing a cop in this situation, he'd have him deep into the suspect's life at this point, digging out everything. Everything. Looking for a fracture line that could be pressured into cracking wide open.

Why is this happening? A wail builds inside him, choked off because it wouldn't be manly to fall apart. There's too much at stake. He has to hold it together. For himself. For Olivia.

He doesn't like the way he feels right now. Defensive. Frightened. Confrontational.

Desperate.

He slams his hands against the steering wheel again, and again. His whole life is coming apart, and he can't control it. And the manuscripts from his safe are out there in the world somewhere. What happens if they leak? If the police find them before he does, everything comes apart, that's what.

A car whips around the corner and honks at him, long and angry, pulling him from his reverie. It whizzes by and pulls into the driveway of the charming cottage he's been scouting.

Her. It's her.

He watches Scarlett—*my daughter*—get out of her car and is seized with the sudden urge to speak with her. He pulls his car to the front of her house. She stops on the neat slate sidewalk between the drive and the house, watching him suspiciously.

Beautiful. She is so, so beautiful. Long legs, curly red hair, heart-shaped face, a dimple in her chin—she could be Lindsey at sixteen, though that red hair—my God, she looks like his mother. He is filled with pride, and wonder, and something else, an instantaneous affection. She is his. She belongs to him. He wants to know everything about her. Wants to talk to her all night.

Will it be the same with the others? Will he feel the same sense of pride and possession and infatuation with the boy who thrust them into this mess? Does a parent love their child regardless of the terror they bring, the mistakes they make?

Murdering a woman is not exactly a mistake, though, is it?

Their eyes meet. He wants to get out of the car. He wants to put down the window. Something. Anything.

And realizes, here he is, a man in a car, a stranger to the neighborhood, staring at a young girl. This doesn't look good. This isn't the way.

Panic seizes him, and he smashes the gas pedal. The car fishtails away, and in the rearview, he sees his daughter looking after him, then running for the house.

Stupid, man. Really stupid. Now she'll think you're a stalker—or worse.

This is all Olivia's fault. She made him feel small, and he crawled over here to make himself feel better.

Way to go, asshole. It's always someone else's fault.

At home, Park stands by the front door, looking out the sidelights toward the street. The lawn needs cutting, he's suffused with a low-level panicked buzz about the manuscripts that were taken, and he's embarrassed by his actions in front of Scarlett, but honestly, he's started debating whether he should pack a bag and disappear. Olivia has tons of clients who have second homes; he's sure it would take a single call to the right person, and they could be lounging on a beach somewhere, looking at the ocean and trying to make sense of all of this in private.

Running would be stupid, he knows this, but he can't just sit here and wait for the world to collapse around them. Now that another woman is missing, this is all going to explode.

He has to do something.

He flees to the shed, takes a seat at his computer, and looks up Winterborn. The website is slick, three-quarter-screen shots of smiling partners standing in a field of tall grasses, holding the hands of a beatific child, couples hiking among redwoods with a baby in a carrier strapped to a chest, moms and kids jumping into shimmering blue lakes.

Apparently, sperm donation equals a happy, active life outdoors.

He locates the number for the facility and dials it. An actual person answers, chirpy and hopeful.

"Winterborn Life Sciences. Amanda speaking. How may I direct your call?"

"I'd like to speak to the director." He skims the About page, lands on a name. "Thomas Slade. I am a donor, and I have an issue I need to discuss with him."

"Oh, I'm afraid Dr. Slade is busy at the moment. Perhaps I could route you through to his lab assistant and you can leave a message with him. Hold please."

Chirpy Amanda is gone, replaced by the deeper lilt of a man who identifies himself as Juan.

"How may I help you?"

"I'm a donor with an issue. I need to speak to the director. It's urgent."

"May I get your name, sir?"

"I'm—"

"Get off the phone, right now." Lindsey storms into the shed, abject horror on her face. "Seriously, hang up."

"I'll call you back," Park says into the receiver. Then to Lindsey, "What the hell?"

"Park, what in the name of God were you doing?"

"I—I wanted to find out the names of the women who used me as a donor, so I can start figuring out who he is."

Neither of them need to qualify who "he" is.

"Don't be daft. You can't go off and play detective. The police are all over that, though the privacy laws are making their lives difficult. But you—you have to stay away from this. We need to plan this out. I want you and Olivia to sit down with my friend Lucía Perez. She's the best crisis management lawyer in town, and I've already cleared it with Olivia. Where is she, by the way?"

"At therapy," he replies absently. "Crisis management lawyer? We don't have the kind of money it would take—"

"Park. You don't seem to have any real concept of what's happening. Lucía will run you through how you need to act going forward. We can't have the police dragging you in for questioning again. They are not your friends."

"Technically, they didn't drag me in. Olivia was giving them a statement about the guy who broke into her build this morning. They think it's the same person who tossed this place overnight. I went to give her moral support."

"Moral support?" He hates that smug raised brow she gives him that makes her look like a sulky thirteen-year-old again. "The police suggested you come down to give Olivia moral support? I suppose they didn't ask you anything about your past?"

"Olivia asked me to come. And yes, they mentioned they learned Melanie was pregnant and they're exhuming the body—"

Lindsey groans and flops onto the crackled leather chair. "No more talking to the police without me, do you understand? We need to have a conversation with Lucía. I called her from the car, she's on her way. She needs to talk to Liv, too. It's going to take all of us working together to keep your heads above water."

"I don't—"

"Do you remember when Melanie disappeared?"

"Of course I do."

"When you were suspect numero uno, we were inundated."

"It wasn't that bad."

Lindsey stands, hands going to her hips in a move so reminiscent of their mother in moments of extreme unction that he fights back a laugh. "Park. Are you slipping into early dementia? You seem to have lost your memory. They interviewed me. They interviewed Dad, and Perry, and the local news heard about it and ran stories. The moment the media put you and your biological son together with Melanie's death all those years ago, they will smell the blood in the water and attack. Trust me."

"But I didn't do anything." He sounds weak, even to himself.

"Honey. The media doesn't care. The cops don't care. It's a story. A juicy one. The suspect in a splashy murder is your biological kid. That in and of itself would be raw meat to the dogs. And there's a bunch more biological kids you didn't know about, which is another great angle. But now they've found Beverly Cooke dead in a lake, and another woman is missing. And apparently they're talking about exhuming the body of the woman you dated in college who was murdered. Think, brother. It doesn't take more than ten minutes to put you in proximity to another similar murder. You are on their radar. Maybe you thought it was moral support, but trust me, it was anything but. You're a suspect. Again. We don't even know that they're telling the truth about the DNA."

"I didn't do anything wrong!" he roars at her, and she steps right into his space and yells back, enunciating every word in tight, clipped fury.

"They don't care! Don't you understand? They want to solve this case, and you're in it up to your eyebrows, regardless of what you did or didn't do. I refuse to let them railroad you—"

A loud knock, and they both jump. An elegant woman in her fifties, dark hair in a side-swept pixie bob sprinkled with silver dust, wearing thick pastel-framed glasses, sporting bright red lipstick and a white shirt with a popped collar, stands in the doorway. "No one answered the door, and I heard voices, so I came around the back. Am I interrupting?"

Lindsey runs a hand through her icy hair. "No. Of course not. Hi, Lucía. This is my brother, Park Bender."

Park is still fuming but takes a huge deep breath and gives the lawyer a tight smile.

"I'd say it's nice to meet you..."

"I understand completely. No one calls me when they have good news. Is there someplace we can all sit down?" Her voice is low and warm with just the hint of an accent, and makes his shoulders drop a notch. The shed isn't big enough for a team meeting, that's for sure.

They troop into the house, Park cursing Olivia for bailing on him to go talk about her feelings—*not fair, Park, totally not fair*—and puts on a pot of coffee. Lucía makes herself at home in the dining room, spreading out notebooks and file folders like she lives there. He ferries in the cups and milk and sugar on a tray like a goddamn fifties housewife, and Lucía takes a sip and smiles.

"Good stuff. Okay. Have a seat, and let's talk."

He sits, and Lindsey sits by his side. Lucía hands him a legal pad and a pen with a kind smile. "You may want to take some notes."

He's immediately relieved that the pen doesn't have a name and logo like he would get at the dentist or pharmacy. She doesn't seem smarmy at all. She seems like a beacon of hope, if he's being honest. She's the first person he's seen in days who isn't giving him pitying glances under their lashes.

"Should we wait for Olivia?" he asks. "Or should we talk first without her?"

Lindsey glances at Park. "Let's catch Olivia up later."

Lucía nods. "All right. So, Mr. Bender, the first rule of crisis management is to not get into trouble in the first place. From what Lindsey has told me, right now you're still in this category. My job is to make sure you stay there. I want to help you avoid a crisis. You're going to be a curiosity to the world because of your status as the unknown biological father of a number of children. Add in the police investigation, and you become more enticing. Lindsey tells me you have a past with law enforcement, a girlfriend who was murdered?"

Park shoots Lindsey a look. She's sitting with one leg bent beneath her, playing with the tips of her hair, looking innocent but concerned.

"Yes," he replies.

"Tell me. Just the broad strokes."

"There's not much to tell. I was a senior in college at UNC Chapel Hill. My on-again, off-again girlfriend went missing and was found dead several months later in a lake. The police arrested my roommate, who was convicted and went to prison. He died soon after. The end."

"Were you a suspect at any time?"

"No."

"You weren't interviewed, give any samples, fingerprints, DNA?"

"Well, yes, I—"

"Then you were a suspect. Tell me about the sperm donation. Again, broad strokes."

Lindsey smiles. "Pun intended?"

"Gross, Linds."

Lindsey starts to giggle. Park sits there rubbing his eyebrow with his thumb, trying to massage away the sudden headache that's taken hold while his sister loses it, going off into gales of laughter, hitting that weird moment of hysterics that makes her shake and cry with no sound coming out, even when the moment isn't terribly funny. He used to love making her laugh that hard. Lucía starts laughing at Lindsey's reaction, throaty and deep, and then they're both lost.

"Sorry," Lucía finally says, gathering herself. "Stress reliever. The donation?"

Park tries to stay dignified. "A friend suggested I donate. It was a good way to make a little bit of cash, and I liked the idea of helping people. It was really no big deal. They had me fill out an extensive questionnaire, get a physical, but it was my… sperm that they were excited about. I fit some weird box for them. I donated for six, eight months or so. They contacted me once a few years later and asked if I'd be interested in donating again, but I declined."

"Did they send you any paperwork at that point?"

"I don't think so."

"No new releases that they might have on file saying you are aware of your samples being used multiple times?"

"No. Nothing like that. They said something about the limit being ten, but that was it."

"And you have the paperwork from the initial donation?"

"Yes. That's part of what was stolen from my safe last night. Though whoever took it left it at Olivia's build site."

Lindsey looks confused.

"I hadn't had a chance to tell you. Some of the things that were stolen from the safe were left for her to find. Someone wanted her to know."

"Your wife was unaware of your donor status?"

"Yes. I…hadn't found the right moment to share the details with her."

Lucía seems intrigued. She sits back in her chair, takes a sip of the coffee. "Someone's sending a message."

"I agree," Park says. "Someone wants Olivia to know about this. But she does now, so that was a pointless act. Listen. I did nothing wrong here. Olivia hasn't either. I understand that we need to get out ahead of the craziness that's coming with the biological kids and the criminal aspect of our connection. You're right, the media's going to have a field day, and I want Liv to be protected. She's had a hard enough time with the infertility treatments and miscarriages. This is going to push all of that to a nasty head. But Chapel Hill—I won't discuss it. The case is closed, I wasn't involved, and there's nothing there for the police to hang on me. It's a cruel coincidence, that's all."

"Except they are exhuming the body because the girl was pregnant, and no one dealt with that back then," Lindsey says. "Park says it's not his, but until we know for sure…"

Lucía taps her pen on her notebook. "Have you stopped to think that perhaps the killer is trying to get your attention? That he's mimicked your girlfriend's murder to send you a message? It's not out of the bounds of reason to think the break-ins are tied to him, as well. Either someone wants your attention, or someone's trying to frame you."

"I—" Park stops, aghast. He *has* been thinking this, he just hasn't voiced it aloud. Someone is definitely trying to get their attention. Attack them. But to be framed for something he didn't do… "That's too twisted for words."

Lucía smiles. "And yet, Mr. Bender, it appears that's exactly what's happened."

Park can't help it, finally acknowledging this sends chills down his spine. "You really think the killer—my son—is the one who broke in?"

"Highly likely. I'll assign some security to you and Mrs. Bender. Just in case. They'll serve two purposes—keep you safe and keep the media from pestering you."

His initial impulse is to say no, no way. But if Lucía is right, and Olivia was in any kind of danger this morning, he'll take the security muscle, and welcome it. The cops are already circling the neighborhood.

"We also need to have a conversation with Winterborn right away. I'd like to hear what they have to say about the excessive number of children conceived from your donations. I want to get as far ahead of things as we can before the media gets wind of this."

"How can we possibly pull that off? The police already want to reveal my ties to the cases."

She flashes him a knowing smile, and even Lindsey looks smug. "Because we're going to tell them. You're going to come to my office right now for a bit of media training with my people, and you're going to do the interview with Erica Pearl. Tonight."

26

THE WIFE

Park isn't home when she gets there, and Olivia makes a cup of tea and goes to his office. She stands in the doorway, staring into the room she designed for him. It's the place she feels closest to him. There's more of Park here than anywhere else in the house. It's his personal space. He trusts her not to snoop, and besides, Olivia has never been the suspicious wife type.

She and Park share a family email, their bank accounts are joint, and the combination to the safe in his office is taped to the underside of their kitchen junk drawer. She knows the security key to his password manager, and he has full access to her studio. They are equitable with one another's privacy. Park hasn't given her a reason to distrust him for a long time. She also hates the very thought of doubting him.

But standing in his empty office, wondering why he didn't come clean with her when he had the chance, gets her thinking about the package of items from his safe that was left behind in the Jones build.

Why? Was the goal to make sure she knew about Winterborn? To cast doubt on his past in Chapel Hill? She hadn't gone through the stack piece by piece. Has she missed something that she should be aware of? Was the cop right, a message was being sent? What else might he be hiding from her?

The idea that he hasn't been entirely truthful, that he's concealing parts of himself from her, sets her teeth on edge. Their marriage has been a happy one, for the most part. He has no reason to keep secrets.

But the grainy photo with his arm slung so casually across Melanie Rich's bony shoulders has planted the seed. Why would he have kept that picture in his safe? Worse, are there others?

Her husband is a good man. A kind man. A provider. He loves her. He will make an excellent father.

She shouldn't be suspicious of him. But now she is.

It's the reaction she'd had when the police showed up that's nagging at her.

Beverly Cooke, dead in a lake, and there she was, imagining Park guilty. She had him convicted and in jail without a moment's hesitation.

Why?

Because he's been acting strange lately.

The thought hits her like a bomb. She's been so caught up in her own roller coaster of emotions that she's written it off to his grieving process. The past several months have been elegiac in their pain. They'd lost the first two in vitro implantations in March and July, respectively. Neither pregnancy made it past the eight-week mark. It was truly a leap of faith for her to try another so soon, but she'd insisted. She had that clawing fear chasing her, the horrible sense that things wouldn't go the way she wanted them to. That her time was running out.

She touches her stomach lightly. She really thought this was the one.

Park has been a rock for her through the fertility treatments. Such a rock that Lindsey joked they should name a kid Gibraltar in his honor. They've been trying for a baby for over five years now, and never once has he been anything but steady, calm, and supportive. Finding ways to make it easier on her, offering himself for the hard parts of the process, from googling all the best ways to make giving her the shots easier to stockpiling her favorite indulgences when she miscarries. He's been a damn prince through it all. Solicitous to the point of annoyance.

What an uncharitable thought, Olivia. God forbid your husband give a shit.

Looking back, though, she realizes that yes, these past few months, he has been overly kind. Overly, and overtly.

She recalls a conversation with a client who recently divorced her husband for cheating on her. She said she suspected something was up because he was suddenly so attentive. There was no lipstick on his collar or late nights at the office, but he had been smothering her with his attentions.

Overcompensation, Dr. Benedict would say. Misdirection.

So, what is Park overcompensating for?

She takes a Post-it note and a pencil and retrieves the safe combination from the kitchen, noting in slight horror the date corresponds to her first miscarriage. *Jesus, Park.* She pulls out a tape measure from the drawer as well. If he comes back before she's finished and catches her rifling through his things, she can say she's gotten a call from one of her clients who wants the same live-edge desk installed and she's double-checking the measurements.

Planning the lies to tell your husband. Not great, Olivia.

The safe opens on the first try. The stack of paperwork she found at the Jones build, along with his passport, have been returned to their home, released by the police. She searches through them, but nothing seems out of place. Granted, she has no idea what she's looking for, but this isn't it.

She's been operating under the assumption that the paperwork was left to tell her about Park's relationship with Winterborn. And to rub his relationship with Melanie Rich in her face.

Could there have been a deeper message?

She stares at the room, taking it in sections. Nothing new, nothing out of place.

She sits at the desk and carefully looks at the papers on the wood top itself, opens all the drawers, runs her hands along the undersides. She unlocks the filing cabinet. It is organized alphabetically, perfectly labeled, and contains notes, house contracts, and teaching materials. Hardly suspicious.

You're tossing his office because he's been too nice to you lately. You are definitely losing your mind.

She runs her hands along the bookshelves, catching bookmarks, but not much else.

Frustrated, she plops down in the battered leather chair—she absolutely must talk him into a new chair, this one looks like someone's cat decided to make a nest in it. The edges of the cushion are literally torn open. She knows he loves the stupid thing, but can she at least have the cushion restitched? It's so unsightly.

She stands, dragging the cushion off the chair. And there it is, something out of place. An envelope stashed in the crevasse between cracked leather and high-density foam.

She fishes it out. This could be nothing, the detritus of her husband opening the mail in his favorite chair and a piece slipping below the cushion. But the feminine handwriting, a perfect flowing cursive, makes her blood pressure spike. She unfolds the letter.

Dear Mr. Bender,

I am so grateful you are willing to talk to me about Brandon. When Winterborn told me you'd agreed to allow me to contact you, I was over the moon. Brandon is too. All he's ever talked about is meeting his father, and now, thanks to your generosity, I get to make his dream come true.

Thank you also for the train set. I never thought Brandon would get over his dinosaur obsession, but the Pennsylvania Flyer is his pride and joy. I hope one day soon you will get a chance to play trains with your son. My number is 629-555-9089. Whenever you're ready to meet Brandon, please give me a call. We are happy to drive to Nashville to meet you.

Yours truly,
Fiona Cross

Olivia sinks into the cushion-less chair, a hand over her mouth. A small school photograph tips out of the envelope into her lap. The boy is young, gap-toothed, grinning ear to ear, sporting a clip-on tie and a severe blond cowlick. "Brandon, 1st grade, 6 years old" is painstakingly printed on the back of the photo in blue ink.

She looks at the post date on the letter. It is three years old.

Three years old. Brandon Cross would be nine now.

Olivia feels the small break in her heart widen. Tears come again, tears of wrath. She crumples the letter in a fist, wadding it tightly, and throws it on the desk. She rips the photo of the child in half, then halves it again, and again, until there is nothing left but shreds of tooth and cowlick. She sweeps her arm along Park's newly cleaned and organized desk, knocking laptop, notebooks, pencils and pens to the floor. She stamps on the mess, the pencils cracking underfoot, the screen of the laptop breaking with a satisfying crunch.

More than an omission. More than hiding the truth to spare her feelings. More than trying not to hurt her.

Park has known about his donor children all along.

27

THE WIFE

Furious, Olivia races to the Jeep. She wants to be away. No idea where, just gone.

The build, she thinks through the haze of red. Go to the Jones build. Work always fixes things.

A thought of Park at the police station, forlorn, watching her leave like he knew she might not come back. She'd had to steel her heart to walk away. Now she wants to murder him.

Before, when she was consumed with conflicting emotions—one minute wanting to hurt him, the next, kiss him—she blamed it on the hormones. Her body was warring with itself, why not her mind, too? That's what happened when they were doing the shots for the first round of IVF. "Menopause in a bottle," Brigit Blessing had warned with a saucy grin. "You're going to get a dose of what it's like, and trust me, it will be hard to keep your mouth shut. I'd advise you learn how to count to ten before you speak."

Too right it was hell. Olivia had prided herself on not becoming a harpy, though the urge was overwhelming. A fine-grained rage simmered inside her at all times.

Now she is consumed with the flames of anger. She wants to take the brakes off her tongue and lash Park around the edges until he is ripped and bloody. She wants to scream. To hit. To unleash herself.

But she swallows it all down. It's not right for her to lose control. The shots, that was different. She was being injected with medications that made her irrational. This is real. She doesn't have the buffer of medication as an excuse.

Benedict's voice pops up. "This fury is an emotion you're allowed to feel. Anyone would feel the same if they were in your shoes."

Olivia's own inner monologue argues back.

Ah, but you're not in my shoes. You have no idea what this is like. What he's done, it's betrayal on an epic scale. Isn't it?

Is it? Who betrayed who first?

Olivia is hit by a memory, her prom dress discarded in the back of the limo, the shy, warm strength of Perry's arms. The pain she'd felt in the moment of their first joining was sharp and welcome, because it was something taken away from Park. He would never get this honor, and she was glad.

The pain of the repercussion of their trysting was her own punishment. Taking a couple of pills would have been so much easier, but according to the sketchy clinic, she was too far along. Instead, she'd had to do it the old-fashioned way, surgically, a full-blown D&C, and she knew in her soul she would never, ever be the same again. It was as horrible as she feared it would be. After, as she lay among the sister brethren of the morning's surgeries, packed full of gauze, dazed—regretful even—at what she'd just done, the nurse had given her a prescription for birth control pills like she was an idiot who didn't know how to prevent a pregnancy. When Olivia declined, the woman pushed the script into her hand and said, "Take it. I don't want to see you here again. You're better than this."

The nurse's derision was a harsh, horrible moment to cap a terrifying ordeal.

You're better than this.

What a message to give a mournful teenager. It certainly struck home. Olivia vowed never again. She wouldn't be a victim. She wouldn't exist for the whims of a man. She would stand tall, succeed, be strong.

And look where it's gotten her. With a man who is hiding parts of himself from her. She is a fool. Love has room for secrets, yes, but not lies. And not telling her about the child he's aware of, pretending to both her and the cops that he knew nothing about his donor children, is the worst lie of all.

She's been driving in circles as she replayed these awful memories, and realizes she's closer to Lindsey's house than her own. Maybe Lindsey has talked to that crisis management chick, and they have a plan in place. Maybe they'll do a quick bit of late afternoon drinking. It's almost five o'clock, and God knows she needs a drink.

Strong she might be, but made of kryptonite, no. Sometimes, a girl just needs her bestie and a huge glass of wine.

The white Tudor looks as relaxed and friendly as she could have made it and still stick to Lindsey's modern aesthetic. Olivia loves this place; knows she did a good job on it. It's elegant and functional, and Lindsey always keeps it show house ready. Olivia uses it in all her portfolios.

She pulls into the driveway, mounts the stairs, rings the bell. Nothing.

Pulls out her phone. I'm on your doorstep. Where are you?

The answer comes immediately. At your place. You should

come home, now. Park says his office is trashed. Not from the break-in, something today.

Three dots.

Honey, are you okay?

Home. Olivia has exactly zero desire to be home. To help Park find his way out of this mess. Serves him right.

She ignores the text, ignores the vibration and ring that come moments later, too. She puts the phone into her back pocket, swipes the notification off her watch face, and is down two steps when the door opens behind her, and a deep voice says, "Liv?"

She freezes on the stairs, grabbing onto the handrail.

His voice. Vertigo. Her world spins, a kaleidoscope of possibilities. The offers, the joys, the regrets, smash cutting into this moment. His voice again, softer, aching.

"God, it is you. Aren't you going to say hello?"

She turns into the face of the sun and is blinded.

Perry has grown since she's last seen him. He's two inches taller and fifty pounds heavier, but it is all muscle, easy to tell because he is shirtless, skin gleaming, and his hair, longer than she's ever seen it, even in photos, runs in wet rivulets over his shoulders. He's bigger than Park, fitter, too. Park's physique, while still trim, has begun to blur around the edges lately—too much stress, too many bottles of wine, a sedentary office job. Perry is an outdoorsman, and it shows, long, ropy, all the way down to the grooves of muscle that disappear beneath the folds of the white towel hitched low around his hips, being held with a single hand. Not that she's looking.

"Perry," she says, the word a slow, deep breath. "You're home."

He grins. "And I'm soaking. Come in while I get dressed?"

"I shouldn't. I..." She falters and shakes her head. "Sure. Of course."

He disappears into the guest room; she makes a cup of tea. Grabs a second cup, just in case. He's back before she's had a chance to decide what to say, smiling again—why is he smiling, like he's happy to see her?—and saves her.

"Oh good, tea. Thank you."

"You still don't drink coffee?"

"No. Nasty stuff. Give me a good old-fashioned cup of English Breakfast any day. How are you, Liv?"

From anyone else, this would be a simple interrogative. From him, it feels like being shriven. They'd been close friends long before they were lovers, and she realizes with a start how much she's missed him.

"You're doing really well for yourself." He waves a hand. "The business suits you."

"I assume Lindsey has filled you in?"

He gives her a look, one she recognizes from high school, the familiarity of it juddering through her spine. When they were young, he would have said, "Duh, dummy," and she would have punched him on the arm, both of them hooting with laughter. Now he only smiles, the adult version of their old game.

"You are rather popular. And you have a website, social media. I check in."

The juddering turns into a flutter, mid-abdomen, and she smiles despite herself. "You do?"

"I mean, not all the time. Only when I have Wi-Fi."

"I've seen your work, too. You're a bit more famous than me."

"I am hardly famous. Let's go with well-known in certain esoteric circles."

"But the photographs—they're beautiful."

"I still have the camera. I use it all the time."

A spike of pleasure. "The one my dad was going to sell on eBay? My grandfather's Olympus?"

"Penny the Pentax. The very one. She's in my bag right now. Fantastic camera. Still my go-to when I want to shoot on film."

Olivia is deeply touched by this. She tries to cover her discomfiture by staring over his shoulder at the kitchen, then at her lap. Anywhere but at him. She takes a sip of the tea. It's already cooling. "I should find Lindsey some new cups. These don't keep their heat."

"So Linds may have mentioned you and Park were having some difficulties."

"You needn't be oblique."

His brows arch. "Okay. Yes. She told me what's happening. The miscarriages. I'm sorry, Liv. If I'd known..."

"It's not exactly something I'd post online."

A flicker in those gray eyes. She's hurt him. She is so good at that.

"It sounds like you've been going through hell."

"Thank you," she musters, with as much dignity as she has left.

"I hate that you've been suffering. I really am sorry. I didn't know. I've been...absent, for a while."

She can't take this. Even being in the same room with him feels like cheating, though they are appropriately distanced and both on their best behavior. He smells the same. Good. Of the outdoors. Of man and cedar and lime and tea. Of a simpler time. Aphrodisiacs. But the olfactory delights are overwhelmed by the memories flooding back. Him walking away. Their fight at the airport. The clinic. His rough palms on her thighs. All of it.

The secrets she's kept her entire adult life.

She cannot separate Perry from her past, and she absolutely can't allow him in now. She is a strong woman, but everyone has their breaking point. She needs to get away from the Bender boys.

He is watching her. Of the two boys, Perry is still the quieter one. Park always jumps in, runs the conversation, fills the room with hearty jokes and love and laughs. Perry simply is.

She sets down the tea. "Why have you come? Why are you here now, of all times?"

He leans back in the chair, the two front feet coming off the ground. His legs are long enough to balance him perfectly. "Instinct, maybe? I had a chance at an earlier flight. I've wanted to see y'all for a while, and I had some time between shoots. Lo and behold, I come home to find my family is in trouble. Who knows? Maybe the universe thought now was the right time to set things straight. At the very least, I'm here if you need me."

She picks at the side of the cup, her nail making a soft ticking noise. "That's very…nice of you."

He stares at her. "When did you get so cold?"

That rage, that incandescent rage, courses through her. "What?"

"You didn't used to be so contained. So remote. The girl I knew—"

"I've grown up," she snaps. "Some of us didn't run away. Some of us stayed and gutted it out. You have no idea what you did to me, leaving like that. You have no idea what it did to Park. You drove us together, and we've been doing just fine. Suddenly you're back in town and our world is exploding. Coincidence? I think not. I… I have to go."

He catches her hand as she flees. She halts, and for a moment, it seems he will apologize, that she will accept and sit down again, but the moment ends. She rips her fingers free and walks away.

In the Jeep, she moves on instinct. Start, Reverse, Drive, steer, brake. She aims the car toward her house. This is her refuge and her punishment, this life she's chosen. She will not think about the hurt in Perry's eyes, she will not think about the cramps in her belly, she will not think of Beverly Cooke's dead body, bloated and peeling skin. She will not think about the police, about this new missing woman. She will not think about the children, real and wished for. She will not think about the gap-toothed smile of a little blond stranger. She will go home, she will confront her husband, she will find them a path through this.

She might not be able to bear him a child, but she sure as hell can be his rock right now. She chose Park back then. She should choose Park now. Perry might be a part of her past, but Park is her future. Park is her husband, for better or worse. She's always taken their vows seriously, thinks he does, too. He might be a liar, but together, they can weather the storm. Together, they can fight for their marriage, their lives, their very souls. She will be righteous, and virtuous. He will be apologetic, and gallant. He will want to fix things between them; he always does, he always has. She will be rewarded for her loyalty in some way, she knows.

This is what Perry's attentions have always done to her. Her guilt drives her right back to Park like a snapping rubber band.

She blocks Perry's soft gray eyes, hurt and confused, from her mind. She cannot allow him to wreck everything she's built. Not now. Not when things are at their most tenuous.

The setting sun is bright and reflective, and a glance at the rear view shows a van following her, too close. A moment of panic—is that him? The van from this morning? Griffin White?

She slows, thinking he'll go past, and doesn't see the deer until it is too late. The buck darts in front of the Jeep, and she only has time to swerve before the sickening crunch of impact. The airbags explode, cushioning her, but the windshield cracks wide, the huge antlers breaking through the glass with such force that one branch impales her shoulder, pinning her to the seat. The deer is not dead, it is thrashing and screaming, and the pain is too much, and she feels the faint coming on and fights to stay awake, stay focused. The crash hasn't hurt her badly, but the convulsing deer will, she knows this instinctively, even through the fog of shock and pain. She must get unpinned.

Glass smashes near her ear, and hands reach in to help. She can't turn her head to see this angel who has stopped to save her, but listens to the faraway voice patter, lets it soothe and calm.

"Stay steady, stay relaxed, it's okay, I'm going to free you."

A wrenching pain in her shoulder, then an overwhelming sense of freedom. She takes a breath and cries out at the pain. The buck runs off the side of the road, streaming blood—her blood, she realizes; the damn thing seems to be unhurt despite barreling through her windshield antlers first.

A piece of antler protrudes from her body like a narwhal's horn. There is warmth, and wet, and her right arm tingles. She's fading, shock setting in, overpowering the adrenaline. The voice, it is a man's voice, familiar in an unfamiliar way, speaks again, urgent and calm.

"I'm calling an ambulance. Hold tight. You're going to be okay, Olivia. I'm so sorry you're hurt. You're so beautiful. Oh, my darling. You don't deserve this."

And she is gone.

28

THE DETECTIVES

Walking back to her car from court, running testimony through her head as she always does, Joey gets a text from Osley.

You ain't gonna believe it.

She calls him immediately, crossing the downtown street, jaywalking.

"What am I not going to believe?"

"We just got another tip on the Cooke case. About Kemp this time. You gotta get back here, stat."

She starts to jog, thankful for the boots she's wearing. Her car is in the courthouse parking lot. It will take her ten to get back to the office.

"What is it?"

"Not over the phone."

This case is about to break wide open, Joey can feel it. They just need to find Jillian Kemp before she gets killed.

Osley is waiting at Joey's desk. He's been chewing cinnamon gum; the scent is overpowering.

"Joey Joey Jo Jo. It's been quite a day, hasn't it?"

"Why are you looking so cheerful? There is another woman missing."

"Am I cheerful? Hmm. I was thinking more…international man of mystery."

He strikes a pose, hands together holding a pretend gun, and she smiles despite herself.

"What's the tip, Will?"

"We got a call from a woman who moderates a private Facebook group. It's a support group for families who have used sperm donation. We already know Jillian Kemp used a sperm donor to father her kid."

"And… Come on, Will. Spit it out."

"Beverly Cooke was a part of the Facebook group, too. She also used a donor to get pregnant. It's very hush-hush. She didn't tell her husband."

"My God. So someone is targeting this group? Do they all have the same donor? Are they all Bender's?"

"No. It's a wide-ranging group, variety of ages, multiple donors."

"Too much to hope for. Tell me you checked on who Beverly Cooke's donor was. If that's our tie…if her kid is Bender's—"

"Not gonna get so lucky. I put in some paper to get the details about Cooke's situation, but looks like it was a place here in town. Not Winterborn. And the woman I talked to, who called it in, is from Colorado and used a firm out there, so I don't think that's the tie. But. Two women who belong to a private support group go missing, and one's dead. Tells me we got a lot of targets to protect, and a place to start searching for this creep.

I already talked to the lieutenant. We've got as much overtime as we need, and she's tasking us three more detectives, that kid from forensics who can break into any computer, and as many rookies as we need to dig through the data and figure things out from that side."

Joey smiles. "You've been busy. Looks like I'm buying the pizza to make up for lost time."

"Some of us didn't have court today," he says with a half smile. "There's more."

"You're making me a happy girl, Will. Keep talking."

"How'd it go with the lovebirds earlier? They seemed a little tense walking out of here."

Joey blows out a breath. "Mrs. Bender gave a solid description of the suspect inside her build to Roger. He's getting the sketch into the system so we can release it tonight. I rattled Bender's cage a bit about Melanie Rich. He seemed genuinely surprised to hear she was pregnant. He fell apart and stopped chatting, wants a lawyer."

"Does he, now?" Osley hands her a file folder. "We've been running prints from the Bender crime scene this morning. There were multiple sets collected, so it might take a while to sort through all of them. But there was a match right off the bat."

She opens the folder. Park Bender's face stares up at her. He is much younger and quite good-looking, his hair too long and the hint of a scruffy beard around his chin. A nice fat thump in her heart, one she recognizes and loves, the wonderful moment of suppressed excitement when something unexpected pops on a case.

She flips a page. "Wait. This is from Daytona Beach." She reads further. "No. You're kidding me."

"Not kidding at all. You know how those spring break parties get out of hand. Everyone gets wasted, folks go for a late-night swim in the ocean, and sometimes, people drown. This girl just happened to be from Vermont and was staying at the same hotel as Mr. Bender, Mr. Johnson, and a few other frat boys from UNC Chapel Hill. Made the papers for a minute at best. Nothing suspicious, just a terrible accident. They took everyone's prints, just in case, and let them go. The boys headed back to Chapel Hill the next morning."

She reads it aloud. "'It was our last night, and we'd been partying pretty hard. We decided to go for a final swim since we were heading out in the morning. We arrived at the beach just as people started to shout for help. I ran back up to the hotel and called 911.' God, he's the one who called the authorities?"

"Ironic, isn't it?"

"Why in the world did he not mention this? Get out ahead of it. He wasn't a suspect; they just took his statement. And his prints, of course. Good on them for them being cautious."

"Would you offer that up to us? It's a prime piece of bloody steak. He's on scene when a woman drowns, and six months later his girlfriend goes missing, and is found murdered in a lake? Makes him look guilty as shit. Proximity to two women, dead in bodies of water? Now we're up to three—and this one, we know has connection to him. Yeah. I wouldn't have offered it up, either."

Joey closes the file and taps it with her fingernail. "Do you think we're dealing with some sort of serial, Will? Is Bender a monster, disguised as a suburban wannabe dad?"

Osley shakes his head, as serious as she's ever seen him. "I honestly don't know. But it's time for us to tear Park Bender's life apart."

29

THE MOTHER

"Mom!"

Darby is napping in the chair in the living room, where she sat down for just a second, her biorhythms still completely screwed up by switching her days and nights. At her daughter's call, she leaps to her feet, ready to take on the world, to fight to the death whoever has harmed her baby.

Scarlett skids to a stop in front of her.

"They have a drawing of the suspect."

"You're okay?"

"Duh. I'm fine."

Darby puts a hand to her heart. "You scared me to pieces, screaming like that. I thought you were hurt. What are you yelling about?"

Scarlett speaks lower and slower. "The police have a drawing of the suspect in that woman's murder. And another woman is missing."

Now it's Darby's turn to get agitated. "They do? How do you know? Who is it?"

"I just know, okay? I don't know who it is. I don't think they've released her name yet."

"No. Not okay." Darby gets up and stretches. "I thought we'd discussed this. No more sneaking around. Who is feeding you this information?"

Scarlett looks entirely incensed at this accusation. "I'm not sneaking around. A friend told me. And it's going to be on the news. Don't you want to see? I mean, I'm related to whoever it is, right? It's one of the Halves. I just wonder if it's one I've already talked to."

Of course Scarlett wants to see who this mystery sibling might be. Darby wants to know, too. Still.

"What friend? I'm serious, Scarlett. This is a dangerous situation, and I refuse to let you play coy with me."

"It's one of the Halves. Her name is Jezebelle. Well, that's her handle. Remember, we don't use real names, to protect ourselves. But there's no way it's the killer—she's a girl. I think her mom must work with the police or something. She finds things out."

"And you believe her?"

"She hasn't been wrong yet. We've been talking for a while."

"How do you know it's a girl? Anyone can pose as someone else, Scar. I've told you this time and time again. You are being reckless talking to strangers online."

Scarlett's eyes fill with tears. "I'm being careful. I'm not an idiot, Mom. It's not like we're making plans to meet up for coffee. And I know it's a woman because of the way she talks about things. Like, personal things. I mean, we talk about all the stuff happening in the world now. People are more open about themselves. She's cisgendered, pronouns are she/her. Why would she lie?"

Darby relaxes a fraction. She still has a bad feeling about all of this. "My darling, something you need to realize is people can misrepresent themselves, especially if they're trying to fit in."

"You don't understand. Why can't you trust me, for once?"

Because you're sixteen and too damn precocious and I want to keep you swaddled next to me forever.

Darby closes her eyes and counts to three. "I do trust you, baby. The news isn't on for a while. We have plenty of time. Let's make dinner. What do you want? Anything goes."

"Anything?"

"Within reason." Darby smiles. Concessions are rare in their world. She hopes Scarlett recognizes this isn't the new normal.

Scarlett's eyes twinkle. "Pizza. That cauliflower crust one from Costco. With mushrooms."

Pizza is reserved for Friday nights, so this is special. Darby is just glad she didn't ask for some sort of complicated dish that would take an hour to put together. She is so tired.

"Done. Why don't you do your homework and I'll call you when it's ready. And Scarlett? No Discord. No Halves. Not until we know what's happening. Got me?"

Her lovely daughter casts her eyes to the floor and nods. She starts toward the stairs, but Darby calls, "Have you checked online to see if the sketch has been released yet?"

Scarlett whips out her phone and her thumbs fly. "No. Nothing yet. Though…they identified the other woman who's gone missing. Her name is Jillian Kemp. God, this is so scary."

Oh my God.

Scarlett is looking at her. "Mom? Are you okay?"

"Hold on, Scarlett." Darby slaps open her laptop and goes to the news website. The headline screams:

Another Nashville Woman Missing

Darby reads the article in disbelief, then opens her private group for the first time in days to see a hundred new entries and multiple private messages. While she wrestled with her conscience, the decisions were being made for her.

Moderator: It has been decided by a nearly unanimous vote to make the police aware of Beverly Cooke's involvement in the group. We can't have Jillian end up like Beverly. I have alerted Metro Nashville police to the possible connection. Please co-operate with the investigation if detectives contact you. If you have any information that could lead to finding Jillian Kemp, please get in touch with Metro Nashville detectives immediately. No tip is too small.

A string of phone numbers and emails follows the entry.

Darby shuts the laptop.

Is someone preying on their private Facebook group?

Oh, come on. That's ridiculous. It has to be a fluke.

"Mom?"

"Yes, honey."

"Did you hear me? I'm freaking out here."

"I heard you. This is very scary, I agree. Come here." She gives Scarlett a long hug. "We're going to be okay, you understand? I won't let anything happen to you. Not now, not ever. But I do need to talk to you about something important."

"If this is about the argument we had… I said I was sorry."

"You did? I must have missed that."

Scarlett blushes.

"I appreciate the apology. It's not about our disagreement. Well, it is, but in a tangential way."

"Twenty-five-cent word, Mom."

Finally, a little normalcy. The color is coming back to Scarlett's face, the fear receding from her eyes. The thought of her daughter scared just about kills her.

Darby smiles, gets up, and drops a quarter in the jar on the counter. When the kids were little, instead of a swear jar, she instituted a vocabulary jar. She figured it was a better game to reward than punish, because at what point does it become okay for them to swear? What less profane words were all right? What filthier words were out of bounds? No, this worked better for her little brood. Neither of whom swore in front of her, thank you very much.

She returned to the table. "You have your own group, and while I'm not happy about it, I understand why you've done this. I don't blame you, and I'm not angry with you. I have a group, too. It's bigger than yours, made up of families all over the country who've used sperm donors. It's a support group of sorts. A lot of good friendships have been born there. But it's a secret place, because some people who use sperm donors are ashamed, or embarrassed, or trying to save face." She fends off the incipient question: "There are many, many reasons someone might need—or want—a sperm donor, and a thousand more why they might want to keep it private. It is not up to us to judge how anyone chooses to have a family or what they want people to know about them."

"Yes. Of course."

"Good. Anyway. The woman who's gone missing, Jillian Kemp, is a part of my group. I'm very, very worried about her. The problem is, Beverly Cooke was as well. She's one of the ones who was there in a very private way, do you understand?"

Scarlett's eyes are wide, recognizing the significance of this. "I take it this is a secret you're sharing with me alone?"

"It's something I'd appreciate you not discussing with anyone, yes. It's not your story to tell, do you understand?"

"Yes."

"Thank you. Now. The group made the decision to talk to the police because there is a connection between the two women."

She sees the realization flash in her daughter's eyes—if these two women who were in a group together went missing, her mother might as well. Darby hates it, hates that Scarlett is now even more frightened. Scaring her kid is not on the family game plan.

"Nothing is going to happen to me. I promise."

"But you don't know that." Scarlett's voice is small, the voice of a child who's had a terrible nightmare and doesn't want the light turned off again.

"I do know that, because we're going to take a little trip. We're going to scoot right on out of here so we don't have to worry about anything."

"What about work?"

"Unfortunately..." She sighs. "I haven't been telling you the whole truth. I got laid off. They had to cut two salaries, and mine was the highest. I have unemployment starting, and a full recommendation, and I will find another job. That's what I'll be doing while you get those glorious long legs tan, looking for a new position."

Scarlett looks scared again.

"But school...how will you afford..."

Darby rubs Scarlett's arm affectionately. "Let me give you a life lesson, my darling daughter. Always, always, always keep at least six months of savings set aside to handle a situation like this. I'm highly specialized. I'll find another job. In the meantime, I have a very hefty emergency fund."

Scarlett looks oddly proud to hear this. "If Peyton's back from his camping trip, can he come too?"

"Of course. We can drive by campus on our way to Destin and pick him up."

"I have a big test tomorrow."

"I will get you excused for the rest of the week, and you can make it up when we get back. Okay?"

"Okay!"

"Good. Pack, and then finish that history report so you can turn it in before we go. We'll leave first thing in the morning."

Scarlett starts for the stairs, then turns back and hugs Darby hard around the waist. "I'm really sorry about your friends," she whispers, then darts up to her room.

Darby stands with the echo of her daughter's arm and knows this is the right thing to do. An impromptu vacation *is* being reckless with that robust emergency fund, but getting away suddenly seems like the best way to handle the situation.

She goes online and finds a very inexpensive rental, a two-bedroom condo at a little spot near Destin that they've visited before. The season has just ended, so she gets it for a steal. Almost a steal. She books it for four nights. Come morning, they will be seven hours away from this madness.

Darby pulls the pizza from the freezer to give it a chance to thaw before she puts it in so it will get crispier, chops some mushrooms, straightens up the kitchen, pulls the laundry from the dryer, and carries the basket upstairs. Scarlett is whirling through the hallway from bedroom to bathroom, a grin on her face.

"Do you know where my red bikini is?"

"In your bottom drawer."

"Peyton is going to be so stoked! I wish he'd call me back already."

A thought strikes Darby. "Have you talked to your brother about the DNA matches?"

Scarlett looks down immediately, and Darby recognizes her daughter's tell—she is trying to figure out how to answer. Not formulate a lie, just trying to decide what Darby wants to hear.

"Yes?" Darby raises her brows in question.

"I did tell him about the donor thing."

She tries to keep her tone neutral. "You did?"

"It's one of the things the Halves are really into, making sure everyone gets their siblings' DNA into the system. It didn't seem as big a deal since we have different donors, but they wanted to be sure. I asked and he said he would, but you know him. He's never been worried about not having a dad, you know?"

Darby ignores that little stake to the heart. "You two talk about this?"

"Sure." Scarlett pulls her hair up into fluffy ponytail; the scrunchie has trailing ends so it looks like she's tied a polka dot scarf in her hair. "You like?"

"I do. Cute. Great for the beach. So, what else did Peyton have to say?"

"I mean, I asked him once if he was interested in meeting his donor, and he was like, no, no way, I don't want to know anything about him. He thought I should leave well enough alone, too, but..."

Darby bites her lip and nods.

"Well, we'll give him the option again of participating if he wants, but don't push him. He has never expressed any interest to me either. I don't want him to feel like there's something wrong that he's not interested, especially given how keen you are to find out everything you can."

"I get it. Don't forget the towels," she calls, whirling back into her room, and Darby grabs them from the linen closet and takes them into her own room to pack.

Her mind is whirling as surely as her daughter's body.

My God, what if Jillian Kemp's twins are related to Scarlett?

What if we're closer to this than we know?

Darby paces her room, glances out the curtains, then pulls them closed. Goes to the basement and double-checks the door and windows are locked. The odds of someone coming for her are astronomically low, she knows this, but it makes her feel better to have the house buttoned up. She doesn't feel foolish at all retrieving the baseball bat she keeps under the bed and setting it against her night table.

Poor Jillian. God, Darby hopes she's just let the battery die on her phone or had a fight with her wife and took a road trip to clear her head.

They'd hoped that about Beverly, too. Then days turned into weeks turned into months, and they all knew she was dead.

Darby rarely, if ever, watches the local news unless there's some sort of disaster she needs to follow, but tonight, she and Scarlett set up to tune in together. This almost feels like a luxury, or would, if it wasn't an enforced home stay and they weren't trying to track a killer.

After the pizza feast, Darby indulged her daughter further with homemade cocoa, and poured herself a very large glass of wine. Then another.

It feels a bit like the days of old, when both kids were home, and she could appease them with special treats and normal hours. It was hard having a mom on the night shift. Hard to have an overnight babysitter instead of a mother down the hall. When Scarlett declared herself old enough to stay home alone at night, Darby had balked. With Peyton off at school, she didn't like the idea of Scarlett being alone. But Scarlett did. She always had been so fearless. So independent.

Even with all the drama and arguments, it's been nice being around overnight again, not having to worry about her baby's safety—that little gremlin in the back of her mind always reaching out to say *hey, something bad could be happening to her and you let her stay alone* has been silenced.

Of course, nothing did hurt her.

Until now.

Darby feels so ashamed, though she doesn't know why. She's done nothing wrong. Winterborn is to blame here. Winterborn is the reason Scarlett has more than two dozen half siblings. Winterborn is the reason one of them is a killer.

This is all going to come spilling out, she knows it. There's no way to keep it quiet. The waves are getting bigger, crashing further up the beach. They will be swept out with the tide if she's not careful.

Scarlett is barely awake on the couch beside her. Ten is well past her normal bedtime—her sweet girl almost always turns in early. "News is on," she says to Scarlett, who mumbles and burrows a little deeper into the couch pillow. Even extreme excitement can't stop natural circadian rhythms. Darby slops a bit of wine on the blanket as she reaches for the remote to hit Record and turn up the volume. The anchor has been on the air since she can remember and doesn't look like she's aged at all.

I want your plastic surgeon, lady.

"At a press conference this afternoon, Metro detectives discussed the ongoing investigation into the disappearance of Jillian Kemp, last seen on Monday night leaving her gym in Brentwood. Metro sees no connection between Beverly Cooke and Jillian Kemp at this time, though all avenues are being pursued. This story will continue after the break."

A commercial for a local car dealer blares three times louder than the news broadcast, but Darby doesn't hear it. She goes to the kitchen, a little unsteady now, and pours the last bit of wine into her glass. Maybe this wasn't the best way to deal with her fears, but it is certainly taking the edge off.

"Mom!" The word is strangled, a call of genuine fear.

Darby's adrenaline shoots through her system. She runs back into the living room to find Scarlett sitting upright, the remote in her hand. Her face is ashen.

"Honey? What's wrong?"

Scarlett points the remote at the television. The commercial is over; the story has continued. Her daughter's hand is trembling.

"What is it?"

"The sketch. Mom. Oh my God."

Darby turns to face the TV, and Scarlett hits Play.

★ ★ ★

"Metro has just released a sketch of a person of interest in the Beverly Cooke case. The suspect is using the name Griffin White, though police believe this could be an alias. If you've seen this man, do not approach, but call 911 immediately."

The charcoal lines capture him perfectly. The square jaw. The beard. The only thing that's wrong are the eyes. The eyes are dead. Cold. Cruel. Empty. A void of horror. A void she hasn't seen in over a decade.

"Mom," Scarlett says again. "Mom? What do we do?"

Darby is speechless. Scarlett rewinds and clicks Pause, and her son's handsome face freezes on the screen.

30

THE MURDERER

One last hug. One last "I love you." That's all he wants.

He doesn't think he's going to get it.

The phone in his pocket rattles to life with the notification from the news app he downloaded. It's the third burner phone of the month. He's been so careful to leave his real phone in all the places he's expected to be—Murfreesboro, mostly. He's been stashing it in the wheel well of his roommate's car, taped to the metal with only the charging port exposed. Attached to that is an extended-life solar battery pack. The wire feeds up through the trunk, and the small panel is glued just to the left of the wiper of the back windshield. It's almost impossible to notice, and so far, has worked perfectly.

But time is running out.

He's not stupid. He knows that if it comes down to it, if he is caught, if he says the right things, chances are he'll go back to the hospital. But in case they want to go the trial route and try to send him to jail, he needs something, anything, that will make him look innocent. He can't do that to his mom, can't go to jail. It would break her. The hospital is a different story. People can forgive insanity.

Circumstantial as it is, the cell phone pinging in the proper places while women are going missing forty miles north gives him a defense. Today he needs to attach it to another car, of a former friend who is going to the mountains, and let that be his alibi.

He hates having to think like this. But he's always been self-aware. Too much for his own good, his doctor told him once.

Time is running out, but he can forestall a little while longer.

Campus is quiet in the dark. He finds the car, gets to work. Thinking. Always thinking. He can still smell the blood on his hands. Blood, and flowers.

When Scarlett told him about the Halves, he made up a name and sent in his DNA. Matched to her, and to all the others. He is known in the program as Male Sibling 13, though he is really number one. The first of his kind, the first of his name.

Of course, putting his DNA in ended up being a mistake, but really, maybe it was for the best. This lifestyle isn't sustainable. And it drove him to find his father, and that was how he found her. His darling Olivia.

Oh, her pain. The tears. The strength she shows. He's known no one like her before, his blessed soul mate. It was bound to happen; he'd always known he'd find someone who understood him. That's why he did so much introspection. He wanted to be right for her. To do things she likes, to make her happy.

He's only curious, after all. About himself, about his mind. In the hospital, after talking to his doctors about why he was experiencing such violent thoughts and urges, he'd done copious amounts of research about the MAOA gene, the warrior gene, and its link to aggressive behavior. The sexier, and less accurate, name was the murder gene. According to one study he memorized, of nine hundred criminals in a cohort in Finland, the group had committed over eleven hundred murders. Were they destined to kill? Compelled? Was this murder gene a real thing? He didn't know, but wow, he was fascinated by the possibility.

He'd always been convinced the urges he was feeling were organic, though he held back with the doctors on just how intense the impulses were. He was smart; they all knew he was smart, so they dug, deep, into his psyche. They tried everything to pull out the seeds that were germinating inside of him, but he was able to control what he told them, what he said. He didn't want to spend his life in the hospital, and he knew he could control his compulsions if only he understood himself. This was a dopamine thing. A serotonin thing. A coiled snake that lived in his head, not created by his environment. He'd had a fantastic upbringing with a wonderful mother, so where did his darkness come from?

His genes.

His father.

Yes, there was free will. Yes, there was socially acceptable behavior. Yes, he could be conditioned to not hurt people.

But in order to quell a craving, first you must slake the thirst.

It took him forever to get the name out of Winterborn. He'd befriended a woman who worked there, seduced and cajoled and flattered and begged and maybe did a tiny bit of threatening until she finally broke the rules and gave him the details.

He'd left her by the side of a quiet Georgia road, inside a thick field of cotton. An inelegant solution, but as far as he knew, her body had never been recovered. He missed her sometimes. She'd been so nice to him, in the beginning.

Once he had the name, it had taken him all of ten minutes to find his father. Living in Nashville, only miles away from his childhood home. Not a huge surprise; Winterborn was a popular regional sperm bank. He'd probably seen his father in the store or driving downtown sometime.

He followed. It's what he did.

His father and stepmother were a typical Nashville couple, did all the typical Nashville things. It was fun watching them, getting to know their tastes and patterns. Until he trailed them to Charlotte and 23rd Avenue North and saw them enter the building that would change all their lives forever.

His father, with his beautiful fragile, lovely wife, at a fertility clinic.

Olivia had given Peyton a tremulous smile in the building's elevator, and Peyton fell in love with her in an instant. Fell, hard. He couldn't stop thinking about her. The more he watched, the more he wanted her. She was his ideal. Perfection, in so many ways.

Oh, and their terrible problems. His heart really did go out to Olivia. She wanted it so much. She wasn't all that different from the women who were pouring out their hearts to his mother online, night after night. They wanted this commonality, they wanted to carry, bear, and raise children. Some didn't want a partner; some had a partner who couldn't give them what they wanted. Some were gay, some were straight. Some had no kids, some full families they wanted to add to. One who needed to get pregnant again with a genetically matched child who didn't have the crippling disease her other kids suffered from so "it" could be used as a bone marrow donor. She figured a different genetic stream might provide a healthy child or two. She had actually called the possible child "it."

That bothered him, the harvesting of other children, but it wasn't his problem.

Point was, the stories were endless, varied. Every life, every need, every desire, different.

Did they ever stop to think that the children might not be

what they wanted? That a child would not heal the emptiness in their soul? That a child might tear a hole in an otherwise perfect life?

Online, his mother tried so hard to warn them. She tried to make them aware there could be issues, that everything wasn't always sunshine and roses. She spoke from experience. She spoke from the heart. She spoke of his problems so eloquently while still protecting him. So loyal, his mom.

When he'd realized he was different, that *he* wasn't sunshine and roses, he'd done everything they'd asked of him and more. He wanted to be good for his mother. He loved her. Loves her.

Those people in her group, they never listened.

He finishes placing the solar panel, taping it securely, and steps back into the darkness. The last traceable part of his previous life is journeying to its last stop. It's heading east to the mountains, and he is not. He doesn't feel sorry to see it go.

The phone shivers again, and this time he takes it out and looks at the breaking news alert.

He almost feels relief. Almost.

It's over. As he feared, there will be no goodbye.

31

THE MOTHER

It is nearing dawn, and Darby hasn't slept.

How could she? She's been calling Peyton every five minutes for the past several hours to no avail, alternating frenetic speed-dialing with laps around the bottom floor of the house. Her calves and thighs ache. Her heart aches.

This is not the situation she ever thought she'd be in, faced with an impossible choice.

Confront her son and ask if he murdered a woman or call the police and tell them she knows the man in the sketch they're circulating. And hope to God she does it before a stranger does.

The boy. He's barely a man.

Apparently, he's man enough, her mind helpfully provides. Man enough to rape. Man enough to strangle.

Her boy, that darkness in him. The rages. The altercations. The push and pull of love and hate.

It can't be him. Her Peyton did not do this. The police have made a mistake.

Ah, but you were afraid of him when he was ten years old. Could they really have fixed him so easily? Did he not grow out of his problems, as the doctors thought, only found a way to channel them? To hold them close to his heart and never share them again? Have they finally risen up and overwhelmed him? Has he been hiding his true self this whole time?

No. It is not him. Of course it's a mistake.

It started with night terrors. Peyton had slept alone for years with no problem, but after Scarlett was born, suddenly needed to be in Darby's bed or he would scream in fright all night, waking the baby, who would join in the chorus.

Then the tantrums began.

Not typical tantrums, not crying because he couldn't have candy at the checkout tantrums, but full-blown rages that forced her to lock him in his room so he wouldn't hurt her, or the baby. Frustrated by the lack of targets, he would bang his head on the wall until huge lumps formed on his forehead.

She took him to his pediatrician. To specialists. There were brain scans, MRIs, drugs. So many drugs. He'd cry his little heart out at the kitchen table because he couldn't feel anything anymore, then tear through the house ripping paintings from the walls and overturning tables if she tried to console him. *You're doing this to me. You hate me. You love her more than you love me.*

More drugs. Higher dosages. They zombified him, and he sat, staring blankly at the walls, losing weight because she couldn't rouse him to eat. He was tall and thin, a wraith with a shock of brown scarecrow hair and dead eyes.

She tried everything. Every drug. Every doctor. With every new specialist, a different diagnosis. *Autism. Bipolar. Borderline. ADHD. Early-onset schizophrenia.* She changed his diet, eliminating gluten, dairy, soy. Skipped his vaccinations. Anything, everything, she tried it all.

He was eight when he accused her of trying to kill him. He was nine when she caught him in the bathroom, Scarlett in the bathtub merrily splashing away and Peyton with his dead eyes, a knife raised over his head.

She had no choice at that point but to try inpatient treatment. She had to protect Scarlett. And she was so tired. So tired.

The horror of her choice wouldn't let her rest. She'd chosen her daughter over her son.

Her safety, Darby. You chose to keep her safe. Big difference.

The hospital that specialized in childhood-onset psychological disorders was in Maryland, so she moved them there to be close. And miracle of miracles, it worked.

After the first few months, they experimented by weaning him off the drugs. Her little boy was clear-eyed again. After a year, they let him do an in-home visit. He cuddled with Darby and played dolls with Scarlett and seemed so happy again.

When he was thirteen, after they'd definitively determined the psychotropic drugs he'd been given in the early days of his disease were inducing schizoaffective disorder and got him on a small dose of antidepressants daily with good vitamins and lots of clean food, he returned to the sunny, bright, precocious child he'd always been, and was deemed stable enough to be sent home permanently.

He never blamed her. This he told her the first night after Scarlett had been put to bed, round-eyed that her big brother was home. They'd sat at the table, Darby with a glass of chardonnay, Peyton with chamomile tea, and he told her his heart.

"I don't blame you. I was terrified of myself. You did exactly the right thing, making sure I was safe, with specialists who could help me. It was beyond us both, Mom. If I'd hurt Scarlett..." He'd closed his eyes and shuddered. "I love you, Mom. Thank you for saving me."

She thought about locking the bedroom doors that night. But she had to trust him. Had to trust that the doctors were right.

And they were. Peyton outgrew his problems. The darkness was no longer. Now it was only light. The frightening chapter was closed for good.

Or so she'd thought.

Her mind wars, the thoughts tumbling against each other. It's a mistake. He isn't the one. This is just a man someone saw and thinks is involved. It's not him. It's not. She knows in her heart her son could never do such a thing.

Doesn't she? Doesn't she?

Yes. He could never hurt someone like this.

Ah, but he could. He might have if you hadn't stepped in and put him in that place. If you hadn't had the strength to get him help.

No. This isn't happening. He couldn't be capable of such a thing.

Darby needs to talk to her son, and she needs to do it right now. Before anyone gets their hands on him. She wants to look him in the eye and hear him say the words.

I didn't do this, Mom. I swear it.

What if he said, *Oh God, Mom, I lost control again. I didn't mean to do it. It was a mistake.*

Could she still love her son properly if he admitted his darkness had become a real, tangible thing? That he had raped and strangled a woman Darby herself knew? And, dear God, possibly taken another?

She had found the strength to love him before. She would again.

But it's not him. It's not.

Is it?

She hates herself for the tiny seed of doubt, rushing back in the glint of the knife raised over his sister's unknowing head, in the bathroom of their house, all those years ago.

"Mom?"

Scarlett slinks downstairs, hair in a wild bun on top of her head. She'd alternated between trying to reach Peyton and chewing her nails down to the quick until her body revolted and she had to sleep. Strangely, she hadn't cried.

Darby hadn't shown such restraint. The moment Scarlett declared it was all a mistake, that when her brother returned from his camping trip, he would tell them all how silly this was and marched herself off to bed, Darby had broken. She hadn't cried so hard in her entire life. Nothing, nothing, shattered her, but this did.

You think he did it. You are a terrible mother, to think he could be capable of such a thing. You have failed him, you have failed Scarlett, you have failed yourself. How could you think he's responsible for this?

How can you think he isn't?

The noise from the call. The sound of a woman's voice, a scream of fear echoing through her brain. A video, he claimed. A video.

And now he's off camping? Without phone access?

Jillian Kemp is missing...could he have taken her? Her baby? Her boy?

No. Just...no. *Please, no.*

Darby's thoughts swirl so fast, so strong, a current dragging her downstream, that she barely notices Scarlett has made and poured coffee for them both until her daughter presses a cup into her hands.

"Did you sleep?"

Darby shakes her head.

"Did he answer?"

Another shake.

"Okay. Okay. What do we do? I can't imagine someone won't recognize him and call the police. It was a good likeness. Sort of. His eyes were all wrong. Scary wrong."

"I'm going to Murfreesboro."

Lightning has struck, at last. Of course she must go to him.

Darby is on her feet before the words have left her mouth. "I want to see firsthand that he isn't there, that's he's really off camping. Maybe his roommates will know something. Know how to reach him."

"I'm coming."

"I don't think—"

"I'm coming." The finality of her daughter's words hangs in the air between them. They stand nose to nose—no, Darby realizes, she's actually looking up a touch. Scarlett is suddenly taller than she is. Her daughter touches her cheek, gently, so gently. A caress reserved for mother to daughter, not the other way around. "Brush your hair, brush your teeth, and I'll drive. You haven't slept, Mom. It's too dangerous for you to drive like this, tired and distracted."

"I—"

"You're upset, you haven't slept, and I am driving. Now, go."

Scarlett has the audacity to give Darby a tiny shove toward the stairs.

The role reversal stings, but Darby heaves in a breath and complies. She is so weary, so very weary. Her mind is being torn asunder, and her daughter is the one taking control.

You've taught her how to be a woman, Darby. Be glad that when the crisis came, she stood up for it.

The drive south is uncomplicated. They are on the road early and going against traffic. The miles fly by, and Darby finds herself standing in the parking lot looking up at the balcony of the apartment she'd secured for Peyton at the beginning of the semester. It is a mile off campus, easy enough for him to ride his bike or walk on nice days, drive on bad ones. They'd both been tickled with the location, and the price. The roommates she could take or leave—they seemed nice enough, but she could tell Peyton wouldn't be hanging out with them.

Not that it mattered. Sharing a kitchen and living room with a couple of people you don't get on with is a life prerequisite.

Now she wonders if they influenced him somehow. Gave him drugs. Challenged him to drop down into the gutter with them.

It's their fault. Not his. Not hers.

They climb the two flights in silence. Scarlett gets to the door first, knocks hard. It is 6:15 a.m. These are college students. Chances are they will still be asleep, having rolled home only a few hours earlier.

Kids still did that, right? Get out from under their parents' thumbs and turned into booze-soaked loons for a few years until they figured out how boring it is waking up feeling like crap all the time?

"Coming," a girl's voice trills. The door opens to reveal a willowy girl dressed in yoga clothes, hair up in the same type of messy bun Scarlett is sporting. Like they watched the same Instagram Reel on how to pull it up, fold it over, secure, fluff the front…

"Can I help you?" she asks, chipper as a puppy. Not the hungover slouch Darby was expecting.

"We're looking for Peyton. Is he here?"

"Peyton? I don't know anyone named Peyton."

A young man Darby recognizes joins the girl, looping an arm possessively across her shoulders. He, too, is dressed in workout clothes, his eyes clear, breath minty fresh, beard trimmed, hair twisted into a small bun on top of his head. Darby scolds herself internally for a moment for making assumptions, but Scarlett charges in.

"Peyton Flynn lives here, doesn't he? Or do we have the wrong apartment?"

"Hi, Mrs. Flynn," the boy says. "Peyton moved out, a while ago."

Darby's heart quite literally stops for a moment, then rages ahead, dumping so much adrenaline into her system she has to take a few quick breaths to control it. It's the same feeling she gets when they have a code blue at the hospital, everyone charging toward the room in question to try and save a life.

"What do you mean, he moved out? David," she adds, the boy's name finally penetrating her senses.

"Yeah, it was pretty uncool of him. He took off in July."

July? It is September now. Where in the world has her boy been living? "But the lease was signed through December of this year."

"Yeah, I know. I had to scramble to find another roommate who was taking summer school and needed a place and would stick around through fall semester."

"Did he tell you where he was moving?"

"No. He came home one night just rocked out of his mind and took off the next day. He looked like he'd been in a fight. I haven't seen him since. I've been keeping his mail. You should probably take it. There's some stuff from school in there. Hold on."

Darby can't meet Scarlett's eyes. Peyton has been lying to her for months, apparently.

The willowy girl moves deeper into the apartment, away from the drama. Darby can hear whispers. David comes back to the door alone and hands her a brown Whole Foods bag full of mail.

"Did he leave his furniture?" Scarlett asks, and David shakes his head.

"No, he packed everything up into an old van and bounced. Sorry I can't be more help. Gotta go, we have a class. Willow is a yoga teacher."

The willowy girl is named Willow. Of course she is.

Darby thinks she might just be losing her mind a bit.

"Thank you," she says numbly, and follows Scarlett back to the car. Darby leans her arms on the doorframe and her head onto her arms. Scarlett riffles through the bag of mail like a terrier after a rat. She rips open an envelope, thrusts the paper toward Darby's nose.

"He dropped out of school, Mom. This is confirmation his tuition refund is being processed." Finally, finally, Scarlett loses it. The tears course down her face. "Why would he lie to us?"

Not to *you*, Darby thinks. To *us*. What small comfort that tiny word brings.

"I don't know, honey," she says, gathering her weeping daughter in her arms. "I don't know."

Scarlett hiccups and wipes her nose with the back of her hand. Darby automatically reaches into her pocket for a tissue. Scarlett wipes her face and gives a great, shuddery sigh.

"So now what do we do?" she asks, infuriatingly calm for a girl who's just had a massive breakdown in an apartment complex parking lot.

"I don't know. But it's only a matter of time before someone sees that sketch and recognizes him. Maybe we need to go to the police."

"Oh my God," Scarlett mutters. "This isn't happening. Try him again."

Darby calls, again. No answer, again.

She stashes her phone in her pocket. "All right. Let's go back home. We can discuss what we should do when we get there."

They are on the outskirts of Nashville when her phone rings. Hope flares—*Peyton, please be Peyton*—but she doesn't recognize the number. The car's system picks up the call, and Darby reaches over and presses the phone button on the steering wheel.

"This is Darby Flynn," she says.

"Mrs. Flynn? My name's Detective Osley. I'd like to talk to you about your son."

32

THE WIFE

Olivia wakes to the sound of beeping, and the heady, unwelcome stench of lilies. It takes her a few moments to piece her world back together.

IV. Bright light. People bustling about. Hospital.

Her throat is sore.

A quick heartbeat of elation. The procedure is over. Her hands go to her stomach, caress the flat planes.

As of this moment, she is officially pregnant. Of course they must wait for the test results, but she can already tell, can already feel them inside her. Her babies. The doctors were thrilled; they had several excellent, healthy embryos to implant, and two possibles that were still being analyzed as she was put under. Here she is, with them inside her.

Amazing, even with the haze of the leftover medication they gave her to help her relax while they did the transfer, how quickly she is attuned to them. They are her, and they are apart, floating in their safe, happy home.

"Hello," she whispers. "I hope we get to meet one day soon."

"Oh, finally. You're awake." Park takes her hand. "I've been so worried."

"It went well?" she asks. "The babies are okay? How many did they put in?"

He seems to be struggling for composure, and her heart sinks. Did it not work? But she can feel them.

"Honey, you're confused. We're not at the clinic. We're at St. Thomas. You had a car accident. You've just come out of surgery."

But she can feel them… Nothing makes sense.

She struggles to sit up, is forced back by a searing pain in her shoulder. Her arm is strapped to her side. Park gentles her back down as if she's a spooked horse.

"No, no, you need to stay lying down until the nurse comes."

The pain clears her head a bit. "Oh God, that hurts. What's happened?"

"You hit a deer. The antlers impaled you. It's a miracle, a few inches lower… Your collarbone was broken, badly. The doctors pinned it together, removed some pieces of shattered antler. Do you remember?"

A flash of white, an eerie screech, the impact. The rolling black eye. The blood.

The searing physical pain is replaced with a deeper, primal soreness. Blood, and cramping. Her heart, broken.

"I lost the baby."

"That was earlier. Not because of the accident."

"Oh, Park." Her voice is thick with tears and leftover anesthesia. She is chilled, and begins to shake, the movement jarring her body. Park pulls up the blankets and clings to her good hand.

"You're going to be in a sling for a while, but they say you can come home this morning. I called your parents. They want to fly home, but they have to get to the next port first. You scared me, honey. When the police called to say you'd been hurt, I rushed here immediately. They let me see you for a minute before they took you to surgery, but you were out cold. You've been asleep since. I'm so glad you're okay. If something worse had happened, I don't know what I would have done. Oh God, Olivia. I—"

A fuzzy sense fills her. She should be mad. She is mad. But she's not sure why.

"Shh. I'm all right. I'm okay, Park. Call my folks again and tell them not to come. I can't be the reason they leave that cruise. I promise, I'm fine." There is a vase of white lilies on the tray by her hand. She hates lilies. They smell like death to her. "God, can you get rid of those flowers? I'm sorry, the scent is making me nauseated."

She catches his frown. "I don't mean to be harsh. It was sweet of you to bring them—"

"I didn't. I would never bring you lilies. I know how much you despise them."

"Thank God. I thought you might be punishing me." She gives him a wan smile, and he smiles back, just as tremulous. "Who are they from? Is there a card?"

"No, no card. I went for a cup of coffee, and they were brought in while I was gone. Let me go donate them to someone else."

He disappears for a few minutes, giving her time to gather herself. The scent lingers, rot and loam and perfumed air.

An accident. She's been in an accident.

But she can still feel them inside her.

You're confused. You're just confused.

Park returns, washes his hands with the antibacterial foam at the door. The chemical scent is more welcome than the bitter scent of the flowers, and she relaxes when he sits again.

"Better?"

"Much." It is starting to come back to her, bits and pieces, flashes of shattered glass and fear. "The Jeep?"

"Other than the windshield and driver's window, it's almost unscathed. The police think the deer must have been midair when you impacted. His antlers came through the windshield and pinned you. When they got there, you were unconscious, covered in blood, with a chunk of antler sticking out, and the deer was nowhere to be found."

The crash. The fear. That disembodied voice. *Oh, my darling.*

"What about the man who helped me? Did they find out who it was? If not for him, I'd have been hurt worse. The deer was freaking out."

Park shakes his head. "No one mentioned a Good Samaritan. The police said you were alone."

"That's weird. He broke the side window. I know he did. He said I was going to be okay. He called me by my name. I thought it might have been Perry, but the voice was different. I didn't get a good look at him."

"Perry?" The chill in his voice is palpable.

"He was at Lindsey's. We talked."

"Oh, really? That's where you were all afternoon? With Perry?"

The sneer is too much for her to take. She can't do this right now. Her head is fuzzy, she hurts, and she's beyond annoyed with his attitude. Why is she so mad at him? She can't remember, but it must be important.

"No. I was at therapy, and stopped by to see if Lindsey was home, and he was there. It wasn't more than fifteen minutes. We had a fight almost immediately." She waved her good hand. "It doesn't matter. But it wasn't Perry at the accident. The voice was wrong. It was familiar, but not that familiar."

"Then maybe whoever your stranger was asked your name and you told him."

"No. No, I'm sure he didn't. I'm sure he knew me. There was something in the way he said my name. And he said...he said I was beautiful."

"Honey, you've had a trauma. You had anesthesia. It's possible—"

"No!" The beeping grows in intensity. The racket is quickly followed by a nurse in blue scrubs.

"Okay, okay, calm down," Park says, and the nurse fiddles with the machine, which promptly stops squawking. She is in her forties, comfortably round and clearly competent.

"Excuse me, sir." She steps to the bed, checks the blood pressure cuff wrapped around Olivia's good bicep. "How are you feeling, Olivia? You gave everyone a good scare."

"I'm fine." Though she is anything but; it's a reflex answer. *I'm fine*, but I'm not. *I'm sorry*, though I did nothing wrong. The two phrases trained into almost every woman from birth.

"Let's keep that heart rate down, okay?"

Olivia shifts uncomfortably. "When can I go home?"

"Dr. Oglesby will be by on rounds shortly. You're lucky he was here when they brought you in. Best surgeon in town in my opinion. He heard what happened and offered to work on you. You're going to be just fine. When he gives you the high sign, we'll get you discharged."

Olivia lays her head back on the pillow while the nurse takes her vitals. Park helps her to the bathroom, and when she comes out, the surgeon is waiting. He is kind, and handsome, and very, very tall. He explains the procedure he's done and gives her instructions for problems to watch for. He gives Park a stack of paperwork and tells her to come see him in two weeks to get her stitches out.

"No more deer hunting, Olivia. Okay?"

"Okay."

The nurse comes in with another stack of papers, plus instructions for how to care for the incision and a prescription for painkillers.

"Don't be brave, take the pills on time. You want to stay ahead of the pain cycle. You won't need them for more than a couple of days. Here's two to get you started. Be safe, they might make you a little dizzy. Go straight home and get into bed. You'll want to be propped up, you won't want to lie down flat for a few days. If you have a recliner, that's even better. I'll get a wheelchair for you."

Olivia gobbles the pills as if they are water in a vast desert, hoping, praying, for oblivion. This pain is too intense. Her shoulder and collarbone hurt, too, but the pain she needs relief from is internal. Her heart. There is something wrong with her heart.

The wheelchair arrives. She is very blurry now. The walls of the hospital flash by. Outside, the bright morning sun gleams into her face.

Park gets her settled in his BMW, and then they are free.

Olivia drifts.

Park is speaking to her, but she can't make out the words. They pull into the drive and she sharpens, focusing when he says, "We were supposed to talk with the reporter last night, but Lucía moved it to this morning. We can wait for a few hours. If you can't do it, I will. It's all good. You just rest."

Reporter.

The rest of it all comes flooding back. And something else... Her mind finally latches onto reality.

Little Brandon Cross. Park's son. Another son.

She wants to confront him, to yell and scream and hit, but she is too high to do anything but allow Park to help her walk into the house, move slowly up the stairs, and swing her legs onto the bed. A recliner. She almost giggles at the thought. Olivia is not the recliner type. She has a fabulous 1940s French chaise in bottle-green velvet she found at an estate sale eons ago, but it's in the living room, and she feels fine here in the bed, bolstered on all sides by fluffy pillows.

Park reappears with water in her favorite thermos, the straw top open and waiting, and a plate of sliced apples. Solicitous Park is back.

"The nurse said you should start with something light."

She nibbles an apple and has a few sips of water, but she is tired, so damn tired. She examines Park's features, looking for the truth. He looks just the same. It is she who's inexorably changed.

His voice is gentle. "You want to tell me why you trashed my office and raced off?"

"You really don't know?"

He shakes his head.

"Brandon Cross."

His face goes comically blank before his eyes close. He takes a deep breath through his nose before he opens them again.

"I wanted to tell you," he starts, but she holds up her hand. "Just don't. I don't have the energy to listen to any more lies."

"I'm not lying. I only met him once. His mother was looking for a handout. When I didn't give it to her, she found another guy. They live in California now. She's never reached out again."

"How do you know they're in California, then?"

He has the decency to look abashed. "Social media."

She turns her head away, tears sparking in her eyes. Park strokes her hair and whispers, "I'm so sorry. So sorry. You're going to be okay, darling. We're going to be okay."

"Don't call me darling," she manages before she slides into the darkness.

When Olivia wakes again, she can hear many voices. She shifts—gasps a little at the sharp pain—then swings her legs to the side and manages to sit up. An argument, happening downstairs, harsh whispers. Lindsey. Park. Another woman. Her mom? No, can't be.

She wavers a bit as she stands. She desperately needs the bathroom. Let them fight. There's nothing she can add anyway.

Once the awkward job is finished, she glances in the mirror. She has a black eye and bruises creeping up her neck like a fungus.

The arguing has stopped, and Lindsey appears in the doorway. "Hey there. I thought I heard you moving around. Jeez, girl, you look like hell. Come get back into bed."

Olivia allows herself to be towed to the bed, gently tucked in. "What's the fuss downstairs? Who is that woman I hear?"

"That's Lucía, my...your lawyer. She and Park are trying to hammer out what he should be saying, and she's giving him an earful because he's trying to tell her how to do her job, and Perry keeps telling him to shut up and listen to her. The reporter will be here within the hour. Do you feel up to talking? I could put your hair up in a twist and cover up that shiner. Nothing to be done for the sling."

Olivia tries—and fails—to compute all of that. All she hears is *Perry*.

"Perry is here?"

Lindsey coughs a little laugh. "Yeah. Wild horses couldn't keep him away. He was at the hospital, too, we all were. Your folks are catching a plane. They won't be back for at least a full day—"

"No, no, please, I told Park I don't want them to come back. Bring me my phone. I'll call them and tell them to stay. They've been excited about this vacation for months. There's nothing they can do here now anyway."

"They were already heading to the airport the last I heard. We didn't know if you were going to be okay for a while there. You got lucky, Liv. Everyone wants to help. Just let them. All you need to do is sit tight."

"You know how much I love help."

"For once, please?"

Olivia sighs. It hurts to breathe. Maybe it's time for another pill. "Okay. I trust you. But I don't want to sit up here while everyone is downstairs deciding our fate. Let's do my hair and makeup."

Fifteen minutes later, Olivia is presented downstairs like a stoned, bedraggled debutante to the oohs and awws—not in excitement, but pity—of her family.

Both Park and Perry start for her, but Perry draws up sharply and picks up a framed photograph from the table. Park, shooting his twin a death glance, reaches Olivia and helps her to the sofa. She tries not to flinch away from him. She is introduced to Lucía, who she vaguely senses is lovely and extremely put together. She is fussed over, made comfortable with pillows and a cozy throw, a cup of spiced chamomile set by her good elbow.

She takes as deep a breath as she dares with the pain and is immediately assailed with the scent of lilies. Again. She spies a vase sitting on the massive island in the kitchen—it is one of hers, a wedding gift, crystal cut with a wide lip and fluted edges—and is overflowing with white lilies, ripe and lush, their stamens open and disgorging stinking orange pollen all over her marble.

"For God's sake, why did you bring those flowers home from the hospital, Park?"

He glances wildly over his shoulder, spies the vase on the counter. "I didn't. That's bizarre. I didn't even notice them. Lucía, did you bring them? Perry? Lindsey?"

At the trio of shaking heads, Park gives Olivia a concerned glance.

"I'll just go get rid of these."

"Park, wait," Lucía says. "If no one brought them, how did they get here?"

Silence. Uncomfortable silence.

She continues, "Are you sure someone hasn't been in the house? You've had two break-ins already."

He shakes his head. "We would get a notification from the front door, and there would be a history on the other doors, too. We always set the alarm when we aren't home. I sometimes forget to set it if I'm just going into the back yard, but after yesterday...no, I set it before I left for the hospital, because I turned it off when we got back this morning. I don't have it set to capture every movement around the house, because we were getting a thousand alerts a day. It's quite sensitive, and birds and squirrels were setting it off. You can't come into the house without tripping the alarm."

"Better check. Just in case. You were upset. You might have forgotten."

Olivia watches as Park opens his security app and looks at the timestamps of movement from the front door, stomach twisting into knots. He scrolls back to 5:00 p.m., right before he got the call that Olivia was being taken to St. Thomas. Yes, the alarm is on, and there he is, hustling out the door. She can see his car leave the driveway.

There is only one other taped event. At 11:28 p.m.

A man approaches the porch. He is wearing a hoodie with a zipper up the front. There is no car on the street; he seems to be on foot. He is carrying something in his arms, wrapped in brown paper.

The man comes to the door, moving quickly, then disappears inside.

"The alarm was disengaged at 11:29 p.m."

Olivia feels faint when Park looks up in horror.

"Oh my God. He has a key to the house and knows our alarm codes."

33

THE DAUGHTER

Scarlett's cell phone has been pinging, notification after notification, the Facebook group blowing up as Peyton's name gets out, and she's tuning it all out, watching her mother talk to the detectives.

The cops were waiting at the house when they got back from Murfreesboro. As she expertly slid the car into the drive, Darby had admonished Scarlett—"You do not say a word, do you understand me? I will handle this"—and so far, Scarlett has stayed out of it.

They're both still in shock. But Darby is surprisingly composed, considering. Scarlett is totally rattled, screaming inside, has been since they'd been standing at the apartment door, face to face with the yoga power couple, realizing Peyton wasn't living there anymore.

Peyton lied. He lied to them. He lied to her. He might as well have shoved a knife into her heart.

She texts him again.

Where are you? The police are here. They are taking things from your bathroom to test. Tell me you didn't do this. Tell me this is just a big misunderstanding.

A text, almost immediately…but it's not from Peyton. It's from Chastain.

I always knew he was a creep, this is why you have no friends. Your brother is a murderer.

Check your socials, freak.

She does, already cringing at what she will see. It is as bad, and worse, as she can expect. She has been tagged in a number of posts, but the entry, from the school's darling, Chastain, her former friend, her former confidante, is the one that breaks her. The post is long, and detailed, but the part that leaps out makes Scarlett want to crawl into a hole and die.

…so after that, I went to a sleepover at their house once. Once. Her creepy brother showed up and was all slick and charming, offered to get us some beer later if we wanted. That was cool and everything, but later that night, when I went to the bathroom, I saw him sitting in the hallway outside her room with his hand down his pants. He was listening to all of us in there, sleeping, breathing, and getting off to it. The way he looked at me, I was sure he was going to leap off the floor and attack me, but he just smiled and patted the floor next to him, like, an invitation or something. He said "why don't you come here and let's chat."

I was totally weirded out and went to the bathroom. I locked the door but I didn't realize that it was a Jack and Jill, so he came in the other door. I was trapped in there. He came up beside me and started playing with my hair. I was so scared I couldn't even scream. I just wanted him to go away. He leaned over and smelled my neck and kissed my cheek. "Don't you want to come back to my room and have some fun?" he asked and when I shook my head, he shoved me, hard, against the bathroom counter. I thought he was going to hurt me but he left then. There was something in his eyes, something terrifying. I practically ran back to the bedroom and I made sure to lock the door but I couldn't sleep knowing he was out there. I stayed awake all night to make sure we were all safe. And didn't EVER go back. I knew something was wrong in that house. Very wrong.

I feel sorry for Scarlett, I really do. I can only imagine what was happening behind closed doors when people weren't around, if you know what I mean.

Scarlett swallows down her tears. God, that's why they'd all abandoned her? Because of Peyton? And what was Chastain insinuating, that Peyton would lay hands on Scarlett? That he had done something to her?

She gets through five more horrific comments before she logs out. The girls of Bromley West, piling on. It seems everyone has a Peyton story. All are similar. So similar Scarlett thinks she might legitimately be sick. My God, how could she have been so blind?

And now the most traitorous thought. Could he have killed that woman? And kidnapped another?

None of this jibes with the brother she knows, who's always been chivalrous and kind, but now, she is confused enough to worry if it might be true. She feels terrible and disloyal at the thought, but if the schoolgirls she's friends with are leading the way into this fray, and the police themselves are pretty convinced Peyton did something wrong, something very, very bad. What else is she supposed to think?

They're all arranged in the living room—her shattered mom, the disapproving cops. The man is grilling her mom.

"Does your son have any history of violence?"

Darby shakes her head. "No. I mean..."

"Mrs. Flynn—"

"Ms.," Darby snaps. "I am not married."

The detective doesn't miss a beat. "Ms. Flynn, I get the sense you are holding something back. Trust me, we only want to find him. There's probably an explanation, like you said, for why his DNA was in Beverly Cooke's car. Maybe even an innocent thing."

His voice hardens, and Scarlett is suddenly afraid.

"But if there is any chance at all that Peyton did hurt Beverly, and if he has taken Jillian Kemp, both women you know, both women you have a very intimate tie to, then we need to find him. We need to know everything we can about him. I get how hard this is. He's your baby. If I was in your position, I would be torn to pieces right now. But if he didn't do it, that will also come out. If he's just a bystander, and it's circumstantial, we will not press any kind of charges against him. We aren't in the business of railroading suspects. That's not how Detective Moore and I work. We are only interested in one thing—making sure Jillian doesn't end up like Beverly. With Peyton's background, we have to look at this very seriously. Obviously, we can get a warrant for the records, but it would be much easier if you'd just tell us what happened."

Peyton's background? Records? What in the world?

Scarlett's confusion must show on her face, because Darby nods once, twice, almost to herself, then sighs. Scarlett senses the shift in her mother, as if she's come to terms with a horrible, inevitable truth. When she speaks, Scarlett is transfixed.

"Your brother spent some time in a facility in Maryland when he was a boy. He was exhibiting aggressive behavior after your birth. It started when he was five and continued until he was twelve. Medications didn't help, only seemed to make everything worse. We went through a number of diagnoses, doctors, and numerous medications until I was forced to place him into a hospital that specialized in his behavioral issues. They suspected he was having a rare side effect to the psychotropic medications, which were causing him to have hallucinations, delusions, and manic behavior. They diagnosed him with drug-induced schizoaffective disorder. They immediately took him off the medications other various doctors we'd visited put him on. He was better within weeks, and exhibited no more signs of anger, delusions, or dysfunction in any way. I brought him home when he was thirteen, administering a single antidepressant med for a year, and then weaned him off everything. He's been fine ever since. He was basically having an allergic reaction to the heavy-duty medication the doctors kept throwing at him, none of which he needed. He was simply adjusting poorly to a new presence in the home. He wanted more attention than I could give for a while there."

Scarlett is staring. She knows this because the woman detective is ignoring her mother and watching Scarlett's reaction instead. Scarlett doesn't care. She feels betrayed that she's just now finding out about this side of her beloved brother.

"He resented *me*? He had to be hospitalized because he hated me so much? You never told me that," she said, and Darby shakes her head vigorously.

"Hey, that wasn't the case, not at all. He was a little boy. Sometimes, kids don't act like adults want them to all the time, and we rush to fix them when they aren't broken in the first place. It was a time when doctors misdiagnosed any sort of negative behavior and put children on medications their bodies and brains weren't capable of handling. Peyton was a little jealous of you when you first came. That's totally normal. But his pediatrician convinced me it was something more. That he was sick. The medications caused the problems. Once we took him off of them, he was fine."

The detectives are making notes as fast as their pens can scratch.

"But you didn't tell me. You said he went to a special sleepover school."

"Peyton and I decided not to share this, together. We didn't want you to worry that you might go through the same thing someday." Darby slides a comforting hand over Scarlett's, and she can't help but pull away, still too hurt, too confused, to want to be touched.

With another sigh, Darby turns to the cops. "I want this to be very clear," she says, voice strong. "There is a terrible stigma associated with mental illness. If—*if*—Peyton is behind these crimes, I want it known Peyton needed exactly zero intervention after we discovered the problem was not organic but was being caused by his medications. This isn't a well-documented syndrome, but you'll find that the literature available is both fascinating and compelling. I even agreed to let the doctors use Peyton's case for teaching, helping doctors and pediatricians recognize the signs of medication-induced schizoaffective disorder, so more children aren't misdiagnosed and forever labeled. I would be happy to share the names of his treating doctors, who will confirm what I've just told you."

The detective nods, his head bobbing in time with Scarlett's heartbeats. "This is very interesting information, Ms. Flynn. We appreciate your honesty. Those names would be a great help. We'll certainly want to talk to his doctors."

"Fine. I'll get them for you."

"And you're sure you don't know where Peyton might be now?"

"I don't. He apparently has dropped out of school and didn't tell me that. He told his sister that he was going camping this weekend. Scarlett?"

Scarlett is too shocked not to answer. "He said he was heading to the Blue Ridge with friends. He went a few weeks ago, too, but this time they would be out of touch. His phone wouldn't be working." Her voice is flat. She notices Darby is trying—and failing—to hold it together. She scoots closer to her mom on the couch, puts an arm around her. "This has to be a mistake. Peyton couldn't do this. I know my brother."

Freak. Your brother is a freak.

The female detective looks at her phone. Someone's been texting her for the past few minutes; the phone has been vibrating frantically in the woman's pocket.

"Osley," she says, and he breaks eye contact with Scarlett to glance at his partner.

"Channel Four is teasing an interview about to go live. Park Bender is going to talk to Erica Pearl. It's on the station's app, and it's all over social media."

"Park Bender?" Darby asks.

The cops exchange a brief glance, and the woman nods. "It seems Peyton has been in contact with both him and his wife. That's how we got the sketch. He broke into Mrs. Bender's work yesterday. She confronted him, and he left," Osley says.

"But Peyton is camping in the Blue Ridge," Scarlett says. If she says it enough, maybe it will be true.

The detective shakes his head. "He's not. I'm sorry, both of you. I know this is hard to wrap your heads around. But as of yesterday, we know for a fact Peyton was right here in Nashville, driving a van he purchased in August for $500 from a man in Hermitage. We have both the van's license plates and the details of the transaction. There is currently a BOLO for the van."

"BOLO?" Scarlett asks.

"It's a term we use for other police to 'be on the lookout' for a van matching the description. Has Peyton ever shown you his van, Scarlett?"

"No. Of course not. He doesn't own a van, he drives an Accord. This is just too weird. Wait. I know something that might help. There was…there was a man, yesterday. Sitting at the corner of the street. He came to the end of the driveway and was watching me go into the house. He creeped me out."

"Do you know what kind of car?"

"It was one of those quiet ones, electric. A red BMW hybrid. Chastain's father has one, but it's silver."

The cops look at each other again.

"Do you know who it was?" Scarlett asks.

"I think we have an idea, yes. Park Bender drives a red hybrid BMW."

Scarlett watches her mom, waiting for her reaction. She needs to tell her about the Facebook posts and comments, but she doesn't want to do it in front of the cops.

"Who is this Bender person? Why is he hanging around my kid, and why is he sitting down with Erica Pearl? Is he going to accuse my son of something?" Darby asks.

It's the woman who responds. "This is going to come out, so we might as well deal with it now. Park Bender is Peyton's biological father. Scarlett's, too. He is their donor."

Silence. Darby's hand goes over her mouth, but Scarlett says, "No, you're wrong. Peyton is my half-brother. Not a full sibling."

"I'm afraid that's not true."

Darby shakes her head in disbelief. "There's been a mistake. Scarlett is right. They don't have the same donor. I should know, considering. They had to send me a completely different donor because Peyton's was tapped out. They limit the number…or they're supposed to. But the man I chose for Scarlett—I have all the information. He's different."

"Well, Ms. Flynn, this case gets curiouser and curiouser, because the DNA we retrieved in Beverly Cooke's car, the DNA that matches your son, also has a patriarchal link to Mr. Bender. He is your son's father, there's no question about it. We can back this up with some testing of our own, but it seems Winterborn lied to you, ma'am."

"This is impossible. You're saying Peyton and Scarlett are full siblings?"

"That seems to be the case."

Her mother turns to her. "Scarlett. You told me Peyton declined to be a part of the group, that he wouldn't give you DNA. Is that true?"

"Yes. Originally, he said he didn't want to know. He didn't care about having a father. Then he agreed, but I don't think he did it. Maybe it was just…maybe he knew it would get him in trouble."

"I can't believe this," Darby says, leaning back into the couch and covering her face with her hands.

It's the woman who asks, "Scarlett? May we test your DNA to confirm Peyton is your full-blooded sibling? It will help us to know if we've made a mistake or not."

"I don't think that's necessary—" Darby starts, but Scarlett raises her chin. "Yes. Of course." To her mom, who is looking utterly betrayed, "Mom, we have to. We can't help him if we don't know the whole truth."

"Interview's starting," Osley says. "We should go."

"Wait, that's my father the reporter is talking to, right?" Scarlett says. "Mom, can we watch?"

"I think we should all watch," Moore says under her breath, shifting from foot to foot. Even with the shock and craziness of the past hour, Scarlett finds the woman interesting. They've been studying body language in psychology, and this woman is so contained, but there is something simmering beneath the surface that seems ready to explode.

Osley nods. "I'm surprised Erica Pearl isn't here, right now, banging on the door wanting to talk to you, Ms. Flynn. She must have something big."

Darby grabs her iPad from the side table, unplugging it and whipping back the cover. "Then let's see what she—what he—has to say."

34

THE HUSBAND

Park has retrieved his laptop from his office and has the computer open, searching through the security feeds for any hint of their intruder.

He has a notebook next to him, where he logs every instance of the man coming into their house.

So far, he's found at least seventeen intrusions over the past month. They almost always seem to coincide with Park and Olivia leaving, but damn if there aren't at least three that happen when he thinks they were home.

Olivia refuses to go upstairs and lie down and is sitting on the couch in the den, feet pulled up, looking wan and not a little terrified. Perry—goddamn him—is ministering to her like she's a wounded cat. Practically petting her. Can I get you some tea? Are you hungry? Are you sure you shouldn't be lying down, Liv?

She's brushed him off so far, is keeping her distance, but every query makes Park's blood pressure shoot up, higher and higher. Lucía and Lindsey are arranging everything for the interview, which has left the three of them, in their lopsided triangle of love and hate and discomfort, stuck in the den, examining the security footage to ascertain just how deeply this creep has gotten into their lives.

Perry quits hovering over Olivia and stands behind Park. "Anything new?"

"Other than this asshole has been stalking us?"

"For how long?"

Park sits back in the chair, running a hand over his chin. "At least a month. My feed only goes back so far. Even if I reached out to the security company, they'd only have it for so long, too. He's been waltzing in and out of here like he owns the place."

"Has he taken anything?" Perry asks.

"I think he's been taking my clothes," Olivia says.

The brothers respond as one. "What?"

She shifts her sling, looking utterly miserable. "I'm missing a few things. A top. A bra. Some panties. I just assumed they were lost in the wash, or the dry cleaner screwed up."

"It's time to call the police," Perry says.

"Actually, it's time to talk to Erica Pearl," Lindsey says. "She just rolled up. Liv, why don't we get you upstairs. Even with my mad makeup skills, you're not looking up for this."

"I'm staying."

The three Benders meet eyes. All three of them know how stubborn Olivia can be.

"Maybe this isn't such a great idea," Perry says, but Park puts up a hand.

"Stow it, okay? There's no right or good decisions in this. I want my side of the story out there."

"You should call the damn police and tell them about this."

"They'll hear about it in five minutes when I bring it up to the reporter. They haven't done us any favors. Why should I help them?"

"Park, he has a point," Olivia says.

"So you're taking his side against me, is that it?"

Olivia bites her lip. "Please stop attacking me. I am just saying that in light of this new information—"

The reporter shows up at exactly the wrong moment. Or maybe the right one, he doesn't know. All Park can do is stow his worries, his hurts, and put on the show he knows he must give. There will be time later for them to talk. He realizes they haven't been properly alone in days. Haven't had anything more than an argument all week.

He misses his wife.

The worst thing? She doesn't seem to miss him.

"Hi there!" a bright voice calls from the hallway. Lucía enters the room, followed by Erica Pearl, who swans around the den, looking around at the floor-to-ceiling shelving surrounding the fireplace, the shiplap and stone, the comfortable sofa and chairs. This is a relax space for them, a place to chill, watch a movie, play a game of cards with friends. It's always been one of Park's favorites, but it's becoming decidedly less so right now.

"Are you all set? The light is pretty good. If you're comfortable, we can chat here. I like this room. It's homey. Less showy."

"This room is fine." Olivia says. "I don't believe we've met."

"We haven't. I'm Erica Pearl, Channel Four. My goodness, are you all right?" The teensiest bit of accusation lingers in the air—did your husband do this to you? Park bristles, but Olivia smiles, graciousness personified.

"Car accident. I hit a deer. I'm fine."

"Oh, that's so scary. I'm glad you're okay. You sure you're comfortable giving an interview right now? I could always reschedule."

Like hell they're rescheduling, Park thinks. They need to get this over with.

"We're good," he says, watching Perry out of the corner of his eye. His brother slinks from the room disapprovingly.

Five minutes later, Park and Olivia are miked, and watching Erica Pearl straighten her shirt and adjust the lavalier mic attached to her lapel.

"My lav's set. Sound check, one, two, three. All's good?"

The photojournalist nods, gives a thumbs-up. Park takes Olivia's hand. It is cold and weak in his.

"Okay, Mr. and Mrs. Bender. We're going to run through the whole story, and you can tell us what you know."

"I don't know anything," Park says. "That's the problem."

"Then let's start at the beginning. I understand the day Beverly Cooke was found, the police came to your front door with some rather shocking news."

"Yes," he says, and they're off. He recounts all the things that have happened so far, of course leaving out a few particulars—the fights with Olivia, the drive by at his daughter's house, the interrogations by the police. Lucía has coached him, and he has had time to think about what he wants to say. He frames everything in as straightforward language as he can.

He mourns with the rest of the city at Beverly Cooke's death.

He is horrified and scared for Jillian Kemp and is praying for a quick and happy resolution.

Yes, he has been told that there is a DNA match to a biological son he wasn't aware of.

Yes, he is cooperating with the police.

Yes, he is now aware that he has twenty-eight biological children.

No, he didn't know about these children.

Yes, of course he wants to meet them. It will be the greatest joy of his life.

He doesn't look at Olivia when he says this, knowing it must be a stake to her heart. Her free fist clenches in her lap.

Finding Beverly's killer is paramount, and all he's currently focused on.

Please, if you're seeing this, as your father—though I know I don't deserve that title—please come forward. We will figure this out.

And when Pearl brings up Melanie Rich, he answers the way he wished he had all those years ago.

A tragedy. An absolute tragedy. My heart goes out to her family. No one should lose a child.

The reporter is eating it up. This is gold. He knows it, she knows it. Scoop, with a capital *S*.

And then it all goes sideways.

"I think we all feel your pain and understand. I so appreciate your honesty. Just one more thing before we wrap up. Is it true you were on the scene of another death, in Florida? A teenage girl drowned during your college spring break, isn't that right?"

Olivia tenses beside him, pulls her hand away in reflex. Unprepared, Park, heart pounding, sputters. "How did you find out about that?"

He hears how badly it sounds as he says it, and Pearl, smelling meat on the grill, doesn't let up.

"And according to police records, when you were ten, a neighborhood girl went missing. Annie Cottrell. Her parents told St. Louis police they'd seen her playing with you and your brother an hour earlier. She was never found, isn't that right?"

Lucía strides into the den, stepping in front of the camera. "We're done here. You've gone outside the scope of this interview. Thank you for your time, Erica. Because you didn't follow the rules of our agreement, we rescind our permission to have this shown on the news."

Erica doesn't look incensed, only prettily confused. "Lucía, we've been live this whole time on the app. I told you we would be."

Park feels the blood drain from his face. "We're live?"

Erica Pearl's smile is nearly Cheshire. "Of course. Still rolling," she adds sweetly.

Olivia steps in. She is steel, and she is Valkyrie furious; Park can't remember seeing her this angry since they were teenagers. "Then we need to discuss one more thing. A stranger has been breaking into our house. We have footage from our security cameras. A white male, wearing a dark hoodie. He has a key to our home and knows our security codes. Personal items are missing. We have been violated by these intrusions, we have been shocked by the news this week, and we will not stand idly by and have any sort of accusations, oblique or otherwise, cast our way. For you to pretend to be taping an interview yet broadcast it is not only disingenuous, you're taking advantage of a horrible moment for our family, for our friends, and for the women of Nashville, who are all terrified right now that they might be next. I hope you're satisfied. Now cut your camera. We're done."

A bell cannot be unrung.

Cameras off at last, Lucía and Erica go at it hammer and tongs, but the interview is already out there. They are screwed. Park is screwed.

It doesn't matter if he isn't involved in the murders or disappearances. It doesn't matter that Olivia dealt Erica Pearl a deathblow live. Public opinion has already judged him. Their phones have been ringing off the hook, and when he hears Erica Pearl say the word *Dateline*, he retreats to his trashed office, nauseated.

What has he done?

His office is a perfect replica of his brain at this moment—a convoluted mess.

Olivia ruined as much as she could find.

He retrieves the pieces of the laptop and sets them gingerly on the desk.

Replaces the slit cushion where he hid the demise of his life.

Pulls the bottle of Scotch from the side table drawer and pours a healthy slug into a glass. Shoves the rest of the mess around with his foot so he can sit without crunching anything else.

Brandon Cross. His tiny son. It won't matter to Olivia that he only met the boy once. He hadn't lied when he told Olivia that Fiona Cross wasn't looking for a father for her child, but an easy paycheck.

He could have given her some money, but he knew where that train was headed, and balked. He talked to Lindsey about a "theoretical situation for a novel" in which the scenario played out, and she said it was "a disaster in the making. The perfect fodder for a plot. Can you imagine how messy that would be? You could have the guy swoop in and rescue the kid, or you could have him blackmailed into submission. Legally, though, as a donor, the guy is protected by the agreement he signed with the company. If he declined support or contact, the mother is breaking the contract she agreed to, and he would not be culpable."

He's always known this could happen. And like a damn fool, he hasn't told Olivia about the possibility. Even after the Fiona Cross catastrophe, when it was an awkward but manageable situation, he hid this from her. Was he afraid to lose her? Yes. Or was he trying to push her away? Avoidance? Guilt? Shame?

His darling Olivia, who—understandably—has now put up an impenetrable wall between them. Just when he needs her the most, she is slipping away.

It was Perry the sainted white knight who had taken Olivia upstairs after the interview fell apart, practically carried her, and seeing them together cuts Park's soul. It always has. Knowing they slept together, carried on their little revenge affair—it was an affair, Olivia was *his* girlfriend, damn it—until Perry left for school and Olivia spent the next few months grieving, not speaking to anyone, about killed him. He'd been overjoyed when their brief fling was over. Yes, he'd dated other girls, yes, he'd pretended not to care, but inside, he seethed with resentment. He stopped speaking to Perry—his twin, his closest friend—and bided his time until he made contact with Olivia again, hoping she would come around, and sure enough, she had. Maybe she felt sorry for him in the aftermath of Melanie's death, maybe she missed him, maybe she even loved him like he loved her, completely and forever, but their lives had started over that day, and he had no regrets, none at all.

Olivia does. He saw the look on her face when that nasty reporter tossed St. Louis at them. Her recoil, her hand yanking away from his as if she couldn't bear to be touching him anymore. He is losing her, he knows it, and he needs to find a way to keep her, and fast. She has to believe he isn't capable of murder. That all of this is just coincidence.

Damn it, how did Erica Pearl, of all people, find out about St. Louis?

Poor little Annie Cottrell. Everyone in the neighborhood knew there had been a creep driving around, asking kids if they'd seen his puppy. It had been happening almost the whole summer. Everyone knew it had to be that creeper who took Annie. Everyone knew it.

But a vicious whisper campaign had started up among the neighborhood moms. The Bender boys had been paying too much attention to Annie Cottrell.

Without a clear suspect, the neighborhood had turned on them. Accused the boys of such terrible things. He and Perry hadn't even been near Annie's house when she went missing. They were at the field, Little League pregame batting practice underway. Park remembered the day vividly—he'd hit a homer and run the bases with a carefree smile, not knowing hours later their world would be under attack.

The police searched their house, talked to the boys, to Lindsey. Annie was their sister's friend. Annie and Lindsey were playing by the fence, Lindsey had gone inside to get popsicles, and when she came back out, Annie was nowhere to be found. Yes, Park and Perry had seen her on their way to the field, but that was before. She'd been on her way to their house to play.

The creep was arrested a few months later exposing himself to another girl a town over. He denied knowing anything about Annie Cottrell, which fueled the flames all over again.

Eventually, their parents had decided they should move. They packed up and came to Nashville, and the course of all their lives had been altered.

Olivia Hutton lived across the street from the new house.

Olivia, with her scratchy voice and her sable hair and her budding, ripe little girl on the cusp of womanhood body, who worshipped the ground the Benders walked on. She was smart. She was funny. She was talented. Park's parents—his mother especially—adored her. The Huttons and the Benders became fast friends, going out to dinner together, leaving the kids with a sitter, vacationing together, camping trips and beaches. It was natural that Olivia befriend their sister, and the boys, too. The boys played with her, protected her, and fell in love with her. Olivia became the north for the entire Bender family compass.

That has never changed, nor will it. The history they all share is too intertwined. She chose him, damn it. Park. Not Perry. It was she and Park who were childhood sweethearts. Madly in love. Yes, they'd had a spat, a breakup, some hurt feelings while she dated Perry, but she came back to him. Then came marriage. Joy. Love and happiness. Attempts to have children.

It's only been recently that he's felt things slipping. That the feeling he had when they were in high school and she wouldn't talk to him crept back in. She's closed herself off now like she did then, and it is Perry, again, who has swooped in to pick up the pieces.

Olivia was and is and always will be Park's entire world. When she was hurt last night, when he'd gotten the call that she'd been in an accident, Park felt like part of his soul had ripped apart.

And now, circumstance and an ill-advised decision twenty

years ago is going to drive them apart. He feels the chasm growing, inch by inch, day by day.

He pours another Scotch, shoots it down. And another. Gets angrier by the gulp.

Why is he out here in the proverbial dog shed revisiting hellacious memories alone while his brother is inside with his wife?

He hears the buzzing, the murmurs, the car doors. Looks out the door to the shed and sees the line of vans, satellite dishes pointed to the stars.

The press has arrived.

Now the real fun is going to start.

35

THE MOTHER

Darby closes her iPad gently, staring all the while at her daughter. Her beautiful, precocious sprite of a daughter, who resembles her donor father in ways Darby has never imagined, if only because he is not the man Darby thought fathered her youngest child.

"I can't believe this," Scarlett mutters, and Darby nods. *I have failed you*, she thinks. Her world—their world—has tilted on its axis, and all she wants to do is hide. But she can't. She can't. Because the police who are going to arrest her son and incarcerate him for life and maybe kill him before they get the chance to slap on the handcuffs are standing five feet away, their faces arrayed in both shock and delight.

Delight, for that is the only word that fits.

The thought hits her, clear as a bell. *They think Park Bender is guilty of something.* Then another.

Maybe this will take their attention off Peyton.

Should their attention waver from her son? She doesn't know. The war raging inside her mustn't show, because they're looking at her, curious what she might say, but not leaning forward in anticipation of her giving up her son. She's already done all she can for him. She has given him a baseline for an insanity defense. Do they know that was her goal? Do they know she is wondering if he is insane? That in case of the unthinkable, she had a plan? Do they know that this has always been her deepest fear, the one thing she's spent her entire mothering life worried about? She's known Peyton has a darkness in him. She's seen the blank stares following women in grocery stores, the withdrawal after interactions that didn't go as planned, the lack of dates, the absence of female friends.

She's known, empirically, this could happen. But she thought that maybe, maybe, he had himself in check.

Too much to ask.

Get them out of here.

"Looks like you have work to do," Darby says, gesturing toward the iPad, and the cops fixate on her briefly, then nod in unison, standing and straightening and heading for the door, anxious and intent.

The woman stops in the doorway. "Please be in touch if Peyton reaches out, Ms. Flynn. This will all go easier if he cooperates with our investigation."

Darby nods, still hollow. She closes the door behind them and leans against it. When she hears their car pull away, she hurries to the kitchen.

"Scarlett. Have you heard from him?"

"No, Mom. But you need to see this." She flips her phone around. "I'm going to have to delete my account."

Darby scrolls through the comments, reads the accusations, the unease she'd been feeling earlier swamping into full-on terror. Here it is, in black and white. More confirmation of her worst thoughts. He hasn't been controlling himself. The darkness wasn't back. It had never left.

"This is all my fault," Darby says softly. "And I don't know how to fix it."

"How could this be your fault?" Scarlett is incensed, immediately, and turns on Darby. "This is Peyton's doing. Peyton is responsible. Not you. You're the best mom anyone could ask for."

Darby hugs her daughter tightly, knowing the words are lies.

She can't escape the thought she's been having since the sketch appeared on the television.

Was Peyton's darkness something she did?

She's never blamed herself for her son's problems, but now? Now, she's wondering how much of his insanity must have been passed along by this man, this stranger, who has ties to the missing and the dead three times over, and how much is on her? Because to think she alone created a child who murders, who rapes, who hunts, is too monstrous for her to fathom.

She'd love to blame it all on Park Bender. That's the easy way out.

But what if it *was* her? What if it's something inside her own DNA, something dark and unforgiving? Something wrong. She'd been forced to leave Peyton in daycare, with strangers, as she went through extra schooling certifications, and of course, years on the night shift. If she'd been there to read him a story as he fell asleep every night, would that have changed things?

And Scarlett. Scarlett's birth had triggered the first episodes of darkness. It's not like Darby could blame Scarlett, of course not. But again, was it Darby's fault for not being happy with just a single child, for having the joy of a son?

You know it wouldn't have. You know his darkness is not your fault. Nor his. This is something organic that happens. And not everyone who has this issue falls off the deep end, goes into the baser instincts. Unless Bender is some sort of monster, and he's passed along his maniacal genes.

"What are you thinking about, Mom?"

Darby drags her attention to Scarlett. Her daughter is watching her, of course she is. She needs direction. She needs guidance. She needs to be told that she is safe, that she is loved.

And Darby's just been standing here in the middle of the living room staring into space as her conscience wrestles with itself.

"What?"

"You're lost in thought."

"Just trying to wrap my head around all of this, sweetie."

Darby's phone rings, and they both jolt, nearly hitting heads in their haste to see the caller ID. It is Scarlett's school. After what she's just seen online, Darby is not surprised.

"Ms. Flynn? This is Dean Barker. Principal Rutger and I have just come from a conversation with the board, and we think it might be best if you keep Scarlett home for the rest of the week."

Rage flares, incandescent inside her. "And why is that?"

"Well, Ms. Flynn, with Peyton…this is an awful situation. I'm sure you've seen the social media feeds. We are doing everything we can to make sure these aren't just malicious rumors, but it's not like we can ask the girls to stop posting. If they've experienced these…atrocities, they need a safe space to let out their stories. I'm afraid it's out of our hands. Now that the police are here talking with the students, it's become too much of a distraction. Let's just excuse Scarlett from classes for the rest of the week, and we can reassess on Sunday night. All right?"

No. Not all right.

"Don't you dare even think you can keep my daughter from school. She has every right to be there. Every right to be treated with dignity and respect. How dare you—"

Scarlett wrestles the phone away and pushes Darby lightly toward the kitchen. She raises the phone to her ear.

"Dean Barker? Keep your damn school. I don't want to come back."

She ends the call, smiles weakly at her mother, who feels herself turning various shades of red.

"What have you done? Do you know what it takes for you to go to that place? I've been killing myself—"

"That 'place,' as you call it, is full of snotty bitches, and I'm bored in my classes. I'm better off getting a GED and doing a year at JuCo, then transferring to a four-year school somewhere. It's not the right environment for me, and now? My God, Mom. Peyton has been harassing the girls there for years. I can't go back even if I wanted to."

Darby feels faint. Quite literally, faint.

"We don't know—"

"Mom, think. If what they're saying is true, if Peyton assaulted Chastain, if he even looked sideways at one of the golden girls, then it's all over for me there. And that's fine. I hate them. I will not miss anything about that school."

Scarlett marches to the fridge and pulls out a bottle of water. She offers one to Darby, who accepts gratefully. She is hungry. How is that even possible? Her son might be a murderer, and she's thinking maybe a BLT will assuage her.

"Apple?" she asks, and Scarlett grabs one, cutting it neatly in half and removing the core, then slicing it into fourths. She takes a slice and hands the rest to Darby. They munch in sync, wash away the sticky sweetness with the water.

"Why didn't you tell me you were unhappy, Scar?"

"What would you have done? Told me that it's like that in high school, that friends come and go, that I will find my tribe, that I'm smart and beautiful and none of this matters. All things you as my mother have to say so I don't lock myself in my room and refuse to ever come out again. Trust me, I'll be better off somewhere else."

Scarlett sits across from Darby, a small frown on her lovely face. "It's time, don't you think? To meet him?

"Meet who?"

"Park Bender. My donor. Our donor."

Panic blooms inside of Darby. This is exactly what she's always tried to avoid. "Oh, Scarlett. There's time for that when we aren't in the middle of a huge crisis."

"But what if there's not? What if we all have some sort of time bomb inside us that's going to blow and do horrible things to people?"

Darby gives her a level look. "There's not a time bomb inside you, honey. And I think Park Bender is having a rather bad day. He may not want company. And his poor wife, she looked terrible."

"She was beautiful, though, wasn't she?" Scarlett is winding her hair around her fist, then holsters it on top of her head in a messy bun. "So contained. She looked like she hurt, hearing all of those things about her husband. I think it would kill me."

"When did you get so wise, little girl?"

"I'm not a little girl anymore, Mom. I haven't been for a long time."

"Drinking coffee doesn't make you a grown up, Scarlett. You're sixteen."

"And my brother is a serial assaulter and alleged murderer. I think that might give me an edge over some of my peers."

"We don't know—"

"Yes, we do. At least, I know what the girls at school are saying is true. Maybe not the details, but after that sleepover, most of them wanted nothing to do with me. I've never known why. Now I do."

Darby is again washed with shame, and something more, something deeper, a guilt that eats her from the inside. "You didn't tell me. Why didn't you tell me?"

"What would you be able to do about it? They're teenage

girls. They're horrid, and mean, and I'm glad we aren't friends anymore." There is a bitterness in her daughter's voice that tears her in two. As her mother, she should be able to fix things. Fix all of this. And she can't. She's brought this on them.

"I want to meet him," Scarlett repeats stubbornly.

"It might not be safe, Scarlett. This man is a stranger to us both, he's on the police's radar, and what if he was responsible for that little girl's disappearance? What kind of mother would I be launching you into his world without knowing if he's guilty or not?"

"Mom, come on. You're being paranoid. Besides, you'll be there with me. I swear, if we get even a hint of weirdo off of him, we'll bolt."

Darby blows out a breath. She wants to shut this down before it starts, yet she has to admit, she is curious. Curious to see what of this man helped create her possibly monstrous son.

"We can reach out to Park Bender if you want, but don't expect anything. And try your brother's phone again."

"I just did." Scarlett flops heavily in the kitchen chair. "Mom, could he really have done these things?"

She sounds like a little girl and Darby so wishes she could just shake her head and deny it is remotely possible, but that is a lie. And she's not going to lie to Scarlett, ever again.

"Yes. He could have. I'm sick to my soul to even think it, but yes, it's possible. But let's pray they are wrong about your brother."

36

THE WIFE

Perry brings Olivia a glass of water and a painkiller, which she accepts gratefully.

"You should eat something with those. They'll wreck your stomach."

"I haven't been very hungry," she admits. "Perry. How are we going to fix this? They're making Park look like some sort of serial killer."

She knows he hears the question in her statement—*There's no way these things are true, are they? Have I misjudged my husband from the beginning?*—because he shakes his head automatically.

"You know he's not."

She shifts, adjusting the sling and grimacing slightly.

"Maybe..." she says finally. "I never thought he was that kind of man. His darkness lies elsewhere, and he channels it into his work. That's why he loves writing so much. He gets all that creepy stuff out of his head and onto the page, and people eat it up. It amazes me how well those books do."

A slight frown of confusion darkens Perry's brow.

Oh, damn. "You don't know, do you? Crap. Park will kill me if he knows I've said something."

"Awful phrasing, babe. I thought Park was an English professor?"

"He is. He's just on a sabbatical right now, doing a side project. Can you just pretend you didn't hear me? I'm stoned. I'm rambling."

"A side project, writing books? That's...amazing. He always wanted to be a writer." Perry sounds genuinely surprised and happy. Despite the brothers' distance, their competitive streak, their furious hatred of one other, they are still brothers, twins who shared a life before Olivia. One that has more secrets than she ever knew.

"When we were growing up, remember he was always dragging around that old journal? Thought he was Hemingway. He kept saying we needed to move to Spain and become matadors."

"I didn't know that," she says. "I remember the journal, though. He has stacks of them in his office. They take up three shelves."

"Oh, yeah. Being a matador was his dearest wish."

"I can't even imagine." Can she? Can she envision Park, stable but broody Park, strutting around an arena with a red cape, challenging a beast? Standing his ground as a thousand pounds of fury stamps and snorts, waiting for the perfect moment to charge?

She can't. She truly can't. And that he'd never told her... maybe he couldn't imagine it, either. Maybe she killed that dream for him.

"Just do me a favor and pretend you don't know anything about it, okay? It's top secret stuff." At least she had herself together enough not to have mentioned that Park was a ghost. That really would have been a betrayal.

Perry settles himself on the end of her bed, pulling the throw up over her feet.

"What a mess," she says quietly. "If it isn't bad enough that Park's spawned all these random kids, now we have to deal with the media reporting about it *and* thinking he's some sort of monster."

"We'll fix it. Don't worry." A beat. "Are you okay?" he asks. An impossible question.

"I'm fine. A bit worried about the deer," she says ruefully.

"I'm not talking about the accident."

"I know you're not."

They trail into silence, and Olivia can't handle the quiet. Perry has a stillness inside him, a peace that she wants to touch, to wrap herself in like a cozy blanket and relax into its warmth. He always did have a gentleness, a reserve, but now it's the assurance of a life well-lived, a man content with his choices. He is a man now, no longer a boy, and she can't help but feel like she's lost him, though he wasn't hers to lose. These emotions are confusing her. That she's still so attracted to him, all these years later, even after all they've been through, makes no sense. She's sitting here half-stoned, in pain, stinking of betadine and hospital, blood in her hair, and she's wondering what it would be like to lean over and take him in her mouth, coax him to life, graze her teeth along the length of him until he cried out her name.

"Why didn't you ever come home?" she asks softly.

His eyes spark with something like pain, but he doesn't answer. Instead, he takes her back to St. Louis.

"When we were boys and that girl went missing, Park was beside himself. Absolutely wrecked. With the neighborhood moms jumping all over us, all of our friends looking at us like we'd done something wrong, it got worse and worse. He felt so attacked—I mean, we both did, but he had it worse. He was always so sensitive about things. I knew we'd done nothing wrong, so I ignored it, but Park, he got paranoid that everyone was out to get him, that the police were going to come arrest us. He obsessed about the girl, riding his bike by her house, going to the library and getting on the computers, reading all the articles in the paper. He tried to talk to her parents, to assure them he'd had nothing to do with it. They threatened to get a restraining order, and that got him upset. He withdrew from everything, from everyone. He was really depressed. So much so that it scared me. I told our parents, and Mom took him to our doctor. He sent them to another doctor, a psychologist, and she got him straightened out. She was the one who suggested to Mom that we move, that Park would be better off in a new environment, one without the constant reminders. Dad didn't want to, but Mom insisted. And it worked. We moved here. Park was able to put the worst of it behind him and move on. Meet you. Fall in love." A hint of bitterness in his tone.

"He's never told me any of this."

"Why would he? When we met you, you became his new obsession. It was like St. Louis had never happened. From the moment he set eyes on you, that was it. You were his future, he knew it, and he didn't care about anything—or anyone—else. He never mentioned Annie Cottrell again."

She feels betrayed, but also protective. This illuminates so many little things about their lives together. Park has willingly gone to therapy on and off throughout their marriage, jokes that this is why he is so stable. It's why he encouraged her to, as well. He never said he started going as a child. She just assumed it was something that started after Melanie's death.

Now, the pattern revealed, she finds it disconcerting. Girl goes missing. Park goes to therapy.

How many times has this happened?

Perry's hand sits lightly on her foot. "That's why I didn't

come back, Olivia. What was the point? You've always been his. And from what I know, you've wanted it that way. If you didn't, you could have reached out. You could have asked me to come home."

Olivia doesn't like the way this is headed. She is starting to feel fuzzy again, the pills kicking in. She takes a sip of the water.

"Is there anything else out there that the media can dig up, Perry?"

"Yes, *Perry.* Since you're so prescient about everything in my life, why don't you answer that for my wife?"

Park is standing in the doorway, arms crossed, fury bleeding off him in waves. Olivia can smell the alcohol; his eyes are red as if he's been crying. He hasn't changed his clothes since yesterday, is rumpled and hurting. She hates him. She loves him. She is torn, especially seeing the two of them in the same room. The intimacy of the conversation she's just had with Perry floods her with shame. Perry is not her husband. She has not shared her life with Perry. She has not loved and laughed and cried with Perry, not for a very long time.

She puts out a hand, calling Park to her, but he shoots her a quelling glance and leans more firmly against the doorframe.

"You're drunk," Perry says flatly. "That will solve things."

"I'm not drunk. And if I was, who cares. I'm an adult. It's my house. I'm not hurting anyone."

Lindsey pushes past her brother into the room. Her hair has come down from its bun and floats in white waves around her face.

"You guys, there's a bunch of media vans out front."

Park points a finger at her. "That's your fault, little sister. You talked us into your lawyer friend, who managed to hook us up with the one reporter in town who decided to dig into my life and ruin it. I think I'll let you pay for Lucía's services. I sure as hell am not."

Lindsey face falls, wilting under her brother's attack, and Olivia honestly doesn't know whether to laugh or cry.

"Lucía says we were ambushed and is already making noises about suing Channel Four. You want her to stay on your side for now, Park. She's going to fix this."

"How?" he roars, banging the side of his fist against the door. "Suing them won't fix this. We're going to lose everything because you talked me into sitting down with a reporter."

Lindsey is nearing her limit; Olivia recognizes her best friend is about to blow. Park always has been able to push his sister's buttons.

"We had very clear parameters, in writing, about how this interview was going to proceed, and the reporter broke them. She's in major trouble from all sides."

"It's too late. You've ruined everything!"

Perry is up and across the room in a heartbeat, wrestling Park into the hall.

"Stop it. Stop shouting at her. That's not helping."

"Oh, and you are? Here to help, *brother*? I bet you're the one who talked to the reporter in the first place. Told her all those things about our childhood so she could embarrass me live, on air, ruin my reputation, ruin our lives! With me out of the way, you can sweep in and steal Olivia from me. That's all you've ever wanted anyway, isn't it, Perry? Can't stand losing her, so you take me down—"

The diatribe is interrupted by the heavy, wet *thunk* of a fist connecting with flesh, and there is mayhem in the hallway. Lindsey rushes out to help, and Olivia shuts her eyes and leans back into the pillow.

She doesn't know who hit whom, though she assumes it was Perry smashing his fist into Park's mouth to shut him up. She doesn't blame him; she would have too under that blistering attack. Park's weird possessiveness of her hasn't reared its head for so long, but it isn't fair to blame Perry for everything.

He hasn't even been in the States, much less have had time to correspond with a reporter. She's not happy with Lindsey and Lucía either, but taking it out on Perry is counterproductive.

A small thought wanders into the back of her mind. How *did* the reporter find out about these things?

Park comes back into the bedroom, fuming.

"Pack your things," he says tightly. "We're leaving."

She opens one eye, then the other. Park's face is a mottled red, and he has the beginnings of a black eye. *Spot-on there, Hutton*, she thinks with an internal smile.

"Park. You've been drinking. I'm hopped up on painkillers. We aren't going anywhere. You want solitude, kick Lindsey and Perry out. You need to settle down."

"I already did kick them out. The damn lawyer, too. But we need to get away, Olivia. Press are all up and down the street, and they are baying for blood. My blood." His voice is shaking, full of rage and pain and horror. She feels even worse for her transgressive thoughts.

"Well, you certainly can't drive, and neither can I. So lock the door, shut off the lights, and come to bed. We'll fix things later."

"It's barely noon."

"I know. But I can't stay awake a moment longer, and you need to sleep it off."

He stares at her for a moment, then surprises her by bursting into noisy tears. Park never has been a good drunk.

"Park?"

"It's just not fair," he gasps out, coming to the bed and plopping down, hard enough to jolt her. She lets out a squeak of pain that he doesn't notice. He lies by her side and swipes at his eyes. "I can't believe Perry hit me."

"He was defending Lindsey."

"He was defending you, the asshole." The heat has gone from his recrimination. The tears have stopped, too. He smells of Scotch and man, and she is as comforted as she is repelled. It's been a thing with them lately, something in her chemistry that doesn't enjoy his scent anymore. Hormones. Maybe some weird, basic, ancient biological response to the miscarriages; her body somehow knows he can't provide her an undamaged embryo and doesn't want her to couple with him again. The urge to procreate is so ingrained she wouldn't be surprised to learn this biochemical reaction was a verifiable medical phenomenon.

"We need to get away," he says again, softer now. "I can't think straight with all this noise. I need to keep you safe. Whoever has been breaking in here—"

"Your son," she interjects. "Your son, not whoever. You need to start realizing there is no escaping. Not really. We have to stay, and we have to deal with things. But for now, I need to sleep."

The house phone rings. It has been ringing for an hour now, the media wanting to talk, wanting a quote, wanting to schedule interviews. Its incessant noise makes her shoulders hike up to her ears with each trill.

"I thought we were supposed to unplug it," she says. "Isn't that what Lindsey said?"

"Yes, but—"

"I don't even know why we have a landline. We have to be the only people in Nashville."

"You know exactly why. After the Christmas Day bombing, cell service was knocked out for three days. I'm not taking the chance of not being able to reach emergency services in case something goes wrong. And stop trying to pick a fight."

"I'm not."

"You are."

The phone takes a breather, then starts up again.

"I'm unplugging it," he says, striding to the wall and yanking the cord free of its plug. "I will not be railroaded into admitting I did anything wrong here."

"Did you, Park?"

"Did I what?" He waits, standing by the bed, looking down upon her with a mix of tenderness and aggravation that she's grown to abhor lately. She wants the fight, she realizes. She wants to have it out with him. To scream and blame and slam the doors. The words are out before she can stop herself.

"Did you have anything to do with that girl's disappearance? From your old neighborhood?"

"How can you ask me that? You know me. You know I would never—"

"Park. We're past the denials. That reporter got information from somewhere."

The change comes over him as sudden as lightning. He goes cold, lips tight together, face white with fury. She's never seen him so angry. If she wasn't hopped up on pain meds, she might be afraid of him.

"Oh, so you're going to believe a reporter over your own husband? Jesus, Olivia. You're the last person I expected to side with them against me, but I guess I don't know you anymore."

"That's not what I'm saying. I'm only asking if you know anything that you haven't told the police. You've omitted a lot of things lately."

His eyes narrow. "I know you're upset about the donor stuff. But to accuse me of murdering a little girl when I was a kid myself? How dare you?"

"I didn't accuse you, I just asked if—"

"No," he yells. "And screw you for even thinking it. I've never lied to you. Never."

"You lie to me all the time," she shouts back. "All the time. About everything. You say it's okay that I can't stay pregnant, you say we have enough money to handle things, you say you love me. If you loved me, you wouldn't hide these parts of yourself from me. If you loved me, you would open up and be honest. You wouldn't creep around and pretend everything is just peachy keen. And it's bad enough that you lie to me, but you lie to yourself, too. Ghosting for that nasty drunk?" A thought hits her, crystallizes sharply. "Oh my God. You're hiding. That's why you don't want to publish under your own name, you're hiding from all of these horrible things. You can fly under the radar here in Nashville, but if you were on the world stage, they'd dig it up. You're afraid of them finding out about your past."

His mouth is open in shock, hurt flaring in his eyes. He doesn't even try to deny it.

"I would never have thought you capable of this kind of deceit, Park. I see now that I was wrong. You are."

37

THE BROTHER

Perry does not want to leave the two of them alone, but he doesn't exactly have a choice. Park was raving mad, and Lindsey has done her best against him, but punching him seemed to have the desired effect. Park shut up and went cold as ice. Then he booted them from the house.

What a mess this is.

The media scrum lights up as they exit, shouting questions and sticking mics in their faces, but Perry muscles through and gets them to Lindsey's car.

"My house?" she asks, beeping open the locks.

Lucía is already working her phone and gets into the back seat, leaving the siblings up front. He hears her say, "Draft an injunction immediately. Tell Judge Phillips we're coming with enough paper to drown him. We're going to shut this down before it goes any further," and shrugs.

"Depends on how much Scotch you have," he jokes.

"Enough," Lindsey says grimly, easing away from the curb, careful not to hit any of the milling media, as much as he wishes she would.

It hurts him to see Olivia in pain. He didn't realize how strong his feeling were for her, still, until he saw her bruised and pale, trembling against the pain. This is not a good situation. He's feeling very protective of her, and it's not his place. It shouldn't have been him sitting at the foot of her bed like a loyal damn dog. He wanted to touch her. He wanted to kiss her. He wanted her, period.

He wants so much that he can't have, and now he's cursing himself for being such a fool. *You could have had her. And you walked away. You've stayed away. And now all your lives are a disaster.*

Lucía gets out of the car at her office, still going hard at someone on the other end of the line. She's promised to make things right, though Perry has no idea how she can, outside of a lawsuit, which will only draw more attention.

Lindsey lowers her window, calls to her. "It's going to be okay."

Lucía, face strained, nods, says into her phone, "Hold on," and presses the metal against her chest. "I know. I'm going to ruin that woman and enjoy myself while I do it. I am sorry, Linds. I'll fix this. I'll see you later."

She starts to leave, but Lindsey says, softly, "Hey."

Lucía glances at Perry, smiles, leans in briefly, and kisses Lindsey on the lips. She hurries away, and Lindsey gives Perry a shy glance, but he's grinning, ready to give her hell.

"My, my, little sister. An older woman. How long have y'all been together?"

"A while." She backs up, whips the car around and into the street. "We met at a Bar function, right before the pandemic shutdown. Created our own bubble. She's wicked smart and a lot of fun. You're not seeing her at her best. Or maybe you are. She can be a cutthroat bitch when she needs to."

"I'm happy for you. You could have told me, you know. You haven't mentioned her once. And here I thought you were languishing alone in Nashville."

"I wanted to see where things went. No reason to share every date I have."

"But Lucía is different, isn't she?"

"Yeah. She's different. I haven't told many people."

"Including Olivia and Park. Why? Olivia's your best friend. Why would you hold out on her?"

"Oh, she knows I'm seeing someone. They both do. It's just… they've had so damn much going on, and it's been so hard, so sad, watching them struggle, watching her lose baby after baby. I'm happy. I mean, really happy. Shoving that in her face seems counterproductive, you know? Especially because…well, we've had a couple of conversations about having a family ourselves. The idea of me getting pregnant while Olivia suffers…"

The thought of little Lindsey with a baby, with a smart, brave woman like Lucía by her side, makes him glow inside. "I think you might find that Olivia would be thrilled to have something to cheer for. And Linds, you can't hold off on something this important if it's your dream just because it might hurt her. She wouldn't want you to, either."

"Maybe. After today's debacle, Lucía will not be their favorite person."

"This whole situation is a disaster," he says.

The strain is back on his sister's face. "She's changed, you know. The losses have warped her. She feels like Park blames her for not being able to stay pregnant. She doesn't open up to me like she used to. She's retreated inside herself. And I can't do a damn thing to help her. Now all this." She waves a hand above the steering wheel. "Sometimes I think maybe she'd be better off in a different setup. With a different man. A different life."

A different man. Him. She should be with him.

"Whose side are you on? Our brother's, or your best friend's?"

"My God, Perry, there are no sides to take. I was just trying to explain why I haven't been shoving Lucía down their throats. We should get some food. I haven't been to the store, and I'm starving."

They swing through Zoës Kitchen, grab tubs of chicken salad, hummus, Greek salads, and lentil soup.

"Since when do you like hummus and goat cheese?" she teases Perry, trying to lighten the mood.

"You wouldn't believe the things I eat. My palate has become more refined from my cheeseburger-only days."

"Apparently so. Park hasn't grown as much. He still gets pale when I cut open a steak that's the tiniest bit pink. I prefer mine to moo, thank you very much."

Back at the house, sustenance on board and the plates in the washer, Perry pours them both a hefty Scotch and they settle in the living room, sprawling on the couch, a quiet and thoughtful silence surrounding them.

"Olivia asked me why I never came back," he says finally.

Lindsey sips her drink. "I think we'd all like to hear the answer to that." She kicks him lightly in the stomach. "Butthead. I've missed you, too. What did you tell her?"

"I didn't tell her anything. What good would that do now? Besides, I did come back, once."

Lindsey sits up. "What? When?"

"I don't remember the exact date, but it was before the Melanie Rich situation. Dad was going downhill, I'd spoken to him on the phone and he sounded awful. I knew Park was at school, so I wouldn't have to see him. I'd hoped to surprise you and Olivia, but her mom said the two of you were gone for a long weekend. So I saw Dad, and good thing I did, because he died right after that."

"I'm still furious with him for forbidding a funeral."

"Me too. Maybe if we'd all gotten together over his grave, things would be different between Park and me. Anyway, I didn't want to stay away like this. It's just how things worked out. I like my life. I love my job. I miss seeing you, but that's part of being an adult, I guess. We don't always get what we want. At least we have FaceTime, right?"

"Yes." He feels her slip away, thinking about something. "A long weekend with Olivia? I don't remember that."

"Linds, it was years ago. I doubt I remember everything—"

"No, really. I have an excellent memory. The Melanie Rich thing happened my sophomore year. I'd transferred from UT to Hollins. I was getting lost in the crowds in Knoxville, needed a smaller environment. I didn't come home at all that semester because I was trying to get my footing in Virginia. I definitely didn't go on any long weekends with Olivia. I didn't see her until winter break. By then Melanie was missing and Park was being harassed by the police. And Dad was such a wreck. Bah, whatever. It doesn't matter what I was doing. But if my big brother decided to come home from Europe, the least he could have done was call ahead and check to see if his favorite sister was going to be home."

"You're my only sister."

"Shut up, doofus."

Perry laughs. He's forgotten how good it is to be with someone who knows you inside and out and calls you on your bullshit.

"So, if Olivia had been here, what would you have done?"

He shoots the rest of the Scotch, enjoying the long burn into his belly. "Beg. Plead. Propose. Anything to get her to take me back. I was an idiot for leaving, but she pushed me away so hard I didn't know what else to do. I was hurt. Everything was great with us, and suddenly she put up a wall and wouldn't let me in. Next thing I know, she's marrying Park. I mean, I guess that's what she wanted all along—"

"It wasn't." There's a worrying note in his sister's voice.

He pours another drink. "I'm not drunk enough to hear this."

"Me either. Give me some of that." He tips the bottle to her glass, the amber liquid purling. She sips, closing her eyes, either in pleasure or against whatever she's about to say. "She loved you. She did. I'm sure she still does. The way she was looking at you when you were in her room today...trust me, the feelings are still there. It's just a really crappy time for you to be making a reappearance. You'll seem like an option, an escape. I know her, better than you, better than Park. Maybe better than she does. She's unhappy, the wheels are coming off, and here comes Lancelot, her unrequited love, just in time to pick up the pieces."

His traitorous heart takes a happy little leap. Maybe he wants to be the distraction. Again.

"Is she unhappy with Park? Or is she unhappy they can't have children? Because those are very different things."

"Both. I'm totally speaking out of turn here, but damn it, I love all of you, and I just want everyone to be happy. Park isn't happy, either. I doubt the marriage lasts. They've been on fumes for a couple of years now. They're just too stubborn to admit it. Now that he has all these kids? Hell, if I was in her shoes, that would be the last straw. I'd be out. I bet she bolts."

"Is he cheating on her?"

"No, it's nothing like that. They love each other. They do. But the stress of losing so many babies, it's been hard on them both. So hard." Lindsey chokes up, her eyes sparkling with unshed tears. "It's been hard on all of us, but Olivia... Jesus, Perry. I can't believe I'm going to tell you this. You have to swear to me to never, ever, say anything to her. But it might explain things."

His heart thumps hard, and he sets the glass on the coffee table. He notices the stack of books in the center are BBC companion pieces to some of their more famous nature shows, with photos Perry has taken inside. Did Lindsey buy them? Or Olivia?

"Explain what?"

"Lucía has told me a hundred times that secrets kill people."

Lindsey is struggling, and he puts up a hand. "Listen, nothing is—"

"She had an abortion."

"Lucía?"

"Olivia."

It takes a second for that to register.

"Why would she do that? Is she not miscarrying, she's—"

"No, Perry. In high school. After prom."

He sits numbly, waiting for the pain, her words a cut to his soul as sure as any blade.

"You're saying the baby was mine?"

Lindsey nods and the tears spill. "She swore me to secrecy, and I've kept her secret all these years. But now… Perry, I can't hold this weight any longer. It's tearing me apart."

He doesn't want to know this. Lindsey is still talking, purging herself, expecting to be shriven by telling the truth at last, finally, but he tunes her out.

Everything makes sense now. He is up and across the room, pacing. His long legs eat up the space and he is more like a caged tiger, back and forth in front of the fireplace. He wants to run. He wants to get back on the plane and leave. He wants to hold Olivia and cry for what they've lost.

Lindsey is staring into her glass as if the Scotch can fix everything.

"Why wouldn't she just tell me? I would have married her on the spot. Happily."

"Because she didn't want to hold you back, and she didn't want to hold herself back. She was just a kid, for God's sake. Neither one of you could have managed."

"But she could have told me. Let me be there for her."

"She was going to. She changed her mind when you didn't come back for Christmas. And then, you know. Life. Dad died, she was there for Park, and they got back together. I shouldn't have told you. She'll never forgive me. I don't suppose you could just forget I said anything?"

At his annoyed look, she smiles weakly. "Didn't think so."

He plops back down on the couch. "Why now?" he asks.

She swallows the rest of her drink. "Because I think Lucía's right. This secret is eating me alive, and Olivia, too. It's time. I leave it up to you whether you want to talk to her about it. I'll tell her I told you, and—"

"No. Don't. Please."

She cocks her head to the side like a puppy.

"It doesn't matter, Linds," he says. "There's nothing you or I can do to change what's happened. The past is the past. If she wants me to know, she'll tell me." He hugs his sister, wipes the tears from her cheeks. "You've carried this long enough. Let it go. I can bear her secret now."

She gives a shuddery sigh in his arms. "You're a good guy, Perry."

"Yeah, I know. I just have one question."

"Shoot."

"Does Park know?"

He feels her head move against his chest. "No. If he found out, I think that would be the end of them."

What is he going to say? How is he going to approach this?

Perry is good at breaking a major project into pieces, establishing a checklist of all the things that need to get done. Wrapping his head around the way his life could have gone if the woman he loved had been honest with him about her pregnancy? Not so much. There isn't a to-do list manager in the world powerful enough for this.

He takes Lindsey's car and drives to the track attached to their former high school. It's been upgraded recently, the chip seal dark and gleaming, the white lines freshly painted. It's deserted. He jumps the fence and sets a leisurely pace. He loved track in high school. Middle distance, long distance, steeplechase, all of it. He wasn't fast, but he could go for hours. He's stuck with the discipline, uses a good run to clear his head. But here, now, watching the sun go down over the trees, he is assailed by memories.

Their whole lives, but especially as they grew older, Park was the star, Perry was the backup. He was always fine with that. Perry had never been interested in having a crowd around him. He loved his camera, he loved his time outdoors, he loved his brother's girlfriend. It was enough. He didn't feel like he fit in—hell, who did fit into the high school ecosystem, really?—but he was happy, liked his classes, his friends. He dreamed of the world and was ready to get out there as soon as he could. A child, then, would have changed his trajectory dramatically, and he understood why Olivia had made the choice she had. If it would have been an upheaval for him, it would have been sailing the *Titanic* straight into the iceberg for her. A catastrophe for a young girl who'd slept with a boy only to wound her boyfriend.

He thought it was more between them, but when she'd given up and gone back to Park, Perry just assumed he was wrong. Now he wonders if the guilt defined her path as clearly as a runway of lights. Olivia was—is—a loyal person. The whole time they were together, he knew she felt guilty. Park got her first. Perry was always going to be second place.

Slap, slap, slap. His feet find a steady, comfortable rhythm. His mind calms. His heart, albeit broken, is steady and strong.

He is three miles in when headlights shine across the lot. The sun is almost down. He should probably head back to Lindsey's. Regroup. The run has given him some clarity, at least. He doesn't belong here anymore. This situation is not of his making, and it is getting out of hand. He has a life, an established life. And he has work to do. Major prep work for the climb. It's going to be a bear, and he needs to have his head on straight.

You should talk to Olivia before you go, his monologue chimes in. *You really should.* Maybe she'll want to leave with you, his heart chimes in, at which his brain laughs. *What could possibly be different now than it was then?*

He shouldn't be here. He doesn't belong here, in their lives. They all know it.

He follows the fence line to the parking lot, hops over. A woman is standing by the car. It takes him a second to realize it's the reporter who interviewed Park and Olivia. Erica Pearl. Her hair is in a ponytail; she's wearing jeans and sneakers, a windbreaker. Street clothes. There are no cameras, no news truck, only an ancient Land Rover parked three slots away from Lindsey's Tesla. Not even a purse, and he doesn't see her cell phone, either. She has come empty-handed. Her eyes are swollen; she's been crying.

"Go away," he says, clicking the button to unlock the doors.

"Mr. Bender. I'm sorry to track you down like this."

He stands tall. "No, you're not. If you've found me here it's because you followed me. I have no comment."

"Sir, please. My job is on the line."

"Then you shouldn't have broken the deal you made with my brother's lawyer. I can't help you." Perry yanks open the car door and slides in. The reporter gets her hand on the frame and holds tight as he tries to pull the door closed.

"Let go of the door. Now."

Up close, he can see the steel in the girl's face. Steel, guided by desperation.

"I know what he did."

"What?"

He releases the door, and she wedges herself in so he can't close it.

"I know what your brother did to that girl."

38

THE HUSBAND

Park thunders down the stairs, glancing out the front door transom as he does. The vans still line their normally quiet street. Attractive, well-dressed reporters hold selfie sticks with cameras attached, talking into puffy black microphones. The neighbors are out, milling around, necks craning, curious. Being interviewed, damn them. *They're such lovely people. They keep to themselves, don't make noise, always bring a nice dish to the neighborhood potluck. He's always out in that shed in the back, though. Heaven knows what he gets up to in there.*

His heart stings from Olivia's accusations. It's almost as if she hates him. His wife hates him. He has to get the hell out of here, but how? His car is in the garage, but the moment the door rises, the media will be on him. He can drive through them, though. Plow through them. Knock their sorry asses to the ground and grind the tires over their soft, pliable bodies.

He stumbles into the antique olive wood table in the foyer as he turns, making the lampshades tilt and knocking a small decorative glass bowl onto the floor. It hits the hardwood and snaps in half, the edges sharp. He hopes it isn't expensive. No, he can't drive yet. *Way to go, Park. Got yourself smashed and now you're a prisoner in your own home.*

Maybe he should have left with Lindsey and Perry, the bastard.

Maybe he should have done a lot of things.

He wanders into the kitchen, double-checks the lock on the back door. Though it doesn't matter much if Peyton Flynn has the keys and alarm code.

A thought permeates his alcohol-soaked mind. *Change it.* Yeah. He should have done that the moment they realized they were compromised. They aren't secure in here, not at all. The media might keep Peyton from trying to get in, but if they leave, he and Olivia are sitting ducks.

Will he come for them? Will he try to hurt them? Kill them?

That's one way to get through this—in a casket.

Park finds the security company information in the junk drawer and calls from the kitchen phone. After verifying his details fifteen ways to Sunday—Olivia is the organized sort and has the secure password printed on the pamphlet from the install—he tells them what he needs. The attendant is chipper. Clearly, she doesn't know about the fiasco that's happened today.

"Certainly, Mr. Bender. I'm happy to help you again."

"Again?"

Rapid clicking on a keyboard. "Yes. I spoke with you last month when you added the new passcodes. How is your cold? I hope you're feeling better."

Dread builds inside him. "I didn't talk to you last month. I didn't have a cold, either."

"That's odd. I remember it clearly. You were having a houseguest visit, and you wanted them to have their own code so they could come and go securely if you weren't there, but you didn't want to give them your main code. It's smart of you to do that, by the way. It keeps you more secure. I assume you want me to delete the secondary code now that they're gone?"

Park's buzz flees, chased away by the adrenaline rush. "What's your name again?"

"Emily."

"Emily. I'm going to have to call the police and have them talk to you. You probably need to loop in your supervisor, too. Someone impersonated me to change the security code, and I believe they've been breaking into the house." A tiny gasp from Emily, who he can only imagine is feeling some serious panic about now. A feeling he understands; his own stomach is butterflies and cramps. "What other changes did the man make to the account?"

He hears typing. "You—he?—ordered new cameras. I show that they were delivered on Monday."

"I never received any cameras. Anything else?"

"The door chimes are disabled. The delays—pretty much everything about how the system reacts to opened doors and windows was altered. I made notes. We always make notes. You—he—said you were concerned about a break-in down the street and wanted to make sure you were safe." Typing again. "You also changed the safety passwords."

Park blows out a breath. "You mean the one I use if the alarm goes off and you call to see if it's a false alarm or if I'm in danger?"

"Yes. Um… I'm going to get my supervisor now. Can you stay on the line?" At his affirmative response, Muzak floats through the speaker. He knows the song, a Nirvana hit from the '90s. Rendered in symphonic piano, it feels almost upbeat, happy.

Clever bastard. What is his son planning?

The door chimes. Something so ubiquitous, so ingrained,

that he hadn't noticed they weren't working. He opens the door to the garage just to be sure and no, nothing. Damn.

He looks at the security company pamphlet, anger blooming. Olivia's hyper-organization suddenly seems foolhardy. She's left the details of their security system available for anyone to find. Thank God he thought to call. He is saving them from sure disaster.

"Mr. Bender?" A brisk, deep voice come on the line. "Fred Westgate. I own the company. Emily tells me we have a problem. You understand that I can't take any chances here, so I've dispatched the police to your address. In case they call this a false alarm, I'll make sure you aren't fined by Metro."

Just what Park needs with the media camped outside, more cops rolling up. But he is solicitous because he needs Fred Westgate's help. "That's fine. I was going to call them myself."

"Good. This is an unprecedented breach, sir. I assure you this isn't the kind of thing that happens with my firm." The thin wail of a siren bleeds into the kitchen.

"I believe the police are nearly here. Would you mind holding a moment? I need to make another call."

"Sir!" But Park sets down the phone, ignoring the sputters from Westgate for a moment while he digs Osley's card from his wallet. He dials on his cell, and Osley answers right away.

"Mr. Bender?"

"You put my number in your cell phone, Osley?"

"I thought you might reach out. Never know. What's wrong?"

"The police are on their way here, because it seems Peyton Flynn has hijacked my security system and has been breaking into my house."

Osley curses. Park hears mumbling, then, "I'm on my way."

Park ends the call and picks up the house phone. "Sorry, needed to call the guy I've been working with at Metro, get him out here, too. How much security footage do you have from my home?"

Westgate sounds incredibly relieved that Park is back on the line with him. "Enough. I've been accessing it, but you're going to have to confirm your identity with Metro before I go further."

"Fair enough." The sirens are louder now. Park goes to the front door, looks out the left sidelight. Once this is resolved, he's going to rouse Olivia and get a damn police escort out of his house. Get her someplace safe. She might hate him, but he still loves her, still wants to care for her. They have been compromised here. Park knows enough about these things to recognize danger when he sees it.

It hits him then. This whole scenario feels…familiar. Something… Has he read this setup before? Worse, written it? It's a ridiculous phenomenon that he doesn't remember everything he's ever cooked up, but he's written ten books for Barty (*that nasty drunk*, God, Olivia), and drafted three more. He racks his brain—is this something he's done? Has he read it in another story? It makes a perverse kind of sense; how could a kid come up with this by himself? How could he be so devious? Where had he come by this sort of brain?

You gave it to him. You're the devious one. You've been living this dual life for years, one part of you present and accounted for, another fantasizing ways to kill and maim for the entertainment of others. It doesn't matter if it was written before or not. You gave him this identity in his very genes.

Knocks sound on the door, and he opens the heavy wood to see two patrol officers, blandly interchangeable with crew cuts and overdeveloped biceps. Among the crowd, phones are held in the air, frantically documenting this new development.

"Mr. Bender?" one says.

"Yes. Please come in. Detective Osley is on his way as well."

The cops step inside and Park leads them to the kitchen,

handing the landline to one of them while he digs his license from his wallet, only partly listening to the Q and A between Westgate and the cop.

Bona fides established, the cop hands over the phone. Westgate, now utterly solicitous, says, "I'm sending my best tech over to redo your entire system, Mr. Bender. It will be a couple of hours. I'll upgrade everything for you free of charge as well. I assure you this isn't how we do business. I apologize."

What he's really saying is *please, please don't sue me*, but Park has bigger problems at the moment than going down that path.

"Thank you. We'll talk again." He clicks off the phone and puts it on the counter.

"Thanks for coming," he says to the cops. "I need to check on my wife now." He points them toward the door, but they stubbornly hold their ground.

"Detective Osley told us to stick around, sir. Seems like you've got a few issues today."

"Fine," Park says, starting for the stairs. "Help yourself to some water. I'll be back in a moment."

When he hits the stairs, though, he sees Osley striding up the walk wearing his boots and hat and gold glam sunglasses. His style screams country music superstar, not homicide detective. Park opens the door and intercepts him.

"This is completely out of hand," he says, waving toward the crowd outside. "You have to get these people under control. They're a danger to my family, to the neighborhood, and—"

Osley slides past him into the foyer. "Good to see you too, man." Osley flashes him a smile. He follows Park to the kitchen—their de facto war room. He greets the patrols and dismisses them. "Go get the media out of here, would you? They're becoming a nuisance."

Happy for something tangible to do, the two men depart with alacrity.

Osley stows the sunnies in his pocket, one temple in, the

frames dangling across the man's muscled chest like a sunburst. "Wanna tell me what's happening?"

Park does, quickly.

Osley whistles, long and low. "This kid's been sneaking around you for quite a while, hasn't he? How do you think he found you?"

"Has to be Winterborn. Or maybe that Discord group my daughter set up?"

"More likely he matched to you on the DNA site and decided to look up dear old dad for shits and giggles. Developed a fixation. Which would answer why we've found a fresh match—we've got his DNA in the system, and the ancestry database lawyers agreed to share what they have. We catch Peyton Flynn, we do a DNA test, and he matches, we got him dead to rights for Beverly Cooke's murder. Got any coffee hot?"

"No. I don't."

"You should make some. You tied one on?"

Park shrugs. "Shit morning."

"Yeah. I saw the presser." Osley moves unerringly toward the cabinet with the coffee, expertly pulling together the pot and setting it to brew. Park assumes he must have seen Olivia do the same. It's a violation, the cop's familiarity with his home, his life, his thoughts. He wants to rush the man, throw him to the ground, stamp on his head a few times, but stays put. He needs a drink. Badly. But coffee will help, too.

"Yeah, well, I got ambushed."

"No idea where she dug up the St. Louis story?"

Park stiffens. "No. And it's totally horseshit. I had nothing to do with that girl's death."

Osley only says, "Hmm," which is maddening.

Blustery now, Park spits out the words. "I want to know what your people are going to do about keeping my family safe while you search for Peyton Flynn."

"Hmm," Osley says again, but his booted foot is tapping.

Nervous energy, a tell. If Park were to sit down across from him at a poker table, he'd only have to listen for the thick *tap tap tap* of Osley's cowboy boot to know when the man was bluffing.

The coffeepot is now full of steaming dark brown liquid, and Osley helps himself to a cup, stevia, creamer. Takes a slurp, then raises a brow inquiringly.

"Yes," Park says, annoyed to no end when Osley makes him a cup light, with two packets of stevia, like he'd seen him do enough times to make an impression.

Osley joins him at the table, pushes the cup across the wood. "Listen. This is a weird case, no mistake. Personally, I believe ya. You've gotten the short end of the stick, and that's not cool. I don't know if you should be happy about finding all these kids, but the rest, from what I've seen, you've just been cursed with some seriously bad luck. It's all circumstantial coincidences as far as I'm concerned." *Slurp.* "It's Moore who's got her firebrand lit. That girl is serious about her shit, you know what I mean?"

Park sighs and sips the coffee. It's good. Damn good. But he's not going to say that aloud.

Osley keeps on with his soliloquy. Park can't tell if he's playing good cop or if he actually thinks Park is getting railroaded.

"So we got a lot of facets, right? Kid you've never met is stalking you. He's been in your house, he's stolen things from you, he's left flowers for your wife. He's been lying to his mother for months, so I'm thinking he's got a plan. He's building up to something. He's already killed one woman that we know of and has taken another. Might be he kills her, might not. I surely pray we get to her before he does. But then what?"

"He comes for Olivia again."

Osley touches the side of his nose. "Bingo. He comes for Olivia again. But I don't think he wants to hurt her. He's had a lot of chances to hurt her. My gut instinct here? He's a boy in love. Was he in love with Beverly Cooke and she blew him off, so he killed her? I don't know, but now that we have this information about the security system breach, I can go back to Mr. Cooke and look at things from a different angle. Same with Ms. Kemp. I can talk to Ms. Wilde-Kemp and see what she knows. So while this is a scary, frustrating thing, it's also a big help to the case."

"Why them, though? Why Cooke and Kemp?"

"Why does a killer ever choose his prey? Something about them attracts him. Looks, attitude, whatever, they send off some sort of silent bat signal the killer claims to be helpless against. We're pretty sure he's been following along his mama's private Facebook group for women who've used sperm donors, so chances are the two said something that triggered his interest, or they have a certain look. You write this stuff. You know how to build a victimology, yeah?"

"Jesus."

"Don't think he has much to do with this, son."

"Did you actually just call me 'son'?" Park is still slightly tipsy, and this makes him want to giggle. "I must be a decade older than you, at least."

"Probably not. I take care of myself. Anyway, not the point. I'm trying to separate out the weirdness of you having all these kids from the facts, but I've gotta wonder if our friend Peyton is jealous of his siblings, and that's what's driving a lot of this. Or if he's got a mommy complex. That's for the shrinks to play with, not me. Me, I just want to be sure your wife is safe, and I want to find Ms. Kemp before she turns into fish food."

Park's stomach turns. Should he mention Fiona Cross? He hears Olivia's voice in his head. *Now's the time to come clean. Stop hiding things from us.*

He fills Osley in, looking away from the accusatory stare.

"You might have mentioned this before. We'll need to check her out, too."

"I seriously doubt she is involved. Seriously, she went away the minute she realized I wasn't going to pony up. But just in case."

"Yes. Just in case. God, Bender. You really do know how to step in it, don't you?"

"A talent I've been working on my whole life," he answers with equal sarcasm. "So, what do you want me to do here?"

"Sit tight. I'll keep a car on the house. Let the security man load you up." He drains the cup, grins. "Maybe get yourself a new gun."

"You think he's going to come for us."

Osley's face goes deadly serious at last, and the cold remoteness in his eyes makes Park's gnads shrivel. "I do."

Park watches Osley stride to his vehicle, pleased to see the patrols have moved the reporters away from the house. The neighbors have abandoned their posts as well. The street is quiet, and his shoulders relax for the first time in hours. He has sobered up enough to start feeling fear, deep and corrosive, and knows he needs to get them both away from here. Maybe they should go to Lindsey's. Then there will be four of them to take on Peyton Flynn if he comes. Maybe he should leave town entirely. If they're careful, there's no way Peyton can follow them, right?

His cell phone rings, and he grabs it from his pocket. He doesn't recognize the number. He puts the phone to his ear. "We have no comment, and if you call here again—"

"Mr. Bender? I'm not a reporter. My name is Darby. I'm Peyton Flynn's mother. You are my son's donor."

39

THE MOTHER

Darby waits, unnerved by the silence. She's not used to calling people and having them go quiet.

"Hello? Hello, Mr. Bender?"

Scarlett watches her, so hopeful, eyes shining, luminescent, expecting this moment to be something magical, something profound, but Darby still hears nothing on the other end of the phone. The call must have dropped. Or Bender heard the word "son" and panicked. She doesn't even know if she blames him.

"I'm sorry, sweetie. I think he hung up."

Scarlett jumps for the phone before Darby can depress the End button.

"Mr. Bender? Are you still there? I'm Scarlett, Peyton's sister. I'm your daughter."

"I'm still here." There are no pauses, no silence this time. "Hello, Scarlett."

The voice is deep. Soothing. Not the frantic, angry challenge from a moment ago, but the voice of a man who is interested in hearing what she has to say.

"Mr. Bender. Thank you for staying on the line. We…we saw the interview," Darby says.

A small, humorless laugh. "I'm surprised you'd want to talk to me after that."

"I admit, I've had my doubts. But Scarlett… Anyway, I assume the media will be on my doorstep next. When they figure out I'm Peyton's mother, they'll be as relentless with me as they have been with you."

"Where is he?" Bender asks.

"I don't know. He told us he was going camping. He hasn't answered his phone. The police think he took another woman. I wish I knew where he is. I want to…talk to him. Before they do."

Talk. Advise. Beg. She has no idea what she wants to say, but damn it, she needs to talk to her boy.

"He's in Nashville, I know that much," Bender says. "My wife was in an accident. We think he brought flowers to the hospital, lilies. And left a vase of them at our house. But it's not the first time. He's been breaking into my house for weeks. We just discovered someone—I'm assuming Peyton—called my security company and changed all the codes. The entire system was corrupted."

Horrified fear shoots through her. "What?"

"He has the code to my house. We have him on video coming and going over the past several weeks. Olivia—that's my wife—thinks he's stolen from her. Little things that she hasn't missed until now."

Darby is awash in horror. Peyton always has had a penchant for stealing, but she'd written it off as a child's magpie tendencies to see something pretty or interesting and want it for themselves. She can't count the times she did laundry and found something unusual in his pockets. Normally little inconsequential things, but once, it was a diamond and pearl earring, and she had to track down the owner, one of the mothers at school. The woman hadn't been cool about it, had threatened to call the police. On an eight-year-old. Embarrassing, and Darby had laid into the kid, tried to make enough of an impression that he never did it again. Clearly, her attempts failed.

Thief. Rapist. Killer. Does she know her son at all?

Scarlett butts in. "Mr. Bender, I would very much like to meet you. I run a group for all the siblings who've matched together—we call ourselves the Halves. I know everyone would like to meet you, too, but maybe it would be easier if it was just the two of us, to start?"

"I'd like to meet you as well. I have a confession. When the police told me about you, I got access to your address. I drove by your house. I'm afraid I chickened out at the last second, though. Before I left, I saw you, in the drive. You're so beautiful. You look just like my mother."

Bender is still talking, gushing out the words, really. He's anxious, she can tell. "Her dad—my grandfather—had fire-engine-red hair. They called him Red, as a matter of fact. But that's only half the picture. Maybe you get it from your mom's side, too?"

Not from my family, Darby thinks. That red hair is all Bender. What other pieces of this stranger make up her daughter? She's beginning to wonder if anything they know is true, and curses Winterborn. How dare they cheat like this?

"No one on Mom's side has it. We always figured it came from you," Scarlett says, shyly pleased. "Could we come over to your house? Now?" she manages to jam in. Darby shakes her head and gives her a *what the hell?* look.

The pause this time is genuine, and Darby rushes to fill the void. "I'm sorry, Mr. Bender, that was inappropriate—"

"Park. Please. Call me Park. Yes, of course you can. Normally I'd suggest someplace more neutral, considering, but I'm waiting on the man from the security company to show, and my wife is hurt. I can't leave her alone." He rattles off the address, a tony street in Forest Hills, right on the edge of Belle Meade. So they've got money. Darby is annoyed at herself for the thought.

"Thank you. I'm looking forward to it," Scarlett says, and Darby is again struck by her daughter's maturity, her sudden shift from child to adult.

"We'll see you shortly," Darby says, and hangs up.

Scarlett is already bustling around the kitchen, grabbing purses and thermoses of water—ubiquitous to any house departure. As if they're going to the desert instead of across town.

"You're sure?" Darby asks, and her daughter nods, glowing with excitement.

"All I've ever wanted is to meet my father. It's not a knock on you, Mom. You're the best. I'm happy. I love you, and I love the life you've made for me. I've just always wanted a dad."

"Listen to me, honey. I can't promise you he'll want to fulfill that role. He might want to meet you, but you might only be a curiosity to him. We don't know what kind of person he is. Clearly, he has a history, a background, that's murky. We don't want to go in there assuming he's a choirboy and he's going to accept you into the fold like you're his own."

Don't steal her away from me. She's all I have left.

"He's a good person. I can tell. I can hear it in his voice. And it's only fair, Mom. I mean, he'll want to know more about Peyton."

Finally, her baby is back, the petulant naivete, the innocent belief that nothing bad can happen if you're loved, that at their heart, people are good, and don't mean harm. It's what gets children in trouble in the world, and especially online. Anyone can be charming if they choose, especially a predator.

She follows an ebullient Scarlett out the door to the car, biting back the words.

We'll see.

★ ★ ★

The Benders' house is a lovely, modern French country, the brick painted a creamy white with black accents, shutters and downspouts, and a large wood-and-glass door. Darby knows more about them now, knows the background especially of Olivia Bender, the designer, thanks to a quick bit of googling in the car on the way over. Scarlett drove with exaggerated care, the cautious motions of a girl about to do something life-changing, while Darby gleaned as much information as she could from the ether.

Sitting in the drive, Darby is more than a little intimidated by the sheer size of the place, the casual charm of the façade and landscaping. It succeeds in looking cozy and welcoming, and Darby knows it must have cost a fortune. She thinks ruefully about the two plastic pots filled with barely budded chrysanthemums from Home Depot flanking her front door, burning in the southern-facing sun because she always forgets to water them. Nothing about the Benders' house and grounds screams *I'm too busy to take care of my place.* Quite the opposite, it is somehow both summer lush and autumnal in spirit, everything placed just so, like something she's seen on the cover of *Southern Living.*

Maybe Olivia Bender could help rework a few things at their place.

Banish the thought, lady. You can't afford those luxuries, not without a job.

"Wow," Scarlett breathes.

"Yes, it's a very nice place."

Scarlett shoots her a look. "Oh, yeah. Pretty. I just meant... wow, I'm about to meet my father."

"You're about to meet your donor, honey. A lucky sperm doesn't make him your father."

"You know what I mean," she shoots back, getting out of the car.

Park Bender opens the front door, the smile on his face welcoming, but cautious. He is handsome, tall, and looks less than delighted to see them.

Scarlett takes one look and loses her head entirely. She rushes to him and throws her arms around his waist. Darby is shocked to see him wrap his arms around her daughter and lift her bodily off the ground in a huge bear hug.

They are both talking at once, talking over each other, and Darby feels such trepidation. All of their worlds are burning, yet here are her daughter and her donor, chatting and laughing like they've known each other for years. Out of the ashes of this horror show they're living, a connection has been made, one of joy and happiness. Maybe she's been wrong to withhold the knowledge of this man from her child all these years. Maybe Scarlett does need a father figure. Darby's rarely seen this level of enthusiasm from her daughter. It's remarkable, actually.

"Come in, come in." Park is beckoning to her. Scarlett has already disappeared inside like she owns the place. God, are they going to end up sharing some sort of custody? No. He has no parental rights. Though she can hardly stop Scarlett from hanging out here if she wants to. *I'll be at Dad's, okay?*

Damn it. She doesn't want this. She's never wanted this. They don't need him.

The inside of the house is as lovely as the outside. They get a little tour of the downstairs. He offers drinks, and Scarlett follows him to the kitchen, offering to help. He looks over his shoulder at Darby, and she swears his smile grows wider. *Look what we made*, he is thinking.

Look what I made, she replies in her mind. *She's mine. I did this without you.*

They settle in the living room, Scarlett still chattering like a jaybird, Bender responding with surprising enthusiasm. Darby takes a moment to breathe, taking a deep sip of her herbal tea and looking around, awkward and out of place. She shares two children with this handsome stranger. And handsome he is. She'd gotten a sense of it before, but up close, comfortable, in his element, the floppy hair and the light eyes and the breadth of his shoulders and that smile, God, that smile makes her remember just how long it's been since she was last with someone.

She realizes he's watching her, too. A strange pulse of desire shoots through her. Not cool.

She sets down the cup. "Mr. Bender—"

"Park. Really."

"Park." The word is hard on her tongue. "We should discuss next steps."

He shrugs. "The police are all over this. They'll find Peyton soon, I suspect. I'd…like to meet him. I know that might not be something you're interested in pursuing, and I understand if you want me to keep my distance."

Darby is on edge, and this gracious offer upsets her. "And if he's a murderer? If there's something inside him so broken that he's actually done these things they claim?"

"I've been thinking about this a lot the past few days. If what they say is true—and I hope to God it's not—I condemn what he's done. But he's still of my blood. You shouldn't have to shoulder this alone."

He reaches over and squeezes her knee, and Darby is flooded with confusion, and not a little gratitude. *If* what they say is true? "You don't think he did this?"

"Innocent until proven guilty. I have a little experience with being falsely accused. If he didn't do this, we will fight to keep him safe, and out of jail. If he is guilty, well, we'll cross that bridge when we get to it. Together. If you'll let me stand by you, of course."

Scarlett is beaming. This version of a father is exactly what she's been dreaming of. Park Bender certainly knows how to be the knight-errant for them both, doesn't he?

"We have to find him first," Darby says, burying her nose in the tea.

"Find who?" A soft voice comes from the doorway to the living room. Olivia Bender is even more bruised than this morning. Her arm is in a sling, but she's fashioned a vibrantly colored scarf to cover the standard hospital blue, and her hair has been freshly brushed.

Park jumps to his feet. "I thought you were asleep." Is there the teensiest bit of accusation in that tone, or is Darby imagining things?

"I heard voices. Are you going to introduce me to our guests?"

Yes, there *is* an edge. Uh-oh.

"I'm Darby Flynn, and this is my daughter, Scarlett. My son is Peyton Flynn."

Scarlett waves from the corner of the couch. "Hello, Mrs. Bender. Your home is so beautiful."

"We thought we should get together, come up with a plan for how to deal with the media going forward," Park says. Darby shoots a glance at Park. That's news to her, but of course he has an ulterior motive for inviting them into his life. "I was going to wake you. Are you hungry? We can all have dinner. I'll call for takeout. Pizza?" He smiles knowingly at Scarlett—apparently, she's already managed to share her favorites with her father.

Olivia Bender says nothing, a parade of emotions jetting across her delicate and bruised face. She turns without acknowledging them and disappears back up the stairs.

Park laughs, but it's uncomfortable now. "I should, um..."

Darby stands. "We need to be going anyway."

Scarlett cries "Mom" in that crazy multisyllabic manner she's picked up, and Park's face breaks into another smile at the word.

"No, no, please. Stay. We'll order pizza and talk. Let me just speak with her. I'll be right back."

He takes the steps two at a time.

"Isn't he amazing?" Scarlett asks dreamily. "I'm so glad we're going to stay for dinner. This is the coolest."

The coolest. Right. Darby may be rusty in the relationship realm, but she's pretty sure Olivia and Park Bender are about to be kaput.

40

THE WIFE

Olivia is very glad for the painkillers, because while they aren't really fixing the pain in her collarbone, they're dulling the agony of seeing that woman and her pretty kid sitting downstairs in her living room, drinking tea out of her good wedding china cups—*What the hell, Park? Why are you trying to impress her*? How have they even ended up here? And why is her husband sitting there glowing, surrounded by his new family, looking at his wife as if *she* were the interloper to their newfound happiness?

Olivia can't take this. It's an affront. She knows there's no getting around Park meeting his biologicals, but to invite them over for tea, to invite them into their house, without checking with her first? It's the final slap in the face, and she is done with this nonsense. She's so out of here.

She grabs her Tumi carry-on from behind the closet door—

thank goodness it's so light, she can manage it one-handed. She gathers clothes—flowing pants that won't be hard to pull up by herself, a long skirt, two button-down tops, tanks, and a cardigan. Bras and undies, and on a whim, she grabs her swimsuit from the bottom drawer. That's what she's going to do. She knows exactly where she's going. The crazy cat lady has given her the greatest possible gift—an escape hatch. How Annika knew Olivia would need it, she has no idea, but thank God for the kindness of semi-strangers.

Back to the closet for a cover-up, five minutes in the anemically sterile bathroom gathering necessities, and she's almost ready.

She goes back into the closet and wrestles open the small stepladder that allows her to get to the top shelf, where her tall boots are stored. There is a jewelry safe on the shelf, locked with a passcode. Balancing carefully, she inputs the code and opens the door. There's something she doesn't want to leave behind, just in case.

She removes the travel case she uses for her jewelry, tosses it into the bag. Reaches deeper inside. What she's looking for is under the set of pearls she inherited from her grandmother, a choker comprised of sixty-five three-millimeter perfectly matched white pearls as exquisite as it is old.

The space is empty.

Her old journals are gone. The photo of Melanie Rich that was left at the Jones build, the one she snuck from her purse into the safe, is gone. And with them, a worn envelope, containing a single-page letter, addressed but not stamped.

Before she can panic fully, Park shows up in the closet.

"What are you doing on that ladder? My God, Liv, get down."

She slams closed the safe door and presses the Lock button. It bolts securely with a throaty electronic whisper, and she carefully gets down off the small ladder. Her heart is pounding.

"What do you think you're doing?" Park demands, waving a hand toward her suitcase.

"Leaving," she replies.

"You're in no shape to drive."

This infuriates her even more. Park doesn't say *no, don't go.* He doesn't say *Olivia, please, let's talk*. He simply comments on her state of intoxication—which happens to be low at the moment, the adrenaline making her completely lucid.

"Get out of my way."

"Why are you so mad?"

She stops dead and stares at him.

"Really? After all these years, you have no idea why I might be upset? God, Park. You really are something."

She manages the zipper on the bag, but tying her sneakers is a bridge too far. She finds an old pair of Birkenstocks and slides them on her feet.

"Is it Scarlett? Come on, Olivia. You aren't being fair. I didn't ask for any of this."

"Did you even think to check if I was okay with you hosting a tea party with those strangers?"

"Strangers? Scarlett is my daughter."

The dagger is brutal and swift, and leaves her incendiary.

"They're complete strangers. They could be lying. You have no idea."

"She looks like my mother, Liv. And Lindsey."

"How nice for her."

"What's wrong with you? I've never known you to be petty before."

"Petty?" Olivia laughs. "Yeah, you caught me, Park. That's what this is, me being petty. After all the lies, you dare to push me even further? Throwing your biologicals in my face? Enjoy them." She moves past him into the hall, ignoring the ache the weight of the bag is causing in her neck and arm.

"Honey, you can't just leave. Peyton is out there. It's too dangerous."

She pays no attention to him, bumbles down the stairs, the suitcase smacking her left knee. Her purse and keys are on the table in the foyer; she gathers them and heads out, ignoring the startled looks of the two women in the living room. She goes straight out the front door, punches in the code to raise the garage door, pops the trunk on Park's BMW, and throws in the bag before sliding gingerly behind the wheel. She'd much rather drive her Jeep, but it must be at the shop getting the windshield fixed.

Park stands on the porch, at the top of the stairs, watching, no longer trying to stop her, his expression unreadable. Is he happy she's leaving? Maybe. He has a new family now. Why would he need her?

She flips him the bird and is off.

Screw Park Bender. She is not going down this road with him again.

The drive takes a little more than seven hours. She frets most of the way. Not only because she's pretty well certain that her marriage is over. The journals are one thing—it's possible they've simply been misplaced, that they have somehow gotten mixed up with Park's. She has carried them with her for decades, started when she was little and working her way into adulthood, then marriage. She has one by the bed that she's been using for the baby making records, but that she could happily burn. There will be no more baby making. She is never going to put herself through that again. She will live her life, free, happy even, eventually, and be childless. The world will not end if she doesn't have a warm, snuggly, fragrant being to commingle with. It just won't.

Her heart breaks a little. She stands the pain. Relishes it. She is being forged; she will be stronger on the other side.

No, it's the letter that she's worried about. That's something she would never, ever remove from its hiding place.

Olivia stops once, south of Montgomery, Alabama, checking her phone at the gas station she finds just off the highway. Park has texted several times, but she ignores them, instead sends a note to Annika Rodrigue, apologizing for the late hour and that she is taking her up on the offer to redo the house. Annika is, unsurprisingly, thrilled.

Yippee! We've already headed back to Nashville, so you'll have the place to yourself. All I ask is no grass mat. It's just too ironic for me. The rest is up to you. What do you think we can do with 150k? Though I did promise a blank check...

Perfect. No grass mat and a starting budget of $150,000 leaves a broad canvas to play with. She'll be able to source materials from new places along the beach, will live in the reno, as much of a pain as that is. *This is freedom, she reminds herself. The media will have no idea where you are. Six weeks, maybe eight, and you'll have most of it finished. Then, and only then, will you talk to Park. And Perry is off your radar for good. You just can't drag him into this again. It's time to go it alone.*

She feels a spike of pain thinking about losing Lindsey but knows in her heart of hearts her best friend is going to side with her brothers. With her family. It's what Olivia would do in her place.

The pain and planning settle her. She eats a granola bar and drinks a Coke Zero to stay awake the rest of the way. It's after two in the morning when she arrives, yawning and exhausted, her shoulder throbbing.

Annika's house is in Alys Beach, a popular place to have a second (or third) home among the Nashville aficionados of the

30A beaches. A European-style enclave, the houses are nestled together as if they were perched on a Mediterranean hillside instead of the flatlands of the Gulf's beaches. The exteriors are a pristine Greek white; the interiors are designed by a veritable who's who of Olivia's world. Honestly, she's been dying to get down here and make her mark. Who knows, maybe she'll move here, live among the white-peaked homes and sparkling blue waters.

She finds it—the biggest one on the street, naturally; Annika is made of money and then some. The code works. She stumbles into the foyer, drops her bag, makes sure to lock the door behind her. In the darkness, she can hear the ocean lapping against the shore. She follows the noise out onto a deck that juts over the house-edge of an infinity pool. There is a boardwalk just beyond the gate; solar lights glow along the wooden path to the beach. The air is soft and sultry, smells of brine and limes and a hint of mold, that unique scent only found oceanside.

She inhales deeply, letting the aroma and the calm permeate her body and skin inside and out.

Yes, she can escape here. Leave her marriage, leave her business, leave her friends.

Leave her life.

Start over.

41

THE MURDERER

He's always loved open spaces. The peace, the quiet, the stillness. He stands at the entrance to the rundown barn, watching the afternoon unfold. Birds chirp and flit in the trees. A frantic carpenter bee buzzes industriously by the door. A barn cat slinks through the tall grasses by the rusted tractor, happily stalking field mice that she brings back to his bed at night, dropping their half-eaten carcasses on his rough pillow before curling up on his legs, sated and purring under his ministrations. The day has been warm, the humidity heavy and thick, the sun traversing a hazy blue sky.

He doesn't have access to the internet, or to television. This place is as tranquil and calm as he can make it. There's been so much noise in his head lately, a buzzing almost as audible as the bees', and the more he's alone, the worse it gets. He'd searched for weeks to find someplace he could use to escape, finally found this place. It's perfect for his needs.

The barn floor is littered with tools, chisels and plowshares and old bits of harness. It has been deserted for years, and he's made it as cozy a home as he can, sweeping away the moldy hay to make room for his things. The television in the corner—hooked up to nothing, there is no electricity in here, but a television always makes a space feel more like home. A small scratched café table and two cane-backed chairs. His old couch against the wall looking at the falling-down horse stalls—currently a woman reclines upon it, watching him with fearful eyes. His bed, the mattress on the floor, trash bags underneath it to keep it from being infested with bugs. The cat helps keep down the insects, though ants climb over him in the night sometimes, maybe a spider or two; he had a bite on his side that got infected, but he knew his way around the first aid kit, and the fever receded the following day. He knows enough about curing sickness to be dangerous. All those first aid and CPR classes his mother made him take.

And then there are the treats. His prizes. He uses a Jenga-stacked set of old fence posts as bookshelves, lining things up tidily. Knickknacks and old clothes, silverware, jewelry trinkets, a book now and again.

He's gotten very good at getting in and getting out of houses. He'd started sneaking into places in high school, using talents he'd picked up at the hospital, especially how to bend a bobby pin and insert it into a lock. Later, he saved up and bought his own set of lock picks. He had a rake, but it was much too noisy for the quiet places he preferred to investigate.

That's all it was, investigations. Something he practiced because it was fun. Hanging out in the neighborhood, learning people's habits, when they would be there and when they wouldn't. Spying until he learned the security codes. The first time inside, getting a sense for things. The smells, the sounds.

Taking something little, something easily missed, assumed misplaced. Nothing that people would notice, especially not right away. The ubiquitous security cameras and doorbells make it harder, and he avoids those places if he can. But sometimes he is compelled.

Something captures his attention, and he looks toward the barn's interior. Ah. The woman is making noises. She screamed herself hoarse in the van that first day and is still too full of fight for his liking.

He doesn't like it when they scream. It's unnerving. Disruptive to the synapses. He's learned to gag them the moment he gets his hands on them so they won't break his eardrums shrieking.

The tape goes on the mouth first.

But this one struggled. Yelled and cursed and spit fire. She scratched him when he took her, managed to get the tape off her mouth, and wriggled like a worm on a hook in the back, shouting invectives at him as he drove down the interstate toward the farm.

Then you bind their wrists. They're so surprised by their mouths being taped that they won't fight for a moment.

"Just pull over and let me go. Please. I won't say anything. Just drop me off and leave. I swear I won't—"

"Shut up shut up shut up shut up!" he roared at her, which only made her scream louder.

"Why are you doing this? Why? I have a family."

He looked back over his shoulder. "If you don't shut up, I am going to gut you, do you understand? You will die a slow, horrible death, and you will be the only one to blame."

This shocked her into silence, then she started to cry. The tension left his shoulders.

Crying he could handle.

Screaming he could not.

Once he got her in the barn, he stayed away from her—she

was strong, and she was pissed. Like a hornet who's been swatted at too many times. Instead of giving in, she'd gotten enraged, and he could still feel that fury from her sometimes. So he left her alone until she was too weak from lack of food or water to fight back, and then he slipped in the drugs, and she's been nice and drifty since. He learned the trick on a forum. It works, too.

He brought her the remaining lilies, though they've all died now, drooping and stinking in their bucket. He thought that might make her feel better, having some flowers. He'd bought so many they wouldn't fit in the vase—God, he'd been so terrified seeing Olivia hit that deer. He'd saved her life, and he was proud of himself. He'd brought the flowers to the hospital and slipped them into her room while everyone was asleep—so easy to move around hospitals as long as you stay away from the maternity wards. Those are much too hard to infiltrate. But he likes hospitals. Likes being able to walk the halls and look in on the strangers. He liked it when he was a kid, when they would come look in on him, to make sure he wasn't scared, or didn't need someone to talk to in the night. The orderlies and nurses were mostly kind, to drop by and sit, to hold his hand. He was so young, everything scared him then. The hallucinations were terrifying; he shudders even now thinking about them. The gaping maws, the razor-sharp teeth, the sense of slipping away into the unknown blackness, of his soul disappearing. The monsters of his youth fill his nightmares still. Most kids are afraid of a cracked door or something hiding under the bed. He was afraid of the madness he could feel swirling inside him like a molten river. Afraid of what it meant. Afraid he would act on his urges. The fantasies, the visions, always coated in blood and fear.

Later, as a teenager, controlled, always controlled, he used to join his mom on the oncology ward sometimes. He always liked to sit with the kids, their big eyes, their bald heads. They just wanted a friend. Someone to treat them like they were normal, not sick. He got that. He totally got that. He was like the service dogs who came to the ward on occasion; he let them pet him and play games and fed off their smiles.

Now he is the one giving comfort where it's needed most.

The woman is making slightly different noises, and he interprets them in his usual compassionate way. He moves the portable toilet to the side of the couch, helps her sit up, eases off her pants. He looks away while she relieves herself.

He doesn't particularly want to kill her. Or maybe he does. These older women are so much harder to communicate with, but he's felt the need for this kind of companionship, of someone who can nurture him, someone who understands how strange it is, the dislocation of being the child of a stranger. Who better to talk to than the women who've chosen to have children this way? His mother explained it to him once, but he didn't feel comfortable really grilling her more.

So he became a part of her group, and he lurked. He watched. He read their truths and tried them on for himself.

He found out that some of the women did their own inseminations and some let doctors do it for them. Back to the hospital, more research. He knows as much about insemination and fertility as the doctors giving advice. All the information you need is out there in the world. He likes to investigate how things work, loves that he can with only a few clicks.

The woman is finished. He helps her reassemble her clothes and lays her back on the couch. He runs a hand across her hair. She flinches but doesn't fight. She is quite striking, but she isn't Olivia.

None of them are.

Substitutes. He knows enough about himself to know he is working with substitutes. That he has a mild Oedipal complex. He'd sensed something wrong the moment Darby had brought Scarlett home. Why couldn't it have been another boy? Why a daughter? A girl who even as an infant was the spitting image of her mother? He loved Scarlett right away, he couldn't help it, and of course he loved his mother, but he could not stand the attention the girl was getting. He needed to be the focus of his mother's world. He needed the interloper gone.

Scarlett was almost his first. The shame he feels over that is incredible. He very nearly killed his adorable little sister.

His mother was right to send him away. The hospital taught him so many things. He was able to learn how to control himself. If she hadn't institutionalized him, he would have hurt Scarlett. He knows this and is grateful. He loves his sister. He always has, but now he feels it genuinely—especially after finding out they are full siblings. Would that have mattered earlier? He was so young, but Darby had always talked to him like he was an adult. He'd thought Scarlett came from a different donor. But she hadn't. She was his full-blooded sister. Oh, Winterborn, you tricksters.

The woman is protesting through the gag, again pulling him from his thoughts. That's all he does anymore, think. Think, think, think. His meditation practice, the one he learned in the hospital and has carried with him ever since, has been falling apart recently because of all the thinking he's doing. You must let the thoughts rise and let them fall away. Envision a river. Every thought is a petal, dropped into the swirl of the water and washed away.

"What's the matter?" he asks. "Are you hungry?"

She nods.

"You've been very vocal today. I don't think it's smart for me to take off the gag."

She whimpers, and he can't stand that noise, so he walks outside, under the now starry night, and breathes in the crisp air. A cold front has moved through, the dry air chewing up the humidity. When did it get dark? He's lost time. That's not good. It's been happening more and more lately. Too much thinking, still.

He doesn't really want to kill her.

But it's not like he can let her go. Not now. They're too intertwined. He's going to have to do it soon.

He hears a branch snap behind him and turns just in time to see the chisel flying at his face. He is so shocked that he doesn't block it in time. The hard metal connects with his temple, and he goes down, cocooned by darkness.

42

THE DETECTIVES

Joey Moore is in the break room pouring herself a coffee when she gets the call from the switchboard that a highway patrol officer needs to talk to her. Dread fills her. Highway patrol calling homicide detectives means bodies found on the side of the road or in heavily wooded areas. They are never good news calls.

Is this it? she wonders, bringing the coffee to her desk. Another body? Another dead soul on her watch? It's been three weeks since Kemp disappeared. A slightly accelerated timeline from the four weeks between Beverly Cooke's disappearance and her body's discovery and retrieval from Radnor Lake, but close enough.

Steeling herself, she answers. "This is Moore."

"Hey, Detective. This is Major Darden Aldridge. Got something you might like to hear. We just picked up the Kemp woman outside of Waverly, near the bomb factory. My guys found her wandering down the highway, feet bare, totally out of it. She's dehydrated as hell, but she's intact. They're taking her to Three Rivers Hospital. I assume you're on your way?"

A waterfall of relief pours through her. "You bet! Thanks, man. I'll be there as quick as I can."

Moore calls Osley as she leaves the break room, crowing loudly as she moves through the room. "State troopers just found Kemp, she's alive and safe. Someone text me her partner's phone number. I'll update her from the road." There are riotous cheers from the squad room.

My God, finally, something going right. She couldn't take another dead woman on her watch.

But it begs the question.

Where in the world is Peyton Flynn now?

She picks up Osley; it's his day off, but he insists on going with her. He gossips about the Benders as they fly down I-40, lights flashing, cars moving out of their way.

The media has backed off, but word has it *Dateline* is looking to do a story on Park and his halves. Olivia Bender has flown the coop, taken a job out of town, redoing a client's beach house. The chick who reached out to Bender, Fiona Cross, is happily married in California and doesn't want anything to do with her child's donor. "It was a moment of weakness. I should never have reached out. My husband, Thomas, has adopted Brandon. He's his father now."

And surprise, surprise, surprise, Darby Flynn has spent quite a bit of time at Park Bender's place lately. Apparently, they've bonded over their shared children—one so bright and sunny, the other dark and twisted, and, of course, missing.

It's crazy how life meanders on. Tragedies happen. People die, or go missing, but unless you are primary in their lives, somehow, it fades from your consciousness. Those little shocks, those little moments of remembrance hurt, badly, at first. But even those lose their sharp edges over time. Pain is numbed. The immediacy of it tempered, forgotten. Hearts find ways to heal.

It's not that Joey has forgotten about Jillian Kemp; if anything, the opposite is true. She's been obsessed and searching relentlessly for both Kemp and Peyton Flynn. But the Nashville media has already moved on to the next sexy, bloody thing, the murder/suicide of an up-and-coming country music star. Nature of the beast, especially if the beast is pretty and young and wronged.

Out of gossip and recognizing Joey's reflective mood, Osley works the phone, gleaning what details he can, which are sparse. Kemp is still being treated; no one official has spoken to her yet.

This is it, Joey knows. Whatever has happened with Jillian Kemp, they're about to find out so much about their suspect. That the woman is alive is sweet icing on the cake.

Osley revisits the craziness at Bender's place, the alarm security breach, the intrusions, the theft, the flowers. Peyton hasn't been seen anywhere near the house; the security system upgrades have made sure of it.

"This kid is too smart for his own good," Osley says.

"He's a daredevil. He wants to get caught. He'll out himself, and we'll get him."

"You think?"

"Well, once we talk to Jillian Kemp, we'll know more. But yes. He knew he would be caught on camera going in and out of the Bender house. I get the sense he's been playing with fire just to see how badly it will burn. If his mother is to be believed, he's not stable. Which means we have to be doubly careful, because he could decide to go out in a blaze of glory and take all of us with him."

"Like all those fire metaphors, girl."

"Screw you," but she smiles. Osley always knows how to make her laugh.

They pull into the hospital parking lot exactly one hour and ten minutes after leaving Nashville, having made exceptionally good time—driving a hundred miles per hour down the interstate has a tendency to make that happen. Inside, they're directed to the emergency room, where they find Major Aldridge and a few other troopers hanging around in the hall outside a closed door.

Aldridge is in uniform, sports a military-grade high and tight, and looks like a former football player, thick through the shoulders, a solid neck, hands like dinner plates. He and Osley size each other up and find some common ground that leaves them both guffawing within moments. Granted, Osley could find common ground with a paper bag, the man's too outgoing for his own good, but that's fine. She wants cooperation. She's not paying attention to the details anyway. She's trying to listen to what's happening inside the room.

Stymied, she turns to the men.

"Has she said anything?"

"Not yet. We're—"

The door opens, and a doctor emerges. Fortyish, her hair is in an ashy-blond ponytail, and she looks like she might enjoy a glass of wine or two after work. Joey likes her on sight.

"I'm Detective Moore," Joey starts, but the doctor holds up her hand.

"I've seen you on TV, Detective. I'm Dr. Jones. Ms. Kemp is on the phone to her partner right now. As soon as she's done, you can talk to her. She is one seriously pissed off lady."

"Is she hurt?" Loaded question, but she has to ask.

The doctor grins. "Physically, no. But she does think she killed him."

"Could we get that lucky?" Osley drawls, joining them.

"Will," Joey warns, and he puts up both hands. "Just saying. Where's he at?"

"That's the issue. She's not sure. He's been drugging her, so she's a little squirrelly on the timeline. Just FYI, I gave her a sedative as well, just to take the edge off, so she might be sleepy.

She's undergone a major emotional trauma. She's tough, and she's as brave as they come. Regardless, I'm sure I don't need to warn you to take it easy with her."

"I will. You have my word."

They hear a voice call from within the room. "Dr. Jones? Are the police here?"

"See what I mean?" Dr. Jones smiles at Moore, and points toward the door. "Be my guest."

Osley hesitates. "I think I'll let you go in alone. Just in case… you know. I'll listen."

Joey does know. The last thing a recently traumatized woman needs is to come face to face with another strange man who must ask intimate details of her experience. Osley is a good guy, and she appreciates his sensitivity. She punches him on the shoulder in thanks and heads in.

The room is typical hospital, but the sun is shining outside, so it's filled with light and not quite as depressing as it could be.

Joey is pleased to see Jillian Kemp does appear unharmed. She's hooked up to an IV, and there's a finished plate of food on the tray by the side of the bed. A small pudding cup is the only thing untouched. Jillian notices her looking at it.

"I hate tapioca. It's a texture thing."

"I understand completely. I'm Detective Josephine Moore, Metro Nashville homicide. How are you, ma'am?"

"Alive. I didn't think I was going to make it out of there."

"I have to tell you, we're very happy you did. Your wife and son are on their way down. They're very relieved."

A smile. "I talked to Cici and Ellis a few minutes ago. The doctor let me use her cell." Silver sparkles in her eyes, and her voice is thick. "I didn't know if I'd ever hear their voices again. Best phone call ever."

"I can only imagine. Want to tell me what happened?"

Jillian shifts against the pillow, dragging the diamond-patterned gown higher up her shoulders. "He was actually very gentle with me after he got me wrestled into the back of his van."

Joey nods. The van... Sounds like this is their boy. It's Peyton.

"Can you describe your attacker?"

"He's young, with short dark hair. Tall... I mean, nothing really stands out except he has a cleft in his chin. And dead eyes. He seemed so...empty. Devoid of life. Except for when I was screaming. Then he lit up, from inside. It was horrifying."

They've got a six-pack to show her, assembled hastily and emailed to them while they were on the road. Joey slides her phone with the photo array onto the tray. "See anyone who looks familiar?"

Jillian picks out Peyton Flynn immediately.

"Okay. Thank you. Hang on just one second."

She steps into the hall, pulling the door closed behind her. Osley is waiting, brow raised.

"She ID him?"

"Yes."

"I'll take it from here," he says, phone already to his ear.

Joey steps back in the room. Jillian has pulled up her legs and is sitting with them crossed beneath her. She looks much more relaxed. The sedative must have kicked in. Joey can see the tips of bandages creeping around the edges of her toes. *She was barefoot...* Joey does her best not to blanch. Her feet must have been cut to ribbons by the time they found her.

"Is that him? Is that Beverly's killer?"

Joey shakes her head. She can't prejudice the witness by saying anything definitively. "I can't say one way or another at this moment, ma'am. We need to hear everything you've been through if you're feeling up to sharing."

Jillian shudders. "If it will help stop him, yes. Whatever you need."

"Thank you. I want to run through it all, from start to finish, but first... I know this might be hard, but I have to ask.

Major Aldridge said you think you killed him? If that's true, we need to go find his body, so as much detail as you can provide would be really helpful. How he grabbed you, how long you were in the van, things you saw, what happened while you were there, how long you walked after you escaped. We're going to go through it all, okay?"

"That's fine. I'm pretty sure I did kill him," Jillian says, voice quiet. "I hit him from behind. He was just turning toward me, and I caught him in the temple with a chisel. He went down and I ran."

"Were you in restraints?"

"Yes, zip ties. But he got distracted and went outside, and I've watched all the videos on how to break them. My hands were in front of me, thank God. I'd have never managed any other way. Normally he had my hands in the back, but today… yesterday? I don't know how long it's been. Anyway, I hit them on the side of the table by the couch he had me on and they broke. I was going to slip away, but I knew I needed to make sure he couldn't follow me. I snuck up behind him and hit him. I looked back once and he hadn't moved, and there was blood, so much blood."

"Head wounds bleed a lot," Joey says. "And that was a ballsy move. So, a chisel, a couch. What else did you see?"

Jillian closes her eyes, and her breath quickens, hands grasping the edge of the blanket. Psychosomatic response, Joey knows, to reinserting herself into the trauma. "You're safe," she says softly. "He can't hurt you."

"It was a barn. An old barn, abandoned. Falling down in one corner. There were stalls, five of them, and old, moldy hay. There were tools in the yard, which was dirt. An old tractor, completely rusted out. Inside was… He's been living there for a while, that I do know. He had a couch and a television, a table, a mattress, bedding. Lots of camping supplies, very tidy rows of canned foods and water." She opens her eyes. "He's meticulous, but spacey. Like, he drifts away when he's talking—and he talks, a lot. If I wasn't so terrified, I would have found it interesting. He talked about art, about psychology, legal issues. Nothing about himself, exactly, but I got the sense he's been in treatment before. Therapy. It was almost as if he was entertaining me so I'd be distracted from what was happening. That he was going to rape me and kill me, but if he was friendly about it, maybe it wouldn't be so bad. I got the sense that he was… lonely. And that freaked me out even worse, because then I couldn't get it out of my head that maybe he wasn't going to kill me, that he was going to keep me there forever. And Olivia Bender. He talked about her a lot, too."

"Really?"

"Yes. She's an obsession for him. He thinks he's in love with her."

Oh, boy.

"All right. Let's go back to the day you were kidnapped. Do you remember how he got you into the van?"

"It was parked next to my car in the parking lot of the gym. I always park on the far side of the lot so I can get in a few more steps. Under a light, and the neighborhood is so safe, there's never been anything other than a purse or laptop stolen from an unlocked car. I was putting my gym bag in the trunk and felt arms around me. He slapped a piece of duct tape over my mouth and wrestled me into the van. I fought, I kicked and tried to scream, but it happened so fast. A blitz attack." She sounds almost apologetic, like it was somehow her own fault for being attacked.

"Hey, he caught you off guard. It happens."

"Apparently," she says, drily, and Joey is again impressed at her fortitude. "He bashed me on the head, and when I woke up, we were driving, so I don't know how long I was out, but when I came to, I started counting. As best as I could tell, I was awake for at least thirty minutes before he got off the highway. And screaming as much as I could—I was hoping maybe someone in another car could hear me. That got him riled up, and he threatened me, threatened Cici, too. That's something I should have mentioned. He knew me. He knew my name, he knew my wife's name, he knew which gym I worked out at. I wasn't a convenient opportunity. He targeted me."

Joey knows this, though she takes notes as if it's news. He had a whole list of women, with all the private details they thought safe to share. Their hearts, their lives. All for a lurking stranger to acquire through the guise of friendship.

"Do you know why? Did he tell you?"

"He thought I was friends with Olivia. He said Beverly was, and he wanted me to tell him all I could about her."

"Are you friends with Olivia Bender?"

"No. I mean, I know who she is. She's done design work for people I know. But I wasn't about to tell him that. I made up a few stories and stuck to them."

Joey is impressed and says it. "You kept yourself alive sticking to that lie."

"Probably."

"Did he blindfold you at any time?"

"No. Which is what scared me most of all. He was planning to kill me, so he didn't bother hiding who he was. He kept my mouth gagged, and my hands restrained, drugged me enough to keep me low-key during the day, and at night…no, he didn't hide who he was."

"And when you got off the highway?"

"Another thirty minutes going slower, and then another ten over rutted, bumpy roads. He apologized for the rough ride. Can you imagine?" Jillian laughs. She actually laughs.

The combination of sedative, natural strength, an ebullient personality, and the adrenaline pump of rescue from a certain death is going to Jillian's head. She'll come down when her wife shows up, Joey knows. Break apart. When the depth of what could have been lost hits them. In the meantime, Joey needs to keep her talking.

"And he didn't touch you, all this time?"

Jillian's eyes cut away; her voice is low. "If he did, it was while I was drugged and asleep. I don't have any memory of it. I'm not damaged. He was careful."

Joey nodded. "Okay. Your memory may change as you come off the drugs. It may not."

"Let's hope it doesn't," she says, shuddering a bit.

"We can run tests, see if there's any semen or spermicide."

"The doc already took samples, testing for STDs, but I really don't know if he did anything. Not really. And with the baths—he let me take baths. The water was cold, but at least I was clean."

"Interesting."

"The doctor suggested Plan B."

"Do you not want to take it?"

Jillian shrugs uncomfortably. "I need to talk to Cici first. I was gone a while."

"If he raped you—"

"You don't understand what it's like. Building a family the way we have. It wasn't easy. I have PCOS—polycystic ovarian syndrome. Bad. I miscarried a couple of times." She searches Joey's face. "I'm going to take it, I think. But I have to work it out in my head, and with Cici. If he did, and if I am…it's just not as cut-and-dried as if he pulled me into an alley and forced me."

Joey is repulsed by the very idea, but that's her own experience speaking. She knows when to step away from a thread.

"Okay. So after you hit him, and you ran, what did you see? Forest? Lake? Pasture? Other farms?"

"Forest, mostly. I went past a lake. I heard the geese. There was a cemetery, too, on a hill. Not a big one, but at least twenty graves or so. It was sunset, getting dark, and I walked all night.

Flushed a deer or two but didn't see any people. I came out near a fence line and followed it, hoping I'd find the road."

Joey tried to keep it less an interrogation than a re-creation of Jillian's moonlit walk.

What did you see? What did you hear? How long did it take? Was there a path? Was the ground hard or soft? What did it feel like underfoot, damp, dry? How long were you in the brush before you hit the open road? Leaf-strewn or gravel? How long do you think it took to walk between the lake and the graveyard? Did you go over any fences?

They went on like this for several minutes, Joey gleaning everything she could, detail after detail. Jillian was fading by the time they finished, but Joey felt like she had a handle on where to start.

"I'm sure we'll speak again soon, Jillian. I have to go look for your assailant now."

She nodded, and her eyes grew distant. "I hope you find him. And I hope he's dead."

In the hallway, a trooper pointed her toward a staff break room, where she found Osley and Darden with a set of topographical maps. They were doing it the old-fashioned way, the trajectory being mapped with string and pencil to draw a hundred-mile radius around the spot where Jillian had been found.

Osley waves her over. "We're figuring a trajectory that led her to State Road 13, just before the AES explosives facility. That site takes up thirteen hundred acres, and if she walked from sunset to dawn, and passed a lake, we think she came from the southwest. It's pretty isolated back there. She couldn't have covered more than twenty miles, tops, and that's giving her a lot of credit. She's in damn good shape, but she was barefoot, so it had to be slower going. Darden's got his chopper ready for us to go do some flyovers looking for the landmarks she gave us. Maybe we'll get lucky."

He grins, a pirate's smile. "Wanna take a ride?"

43

THE WIFE

Blood. Olivia smells blood.

She drags herself to the surface. She is nauseated, in pain, and the thick, coppery scent makes her want to roll over and put her head in a trash can. Gorge rising, she goes to do just that, but finds she can't move. She swallows hard, twice more, then realizes her eyes are open and it is dark, so dark. Has she slept all day? This doesn't feel like her bed. It feels hard, and smells of gas and oil.

She tries to piece together what's going on, what's happening, but there's a huge blank space where her memory of how she got here should be.

Is she moving? The *thwack, thwack, thwack* of tires on concrete permeates the din of horror and she thinks, *yes, I'm in a car.* A car's trunk, she realizes.

All of this has processed in the space of three heartbeats, and now comes the panic, rising like a tidal wave through her body.

Breathe, she coaches herself. *Breathe.*

When the panic subsides a bit, when she feels like she has a grip on the reality of things, she assesses her body. Her hands are tied in front of her, not behind. A small mercy; her collarbone feels like it's taken on a load of shrapnel. She can't imagine how much it would hurt if her arm was twisted back. She is wearing her silk top and soft fleece pants from this morning—assuming this is the same day, of course. It's possible she's been drugged into oblivion for hours, days, she has no idea.

He's going to kill her. He's just marking time—

A horn sounds, sharp, loud, and Olivia jerks awake with a massive gasp, heart thundering in her chest. It takes a moment to right herself.

She's been dreaming again.

She's had variations of this nightmare since she came to Alys, but this one was by far the worst. The scent of blood commingling with oil, and the terrible pain in her collarbone, which has been mending well these past few weeks, these details are new.

She is healing. All of her. Mentally. Physically. She had her first period since the miscarriage, and it was as sad and awful to start bleeding again as she expected. But being alone, consumed with the work on Annika's house, helped dull the pain in her heart. Next month, she'll have an idea of when her cycle is going to start and be ready for it. It is freeing, in a way, to know that there is no possible chance of being pregnant outside of an immaculate conception. That was the hardest part of the past several years of trying to get and stay pregnant—the damn hope of it all. Hoping that this was the time. Hoping that the two lines on the stick would turn pink. Praying that they were. And when they weren't, waiting longer, three minutes, five, ten; dragging the stick out of the trash can hours later to examine the blank space under the light for any hint of color. Olivia had always stuck with the old-fashioned pregnancy tests. Somehow the ones that screamed Pregnant or Not Pregnant seemed too in her face. The two lines system was gentler on her psyche.

But no more of this emotional roller coaster. Next month, she'll bleed, and there will be no tests, no fears. No hoping and praying. Just a regular woman's body doing its monthly biological duty.

But these nightmares are getting worse.

She rolls out of the bed with a small yelp; the pain from the dream is explained—she's woken up on her right side. Her collarbone aches, her shoulder feels stiff. But it's progress that the pain didn't wake her in the night. It's felt better since she got the stitches out. She does her exercises quickly just to loosen things up.

The sun is rising, and she follows the liminal brightness to the kitchen, setting water to boil so she can take a cup of green tea out onto the deck and enjoy it. The days are growing incrementally shorter, and she knows vitamin D is the best possible remedy for dipping moods. Coming off the failed pregnancy, she was already living clean, but she's stuck with it. No caffeine, no alcohol. She's off the postsurgery pills, too. Loads of water, sunshine, fruit and green tea and exercise, and she's feeling more like herself again.

She hasn't been alone for such a long time. Hasn't been self-sufficient like this since she was a kid, between the Perry breakup and the Park reconciliation.

When she finishes the tea, she goes for a walk. This has become her routine—early to bed, early to rise, tea, walk. She's doing some of the best work of her career on Annika's place. Design is an art form like any other, and she recognizes the stages. She's moving into a new phase of her career, and she likes how it's going. If Picasso could go blue, so can she.

The sand is soft under her feet, packed perfectly for walking but fine-grained, like sugar. There is the tiniest hint of chill in the morning air, dew sparkling on the webs strung between the sea oats. Soon enough she'll need shoes for her rambles, but for now, she relishes the cool water and delicate sand. Seagulls swoop and scold overhead, and the sand pipers are out in force, tearing madly across the strand, zigzagging to and fro; there must be a huge field of periwinkles for their morning feast. She's been using the soft translucent pastels of the tiny mollusks' wet shells as her inspiration for the colors in the renovation. The breeze, gentle when she started out, has picked up, shifting to a more southern flow, eliminating the chill but causing her hair to whip, tangling around her neck and into her mouth. She's forgotten a ponytail holder, tucks it behind her ears and down into her shirt and soldiers on.

It is a mile and one half to the next major boardwalk, which is her usual turning spot. The sun is climbing steadily now, and she's broken into a light sweat. The outdoor shower will feel so good, and then she's going into town for supplies—the marble she ordered is in, she wants to take a look at the slab before she has it delivered, and the French oak for the ceiling should be in, too. She started in the kitchen and has been working her way into the rest of the house like spokes of a spiderweb.

The rug for the living room is next up. It gave her fits, but she's settled on a soft cerulean-and-cream antique Turkish from a store on the mainland; it will anchor the palette of the room and allow her to build off the look. The new doors open accordion-style onto the water view, and she's had four new windows framed and installed and painted the interior walls the same Greek white as the outside to make the space as bright and airy as she can.

A shell catches her eye, and a piece of sea glass next to it. Gasping with pleasure at the find, she scoops it up. It is a big piece, exactly the shade of Perry's eyes, the softest gray with a hint of blue, like the feathers of a tiny bird.

So is the rug.

So is the veining in the marble.

Shit. There she goes again. She's recreating her ex-lover's gaze in textiles.

She's so lost in thought about the color scheme that she doesn't notice the man sitting on the steps of the house's boardwalk until she's almost to the stairs.

"Olivia."

She jerks into awareness, gasps aloud to see Perry Bender in the flesh, as if she's conjured him out of salt and sand and wistful remembrance.

"What are you doing here?"

"Hello to you, too," he says, amusement in his voice. He doesn't move—not to touch her, not to get out of her way. He just sits there with that crooked smile she's been dreaming about in between the nightmares.

"I thought you'd be at the top of the Matterhorn by now."

"I thought I would be, too. But something came up."

"More important than work?"

She sounds sharp, she knows it, but he's caught her so off guard.

"Yeah." His face goes blank. "I need to talk to you about something."

"Come up to the house," she says, playing it cool, when inside her heart is throwing a raucous party, yelling and screaming. He's come for her. Perry has come for her.

The man she wanted to show up, finally has. And she has no idea what this means.

He's brought coffee and croissants from the bakery down the street, the pastry still warm in their bag. She pulls butter and jam from the refrigerator while he grabs plates and mugs. Their movements together are easy, comfortable, as if they've been satellite people rotating around a kitchen sun their whole lives.

The croissants are flaky and delicious, but she has no appetite. Perry looks drawn. Tired. She doesn't, she knows. The past few weeks have been good to her. Being away from Nashville, from Park, from the horror show their life had become is healing her as much as the clean food and exercise and sunlight.

"Have you been paying attention to the news at all?"

Olivia shakes her head. "I have been blissfully unaware of everything and everyone. On purpose."

"They've found Annie Cottrell. Her remains, at least. In St. Louis."

"You're kidding. After all these years? Where?"

"A drainage ditch by the baseball field. Buried deep in a septic hole. They would never have found her if someone hadn't talked."

Dread parades up her spine. "Someone, like who?"

"An excellent question. The police got an anonymous tip."

She tears off a piece of croissant. "Well, that's good, isn't it? Her parents must be so relieved to have an answer, finally. I can't imagine anything worse, not knowing where your child is for all those years." She shudders. "You came down here to tell me this?"

He runs a hand through his hair, forcing it back from his face. It's gotten longer in the past few weeks, curling at the ends. She has an absurd urge to run her hand along the same path.

"Well, in a way, yeah. The reporter, Erica Pearl? She came to find me just before I left. She said she knew what Park did in St. Louis."

"I thought you said he didn't do anything."

"I thought he hadn't. But this reporter, she has a different story. She actually grew up in our old neighborhood. Her mom was in our class. I remember her, Enola Johnson, now Pearl. She was a year behind us. She told her daughter she saw Park alone, days after Annie went missing, near a drainage pipe that led to our baseball field. The same place they just dug out the poor girl's body. She told the police, but no one believed her. And she saw him again, a few weeks ago. Standing in the same spot. And she swears he was there a few months ago, too."

"I'm confused. What are you saying? Park was in St. Louis? No way. I would have known."

"Would you have? You work away from the house. St Louis isn't too far of a drive, and an even quicker flight."

Olivia thinks for a moment. "I don't think he's flown anywhere. He doesn't like to fly, it freaks him out. We have to get him loads of Xanax. So no, he didn't fly."

"But he could have driven."

"Yes. But…"

He leans back in his chair, eyes sharp. "What?"

"I'm just trying to think. He did have to go to Jackson, Mississippi, for book research. Right after I got pregnant the last time. Research trips, they're part of his job. He was going to talk to some historian down there about something, I don't know. I only remember this particular trip because I was barfing all morning and he offered to cancel. I told him to go."

"The timing fits. He didn't go to Jackson. He went to St. Louis."

"You're just speculating. Besides, what are you saying, Perry?"

He pushes his plate aside. "First Annie Cottrell, and then Melanie Rich."

"You think Park killed them?"

"All I know is I talked to Erica's mother for a long time. She's unshakeable. She knows what she saw. And then there are the flowers."

"Flowers?"

"Even though they never found Annie, her parents have a grave for her, with a headstone, at the graveyard of the church they belong to. It has her name on it, Ann Elizabeth Cottrell, her birth date, and the date she went missing. They wanted a spot to visit, a place to be able to have some sort of closure. There were flowers left on her grave the same day Enola swears she saw Park. But here's the kicker. Someone's been putting flowers on Melanie Rich's grave, too. Every year, on the anniversary of the day she went missing."

Her heart thumps, but she shakes her head. "Perry, I'm not following."

"Park is sending flowers to the women he killed. He's assuaging his guilt. Or shoving it in their faces, I don't know."

"Perry—"

"Don't you see? He did it. We need to confront him. We need to get him to admit what he's done."

She sighs, breaks a piece of croissant into crumbs. "Do we, Perry? What good will it do? They will still be dead, and Park will have to revisit the wound that has ruined him. And then what? We get him to admit what he's done and the reporter or someone finds out and calls the police? He's arrested, goes to jail?"

"Justice is served."

"He's your brother."

"He's your husband. You want him to get away with murder?"

She dumps the rest of the coffee in the sink, crosses her arms, careful not to jolt the mending collarbone. "No. Of course not. But I don't see what we have to gain by diving into all of this. Trust me, I'm furious with him. I hate him, in so many ways, for the things he's done, and the things he hasn't done. But murder? This is Park we're talking about. He might be a liar, but he isn't a killer. He didn't kill Annie Cottrell, and he didn't kill Melanie Rich. He just doesn't have it in him."

Perry stares out to the water. Small whitecaps are breaking. The wind is picking up.

"I think this has to happen, Olivia. At the very least, we have to talk to him."

"Even you said you were with him when Annie Cottrell went missing. Unless you were lying, covering for him?"

"I wasn't!"

"Okay. So you know he didn't kill her. But if the police start digging into Park, and his alibi—who is you, by the way—you don't think they're going to dive straight into your life, as well? What will your bosses think about you being the suspect in a murder? I assume you have a morality clause in your contract? They'll fire you. And if you knew anything, anything at all…"

He doesn't answer, wrestling with this. He hasn't thought this through, she can tell. He's driving on instinct, fear. She presses her advantage.

"And Melanie Rich…they had a trial, Perry. Evidence. A man went to jail, and Park was cleared."

"But we know more. There's so much we didn't know before that we do now."

She sits down again, takes his hand in hers. "Listen to yourself. Why do you want to take him down so badly? I don't see what it gains anyone by tearing his life apart. Trust me, I wouldn't mind seeing him suffer, but not with this. Not with accusations that can't be proven. You have no proof at all he's the one sending the flowers. None."

"I can get proof. And what about his son? His son is a murderer. What about all the rest of those kids? Do you think he passed this murder gene along to them, too? He clearly inherited some awful predisposition to hurt people."

"I know I don't need to point out that you share his gene pool, Perry. You're his twin. If Park has it, you might too, and so might someone in your family. Who is that? Your dad, your grandfather? Do you really want to sully their memories with these ideas?"

"Not really. But if there's something we can do, we should. It's like you've forgiven him for all his lies and half-truths."

She shakes her head. "I will never forgive him. But you can't hold Park accountable for what a stranger's done. Peyton Flynn's actions are his own."

"They found the last woman he kidnapped alive. I heard that on my way down here. Breaking news."

A little lightness in her, at last. "That's good. That's a huge relief, isn't it? But there still no sign of Peyton?"

"Not that I know of. I've been a little busy, though. Olivia, this is what we have to do. I can't live with myself pretending I don't know these things. At the very least, we need to confront him. I want you to come back home with me. Back to Nashville. We have to get to the bottom of this."

No. No way.

"I understand," she says. "But let me call him and ask him to come down here, so we can do this on neutral ground. I'm not going back to Nashville. I don't have the bandwidth to deal with that yet."

"Fair enough."

Olivia gets her phone and calls, but Park doesn't answer. "We can try again later."

"I'll try."

Perry calls, but Park doesn't answer for him, either. "Well, you have to admit, the two of us are probably the last people he wants to hear from. I'll try Lindsey. She might know where he is."

"Perry, wait. I don't want to drag her into this until we have to. Legally, she might find something that we're missing and be obligated to report things before we get answers."

He takes a huge, deep breath, looks around as if he's seeing the room for the first time.

"It's pretty here."

"If you can call a construction zone pretty, yes. It is. It's going to be lovely when I'm done. Very beach chic. It's a new direction for me."

"I like it."

That crooked smile breaks her apart inside. "I'm glad. Since you're here, can I borrow your strong back?"

"What?"

She rubs her collar bone. "Still a little sore, and I have a delivery today. I was going to get help from the store, but since you're here..."

Perry's face darkens. He's still upset, and she can't blame him. But she also isn't willing to drive off the cliff of throwing Park to the wolves, either.

"I know," he says, quietly.

"You know what?"

"I know about prom. What happened after. Lindsey told me."

Olivia stares for a moment until she realizes what he's talking about. Lindsey told him? How dare she?

"Don't be mad at her," he says, reading her mind in that crazy way he has. "She couldn't bear it any longer."

"She couldn't bear it? *She* couldn't?"

Olivia storms out onto the deck. Perry follows.

"Liv—"

She whirls on him. "Is that why you're so hell-bent on taking Park out? You're mad at him because of what could have been between us?"

"I've always been mad at him, Liv. But my God, a baby? Why didn't you tell me?"

"Because I didn't want to ruin your life."

He grabs her hand.

"You wouldn't have."

"You don't know that. I was a baby myself, and you were just starting out. Trust me, I've had enough guilt about it all these years."

"I'm not trying to make you feel guilty. I am hurt that you didn't trust me enough to tell me."

"It wasn't that."

"Then what was it?"

"I was scared. I was scared of what it meant. I was scared you didn't love me. You were leaving. You'd made up your mind. I couldn't beg, and I couldn't have taken it if I told you and you'd left anyway."

They are shouting at each other now.

"You thought that little of me? That I would walk away from you, from us, from our family? Liv. I can't believe you didn't have faith in me, after all of that."

"I did. I loved you. I still do!"

Shock ripples across his face. Then his mouth is on hers, the kiss so violent, so explosive, that she has no time to react, only to sink into him, into his body, revel in his arms, the strength of him holding her. He pushes her up on the railing, his body hard between her legs, and the heat of him drives her wild. Her legs go around him, pulling him close. His shirt is off a moment later, and she runs her hands over the broad expanse of his chest.

He pulls away slightly, as if in question, and in response she arches her back, arches into him, every line and contour of her body screaming *yes!* Her shorts are off now, and his pants, and he takes her, there on the deck, under the brightening sky, the seagulls and sandpipers and sea oats the only witness to their passion.

It is over too quickly, and they are left panting in the morning heat, both trying to find a way to get closer, waves of pleasure crashing through them.

"Inside," she whispers, and he picks her up as if she weighs nothing and carries her into the living room.

They stretch out side by side, and she is amazed at how they fit together, even after all these years. So perfectly, as if they're made for one another.

They make love for hours, until the sun is drawing low and the shadows high.

She hasn't been this happy in a long time. Being with him again is just as wonderful as she'd dreamed.

Perry, too, seems more relaxed, though there is still a tension in him. He's probably thinking about Park; she wants to tell him that this is their moment, not to let in the chaos they've managed to flee, if only for a few hours.

"Is this going to be weird?" she asks softly.

"No. Only I don't think I could ever get enough of you," he says, and she smiles, snuggles against him.

"Then run away with me. Stay here. We can start over, together. Take the chance we never had."

"I don't know if that's possible, Liv. Not until we get things settled with Park."

"Is this why you want him taken down? So he's out of the picture? Let me tell you, Perry, you needn't worry about that. Park and I are over. I'm free. My heart is free, I mean. The rest is just paperwork."

"It's not that. I can't live with myself knowing what he's done."

He pulls on his jeans and shirt, leaving them both unbuttoned. She feels so far away from him already, though he's standing five feet away.

"It's time to call him again, Liv. I have to resolve this in my mind. I'll leave it up to you if you want to tell him about—" he points to the living room floor, littered with cushions and clothes "—this."

"This?" She'd be amused if she wasn't so desperately afraid of what might happen next.

"You know what I mean. Us." He looks confused and abashed. "I'm going to take a shower."

"Perry?"

He looks back over his shoulder, and her breath catches.

"Is there an us?" she asks.

His smile tells her everything, but the words are good, too. "If you want there to be."

"I do. Stay with me while I call?"

44

THE MOTHER

Darby is in the back yard taking hamburgers off the grill when Osley and Moore show up at her door. Scarlett calls for her, yelling that the police are there, and Darby has a terrible premonition that that their lives are about to change forever. Again. Her mind touches briefly on Peyton, who has dropped off the face of the earth, and draws back sharply, as if burned. She will be in therapy for years trying to understand her mixed emotions toward her son. The boy she raised, who has killed. Kidnapped. Raped. A man she no longer knows, who she can never understand, but wants to hold tight to her breast, to carry inside her again. If only she could do it all over, if only she could start fresh.

But it is too late for that.

"Want me to leave?" Park asks. He is tending the small bonfire they've pulled together. Hot dogs and burgers on the grill, s'mores for dessert. Not a date. Neither of them want to call it that, but they'd be lying if they didn't acknowledge they enjoy spending time together. Though how she has gotten herself into this situation, on a definitely-not-a-date in her back yard with a married guy who she's never slept with but whose sperm twice created life inside her, one of the resulting children the reason the police have arrived, isn't something she wants to examine closely.

When Olivia took off for the beach, bailing on Park, on her clients, on her whole life, Darby honestly understood the impulse. She almost envied her the escape.

But at the same time, she's happy Olivia is gone. It's given Scarlett time to get to know her father and has given Darby a chance to get to know Park as well. To assess for herself whether he could be capable of deceit.

She's vulnerable right now, she understands this. But she has a bizarre connection to this man, and the more he's around, the more complicated things have gotten. She's attracted to him, and she hates herself a bit for this. She, who has never needed anyone, is suddenly happy for a shoulder to cry on.

Park has been around more and more lately, spending almost all his free time at Darby's and Scarlett's sides. He hasn't shied away from the awkwardness of the situation; instead, after Scarlett goes to sleep, he puts his arms around Darby and holds her while she cries. He encourages her to talk openly about the problems of Peyton's childhood. He reinforces her decision to commit her—their—son. He seems to love their daughter without reservation, delighting in every word, every laugh, every moment quiet and loud.

The romance between father and daughter will end eventually, when Park finally trips up and says the wrong thing, or worse, says no to something Scarlett has her heart set on, but for now, Scarlett is coping better than Darby could have hoped. She'd been planning to get a psychologist involved, but right now, her daughter is doing okay. They agreed she doesn't have to go back to Bromley, and Darby has filed a notice of intent to homeschool her with the Davidson County school system. Scarlett seems quite content with that option. It makes Darby feel better having her close to home now, anyway.

Interestingly, Park's been talking about serving Olivia with papers. "We're broken," he confessed, late last night, as they sat together in the cool autumn darkness, finishing the bottle of wine. "I think we have been for a long time, and I just didn't see it until she left. There's no glue in the world that can put us back together again."

She doesn't want him to leave. Now, or ever.

"Please stay," Darby finally says. "I have a bad feeling about this."

Park nods. "Bring them out here, then. So we can keep an eye on the fire."

Responsible Park. She knows he won't let anything bad happen if he can help it.

Moore and Osley both look tired and rumpled, as if they've been up for days. They decline the offer of drinks and seats, instead preferring to stand, hands outstretched over the flames. The evening is chilly, the autumnal equinox upon them. Amazing how quickly the weather shifts in only a few weeks when fall is marching toward winter. Things die faster than they grow.

Scarlett joins them, hope mingled with fear on her face.

"Can I stay?" she asks, and before Darby can say yes or no, Osley nods.

"Stay. We're all good."

"We found Jillian Kemp," Moore says, but before Darby's next, horrible heartbeat, the cop smiles. "She's alive."

They detail what's been happening—finding Kemp, her health status, her information about where Peyton took her, developing the maps, taking the chopper, the overflight throughout the farmland and hills near Waverly.

"We found the barn where he's been living. Found all his things."

"But Peyton?" Darby asks, voice barely a whisper.

Osley steps in. "Ms. Kemp was positive she killed him, but we found no sign of him other than a pretty extensive blood pool. She caught him in the head with a chisel. Either an animal got him, which is possible, or—"

"He's alive," Darby breathes. "Thank God."

"Have you seen him?" Osley asks sharply, and she shakes her head.

"Nor heard from him. But I'm his mother. Of course I'm relieved he's not dead."

"So where is he?" Scarlett asks. Her eyes are filled with terror, and pain, and it kills Darby to see her upset like this.

Osley clearly recognizes the look, speaks as gently as Darby's ever heard him. "We don't know, honey. But if he's out there, he's wounded, badly. We've got a BOLO out for all the hospitals, but you're a nurse, Ms. Flynn. If he's injured as badly as we think, and he's able, chances are he's going to come home to you."

Darby looks to Park. The cops don't seem surprised to see him, which tells her they've been watching the house and know he's been here before. He nods encouragingly.

"I promise I'll call if he comes home. He needs help. I want to get him the help he needs, and I don't just mean stitches for a wound. He needs to be in the hospital. Not jail," she finishes, voice growing louder. "You can't arrest him and send him to prison. Please. He needs psychological help."

"That's not up to us, Ms. Flynn. There's more. We've been doing some pretty intense work these past few weeks, and we got confirmation tonight that his DNA has matched to three more unsolved homicides. One dates back two years. I'm afraid your son has been keeping some pretty heavy secrets from you."

Darby feels faint. This can't be happening. "Beverly Cooke isn't the first?"

"No, ma'am, she wasn't. There will be a lot more information coming out in the next few days, but we wanted you to hear it from us first."

Darby sinks onto the couch by the fire, and Scarlett cuddles next to her.

"It's okay, Mom. It's not your fault."

Moore agrees. "It isn't something you've done. It's what he's chosen to do. Just promise me you will turn him in if he shows up, and be very careful around him. He won't have much to lose if he knows you're aware of the extent of his crimes."

Osley glances over at Park. "Any word from Mrs. Bender?"

Is Darby imagining it, or was there a slight emphasis on the word *missus*?

"Other than assurances from her client that she is alive and well and hasn't seen Peyton, no. She won't talk to me." He shrugs. "Is what it is. She'll come back, or she won't. Personally, I don't care. It's more important for me to be here right now. Especially if Peyton might come home."

Darby wants to interject *that's not true, he cares, he cares so much it's eating him up inside, can't you see how deeply she wounded him?* but she doesn't. Things are complicated enough without her getting involved.

"I'm sure Ms. Flynn appreciates the bodyguard services. I hear you've met a few of your kids."

Park's face lights up despite the terrible news they've just received. "I have. Scarlett's been managing getting everyone together. And Winterborn has offered a mediation, too. They don't want to get sued, have made it clear they are sorry for what's happened, are changing all their protocols. They'll settle with us, with the kids. I think it's important for the families who feel betrayed to get some sort of compensation. Me, I'm feeling pretty blessed right now. We're up to thirty-two." The note of pride in his voice makes Darby want to smile, but this isn't the time for it.

"Peyton," she says, pulling them back. "Did he hurt Jillian Kemp?"

Moore slaps her hands together over the fire. "Well, that's up for debate. He drugged her, and while she doesn't have any obvious physical wounds, there's some confusion as to whether he assaulted her or not. When she was awake, he talked. Mostly about his life, and Olivia Bender."

She addresses Park again. "We really do need to have some idea where Mrs. Bender is, sir. She's in danger until we can get our hands on Peyton. He's obsessed with her, and we don't want anything bad to happen."

"I honestly don't know exactly where she is. She had my car shipped back to me from Florida somewhere. But the client is one she's worked for before. Annika Rodrigue. I'm sure you could reach out to her and see if she'll share. She won't tell me, but you're different."

Osley brushes his hands along the front of his jeans, a sign Darby's grown to recognize as a signal to his partner that it's time to leave. "We'll do that. Thank you. We should be off, lots to do. We wanted to give you the heads-up though, ma'am, that your son is still out there, and we need everyone to stay on high alert. If you hear from him, you gotta call us right away. Okay?"

"Okay."

"Oh, Mr. Bender?" Osley tosses something to Park. "We found this. Figured you'd want it back."

Park dangles the small thumb drive in the air. "Thanks. Did you look at this?"

Osley flashes that lazy grin. "Only to make sure it was yours."

Park smiles back. "Thank you, Detective. You've saved my career."

Darby sees them out, returns to the back yard. Park has assembled the food for them; Scarlett is already digging in.

"Can you eat?" he asks quietly, and she shakes her head. "Come here, then." He opens his arms, and Darby collapses into them, grateful, so grateful, that he's here.

It is later, after she's promised they'll be safe, after he's gone home and she's finished the wine and cried herself into an almost state of sleep, that she remembers what the cops said about Jillian. "He drugged her."

She gets out of bed and goes to the linen closet in the hall. On the top shelf, she keeps an emergency kit, much more complete than your average first aid kit. It's surgical, has the tools for field dressings and pain relief, IV antibiotics, the works. It seems smart to have something so complete in case of the zombie apocalypse, or some other sort of emergency. With as many tornadoes and floods as Nashville suffers from, she never knows when it might be needed.

She has to get the stool, but she reaches into the dark recess of the closet to find the space where she knows the kit lives, and finds it empty.

A tiny bubble of panic forms inside her. When did Peyton take it? Before he started his killing spree?

Or after?

There are all sorts of things in the kit that could be used to drug a woman, but if she's going to guess, he's been using the midazolam or propofol. It will not only knock her out, but she'll have no memory of anything that happens while she's under the influence of it.

This is your fault, Darby. You've given him the tools to prey on these women. You packaged it up with a bright red bow.

She snaps off the light and sits back in the chair. What can she do? Can she fix this?

"Mom?"

Scarlett comes into the office, ghostly in the darkness.

"You okay, honey? That was some pretty heavy news they delivered."

"No. Do you think he really did these things? That he's murdered all those women?"

She puts her arms around her daughter and holds her close. "I hope not, love. But I'm afraid he might have."

45

THE MURDERER

When he woke, to the trill of birdsong, the sun was climbing the sky like wisteria on a trellis, and the woman was gone.

There was a gash on his temple and blood had poured down his face, onto his shirt, pooling in the dirt beneath his body.

His time was running out.

He managed to get himself off the ground, crawled into the barn, dizzy, so dizzy. The rusty smell of the dried blood turned his stomach, as did the view of the wound in the mirror. It needed stitches, a horrible process he barely managed, the numbing shot done awkwardly with his left hand, the line of black zigzagging and crooked. His eye on that side was swollen nearly closed. Once he'd covered the wound with a bandage, he broke open the chemical ice pack and applied it. Getting the swelling down would help.

He had to leave. If she'd gotten to the police, they could come at any moment.

He changed, packed what he needed—food, clothes, the emergency kit, the gun—and left the rest. He felt a pang leaving his trophies, but they served no one at this point. Maybe he'd come back for them one day.

He drove the van to a truck stop, left it in the corner of the lot, stashed between two eighteen-wheelers on their sleep break. With luck, it wouldn't be found for a while. Long enough for him to get to Olivia's house. Long enough to see her again.

A sketchy trucker let him hitch a ride back to town. With the bandages over the chisel cut, Peyton figured he was safe from exposure so long as he kept the baseball cap on. The guy driving seemed as disinterested in him as Peyton was with the trucker. He dropped him at the exit into Bellevue and didn't glance back.

It took him three hours to make it to Forest Hills. He wanted to go home, wanted to curl up on the sofa in the living room and let his mom make him hot chocolate like she used to, let her clean his wounds and fix him properly, but he couldn't face her. He couldn't face Scarlett, either. Things were too complicated, too out of control. Better to leave his family, the people he loved—if he can ascribe the strange fullness he feels when he looks at them as an emotion people know as love—and finish this the way he started it, with Olivia.

So he hoofed it to the Benders'.

Olivia's Jeep was in the driveway. The sight of it lifted his heart. She was home!

He still had a full set of keys, to the house, to the cars, to the shed, though he wondered if by now, they'd had them changed. The cameras were running again; he could see the small red power light. Going up to the house would be harder. But he didn't care. He wanted things to end. He wanted to die with Olivia's arms around him.

He was about to scoot around the hedge to the porch when the garage door started up. He could hear Park Bender talking. Shit. He rolled to the ground by the hedge and froze. He'd been so careful, but had he been seen? Had someone called the police? Was this going to end right now, with Peyton covered in blood and muck, lying on the ground like a wounded squirrel?

No. Bender got into the Jeep, still talking. He sounded frantic, upset. Peyton listened until he heard Bender say, "Olivia, just don't do anything until I get there. Okay? We'll talk this through. I'll be there as soon as I can."

She wasn't home, but Bender was going to her. Okay. Okay.

If Bender had been looking at the house when he backed out, he surely would have seen Peyton still as a fallen log, lying under the hedge. But he didn't. He spun the wheels and was out of the driveway seconds later.

Peyton smiled.

Change of plan.

46

THE WIFE

Dawn, again.

But this time, not alone.

Olivia has barely slept, but she's also not had any bad dreams, and for that she is forever grateful to the man still prone next to her. It has been a long time since she woke up with Perry Bender's arms around her, pulling her into him as snug as a snail to its shell, holding her through the night, keeping her nightmares at bay. He slept, but she lay there with him, reveling in the safety, the gentleness, his breath moving the hair by her ear, his tiny snores before he fell deeply asleep.

Her heart has been shackled for years; this she now knows. It's remarkable, really, to have been holding herself apart from Park the way she has. Unintentionally. Unknowingly. And yet, the division had been there, and she didn't realize it until she opened herself to Perry again.

She has a lifetime to examine the mistakes she's made. But for now, she must pull herself from this blissful nest. She must rise, stretch, walk.

Confront.

Park should be here soon. He got on the road at midnight, though she'd encouraged him to wait until the morning. She doesn't ask why he didn't answer his phone. She thinks she probably knows the answer to that. She glances at Perry, still nestled in the bed. She can hardly fault Park for finding comfort elsewhere, as she has done.

Assuming he didn't stop more than twice, he should be here in an hour. Enough time.

She sets the water to boil, pulls out two cups, gets the tea. Once it's made, she takes her cup to the deck, drains it, then starts down the boardwalk.

"Wait up!"

Perry jogs out of the house, tying the string on a pair of shorts. Even in the barely dawn light, he is breathtaking. He joins her, matching her steps. Their rhythm is easy, the sand a gentle caress against their feet. It is chillier today than yesterday, and she pulls on the long-sleeved shirt she has tied around her waist.

They walk for several minutes before she speaks.

"I didn't want to wake you."

"You didn't. I realized when you weren't in the bed you were probably walking. But in case Park got here early…"

"You came to save me?"

"I came… Gosh, it really is pretty here."

The sun's glow has turned the sea turquoise. "You should see the storms. They're breathtaking."

"So are you."

"Flatterer."

They find the turn, and are almost back when Perry says, "I do have to go back to work. Maybe you'd consider coming with me?"

"To where?"

"I'm based out of London. I have a flat in Kensington Gardens. You'd like it. Lots of color."

"And if I don't want to go to London? You aren't there often. Would I need to follow you all over the world on your shoots?"

"Maybe? Maybe I'd change things up."

"Would you stay here?"

"Well, I haven't done a lot of work on US soil, and there's plenty around to capture my attention." He stops, pulling her to him. "I want to be where you are, Olivia."

They stand together for a moment, but Olivia hears the slam of a car door and pulls away.

"Park's here."

Perry shades his eyes as he looks toward the drive, which they can see from this spot on the beach, through the outdoor living room by the pool to the street.

"So he is."

Park looks good for a man who's driven all night. He's wearing jeans and a polo she doesn't recognize; his beard is growing in after several weeks without a razor. She doesn't care for beards; she almost smiles to see this new independence flouted in her face. He doesn't seem surprised to see Perry in shorts and no shirt, Olivia in workout gear, looking like they've just taken a walk together, intimately, as they have.

"Is there coffee?" he says, in lieu of physical contact.

It really is over, she thinks, heading for the cabinet. Perry excuses himself for a shower, promising to be back in a moment, leaving them alone.

"So, my brother, huh?"

She plugs in the coffee maker. "We were just taking a walk."

Park gives her a wolfish smile and points to her neck. Frowning, she goes to the guest bath. A love bite, clear as day, just under her ear. At least he isn't foaming at the mouth. Maybe they will be able to do this well. Separation. Moving on with others. There must be scar tissue building in her heart.

Park has finished making the coffee and poured himself a cup. He's leaning against the counter.

"We should probably talk," he says, and she nods.

"Probably."

"Is that what you've brought me down here for? To tell me you're with Perry now?"

"Not at all. It's about Annie Cottrell and Melanie Rich."

She can swear he flinches at the names.

"I just need to hear you say it."

"I didn't kill them," he replies automatically.

"That's what I told Perry. But he's pretty upset by some new information he's found out."

Park pours another cup, cool as can be.

"Like what?"

"Like you went to St. Louis a few weeks back?"

To her utter shock, he doesn't deny it. "Yeah."

"What else have you lied about, Park?"

"Are we doing this now? Here?" He gestures to the kitchen, as if this isn't the perfect place for them to talk. Their lives were torn in the kitchen of their home. It seems only fitting the final rips should come in another.

"There's a spot off the living room I'm making into an outdoor eat-in. We can sit there."

The morning is already warming up, but the roof hasn't been removed here yet. She's complementing the outdoor living room with a full dining area feeding off the kitchen to the deck, a massive loggia. Open the glass doors, let the outside in. The new chairs are still covered in industrial-grade plastic, but Park lounges on one, feet up, as if he hasn't a care in the world. Perry joins them, taking the other. Olivia perches on the thick wooden railing.

"You have to fill me in on what you *think* you know," Park says to Perry. "I'm a little lost."

Perry is grinding his teeth; she can see the muscle jumping in his jaw.

"All right. Erica Pearl came to me a few weeks ago." He lays out the story for Park, not accusingly, trying to be open. "I'd like to hear the truth from you. Tell me what really happened."

Park nods once, almost to himself.

"I didn't kill Annie. But I found her."

The words linger in the air, an admission so heinous that Olivia realizes she isn't breathing.

"You found her?" Perry asks incredulously. "Was she dead?"

"Yes, she was dead."

"Why didn't you tell anyone? My God, Park."

"I couldn't. If I was the one who found her, everything they'd been saying was true. I didn't kill her, you know I didn't. When I found her…it had been a while since she disappeared. She was decomposed, bones already showing. I didn't know what to do. If I went to Mom and Dad, they'd go to the police. No one would have believed me. Everyone was accusing me of hurting her, of lying. To be the one who found her? Even as a boy, I understood how the mob worked. I couldn't take the chance."

"So you did what, exactly?" Perry asks.

"I buried her."

"You were ten. We were *ten*. How?"

"I was walking back from practice—I think you had a cold, and you hadn't played that day. I cut through the field and practically tripped on her. She was mostly buried, but parts of her were sticking up out of the ground."

"You knew it was her?" Olivia asks.

"She was wearing a red T-shirt the day she went missing. I could see the fabric, wrapped around her neck."

"And then what?" Perry is pale but composed.

Park shrugs. "It had rained a lot that week. The ground was

soft. There was a hole by the opening to the ditch. It was really deep. I think it was an old well. I put her down the hole and covered it with dirt. It started to rain, so I stood in the field and let the water wash me clean before I went home."

"Jesus." Perry's face is white as bone, but Park's is flushed.

"I felt terrible. Sick. I wanted to tell you. I wanted to tell Mom and Dad. But I couldn't. Every time I tried... And the neighbors were being so awful. Mom and Dad sent me to therapy, and the therapist told me it wasn't healthy to hold on to the secrets. But I never admitted that I'd buried her. I've let that eat me up inside for decades."

"Why now?" Perry asks.

"The draft manuscripts that were stolen. One of the plots is about a kid missing for years who's found in a well by a baseball field. I was stupid to write it, stupid. I wouldn't have let it be published, obviously. I would have edited out those details. But now... I was afraid someone would put it together, and I went... I don't know, I wanted to see if things were still obscured, I guess. And then all this craziness happened, and the reporter dragged me into it when she asked about St. Louis during the interview. After all we've been through, after all Olivia and I have lost, I realized it was time to give Annie's parents some peace."

Perry is looking at his brother with horror etched on his face. "You just now figured that out?"

"You have to understand, they would have sent me to jail."

"Maybe they should have," Perry says darkly, his voice raw with emotion and loathing, and Olivia holds up a hand.

"So you called the tip line?" she asks. She is determined to get to the end of the story before Perry blows up entirely.

"Yeah. Crime Stoppers. Untraceable. I used a burner I bought in St. Louis and got rid of it immediately."

"Good to know your job has given you the ability to avoid detection in a criminal investigation," Perry says.

"Oh, for God's sake, stop being such a Pollyanna. I didn't do anything wrong."

"Technically, criminally, yes, you did. Morally? You absolutely did."

Park deflates. "Well, the moral high road has never been my battleground, so you might as well go ahead and turn me in now, brother."

"And the flowers? On Melanie's grave? Explain that to me."

"Flowers? I don't know anything about that," Park says with a sigh.

"Really? A florist in Chapel Hill gets an envelope of cash every year, with instructions to put a bouquet of lilies on Melanie Rich's grave. There are regular withdrawals from your bank account in the same sum every year on the same date."

"Coincidence."

"The florist kept the envelopes, you know. The police have them. They're doing a DNA analysis on the adhesive. Will it match you, I wonder?"

Park shakes his head, though Olivia is shocked by how he pales.

"No. I didn't do it. I didn't kill Melanie. I swear it. And I have no idea who is sending her flowers."

"After what you've just admitted to, how am I supposed to believe you?" Perry puts an arm around Olivia, pulls her close to his body. "How are we supposed to believe you?"

"Honestly? Believe me, or don't. I've made my peace with all of this."

A slow clapping sounds from the corner of the room. The doors to the deck are open to let in the sultry breeze, and a young man emerges from the boardwalk, a gun in his hand.

"Hi, Dad," Peyton Flynn says. "Good to know I got it honestly."

47

THE HUSBAND

When a lion circles its prey, it seems almost playful. A big, silly cat, toying with a mouse. A mouse it will later rip apart.

Peyton Flynn might look like roadkill, but he is the hunter. He has the three of them at a major disadvantage, and he knows it.

Park stands.

"Peyton. You're Peyton, right?"

"Very good. The resemblance is clear, isn't it?" He's being ironic; the bandage covers half his face. No one can get a good look at him, but he's smiling, and Park can't think straight. *This is my son. My son has a gun pointed at me. Don't shoot, son.*

"Hi, Liv." The gun stays trained on Park, which is good. He can't let Peyton hurt Olivia.

"My name is Olivia," she says, voice shaking.

"Never, darling. You'll always be Liv to me. That's what he

calls you. It suits you. Olivia is such a proper name. And you aren't a proper kind of woman. Not formal, I mean. You aren't formal."

"What do you want?" Park asks. He can sense Perry shifting next to him; he played enough ball with his brother over the years to recognize the muscles tensing. If there was ever a moment for their childhood ability to speak without speaking to one another like they did during games, now is the time.

"Olivia. I hate that we have to get to know each other like this. I've been trying to do all the right things for you. I saved you after the accident. I sent flowers. Lilies."

"I hate lilies," she says, and Peyton frowns.

"Hmm. That's odd. I'd think you'd love them."

Park realizes Peyton has a notebook in his other hand. One of his, from his office.

"Why do you have my notebook, Peyton? Why did you steal things from us? That's not the right way to get to know people, especially ones you want to be friends with."

He puts dead eyes on Park. "I'm not five. Stop talking to me like I'm a kid. If you didn't want me to take things, you should have hidden them better."

He is talking to Olivia again, and it's Olivia who pales, Olivia who frowns.

"I know you so well, Liv. I know all the things about you. How sad you were when Perry left. You're Uncle Perry, right?"

Perry nods slowly. "I am. Please, Peyton, put down the gun, and let's talk things out man-to-man. Let Olivia go, and your father and I will tell you anything you want to know."

"Oh, I think it's too late for that." He scratches at the bandage with his gun hand, and Park starts to edge to his right.

"Don't move," Peyton says absently, the gun trained on Park again.

"Did you tell him everything, Liv? Have you told Dad the whole truth?"

"Park knows everything about me," she says. "So does Perry."

She's being too damn brave. Park wants to tell her to be cowed, to be vulnerable. But that's not who Olivia is. She is strong. She is a warrior woman. She's been through hell and stepped out the other side unburned. She will not back down to a bully. Even if the bully is deranged and pointing a gun at her.

"Do they know about the baby? Tsk, tsk. If you hadn't murdered your baby, maybe you'd have another right now."

Park sees Perry swallow convulsively. "Peyton, you're being cruel. If you love Olivia at all, why would you be cruel?"

"Oh, you haven't told Dad about the abortion? Terrible. You really should have. 'God's punishing me.' That's what you say. 'God is punishing me for killing my baby. For killing Perry's baby.'"

"That's enough," Park says, though his eyes have narrowed, and his fists are clenched so tightly his knuckles are turning white. "What do you want?"

"I want Olivia to come for a walk with me. It's a pretty day. She and I have things to discuss." He pulls a crumpled envelope from his pocket, along with a bent and battered photograph. "I found your letter. You've been really naughty, haven't you?"

Park feels Olivia stiffen beside him.

"Leave my wife out of this."

The pleasant pretend mood is gone in a flash, and Peyton's face grows dark with suffused blood.

"Fuck off, *Dad*. You and Uncle Perry go inside, now. Or I'll shoot her."

"That's not happening. Put down the gun." A siren starts to wail, and Park risks a quick glance toward Olivia.

"The police are on their way," she says, holding up her wrist with its Apple watch. "I've been having nightmares about you, Peyton. You kidnap me, you tie my hands, you throw me in the trunk of your car. But in all my dreams, I don't have this. I sent the emergency signal, and the police will be here in moments."

Peyton's hand wavers on the gun, and that hesitation is all the Bender boys need. Perry and Park leap for him, exploding with violence at the threat.

Peyton panics, running backwards but also pulling the trigger. The shot is deafening. Perry screams, but Park tackles his son, smashing him to the boardwalk. Peyton is strong, and he flips Park over, a forearm on his throat. Perry, blood streaming from his arm, wrenches Peyton off, and the two grapple. They're both strong, and Perry is the bigger man, but Peyton is enraged. Park is up moments later and launches himself into the scrum just as Peyton explodes upward. Perry is thrown off the boardwalk, going over the edge with an audible thump. Park lunges but trips, going down hard on his knees.

Perry jumps back onto the boardwalk, and his movement disrupts Peyton's concentration long enough for Park to scramble up and charge him again. They connect with a terrible force that knocks out Park's breath, and the gun spins away. Gasping, Park scrambles after it, Peyton holding on to his leg with insane strength.

Park touches the metal of the gun, gathering it into his palm. He whips around and pulls the trigger.

The bullet catches Peyton in the neck. Blood spurts from the wound. He keeps clawing, keeps fighting. He twists Park's leg viciously, and Park feels the hot, sharp pain of something tearing in his knee.

He pulls the trigger again but misses. He kicks with his other leg, connects with the bullet wound, and Peyton's hands release Park's leg. Park scoots across the deck, getting as far away from his son as he can.

His son.

He has just shot his son.

Olivia is screaming. He can hear her shrieking but can't seem to rise to comfort her. Perry drags himself back onto the boardwalk, blood streaming down his hand. His arm looks broken; the angle is all wrong.

Peyton is bleeding profusely, his skin growing pale. He twitches, his brain finally getting the message that he is dying. His legs jerk spasmodically in time with the slow, furious pumps of his heart. Once. Twice.

A few moments pass before the third.

He is almost limp now, and Olivia finally gathers herself and scrambles to Park, helps him stand. Perry crawls to them; Park drags his brother to his feet. And the three hold on, watching Peyton's life's blood leave the wound in his neck. It inches across the letter, the foxed, yellow edge turning pale crimson as the blood soaks the worn linen.

Peyton's last words are a whisper, but loud enough that all three of them hear clearly.

"It was you. I know it was you. I read your letter. Now it's destroyed. Your secret is safe with me."

"Secret?" Park asks, kneeling down, touching his son's shoulder. "What are you talking about?"

But Peyton has eyes only for Olivia. "Don't worry. I'm the only one who knows. I'll never tell."

He dies quietly, the words drifting around them, both Park and Perry staring at her.

"Tell what?" Perry asks.

"I have no idea," Olivia says. She snatches up the bloody mess of paper and photo, looking away from Park's terrified gaze as the police come streaming up from the beach, guns drawn, too late to save them.

48

THE WIFE

But she did.

Olivia only wanted to surprise Park.

The drive from Nashville to Chapel Hill wasn't overly long, less than eight hours, but it was the farthest Olivia had ever driven by herself, and that excited her. She had snacks in a tote bag and a six-pack of Diet Coke in the cooler, her overnight bag in the trunk. Everything organized, everything just so. She'd even vacuumed out her car the night before and sprayed the interior windscreen with Windex, cleaning off the residue so it sparkled. And good thing, too, the sun was bright, and she hated that hazy glare.

She stopped twice, once in Knoxville, once in Asheville, and arrived just as the sun was setting on the campus. She had his address—Lindsey had given it to her ages ago—but she'd never been here, never written him. She hadn't talked to him since Perry left, actually.

This was an important moment for her. For him. For them. She missed him. Gosh, she missed them both, but Perry was gone, and she would never see him again, and that meant she had to make things right with Park.

She'd felt so alone since he'd left for school. She was busy enough with her classes at Belmont. She was in her second year of Architecture and Design and loved everything about the program, even the extra work created by double-majoring in both fields. She dated, had a couple of boyfriends, but nothing serious, nothing that felt like the love she had for him, definitely nothing like the dark love she felt for his brother, desire mixed with shame and horror. She couldn't imagine ever being in the same room as Perry ever again, not after what she'd done. He would never forgive her, so he must never know. Simple as that.

She found a parking space on South Street and locked the car carefully. She didn't want anything to happen to her things, but she also wanted to take a walk around the campus first. All part of her newly embraced independence. She was satisfied with the path her life was on. She just missed Park. She needed him back in the mix, and things would be perfect again, like they were before prom.

She had a three-day weekend, so she figured she'd drive to Chapel Hill and surprise him. No strings, no expectations. Just to see if he still cared. Just to see if he still wanted her.

It was a stupid thing to do, but she was a kid still, ripe and lush and sure enough of her own sexuality that she could lure him back even if he'd found someone else. He wouldn't have, though. Not Park. He was hers, and she was his, and that's just how things were going to be. They'd been planning it since they were kids, and yes, they'd hit a little speed bump, but she was going to make it right, and then they'd get back on the planned path. Together. Going forward, it would be them together. Chapel Hill had a fabulous A&D program. She could transfer all of her credits. She'd already checked.

Park would be thrilled. She knew he would be. She knew him, inside and out.

She wandered across the quad, taking in the huge sundial, the ancient trees with their long arms spread protectively over the redbrick buildings. Everyone was so happy. Smiling, healthy, beautiful people. She felt at home immediately. She felt safe.

She walked around campus for an hour, admiring, then made her way back to the car and drove to Park's address.

She grabbed the bag of chocolate chip cookies she'd made fresh last night from the cooler, leaving the rest of her things in the car. She wanted to greet him with her best smile and a sweet treat, and they could deal with the rest later.

She wound her way up the stairwell and stopped in front of his door. She raised her hand to knock but hesitated when loud voices rang through the thin wood. Park's voice, raised in anger. And a girl, fighting back. Olivia leaned closer to the door, practically put her ear against it. Thankfully no one else was in the corridor; she must look totally ridiculous, eavesdropping while holding a pie tin full of cookies covered in foil. A demented Junior Leaguer.

The argument was at fever pitch; they'd clearly been fighting for a while.

"You're a whore. There's no chance in hell it's mine, and you know it."

"You're the only one I've slept with, and don't you dare call me a whore. What kind of horrible person are you? I'm in trouble and all you can do is accuse me of sleeping around?"

"You've been with at least three people I know of, including my roommate. So just leave, will you?"

"You can't be serious. That's not true. I can't belie—"

The voice was cut off with a scream and a gurgle. There was a huge thump, and then the sound of banging, but soft thuds, like small fists against stronger arms. Or feet hammering the floor.

Olivia tried to imagine what was happening, but she couldn't. Everything had gone deadly quiet inside the apartment.

Then there were cries, and Park snarled again, "Get out."

Steps came closer, and Olivia took off running, ducking behind the fire extinguisher, hoping against all hope the girl went the other way.

She didn't. The girl stormed out of Park's apartment, crying noisily, a hand to her neck, ran right past Olivia without even noticing she was there.

She heard Park growl "good riddance" and slam the door.

This was not how things were supposed to go. She felt sick.

This girl was pregnant? By Park?

Oh, the irony.

She saw the girl sprint from the stairwell, then draw up by a tree, wiping her eyes and pulling herself together.

Olivia set the cookies on the carpet carefully, then went down the stairs. The girl was still there, arms around her own waist, comforting herself.

As she watched, the girl started toward the edge of the parking lot. There must be a path there that led back to campus.

Olivia followed.

The girl hurried down the path through the arboretum, then kept going, onto the street, down toward a coffee shop. Toward Olivia's car. Olivia waited until she passed, then jumped behind the wheel. It would be much easier to follow in the car, especially not knowing the area.

Olivia just wanted to talk to her. To find out the truth. If Park was screwing around with her, or if he was telling the truth and the baby wasn't his.

She was still raw from her own experience. Trying so hard to forget. It was impossible.

Maybe she could reason with this girl. Make her understand that she might regret her actions going forward forever. Maybe she just wanted to let jealousy take the reins and lash out. She didn't know.

The girl was in good shape, moved quickly. She finally slowed by a small overpass bridge, then took a seat on the stone, feet dangling.

That looked so dangerous. It wasn't a huge drop, but enough that the girl could hurt herself if she fell.

Olivia pulled the car into the lot nearby and debated. She hated her, if only because she'd been with Park. But Olivia had a newfound compassion for those suffering the burning fires of desire and desertion.

While she debated, the weather turned. The skies grew dark, and fat drops of rain began to fall. The girl turned her tear-stained face to the sky and got to her feet.

Olivia put the window down on the car. "Need a lift back to campus? You're going to get soaked."

The girl got into the car.

A confluence of events.

Desire made real. A surprise trip. The timing of her arrival. Another five minutes and she would never have known. Instead, Olivia was stuck in an overheated car parked by a lake, listening to a besotted and wet girl crying about her perfect boyfriend blowing her off.

Crying about how much she loved him.

How much he loved her. All the things he'd told her. How beautiful she was. How perfect. How sweet. How no one had ever made him feel like this before. How she was his first true love. That's why she slept with him; he was so flattering, so honest and upfront. And now she was pregnant, and he wouldn't talk to her anymore.

She flipped down the visor, the little mirror reflecting her truth. "He tried to strangle me. I kicked him in the balls, and he let me go. Look at my neck."

Yes. Look. The bruises were growing darker by the minute.

"I heard your fight."

"What?"

"I heard him say you slept with his roommate. Is that true?"

"Why do you care?"

"Is it true?"

The girl's eyes narrowed, and the asp inside reared. "Who are you, anyway? It's not like he'd give you the time of day. You are so not his type."

"You don't think so?"

There must have been something in Olivia's face, because the girl tensed. Got edgy.

And leaped out of the car.

The rain was coming down at a steady clip, and the girl hunched into her jacket, arms around her waist again as she headed toward the lake.

Olivia followed her down the path. Something in her had shifted, broken open. She was furious. She didn't know if she was mad at Park or this girl, but she wanted answers.

The girl whirled on her. "Why are you following me? Leave me alone."

"You want to know who I am? I'm the one Park Bender really loves. I'm his girlfriend. We've been together for years. And I think you're lying. I think you just want his attention."

"Oh, screw you." The sneer was nasty, and she lunged at Olivia, arms up.

Olivia ducked the punch and hit the girl with her own, connecting solidly, across the side of her head.

The momentum and the punch took her off balance, and the girl went down in the weeds headfirst. With the *thump* of her body on the path, the heat went out of Olivia.

Served her right. The girl had tried to punch Olivia in the face. She'd had no choice but to lash out.

Olivia started back toward the car. "Get up. I'll drive you back to campus. Stay away from Park."

There was no response.

A chill ran down Olivia's spine. She walked to the girl's side. Knelt. The girl's eyes were open, wide and staring. As Olivia watched, they went as blank as the darkened sky above.

Panic shot through her. She touched the girl's neck where her pulse should be. Nothing. Blood oozed from a deep, wide cut on the side of her head.

Oh my God oh my God oh my God.

Olivia was frozen. She didn't know what to do. Call Park? The police? How was she going to explain this? It was an accident. The girl was trying to hurt her. She was defending herself. The girl must have hit her head on a rock when she fell.

Fifty lines ran through her mind; none of them were right. Line fifty-one was the only one that made sense.

Hide her.

The lake was close. She could hear the water lapping against the bank.

Thunder boomed, making her body shudder, and a thin streak of lightning showed her the path. The girl was heavy, but smaller than Olivia. She managed to get her onto a shoulder and staggered to the lake. There was a small ledge that jutted out over the water. It would have to do.

She filled the girl's clothes with rocks.

Rolled her closer.

Pushed her off the edge into the water.

Heard the deafening splash.

Olivia cried all the way back to Nashville. And never spoke of her surprise trip to Chapel Hill to anyone. But that letter.

Written to a grieving mother. Not so much a confession as a plea for understanding. It was an accident. I didn't know what to do. I panicked. Please, please, forgive me.

Then someone else knew her secret.

A man, who read her sins, obsessed over them, and recreated them.

EPILOGUE

AN ENDING

Some would say the divorce happened with undo haste, but when two people are determined to be consciously uncoupled as quickly as possible and have nothing left to fight over, the process is simpler. He wanted the house, she did not. She wanted the Jeep, he did not. Their business assets were too individualized to benefit one another, so they stayed with their owners. There were no more embryos to fight over. They agreed to split the proceeds of the memoir and the subsequent documentary; she was such a big part of the story, it was only fair.

Other than that, they quickly faded from one another's lives.

When you share a secret so big that it will bury you both, you take a sacred vow of perpetual secrecy, and move on. A little more than hope for the best, a little less than surety.

Park and Darby married a year to the day after their first face to face meeting. Olivia thinks it strange, their intense attraction. He killed her oldest child, after all. But they shared a second, a vivacious, brilliant, beautiful girl who they both dote on. Darby supposedly understands Park in a way Olivia no longer can and has been instrumental in helping him connect with his biological children. She helped him complete his dreams of having a family. Olivia doesn't resent him, or her, or them. Not anymore.

She and Lindsey rarely speak, one of the situation's greatest casualties. A bridge too far, staying friends with the sister of her ex-husband. The Benders always have been good at circling the wagons.

Lindsey and Lucía are also married now, living in Lindsey's Nashville house that was always too big for one. Lucía hired a decorator, one of Olivia's competitors, to warm up the house, to bring in vibrant colors and furniture people understood how to sit on. Lucía fits into the family with ease; even Park had forgiven her. The Aunties, as they were affectionately known among the Halves, were popular guests and devoted members of nearly every philanthropic organization in Nashville.

Olivia has not heard from Perry. He continues his position with the BBC, racking up awards for his beautiful photography of the relative unknown. She misses him, but she can't really blame him. The shock of their final meeting, to go from such love and joy to such chaos and fear and death, was insurmountable. He knew—or suspected—what Peyton Flynn's secret was. She could see it in his eyes. Though she never admitted it aloud, both the brothers seemed to know what she'd done. They did not forgive her the damage she'd caused. She called. She wrote. Perry never answered. Finally, she stopped trying.

She hopes that one day he'll come for her again, the way he did at the beach, all those years ago. And then he'll know.

The boy is five now. He has his father's soft gray eyes and his mother's dark chocolate hair. He is sturdy, tall for his age, and the happiest child she's ever seen.

After all she's been through, all she's done, right and wrong, sinner and saint, the murder and the miscarriages, the secrets and the lies, the forgiveness, the absolution, to be given the gift of a son who looks so much like his father seems the most remarkable grace.

She named him West. West Finley Hutton. Should she ever decide to tell his father the truth, she supposes they could add a Bender to the moniker, but for now, he is her darling West, her greatest joy, her reason for living. Together, they have made a new life in Monterey. It was an easy sell: Olivia needs to be near the production studios for her show. The area affords her glorious views to work with, a beach to stroll on, access to stunning raw materials, and monied patrons who are in regular pursuit of a fresh look for their lives.

And as much privacy as she can manage, considering the documentary and subsequent memoir made them both famous, for a time. The design show has only made her more so.

The gates are tall, the adobe walls thick, and the path to the beach is studded with cameras.

The past rarely stays hidden. Olivia knows this. But for now, she is safe. They are both safe.

★★★★★

THE MAN WITH MANY FACES

Documentary Script (Draft)

SCENE	VIDEO	AUDIO
1 **The Setup:** **Park**	**B-Roll:** Scenes from a lab, test tubes and centrifuges spinning, scientists in lab coats. **Text:** "Winterborn Life Sciences, Chapel Hill, North Carolina" **Text:** "Helping Create Families Everywhere" **FADE TO:** **B-Roll:** PARK BENDER'S office **Text:** "Park Bender's Home Office" **Observational:** PARK looks up, stares at the window, seemingly lost in thought. **B-Roll:** (SLOW PAN) Framed photographs of multiple children of various ages on a table. **B-Roll:** Close-up of the computer keyboard as fingers fly across the keys. **B-Roll:** Professional graduation photo of a young Park Bender, smiling for the camera. **Exterior:** The brown wooden door to Park's office, and a woman's raised fist.	**Music:** Thomas Dolby, "She Blinded Me with Science." **Narrator:** When he donated his sperm, he thought he was helping families in need. He couldn't imagine the trouble that was to come. **Music***:* Dolby melds into Chopin's Nocturnes, Op. 9: No. 2 in E-flat Major. **Narrator:** A celebrated sperm donor, Park Bender has thirty-two children, and counting. Today, he's meeting one of his daughters for the first time. **Park:** "It started as a way to earn a little extra cash. I was in grad school, broke, like everyone around me. I had some friends who were doing it and they said I could make some cash and help people. All I ever wanted was to help people. I had no idea what this would turn into." **Background:** Three sharp knocks at the door. **Park:** *(Laughing nervously.)* "I guess she's here."

THE MAN WITH MANY FACES

Documentary Script (Draft)

SCENE	VIDEO	AUDIO
3 The Setup: The Murders	**B-Roll:** A calm lake on a sunny spring day. **Text:** "Radnor Lake, Nashville, Tennessee"	**Sound:** Birds chirp, a breeze rustles the trees. Water laps the shoreline. **Narrator:** They found the first body in the lake.
	B-Roll: A set of feet hurries along the path into the woods, dragging a body wrapped in canvas.	**Sound:** Heavy breathing, as someone runs.
	B-Roll: A car rolls away from the lake parking lot.	**Narrator:** At the time, they had no idea how many there were. **Sound:** Tires crunching on gravel. **Music:** Dread-filled violins.
	B-Roll: The Nashville city skyline, sweep pan the river, the bridges, the lights of the city. **Text:** "Nashville, Tennessee"	**Narrator:** No idea how many women he had killed.
	B-Roll: Lower Broadway, the streets filled with revelers	**Music:** Strains of twangy country from the downtown honky-tonks. **Narrator:** Nashville was under siege, and they didn't even know it.
	B-Roll: PARK BENDER'S office **Park Interview:** PARK BENDER, 43 years old, sits at his messy desk typing on a computer. He wears a white button-down and faded jeans. His hair has a streak of silver from temple to nape. The sun shines into the room, illuminating dust motes floating in the air.	**Park:** "I had no idea what was happening. One day we were fine. The next, I was a murder suspect."

THE MAN WITH MANY FACES

Documentary Script (Draft)

SCENE	VIDEO	AUDIO
26 The Setup: Scarlett	**B-Roll:** A rocky path toward a mountain lake focuses on a weathered sign that says "Maverick Pass Campground." **Text:** "The Halves Family Reunion" **FADE TO:** **Observational:** A young woman in a plaid skirt with red hair stands with her back to the camera, watching over a group of people. **Scarlett Interview:** SCARLETT FLYNN, 18, sits at a picnic table, wearing sunglasses, her hair in a bun. **Text:** "Maverick Pass Campground" **Observational:** SCARLETT watching a crowd of people with a smile on her face. **B-Roll:** (SLOW PAN) Men and women of various ages milling around a campground. **B-Roll:** The lake, shimmering, people in inner tubes and a boat pulling a skier. **B-Roll:** A picnic lunch on a long table covered in a blue-checked tablecloth. **B-Roll:** (PAN IN; CLOSE-UP) A fly sits on the potato salad. **FADE TO:** **B-Roll:** A campfire.	**Sound:** Shouts, happy laughter, children's screams of joy. **Narrator:** Scarlett Flynn was determined to get all of the siblings together at least once. **Scarlett (VO):** You don't know what it's like, everyone staring, everyone gossiping. I didn't know anything, but they treated me like I was the one who'd done it. Which wasn't the coolest, you know? Peyton was responsible, and I bore the brunt of it. **Music:** Nirvana, "Smells Like Teen Spirit," from a car stereo. **Narrator:** The Halves, as they call themselves, are trying to find a way forward in the midst of the tragedy that brought them together. **Scarlett:** Having so many siblings is like a blizzard erupting out of nowhere. I felt overwhelmed at first. Everyone's different, but everyone's the same. I've met all the ones we know about so far, but we get new people still. We don't know how many are out there. Incredible, isn't it? **Sound:** Crickets, the soft strumming of a guitar. **Music:** Melancholic guitars.

THE MAN WITH MANY FACES

Documentary Script (Draft)

SCENE	VIDEO	AUDIO
38 **The Setup: The Detectives**	**B-Roll***:* Nashville Police Headquarters. **Text:** "Metro Police, Nashville, Tennessee" **B-Roll:** Inside the police headquarters. **B-Roll:** A long, gray-carpeted industrial hallway. **B-Roll:** (Close-up on sign) "Violent Crimes" **B-Roll:** The rabbit warren of back-to-front desks of the violent crimes team. **Text:** "The Homicide Team" **Will Osley Interview:** DETECTIVE WILL OSLEY, 38 years old, sits in a chair with his cowboy-booted feet on his desk. His gold sunglasses are clipped in his pocket. **Text:** "Homicide Detective William Osley" **Observational:** OSLEY flips the pages of a file. **B-Roll:** A binder full of paper.	**Sound:** Typing, phones ringing. **Narrator:** The police were baffled by the earlier case involving Park Bender. **Sound:** Whispery pages turn. **Osley (VO):** So when we exhumed the body, we typed the embryo. Sure enough, the baby was the roommate's. Created quite a bit of confusion for us because I gotta admit, I really thought Bender was our guy. Just goes to show you sometimes, your instincts can be off. Sure am glad we didn't force the issue, because if we'd peeled Bender's life open the way we were going…well, I'm just glad the right man was convicted. Still circumstantial as hell, but that's a pretty strong tie—DNA in the body is hard to refute. Guess she told her mama the truth about who got her pregnant.

Continue Scene 38

SCENE	VIDEO	AUDIO
	FADE TO: **B-Roll:** Park Bender's home in Nashville. **Text:** "Park Bender's Home" **B-Roll:** A police car.	**Sound:** Suburban bliss—birds chirping, the whir of a bicycle wheel, car doors. **Music:** Building dread violins.
	Observational: A female detective with blond hair watches the house. **FADE TO:** **B-Roll:** The rabbit warren of back-to-front desks of the violent crimes team. Moore has joined Osley. **Text:** "Homicide Detective Josephine Moore"	**Narrator:** His partner disagrees. **Sound:** Resounding silence. **Sound:** *(FADE IN)* Water lapping against a shoreline.
	Moore Interview: DETECTIVE JOSEPHINE MOORE, 29 years old, dressed in a black pantsuit, stands with her arms crossed, shaking her head.	**Moore:** I still don't trust him. There's more to the story that he hasn't told us. But the case is effectively closed, so there's not much more we can do. **Osley:** You're just mad I was right. I'm always right.

THE MAN WITH MANY FACES

Documentary Script (Draft)

SCENE	VIDEO	AUDIO
40 The Setup: Olivia	**B-Roll:** (SLOW PAN) Interior design studio in LA, close-up of kitchen fixtures, pull out to frame glass door, with stylized lettering. **Text:** "Olivia Hutton Designs" **FADE TO:** **Interview:** OLIVIA BENDER, 43 years old, wearing black-framed sunglasses, a no-nonsense pantsuit, and carrying a green leather sample bag, leaves her business and walks quickly down the streets, ignoring the camera. **Text:** "Olivia Bender" **Interview:** OLIVIA stops, whips off sunglasses, faces the camera head-on. **B-Roll:** (SLOW PAN) Sunshine moving across the floor of a high-end kitchen. **Observational:** A wineglass rolls along the marble countertop and teeters on the edge… **SMASH CUT TO:** **B-Roll:** Waves crash on the beach. A fine spray of water covers the camera lens. A solitary figure moves down the beach in soft focus. **FADE TO BLACK**	**Music:** The Ting Tings, "That's Not My Name." **Narrator:** The police were shocked when Olivia Bender left town suddenly. **Sound:** Rapid footsteps, high heels on concrete. **Sound:** Voice calling Olivia's name. **Olivia:** I'm not comfortable being the focus of this. Park and I have made our peace with the situation. I was crushed by the revelation of his children, and clearly, the media intrusion was too much for our marriage to bear. I had to leave. It was the only thing to do. That's all I have to add. Please leave me alone. **Sound:** Glass shattering. **Narrator:** After this single brief interview, Olivia Bender declined to participate further with this documentary. **Sound:** Silence.

AUTHOR'S NOTE

Please be aware, what follows is a frank discussion of infertility. It may be distressing to some readers.

Life imitates art, and art imitates life. These pages belong to the characters within; these are their stories. And yet, much of what you've just read has its roots in reality. My reality.

I don't like being a statistic, but I am one of 10 percent of women who suffer from infertility. Our path echoes Olivia and Park's too closely; multiple pregnancies, multiple miscarriages, fertility treatments and IUIs, cross-country booty calls after early ovulation triggers, failed IVFs. Losing twins was the last straw; we closed up shop and forged ahead, knowing we weren't meant to parent our own children.

We didn't tell many of our struggles because inevitably, well-meaning and invariably kind advice was offered. No matter what you say to an infertile couple—outside of "I'm so sorry, that sucks"—it will be taken wrongly. ("You can always adopt" is particularly egregious.) It's the hormones, you see. Pregnancy brain combined with the delightful cocktail of injectables in legs and stomachs and buttocks that bring your body to the brink of pseudo-menopause only to make your cycle start again in order to get you pregnant...homicidal tendencies have nothing on a woman in a suppression cycle.

I can look back on it now with rueful amusement. At the time, it was scary, frustrating, and painful, on many levels, physical and emotional.

Partners who are not being shot up but have their part to play, especially those providing semen, have their own delightful challenges, physical and emotional. The "Sweet Home Alabama" incident is real. It was after that particular day, in mild hysterics, that my husband mentioned this event should really make it into a book.

Honestly, we'd never planned to have children right away. That we went down the path at all can be blamed on my biological clock kicking into gear. In the library parking lot, two tiny girls in pink tutus danced across my path, and it was as if a bell rang, deep, resonating, and loud, inside of me—YOU MUST HAVE THOSE NOW. This combined with the news of the celebrity pregnancy of one of my film idols (Jennifer Garner, you adorable creature) and I found myself popping open a bottle of the good wine to propose a moratorium on birth control. I joked we'd get pregnant that first time trying, or we'd end up doing IVF. Both were true.

No doctor could pinpoint why, exactly, things didn't work out for us. There are multiple medical anomalies in my chart: an MTHFR mutation, a clotting disorder, seminal antibodies, competitive blood types, on and on. And yet, I could get pregnant at the drop of a hat. I did, actually, quite regularly, almost every three months for several years. (You can do the math on that. I know. It's okay. It really is. As my beloved Hemingway said, we are all strong in the broken places.)

The irony, of course, is the medication I went on for both birth control and migraine suppression in the first place probably rendered me infertile. Or I always was, and all those years of prescriptions were pointless. I suffer from celiac disease, also a known contributor to infertility. Maybe it just wasn't meant to be.

When we decided to stop trying, I turned to my own work and produced several books in a row I am deeply proud of, and only realized after the fact, several years removed, that I was sorting through my feelings in my work. Just read *A Deeper Darkness*, the first Samantha Owens novel, and experience the horror she does when she loses everything, and you will know my state of mind at the time.

I turned to my work, and it gave me power.

I turned to my husband, whose grace and love sustained me. He never blamed me, even when I blamed myself.

I turned to my faith, tattered though it was, and found peace.

I turned to yoga, and found the path to enlightenment that started with taking my first honest and true breath in many, many years to the backdrop of Jeff Buckley's rendition of "Hallelujah." There were tears. I was cleansed.

The idea of a story based on the inciting incident, as we writers like to call it, of my darling getting off in a tiny impersonal cubicle to the strains of "Sweet Home Alabama" to provide me with a slightly designer child, wouldn't leave me alone.

And then, at last, came Olivia.

I knew her as surely as I knew myself. I have rarely been presented with such a wholly realized character—not since Taylor Jackson pulled an Athena and sprang fully formed from my head. I saw Olivia and knew her stories as if we'd been friends for years. She was walking down a beach, alone, arms wrapped around herself. She had just suffered a heart-wrenching miscarriage. She was so very, very sad. The line appeared in my consciousness: *There was blood again.*

It was finally time to tell her story.

I've said to my husband many times over the years that I often feel handicapped as a writer because I don't speak the same language as so many of my peers. What Liane Moriarty did in *Big Little Lies*, for example, the language of the school pickup line—I didn't have that in my repertoire. I wrote characters who had children sometimes, naturally. We don't always have to experience things firsthand to write convincingly and honestly about them; I believe this in my soul. But there was always a little something I felt I was missing.

When Olivia demanded her story be told, I had a realization. I might not be able to write comfortably about what it's like raising children, but I sure as hell could write about what it's like to lose them.

This is the story of a woman who cannot bear a child, despite her many attempts. It is about a marriage broken by too many things to count. It is about the family we think we need, and the ways we survive the hardest parts of living. It is a tale of obsession and a tale of betrayal.

It is also a celebration. I hope to unmask and destigmatize—no, normalize—the conversation about infertility. I promise you, whether you know it or not, a woman very close to you has suffered a miscarriage. It is something so ubiquitous as to be almost commonplace, and yet it is rarely spoken about, and treated with such abhorrence and fear that it remains in the shadows, a dirty little secret too many of us are trying to hide. It's horrible. It's tragic. It's happened to virtually every woman of childbearing age—some of them without even knowing it.

Yes, I am a statistic. I am also incredibly blessed to have a loving husband, a wonderful family, and internal fortitude. I chose not to be broken by the tragedy that befell us. It was a difficult choice, but it was the only one for me. As they say, the only way out is through.

Recently, a woman who is more in tune with the things we cannot see around us did a reading for me. I was suffering from a creative block, not surprisingly whilst writing this book. Fear, most likely, of putting too much of myself out in the world.

Knowing absolutely nothing of my background, my private life, my interior life, my struggles with infertility, she said that when she envisioned me, I was surrounded by small sparks of light. They danced around me. She thought they were beautiful, these invisible fireflies of hope.

Eventually, that woman became a friend, and I felt close enough to her to share my journey. She clapped her hands and said, "Oh! That's what those lights are. The souls of your babies. They surround you with joy and happiness. They're with you, always."

And so they are. In this world, and the next.

ACKNOWLEDGMENTS

I normally start an acknowledgment with a list of people who've bolstered my path in writing a book, ending with my husband of many years. But this time I'm starting with Randy. This is his story as much as mine, and if he hadn't encouraged me to find a place for the anecdotes that plagued our fertility journey, both the horror and the hilarity, I might never have found my way through, much less have discovered Olivia. He has been my rock for three decades, but never more so than during the trials and tribulations of both trying to have children and the writing of this book. There were days when it was just too much, and he was always there, arms open, silent, strong, and steady. I would be nothing without you, my darling. Thank you for showing me the joy on the other side. And for not being a vampire.

On to the rest. My deepest thanks to the following:

My darling agent Laura Blake Peterson, who pushed me

out of my comfort zone and believed I could fly, who gave love, support, encouragement, and ass kicking as needed. Her gasp of excitement when I pitched this idea will live on in my mind forever.

Jeremy Finley, who happily sacrificed his precious time to talk me through the reporter parts. Any mistakes are my own.

Will Osley, for great care with our move(s) and insisting on being a heroic cowboy detective. I hope Osley is exactly what you wanted, and thank you for letting me take liberties with his character for the story.

Mel Osley, for the enthusiastic book discourse and screenwriting chats.

Andrea Baynham, for showing me the stars, then showing me my power.

Connie Gerhman, for the tour of Chapel Hill that made a lasting impression.

Courtney Breslin, formerly my producer at WNPT, for sharing how a documentary should be structured. Again, all mistakes are my own.

Laura Benedict, whose shoulder was cried upon more than once, and who listened, scolded, encouraged, plotted, and supported, endlessly, for all the things, then and now.

Ariel Lawhon, structural dynamo, cheerleader, Wordle partner, permanent queso date, and plotting genius, for, hell, all of it.

Patti Callahan Henry, who was the first one to LOVE this title and is a strategic creative queen.

Paige Crutcher, who lived through so much of this with me, held me when I wept, and gave me the gift of yoga to heal my troubled soul.

The Porch: Paige Crutcher, Helen Ellis, Lisa Patton, Anne Bogel, Mary Beth Whalen, Ariel Lawhon, Laura Benedict, and Patti Callahan Henry, for holding me up when I didn't think I could pull this off, for quarterly write-ins and in-person dates, for the laughs, the tears, and the creative synergies of an incredible group of brilliant women with whom I am honored to share the rarefied air.

My fellow scribes, sounding boards, and brainstormers Lisa Unger, Kerry Lonsdale, Kaira Rouda, Danielle Girard, Hank Phillipi Ryan, Jayne Ann Krentz, Catherine Coulter, Allison Brennan, Barbara Peters, and John McDougall: I couldn't do this without y'all!

Dr. Wills Oglesby, for patching up Olivia—and me! And my indefatigable buddy Bob Smodic in PT for the healing hands. And ice. So. Much. Ice.

Designer Kelly Wearstler, whose incredible Masterclass influenced Olivia's own designs.

Rachel Perez, and the whole team at Aurora Publicity, for oodles upon oodles of support, and the magnificent Trello Boards.

My editor, Nicole Brebner, who understood immediately when I said, "This one is different." She championed the story in-house and made it what it was meant to be.

My publisher, Margaret Marbury, for the brainstorming session that landed us on the right path, at last.

My publicist, Emer Flounders, who grounds me, saves me, and finds me all the best people to talk to.

The entire MIRA team, who do so much to get my stories into your hands. From art to PR to marketing to sales: the list is endless, the people fabulous, and the efforts on my behalf so much appreciated. My long-time art director Sean Kapitan needs a special shout-out for nailing the incredible cover art.

My DNA family, those constant supporters who act as sounding boards, listen to me complain, make all kinds of suggestions, read all the early drafts, and put up with me day and night. Sorry to always call during dinner. And my sweet in-laws, who are always cheering behind the scenes.

Jeanne, Clive, and the Unknown Screenwriter, for suggesting that maybe I write our experience as a short story, and then we'd see what happened…

The librarians, booksellers, Instagrammers, Twitterers, TikTokers, Facebookers, and lovely readers—without y'all, I'd be writing into the void.

For the incredibly talented writing community that I am honored to be a part of—your works challenge me to be a better writer. Thank you for hours upon hours of entertainment, support, enlightenment, and inspiration, for writing books that make me strive to be better, on all accounts.

Thank you, all, from the bottom of my heart.